WHITE MAN'S VISIT

The moment Quanah drew his paint to a halt beside his father at the edge of the village, he sensed a terrible wrong blanketing the village.

Where were the women with their knives and pots ready to claim a share of the meat they brought? Where were the old men with critical eyes to compare today's kill with last week's hunt? Where were his mother and his infant sister, Prairie Flower?

Fear set Quanah's heart to pounding in his breast.

"There." Peta Nocona pointed toward the river's edge.

Quanah saw the members of the band now. Braves, women, and children gathered by the water. The anguished wails came from that direction.

Five tipis had fallen and another two were no more than smoldering mounds of gray and black ash.

"What has happened?" Peta Nocona called to the brave Mo-wi. "Has a windstorm swept through our camp while my sons and I were hunting?"

"A wind on the backs of big *Tejano* horses," Mo-wi answered.

D0817336

BANTAM BOOKS BY GEO. W. PROCTOR

Enemies
Walks Without a Soul
Comes the Hunter
Before Honor

Blood
of My
Blood

Geo. W. Proctor

Bantam Books
New York • Toronto • London • Sydney • Auckland

BLOOD OF MY BLOOD

A Bantam Book / July 1996

ISBN 0-553-57451-5

Published simultaneously in the United States and Canada

Bantam Books are published by Bantam Books, a division of Bantam Doubleday Dell
Publishing Group, Inc. Its trademark, consisting of the words "Bantam Books" and the
portrayal of a rooster, is Registered in U.S. Patent and Trademark Office and in other
countries. Marca Registrada. Bantam Books, 1540 Broadway, New York, New York 10036.

PRINTED IN THE UNITED STATES OF AMERICA

OPM   10 9 8 7 6 5 4 3 2 1

For my brothers and sisters:

Mary
Hap
Barbara
Tom
In order of appearance!

Blood of My Blood

CHAPTER
ONE

Death hung in the air.

Leather creaked when John Teller shifted his weight in the saddle. His gray eyes lifted. Flat plains stretched before him to a featureless horizon, formed where yellowed autumn grass met a blue sky unhampered by so much as a hint of scud white.

That his gaze revealed nothing did little to relieve the doubt that wormed beneath his skin and coldly crept upward from the base of his spine. A man could not trust his eyes and expect to stay alive long, not here, not on the Texas high plains.

The monotony of the vast ocean of grass that fanned out in all directions around him created a deadly illusion. No matter what the eye and brain perceived, the dried vegetation concealed subtle shifts in the face of the land. Ahead, perhaps just beyond the breeze-rustled grasses, lay a shallow buffalo wallow. On the right, or maybe the left, hidden by the same grass, was a dry playa lake. No matter how slight the unseen depression, a Comanche could use it to watch every move of those foolish enough to intrude upon this last stronghold of *Comancheria*.

Trusting his eyeballs had almost cost Teller his life two years ago, while scouting for an army patrol out of Fort Sill. Then, he rode a mile ahead of the troopers, certain the nearest Comanche brave was at least three days from his position. In the time it took him to glance up at a merciless summer sun, five mounted warriors, faces streaked with the red and black paints of war, sprang out of nothingness and charged with bloodcurdling cries tearing from their throats.

Had his own mount not been fresh from a night's rest, he would have fallen to the war lances brandished by the braves that day. Even his horse's speed did not save him from the bite of a flint-headed arrow that buried itself in his right forearm.

The fingers of Teller's left hand eased to the once-injured arm and rubbed away remembered pain. Beneath the fabric of jacket and shirt, he imagined feeling the roughness of the white scar he carried as a souvenir of that ambush.

He pursed his lips and sucked at his teeth. By the time he reached the safety of the soldiers who followed his trail, the five braves had once again vanished into the flatness. A buffalo wallow, sand marking where the braves had forced their ponies to lie on their sides while they watched the lone white man approach, did reveal how the Comanches had hidden themselves before the attack.

No, a man needed more than eyes to keep his scalp intact here on the high plains. He had to employ all his senses and carry a healthy serving of luck with him, Teller thought, as he slowly drew a long breath into his nostrils.

Caution again wiggled along his spine. The smell of death hung in the air beneath the crispness of the October morning. The odor of rotting flesh was something a man did not forget, and Teller had smelled death more than once during his forty years in Texas.

A dead antelope, or buffalo, Teller tried to lie to himself and failed.

The buffalo were gone from Texas, gone from the whole country, hunted to the point of extinction with the unofficial seal of approval of the U.S. Army and the government that supported it. Buffalo hides meant golden eagles to fill the pockets of the men who slaughtered the once endless herds of bison. More important was the simple fact that each of the shaggy giants that fell meant the loss of buffalo steaks a-sizzle over some Indian campfire.

Newspapers carried stories each day of the army's ceaseless actions against the tribes who claimed the plains as their own. Melees of blue-coated soldiers and painted savages made for good reading, but told little of the real reason the army slowly gained the upper hand over its red-skinned enemy. Comanche, Kiowa, Pawnee, Cheyenne, Sioux—every tribe that inhabited the American plains depended on the buffalo for food. Remove the meat from the stew pot and an army, even one as resourceful as one soldiered by Indian braves, would not stand long against a relentless foe.

A gust of north wind filled Teller's nostrils with the pungent smell of putrefying flesh once more. He glanced at the man astride a bay mare to his left. If Charles Dumaine smelled the death ahead of them, he gave no outward sign, not even a twitch of his nose. The New Orleans newspaper man appeared more concerned about the morning's chill than his surroundings. The bay's reins were wrapped about the saddlehorn, and Dumaine used both his hands to worry the top button of his coat into its eye.

"Is there anything wrong, Mr. Teller?" The young reporter's head turned to the older man.

Teller nodded at the reins. "You'd be in a hell of a fix if a prairie dog up and popped out of the ground to spook that mare right about now."

Chagrin slid across Dumaine's face, while his fingers finally managed to fumble the button through its eye to secure the coat snugly beneath his clean-shaven chin. "These Texas mornings are far colder than I anticipated. I fear I would have frozen to death by now had you not insisted I purchase this coat back in Fort Worth. I'm accustomed to the mild temperatures of a delta autumn."

Dumaine began to unwrap the reins from the horn. "I was under the impression that the Texas heat rivaled the flames of Hades itself."

"We're atop the Llano Estacado, the Staked Plains, Mr. Dumaine. That's about as far north as a man can ride and still be within Texas. Head northwest for about a week, and you'll be seeing the Rocky Mountains on the horizon. Fall can bring snow to this country, or summer can linger on 'til Christmas has come and gone."

Dumaine glanced in the direction Teller had indicated. "The Rocky Mountains, perhaps I'll gaze upon their majesty one day—when this country has been made safe for a Christian gentleman who wishes to travel freely from coast to coast without being in constant fear for his life."

Teller hid an expression of disgust when the newspaper man took the reins in his right hand and held them there. A dozen times since leaving Fort Worth, the older man had warned the reporter to leave his gun hand free should the need to free revolver or rifle suddenly present itself. Either Dumaine was slow to learn, Teller decided, or he cared little about protecting his own skin.

The Texan's attempt to conceal his disapproval fell short of success. He felt Dumaine's eyes on him and saw the younger man quickly shift the reins into his left hand. Teller's own attention returned to the dried grass of the plains and the smell of death carried on the breeze.

For the thousandth time since leaving Fort Worth a week ago, Teller wondered why he had agreed to bring this New Orleans greenhorn with his packhorse weighted down with a bulky wooden camera, tripod, photographic plates, and an assortment of trays and chemicals into the very heart of Comanche territory. Only a fool would accept such a job.

Or a man without two thin dimes to rub together, Teller considered. For a man who had spent the past year drifting across Texas, the hundred dollars Charles Dumaine had paid to be guided across Texas to join Colonel Ranald Mackenzie and the troops he led to spearhead the fight against the Comanches seemed like a fortune. Quick money often made a man act the fool. Dumaine wanted to make a name for himself reporting and photographing the Indian wars, and Teller was broke. Who was the bigger fool was yet to be seen.

"Is there something else troubling you this morning, Mr. Teller?" Dumaine asked. "You seem more reticent than my mistake of holding the reins in the wrong hand would warrant."

For an instant, Teller considered mentioning the smell of rotting flesh that assailed his nostrils with every breath he inhaled. He merely shook his head. There was no need to alarm the reporter. The stench *might* come from the stripped carcass of an antelope or a deer ahead. Unlike the buffalo, both were still abundant on the Staked Plains and hunted by Kwerhar-rehnuh bands of the Comanches. After all, Kwerhar-rehnuh meant Antelope-Eaters in Comanche, Teller tried to convince himself.

"Are you certain there is nothing troubling you?" Dumaine pressed. "Perhaps we've strayed from Colonel Mackenzie's trail?"

"Not even a village idiot could lose this trail." Teller barely kept the edge from his voice when he poked a finger at the ground. "Those are the same shod horses we've been following since we picked up their tracks at the edge of the Caprock two days back. And those ruts were left by the wagons carrying Mackenzie's nappy-headed buffalo soldiers. No, we ain't lost the trail. The colonel and his darkie soldier boys are up there ahead of us."

Dumaine rode silently for a long moment. "How far ahead do you estimate the distance to be, Mr. Teller?"

Far closer than the older man wanted to ponder at length. He could no longer ignore the fear that niggled at the back of his mind, fear of what really lay ahead of them. Mackenzie had brought his troops onto the Llano Estacado in search of Comanches. In all likelihood the colonel had discovered more than he had reckoned upon finding. Somewhere ahead in the grass lay the results of that encounter.

Teller shivered in spite of his attempt to suppress the uneasiness that now coursed through his body. He had no desire to ride upon such a scene. His gut had churned and knotted itself when he had read the accounts of the massacre at Little Big Horn. The bloody battlefield left by the Sioux and their butchery of Custer and the 7th Cavalry would seem like a Sunday picnic compared to what the Comanche were capable of doing to Mackenzie and his black soldiers. The Sioux were merely Sioux; the Comanches had ridden as lords of the plains for nearly two hundred years. Their murderous marauding had stopped Spanish, French, English, and American from claiming the great plains as their own.

"We made good time yesterday." Teller leaned to the left side of the buckskin gelding he rode and eyed the soldiers' trail. "Mackenzie's about a day or two ahead of us—maybe three at the most. Those wagons slow him down. We can cover twice the ground in a day as the colonel can."

Abruptly, Teller eased back on the reins to halt the buckskin.

The packhorse he led moved beside his mount before it stopped and lowered its head to graze. Dumaine managed to tug the bay mare to a standstill a half dozen strides ahead of the older man. He twisted around in the saddle and stared back at his companion in confusion.

Teller edged the buckskin beside the reporter. "Mr. Dumaine, I want you to close your eyes, draw a deep breath through your nose, and tell me what you smell."

Dumaine's eyes narrowed and a dubious frown shadowed his face. "Mr. Teller, this is not the time for levity. If we are to join . . ."

Teller waved away his remarks. "This ain't no joke. Close your eyes and breathe deep through your nose."

With another frown Dumaine relented. His nose wrinkled. An instant later his whole face puckered as though he unknowingly had bitten into a sour lemon.

With a distasteful shake of his head, the newspaperman stared at Teller. "It smells like a cat that died in the alley outside my apartment back in New Orleans. When did you first notice it?"

Teller tapped his heels to the buckskin's sides and moved forward. "Got a couple whiffs of it last night, but didn't pay it no never mind. This morning it's gotten stronger with every step our horses have taken."

"There could be a dead animal ahead of us," Dumaine replied, but his expression said that his mind raced to Teller's conclusion.

"A herd of slaughtered buffalo left to rot in the sun might raise such a stink," the older man replied. "But the buffalo ain't here no more."

Dumaine bit his lower lip and lifted his gaze to the northern horizon. "You believe there's been a battle, don't you? That the stench is coming from corpses?"

Teller rubbed a hand over cheek and neck to relieve the itch of three-day-old stubble. "Don't reckon how it could be anything else, not way out here in the middle of nowhere."

"Mackenzie and his men," Dumaine asked, "or Comanches?"

"Don't reckon there's a way to tell without seein' what's up yonder somewhere." Teller's gaze shifted to his companion. "I don't guess there's any way to convince you to turn around and head back to Fort Worth, is there?"

"I came out here to cover the Comanche conflicts for the *Pic-*

ayune, Mr. Teller," the reporter answered with solid commitment to his assigned task. "Whether it's red man or white ahead of us, it's my job to find out what happened and photograph it."

" 'Fraid you'd say that." Teller had seen both white and red men killed in battle, had killed more than one of the latter himself, and did not relish seeing the body-strewn battlefield he knew lay somewhere between them and the distant horizon.

"Don't you think it would be wise if we increased our pace, Mr. Teller?"

Dumaine's expression was one of anticipation, perhaps even a bit of excitement. He had traveled to Texas to write articles about the Comanche fighting. Until this moment all he had done was ride westward, following a meandering branch of the Brazos River. Teller caught himself before his head gave an unconscious shake of disapproval. For the young man, it did not matter whether soldiers or braves lay dead ahead. Either way, he had a story to send back to New Orleans. If Mackenzie and his troopers had been hit, then Dumaine would write of a major military defeat. Were the bodies those of Comanches, then he would report a military victory to his readers.

"No need to rush—the dead ain't goin' nowhere." Teller's concern for sparing their mounts motivated the words as much as his dread of finding what lay ahead. "My guess is that the fight happened in a canyon up north about a mile or two from here. The Comancheros call it Palo Duro Canyon. Comanches been making winter camp there since they first came to Texas. Can't think of a more likely spot for a fight. Mackenzie and his darkies surprised a Comanche band there, or they were ambushed in the canyon."

"Palo Duro Canyon," Dumaine repeated while he dug a pencil and slip of paper from a coat pocket and jotted down the name.

The Llano Estacado stretched flat and featureless for as far as the eye could see. Then in the blink of that eye, a deep, red gash sliced into the earth. This ragged rent, an open wound carved over the centuries by the trickle and torrents of a small stream that ran along the canyon floor to eventually become part of the Brazos River, was the Palo Duro Canyon.

"I don't understand, Mr. Teller." Dumaine stood beside the older man on the canyon rim, staring a thousand feet below. "It appears that fire swept through below, but I don't see any bodies. If this is a battlefield, it lacks the appearance of those I've read about."

Teller silently agreed. Palo Duro appeared as though wildfire set off by a lightning strike had burned from mouth to head. Grass, mesquite trees, and cedars were all blackened by the course of searing flames. Nor could he see the bloated bodies he expected—

"Sweet Jesus."

The words slipped from between the Texan's lips as his gaze followed the circling descent of three buzzards into the canyon. For a moment their dark-feathered forms lost themselves amid the charcoal hues below, then Teller picked them out again when they settled to the ground beside a hundred or more of their winged cousins.

"What is it?" Dumaine strained to see what his companion discerned.

"There's bodies below," Teller answered in a shocked whisper. "But they ain't men—white, red, or black. There's hundreds of dead horses down there."

"Horses?" Dumaine's neck craned to the left and right. "I don't see—" His sentence ended in a gasp. "Lord almighty, they're everywhere. What in the name of decency happened here?"

Teller's head moved from side to side. "I don't know, but Mackenzie and his troops were here. Over yonder's the trail they took below."

"Army mounts?" Dumaine asked while he continued to scan the countless dead animals strewn over the canyon floor.

That Comanches would butcher such a wealth of horseflesh was beyond all Teller knew of the red men. A brave built his status among the Nermernuh, the name the Comanche gave themselves, by counting the ponies he called his own. A pursued warrior might ride a horse until it dropped dead beneath him, but he would never wantonly kill a horse. Comanches were nomadic bands; the horse allowed them to freely move across the plains.

"My guess is they're Indian mustangs," Teller answered. "But there's only one way to make certain—that's to go down and take a look."

Dumaine tilted his head in the affirmative. "I want to get some plates of this."

Stepping to his saddlebags, Teller opened one and pulled out a brown bottle and a blue-and-white neck scarf. He pulled the cork from the neck of the bottle and doused the cloth with the light amber liquid that rolled from inside. "Tie this over your nose. The horse liniment's got wintergreen and camphor in it. It'll help cut the stench."

While the reporter followed his suggestion, the older man poured a healthy portion of the liniment on the red bandanna about his neck and hiked the cloth over his own nose like some desperado set on robbing a stagecoach. Despite the heady melange of aromatic oils soaking the bandanna, the stink of rotting horseflesh found a way into his nostrils.

"They left the wagons over there." Teller pointed to depressions in the grass that marked where Mackenzie's wagons had stopped. As he moved down the trail, leading buckskin and packhorse behind him, he added, "The soldier boys were in the same position we are. This path's too steep and narrow to ride down. They had to dismount and walk their horses down in single file."

"If there were Indians in the canyon, they couldn't have done that during the day," Dumaine commented. "They would have been seen."

"Might have done it at night, but I doubt it. The moon's on the wane. A few soldiers might be able to make it down this path, but to lead a whole army into the canyon Mackenzie would need a full moon." Halfway down the trail, Teller began to smell the stale odor of charred vegetation. "That leaves early morning, just before the sun is about to come up. If there were Comanches camped here, the band would have still been asleep, except for a few guards and sentries. They would have been drowsy after staying alert all night. The last thing they would have been looking for is soldiers coming down off the Caprock."

The newspaperman behind him mumbled something that was drowned in the clip of horse hooves on limestone. Teller did not ask Dumaine to repeat himself. The Texan's mind was too busy trying to piece together a picture of what had happened here. His best guess was that Mackenzie's scouts had come up on the canyon during the night, belly-crawled to the edge, and peered down on a Comanche camp. A rider was then sent back to tell Mackenzie the enemy had been sighted.

The colonel, who had proven himself to be an able Indian fighter against the Cheyenne in the north, was not one to let an opportunity for a surprise attack pass. Force-marching his black-skinned buffalo soldiers through the night, he had brought his men to Palo Duro just as night's blackness transformed to the purples and grays of morning twilight.

Teller stared down at the limestone path he trod. Back in 1871, he had ridden for Ranald Mackenzie under the command of Mackenzie's chief of scouts, Lieutenant Bill Thompson. Had he stood in Mackenzie's boots, Teller would have sent Thompson, his scouts, and a few men handy with a knife into the canyon first. Their task would have been to kill the sentries and establish a line of fire across the canyon should the sleeping Indian band be alerted to the blue-coated soldiers descending upon them. A few men might be able to block a Comanche escape from Palo Duro while Mackenzie sent more of his troopers down the escarpment to join the scouts. The early hour and lack of light would have aided the soldiers and left the Comanche band in pandemonium when the fighting broke out.

Bands, Teller mentally corrected himself. No single band had camped within the canyon. Mackenzie had come upon several bands that believed themselves far from the Army's reach here in the northern extremes of Texas.

"Mr. Teller, I'm going to set up over there." Dumaine pointed to the left when they reached the canyon's floor. "It appears to be an excellent spot to begin my photographs."

"Need any help?" The Texan's gaze scanned the red sand interior of Palo Duro. The scene was worse here than it appeared from above. The bodies of men killed by men he could have accepted; man had butchered man since Cain and Abel. But the stiff bloated carcasses of slaughtered horses churned his stomach, threatening to relieve him of the twist of jerky he had eaten for breakfast.

Dumaine moved beside his packhorse and began unlashing a wooden tripod. "Unless you are experienced with photographic equipment, I would prefer to handle this myself."

Teller nodded. "Then I'll stay out of your way."

"You can assist me in another way, Mr. Teller." Dumaine worked the black box that was his camera free of the packhorse.

"You can read what happened here better than I. If you could ride up and down the canyon and see if there are any clues as to how the fight proceeded, I would appreciate it."

With another tilt of his head, the older man tied his own packhorse to the singed branch of a stunted mesquite, then stepped into a stirrup to swing atop the buckskin. "I'll scout around for you. Mind you watch yourself."

"I'll do that, Mr. Teller. I'll do that." The newspaperman waved his companion away while he busily attached camera to tripod.

A cluck of tongue to roof of mouth from its rider set the buckskin moving deeper into the canyon. Teller doubted Mackenzie was able to bring his whole force down before the fray began. He could only guess at what had happened once the first shot was fired. One thing he was certain of, there was no clear-cut line of battle for either soldier or brave. The scene must have been total chaos. Braves armed with rifles running from their tipis to defend against the growing numbers of carbine-armed Negro soldiers that swarmed down from above.

A thin line of an amused smile slid across Teller's lips. He could imagine Colonel Mackenzie's frustration. The fighting was thick and furious, yet the commander was hamstrung by the fact that half his troops were still trying to descend the narrow path into the canyon. Mackenzie had been unable to make a straightforward charge into the Indian encampment.

Two miles from where the Texan left the reporter with his camera and equipment, Teller drew the buckskin to a halt. Standing in the stirrups, he peered deeper into Palo Duro. The scene remained the same for as far as he could see. Mounds of gray ash, ringed by black, seared grass and bushes, dotted the sandy floor. Here and there lay the decaying bodies of horses.

Mackenzie had stumbled upon a massive Comanche camp. Teller could only guess at the number of bands that had gathered within Palo Duro, but their tipis had lined the stream for over three miles. Chaos had not reigned during the attack, but hell itself. Soldier and brave alike must have fallen beneath a thundering fusillade of lead. The screams of squaws and children echoed—

Teller caught himself in midthought. His head jerked from side to side as he again stood in the stirrups. He pursed his lips and gave a soft whistle.

Bodies, there ain't no bodies! His stomach churned again. Except for the horses, he saw no evidence that the hail of bullets had found a single target.

Lowering himself to the saddle once more, he nudged the buckskin into an easy lope and reined deeper into Palo Duro Canyon. The Army did not bury the bodies of their enemies; they left them where they fell to feed the buzzards and wolves. Yet, there were no bodies of Indian or soldier, nor had he seen one since riding upon the canyon.

"Lord God Almighty," he whispered aloud when he halted again near the head of Palo Duro.

His eyes lifted to the rocky walls around him. It did not take the keen sight of a tracker to see the scattered sand and broken limestone. How many of the Comanches had escaped by clawing their way up the face of the escarpment to the plains above?

All of them, Teller guessed, or there would be bodies here below. The horrible pieces of the battle fell into place one ugly piece after another. He now knew what the fire had claimed. He also knew that the Comanche ponies had been the only targets to fall beneath Army bullets.

He reined the buckskin around and moved eastward down the canyon. He had seen enough, more than enough.

CHAPTER
TWO

"I can see it now from up here." Dumaine peered down into Palo Duro Canyon. "It's like circles of ash."

"Each of them circles represents a tipi Mackenzie's men fired," Teller explained, turning to walk toward the horses staked out a hundred yards from the canyon's rim.

"There's hundreds of them." Awe filled the reporter's voice.

"The Comanches were camped along the stream for at least three miles. I can't even guess at how many bands of the Kwerhar-rehnuh were in the canyon." Reaching a pile of wood brought up from below, Teller began to arrange it for a campfire. He looked up when the reporter, face twisted in a perplexed frown, walked to his side.

"Why burn the Indians' tipis?" Dumaine asked. "Why not just leave them to rot in the coming winter?"

What was obvious to any man, woman, and child within Texas's borders completely evaded the New Orleans reporter. It did not surprise Teller; Comanches were not a day-to-day danger one lived with in the Mississippi River delta city.

"A tipi ain't much more than some sticks holdin' up buffalo hides, but it's a Comanche's home. In that way an Indian ain't much different than a white man. He keeps everything he owns in that home—clothing, food, weapons, geegaws, and keepsakes," Teller answered while he struck a match to a wad of dry grass, blew on it until flames appeared, then stuffed it beneath the pile of wood. "Burn a tipi and you take away everything a Comanche owns. Leave it standing, and a Comanche will come back to reclaim what is his."

He paused a moment to lean down and blow on the flames again. "But like you said, winter's comin' on. Take away a man's shelter and food, and you take the fight out of him. The braves that were down there in the canyon won't be worrying about raiding this winter; they'll be busy trying to keep themselves alive."

Dumaine surveyed the plains stretched around them. "And you're positive the Comanches escaped Mackenzie's men. Certain that they all got away."

"No other way to read it," Teller assured the man. "No way Mackenzie's troops reached the floor before they were discovered. I'd say the braves put up a cover fire to give their squaws and brats time to climb the canyon walls. Then they moved to the walls themselves, hiding behind the rocks and boulders."

Teller watched the growing flames lick at the wood for a moment. "Mackenzie's 'bout the best commander there is when it comes to understandin' Indian ways. He'd never try to rush braves dug in like that until he had all his men in the canyon. Trouble was, by the time the troops were on the canyon floor, the braves had managed to climb up and join the squaws and children above."

"And the Comanches scattered to the four winds before MacKenzie could get back up here," Dumaine concluded.

Teller nodded. "Can't see it no other way. Mackenzie rode upon the biggest gathering of Comanches the Army's ever found, and they all got clean away from him."

As though noticing the older man's efforts for the first time, Dumaine stared at the flickering flames. "May I ask what you're doing, Mr. Teller?"

"Makin' camp for the night. Ain't but an hour or so 'til sundown. The breeze is from the north, and we're back far enough to be away from the stink down there. This spot looked as good a place to camp as any we're likely to find." Teller stood and walked to his packhorse.

"But you've got a fire going. After all the lectures you've given me about cold camping at night, have you taken leave of your senses? Surely the Indians will see our fire." An unmistakable tightness pinched the newsman's voice. "And a camp here on the edge of the canyon? Aren't you being more than a little reckless? What if the Comanches return?"

"A little late to be frettin' about keepin' your hair, ain't it? You're the one that wanted to come out here in the middle of Comanche territory." Teller untied a corner of the tarpaulin that covered the supplies on the animal's back. He worked a hand under the canvas and brought out a smoke-blackened skillet, then a cloth bag of dried beans and a slab of bacon wrapped in grease-stained brown paper. "After all the jerky and hardtack we've choked down for a week, I thought we both could use a hot meal in our bellies. Nothin' fancy, mind you. Just some beans and bacon and a pot of coffee to wash it down."

"As good as that sounds, is a hot meal worth losing our lives over?" The tightness remained in the journalist's voice, and his gaze darted from side to side as though he expected a horde of war-painted Comanches to jump out of the high grass and swarm down on the small camp.

"Ain't no need to be botherin' your mind 'bout the Comach. They ain't nowhere 'round these parts." Teller added water from a canteen to the beans and bacon slices he placed in the skillet, then set the pan atop the fire. "After what happened here, ain't no Comanche ever gonna step foot in Palo Duro again."

Dumaine eyed the older man. "How can you be so certain?"

"Bad medicine," Teller said simply. "Comanches are a super-stitious lot. When something bad happens, they hold that it was a matter of evil magic workin' against 'em. They shy clear of any parcel of land they deem evil. What Mackenzie and his men did down in the canyon was about as bad medicine as there is for a Comanche."

Apparently deciding to trust his companion's judgment, the younger man settled cross-legged to the ground beside the fire. "And you're certain they won't see this fire?"

Teller shrugged. "Don't matter what they see. They won't come scoutin' us out. The canyon's filled with evil spirits now. They'll be afraid of being captured by those spirits. Never been two white men so safe in the middle of Comanche territory as you and me are right now."

While the Texan retrieved pot and coffee from the packhorse, Dumaine stirred the beans that began to boil in the skillet. He glanced up when the older man returned to the fire.

"I still don't understand why Mackenzie destroyed all those horses," the reporter said. "There must be close to a thousand carcasses down on the canyon floor. I've never seen such a senseless, violent act."

Since locating a trail that led them up the north wall of the canyon, Teller had tried to shove the image of the rotting horses below from his mind. The hundred dollars Dumaine had paid him was not enough, not for what he had seen today. A lifetime would be too short to erase the nightmarish scene from his brain.

"Can you tell me why Mackenzie slaughtered those helpless animals?" The tortured pain that hung at the corners of Dumaine's eyes told Teller the sights below had been etched into the young man's memories as well.

"Violent, bloody, slaughter—what Mackenzie did was all that," the Texan answered. "But the one thing it wasn't was senseless. However, Mackenzie and his soldier boys would've been kinder if they'd've put a bullet between the eyes of every redskin they found down there on the canyon floor."

The puzzled expression on the younger man's face said Teller's words were lost on him.

"A Comanche and his pony are one, Mr. Dumaine. Take away his horse and he's good as dead." Teller shifted the coffeepot to the side of the fire when it began to boil. "The Comanches call the horse the 'dog-god.' And that's what the horse is to them—a god. It made them what they are. Without it, they're nothing."

"But the horse isn't even native to this country," Dumaine said.

"That's right. It was the Spaniards who brought the horse with them from Europe. Colorado himself first rode horses on these very plains," Teller replied. "Some say Indians stole horses from the Spanish, others say the mustangs are descended from animals that escaped from the Spanish explorers. Don't really matter which. What matters is that the horse completely changed the Indians that wandered these plains."

Teller explained that prior to the horse, the plains Indians were the weak tribes who had been driven by stronger tribes from the plentiful game to be found in the forests and mountains. "Damned hard for braves on foot to chase down buffalo and antelope, especially when they have to keep close to a water hole. In case you haven't noticed, water's mighty scarce in these parts.

"The horse changed all that. The tribes could follow the buffalo—find new water. Most of all, they could ride down the game they needed to survive," Teller continued. "And none of the tribes took to the horse like the Comanche did."

Astride horses, the Comanches spread across the plains until they dominated lands that encompassed parts of Texas, Colorado, and Kansas. Those who attempted to invade that territory were repelled again and again by ferocious warriors with faces painted for war.

"The Spanish, French, English, and Americans were all turned back by the Comanches for over two hundred years," Teller said while he used a fork to test the beans and found them still too tough. "It wasn't just the whites they fought back. Other Indian tribes fell before them. 'Bout the only tribe that seems to get along with the Comanche are the Kiowa. Lot a times, things ain't that friendly between 'em."

Dumaine pursed his lips as though lost in thought for a moment. "There's no wonder the Comanche are called lords of the plains."

"And it's all because of the horse," Teller added. "As ugly as it was, Mackenzie did what needed to be done down there in the canyon. And things are likely to get a whole lot uglier for the Comanche before it's over. Winter's comin' on quick. Without their tipis and supplies and robbed of their mustangs, the Comanches have been consigned to a slow, painful death."

The Texan remembered when Mackenzie had come upon a large camp of Kwerhar-rehnuh a few years before. Then, too, the Indians had managed to escape, although the soldiers captured the Comanche ponies. The night after the battle the braves returned and stole away with their mustangs, as well as half of Mackenzie's mounts. The army colonel had learned his lesson well. What he had ordered in Palo Duro *had* to be done—if the Comanches were ever to be defeated.

Teller drew a long breath. "The truth is, the Comanche are dead at this very moment. They might not know it, but they're dead just as surely as if they had stood their ground down below and been cut down by Mackenzie's men."

Dumaine rose and retrieved two tin cups from the packhorse. He filled both with coffee and passed one to the older man. "You make it sound like the Comanche wars are over—that I've come here too late."

The coffee felt warm and welcomed in Teller's belly. Simple things become a luxury when a man had been deprived of them for a while. It would not be long before something as simple as a mouthful of meat would be a luxury to the Indians who had escaped Palo Duro.

The Texan found no sympathy within him for the Comanches and the fate they faced. They had robbed him of far too much since he had first come to Texas. Instead he felt relief, a sense that the long-fought war to claim this land for decent, God-fearing men and women would soon be over.

"Is the fighting over, Mr. Teller?" Dumaine asked while the older man drew another sip of coffee from his cup.

"Mackenzie won't quit," Teller finally answered, "not until the last Comanche's either dead or been driven into the Indian Territory. There might be a few skirmishes, but the battles are over. Since the end of the War between the States, we've been driving the Comanche back to the very heart of his lands. Younger war leaders like Quanah Parker have put up a damnable fight, but they've been losing ground every day."

Dumaine took the fork from his companion and tested the beans himself. "I think they're ready."

The older man smiled. "They could use a bit more boilin', but I think our stomachs are ready. There's a couple tin plates right under the tarp where I untied it."

The reporter nodded, rose, and walked to the packhorse. He pulled out the two plates and started back to the fire. "Quanah Parker. I heard that name mentioned several times while I was in Fort Worth. Parker—that's a strange name for an Indian chief."

"He's a half-breed." Teller poured equal portions of the beans and bacon into the plates the newsman held out. "In the past decade every Texan's learned his name—and learned to fear it."

"His mother was white?" Dumaine shoveled a forkful of beans into his mouth and sighed softly. "I didn't think beans could taste so good."

"Cynthia Ann Parker was her name," Teller replied, memories

he tried to keep buried deep in his mind clawing to the surface. "She was no more than a girl when the Comanches took her captive."

"A half-white warrior leading the Comanches," Dumaine mused around another mouthful of beans. "What else can you tell me about this Quanah Parker? There might be enough for a story to file with my editors back in New Orleans."

"What else can I tell you—more than I wish I could, I'd say." Teller leaned back on an elbow and glanced at the graying sky.

A single bright star directly overhead heralded the approaching night. Amid the deluge of memories crowding his head was one of his father giving a name to that star—Vega in the constellation of Lyra. It seemed like only yesterday when he had sat beneath the night sky while his father had pointed out the North Star and the constellations that allowed a man to find his bearings after the sun set.

"Reckon you can say I was there when Quanah Parker got his start," the Texan continued. "It was back in '36—a warm spring day in May when the Comanche band was sighted. I had just turned six and—"

Teller paused and grinned sheepishly. "I'm gettin' ahead of myself. My pa and I had come down to Texas from Missouri the summer before. That was two months after the fever took my ma. After she died, Pa couldn't stay on the farm anymore. He wanted a fresh start. The memories in Missouri were too strong for him. So he sold the farm, bought a wagon and a pair of oxen, packed up all our worldly possessions, and headed south. Pa was intent on reachin' San Antonio 'fore winter. But winter came hard and early in '35. We were damned lucky the folks at Fort Parker took us in."

"Fort Parker?" Dumaine questioned. "The army had a fort in Texas back then?"

"Not likely." Teller chuckled while he scooped another forkful of beans from his plate. "Texas was still part of Mexico then. No, Fort Parker was a small colony of immigrants from Illinois who settled near the present site of Waco. They were religious folks—part of what they called 'The Pilgrim Primitive Baptist Church.' Like Pa, they'd come to Texas lookin' for the land of milk 'n honey. What they found was Texas had as much Hell in it as it did Heaven."

Teller chewed at the beans silently for several moments, remembering the day his father and he had first sighted the fort. After the long journey from Missouri, it had looked like heaven to him.

"So why was it called Fort Parker?" Dumaine pressed, parting the veil of memories for the older man.

"They had built themselves a stockade out of logs like forts the soldiers used to build back east," Teller answered. "It was meant to protect them from the Indians they had heard about. Didn't do 'em much good the day the raiding party appeared. Comanches and Kiowas, they were. Rode up toward the fort as boldly as neighbors come to visit. Like I said, I had just turned six that May, but that day is something I'm not likely to forget—"

"—John, you mind Mrs. Parker and do what she tells you without givin' her any back talk, understand." Calvin Teller, hand solidly on his son's shoulder, towered above the six-year-old. His gray eyes stared sternly down at his only son. "I hear of you causin' any trouble, then I'll have you go cut a switch when I get back this evening. Understand?"

Unblinking, John Teller returned his father's stare. "Yes, sir, I understand."

The threat of being required to cut a switch as the instrument of one's own punishment was part of the morning ritual between father and son. In spite of his tender years, John had long ago learned that if he incurred his father's wrath, it was the broad leather belt the elder Teller wore around his waist that would be applied to an erring son's backside rather than some threatened switch.

More than once the boy had prayed his father *would* send him to cut a switch. In the time required to accomplish that task, his father's anger might diminish or a son's transgression be forgotten. Such luck never rode on the boy's shoulders.

"Don't you worry about your young 'un, Mr. Teller," Lucy Parker said from the threshold of a small cabin. "John there never gives me any trouble. He's a good boy."

Calvin Teller looked up and smiled at the slender woman who brushed a strand of stray brunette hair from her forehead. "A man hopes his son'll do him proud. But more often than not,

John here has a mind of his own and does exactly what he wants."

The young woman glanced at the boy and smiled. "John's never been a trouble, Mr. Parker. He's just a boy bein' a boy, nothing more than that."

"Cal," one of three men who led oxen toward the stockade's open gate called to the elder Teller, "time we were going. The others are already in the fields."

Calvin Teller tipped the brim of his sweat-stained hat to Lucy Parker, gave his son a parting stern glare, then trotted after the men and the oxen.

John stood watching his father and the others leave the stockade. While Calvin Teller was not an easy man, the boy felt more than a little pride in claiming him as a father. Teller, along with Daniel Parker, had served with Sam Houston and the Texician army when they had defeated General Santa Anna at San Jacinto less than a month ago. Calvin Teller was more than just a farmer from Missouri; he was a fighter, a soldier—and one who won battles! Texas was a free republic because of what his father had done at San Jacinto. That Calvin Teller was merely one of hundreds under Houston's command meant nothing to the boy. He *knew* who had fought the bravest and hardest on April 21.

"Half Teller." Lucy Parker's voice cut through the bloody revel of battle ablaze in the boy's mind.

With a slight frown, John turned to face the woman. He did not like the appellation. Although she used it to designate him from her own son who was also named John, the nickname implied he was far less than the man he knew himself to be. "Yes'm?"

"Half Teller," the woman repeated to increase the irritation, "I want you to help Cynthia Ann and John with the morning milk. After you three take the pail to Granny Hawkins for churnin', you can go about your playin'."

"Yes, ma'am!" The boy grinned from ear to ear. The chores required of him at Fort Parker were far less than his pa had assigned on their Missouri farm.

He would miss the fort when his father finally moved them southward to San Antonio, as had been his intent before the harsh winter set in last year. His pa said they were lucky to find the Parkers, that they might not have made it through the winter without their kindness. More important to the younger Teller was the fact that there were children here, something sorely missed as an only child on a Missouri farm.

Six-year-old John Parker greeted John Teller with a broad grin when the boy turned the corner of the cabin. The second boy stood beside his older sister seated on a three-legged wooden stool at the side of a brown-spotted milk cow. John Parker held up two crudely shaped toy rifles carved from flat boards.

"Ma said we could play this morning, Half Teller," the Parker boy announced. "This time I get to be Uncle Daniel, and you get to be Santa Anna."

'Half Teller' did not sound any better from the lips of his friend than it had when Lucy Parker spoke it. But it was the prospect of shouldering the role of the defeated Mexican general for the morning that left a sour taste in Teller's mouth. After all, it was *his* father who had fought at San Jacinto, not John's.

"I got a penny Pa gave me." Teller dug a hand into a pocket. "We can flip it to see who's gonna be who."

Before he could correctly balance the tarnished coin atop his right thumb, Cynthia Ann released the cow's teats and eyed the two boys. " 'Less you don't want me to tell Ma you two didn't help with the chores, you'd best tote this pail on over to Granny Hawkins. I've finished my work, and I don't intend to do yours for you."

John Parker glanced at his sister, then at his would-be confederate of make-believe battles yet to be fought. "I told Ma we'd carry the milk to Granny Hawkins."

Teller slipped the penny back into his pocket and nodded. From a corner of an eye, he saw the smug smile Cynthia Ann wore. With three years separating them, the girl was almost fully grown in the younger boy's eye. He liked her well enough—for a girl—except when she lorded over him like an adult. He had also tangled with the nine-year-old once and learned that those three years also gave her the advantage of mature strength when tooth and nail were needed to settle minor disputes. Being bested once by a girl was enough; he had no desire to bear that humiliation again.

Taking the handle of the wooden pail, Teller tilted his head for John Parker to lift his share of the burden. The half-full bucket of warm, frothing milk stretching their young arms, the two boys shuffled around the cabin. They made it halfway across the length of the fort's interior before their aching muscles required them to stop and switch hands and sides of the pail.

"We need more men for our armies." John Parker nodded to Billy Tobias, who carried an armload of wood into his family's cabin. "Tom Bishop might be done with his chores 'bout now, too."

Both the boys were a year older than John and himself, but Teller did not mind. The more men recruited the better the battle would be. The trouble was, prospects were slim. Most boys in Fort Parker were old enough to accompany their fathers to the fields each morning. Their chores did not end until the men trekked back from their plowing and planting just before sunset.

John Teller often helped carry lunch to the men in the fields. The walk from the fort to the planting was a full mile and a half on the other side of a small hill behind the fort. Had he been a year older, he realized, he would now be working at his father's side.

The young boy glanced around the fort. Except for the two old men left behind to protect the stockade during the day, John and he were the oldest men within the stockade, right behind Billy and Tom. Everyone else was either a woman, a girl, or too young to participate in a battle the magnitude of San Jacinto.

"Half Teller, do you see what I see?" John Parker's voice was whispered fear and excitement.

"See?" Teller's gaze made another circuit of the fort. All he saw were women going about their routine chores. "I don't see—"

His throat tightened and his mouth went dry when his gaze shifted to the fort's wide open gate. "Injuns!"

John Parker's head nodded as though in answer to a question. The boy's eyes went saucer round and remained that way while locked on the ten riders who reined their ponies to a halt a hundred strides beyond the fort's entrance.

"What are they doing here?" John Teller's own gaze froze on the copper-skinned warriors with their long black manes of hair and scowling, hairless faces.

All his short life he had heard adults talk about Indians, but these were the first he had ever seen. They were wilder in appearance than he had ever imagined. Dressed only in buckskin breechclouts and moccasins, they were more naked than clothed, which increased the overwhelming impression that these were creatures born of the wild.

"Comanche." A man's voice came from the boy's right. Another male voice added, "Them three to the left are Kiowa. I seen those markings on arrows down in San Antonio."

John Teller's gaze remained frozen on the ten savages. He saw no war paint adorning either the riders or their mustang mounts. But both braves and horses wore feathers a-dangle from hair or single-rein hackamores looped over the ponies' noses. Nor did the six-year-old see a single firearm among the ten. All carried war lances tipped with either flint or steel. And there were quivers of arrows and tautly strung bows. The hide shields, decorated with brightly painted alien symbols and drawings, held by the Indians, swelled the overwhelming perception that the boy stood face-to-face with untamed savagery that had no place in this quiet colony of farmers.

"What do they want?" John Parker's tight whisper echoed the pounding fear that hammered in Teller's small chest.

"Don't know," was all John Teller managed to push through the sudden dryness that sucked all moisture from throat and mouth.

From the corner of an eye the boy saw two gray-haired men armed with single-shot longrifles lift their arms and wave away the women and children who drifted toward the gate.

"Quiet," one of the men said. "And stay back. There's no need to cause a stir. The winter was probably as hard on them as it was for us. Most likely they're here to beg food."

"We'll send them on their way," the other man added as he drew himself rail straight while he approached the gate.

The men's words were meant to silence the buzz of uncertainty that now worked its way around the stockade. They missed their mark; the whispered questions among women and children increased. Nor did the runaway race of Teller's heart subside. Food was the one thing in short supply within the fort. Even game had been scarce throughout the long winter.

Two riders nudged their ponies forward when the men reached the gate. The warriors rode within six feet of the men before halting. To the boy's ears the harsh guttural syllables they spoke were meaningless gibberish. Yet, even for a six-year-old mind, there was no misinterpreting the Indians' gestures. Again and again their cupped hands dipped into imaginary bowls and rose to their mouths. With equal frequency their fingers touched their naked cooper-hued bellies.

"We ain't got no food to spare," one of the fort's sentries finally answered with an exaggerated shake of his head. "There's nothing here for you."

The other gray-haired man made a wide sweep with an arm. "Go back where you came from. There ain't even table scraps to spare here. Go away. Go on now."

The braves' voices rose and their gestures increased with determination. Their dark eyes lifted and scanned the fort's interior. One of the Comanches held up a hand and used raised fingers to count the cows he saw within. He pointed to the nearest cow and then gestured to himself and the other mounted warriors.

His answer was another shaking head. "Them's milk cows. We got babies here. Got to have milk for our infants. There ain't nothing here for you. Now go on away from here."

"They ain't listenin'," the second guard said. "That, or they don't understand. Maybe if we slam the door in their faces, they'll get the idea there ain't no handouts to be had."

With a disgusted grunt, the old man turned and walked toward the stockade's gate. He tucked his longrifle beneath an arm and reached out with both hands to swing the gate outward.

A high-pitched cry rent the air and transformed John Teller's fear into stark terror. He stared as a brave astride a paint drove his heels into the pony's flanks. The mustang lunged forward. The Comanche's war lance dropped to skewer straight into the stomach of the old man at the gate.

The remaining sentinel fared no better. The brave standing before him charged to drive a flint-headed lance into the white man's throat then wrench the deadly tip free. Rifle forgotten, the weapon fell uselessly to the ground as the old guard's hands clutched at his neck to stem the crimson that fountained there. The effort was futile; the Comanche struck with the lance once more, thrusting into the man's gut.

In the next instant chaos invaded the quiet morning. War cries ripped from all ten warriors' throats. With lances leveled for the kill they charged over the bodies of the two guards into the unprotected fort.

Terror squeezed around John Teller's heart in a tight fist. Try as he did, he could not move. Only his eyes found motion, darting from one side to the other to fill with the bloody horror that reigned within the stockade.

A brave atop a bay rode down two girls no older than Teller. One fell with a lance driven into her chest; the second went down beneath the mustang's hooves.

A scream yanked the boy's gaze to the right. A warrior threw himself from the back of his pony atop two women in gingham who stood at a cabin door. Only the brave rose—with a blood-dripping hunting knife held high while a yipping cry of victory pealed from his throat.

An arm encircled the boy's waist and wrenched him into the air.

"Cynthia Ann, get into the house!" John heard Lucy Parker's voice call before he realized the arm about his middle belonged to the woman rather than one of the Comanches.

With a boy tucked under each arm, the woman ran across the stockade's ground. On her nine-year-old daughter's heels, she darted into the small log cabin and threw the boys toward the center of the one-room structure where Lucy's two younger children stared up from their play. "All of you, behind the bed. Hide yourselves!"

John Teller scrambled beside sister and brother to do as ordered. Lucy Parker slammed the cabin door and threw the locking board in place. She then yanked a hunting rifle from the wall and hurried to join the five children huddled behind the bed.

"Scoot on underneath," she said in a voice that belied the fear etched on her face. "Those heathens are out for our blood. No matter what happens, don't make a sound. Do you understand? Not so much as a whimper."

Teller nodded his head as did Cynthia Ann and her younger brother.

"Good." Lucy tugged back the hammer on the flintlock with a thumb. "Now all of you get under the bed and keep quiet. And pray for God to watch over us. He's the only one that can save us now."

John offered no argument, but wiggled beside the other children. Lucy remained crouched behind the quilt-covered bed, rifle clutched in white-knuckled hands. Above the bass drum of his heart, he barely could hear her whispered prayer for salvation from the red-skinned demons who butchered those caught outside.

The boy's head jerked up when a fist pounded on the locked door. In the next instant the heavy impact of a well-placed foot struck the door. The simple piece of wood used to bar the entrance cracked and splintered. The door swung in to reveal one of the Kiowas with lance raised and ready. John Teller's lips worked silently, praying for a miracle he knew would never come.

The warrior stepped over the threshold and stopped. His eyes squinted to narrow slits while he peered into the interior darkness. Whether nothing within the cabin immediately interested him, or the scream of a woman in a yellow dress who ran by outside caught his attention, the boy never knew, but the Indian spun around and ran from the house.

Now rather than Lucy Parker's soft praying, the screams and cries of those within the fort wailed through the open door to fill the boy's ears. A gunshot was what John prayed for now. No matter how loud and horrible the screams outside were, he knew they would never carry to the men in the fields. The crack of a single rifle would. However, not one of the Indians had carried a firearm; they did their bloody work with lance and knife.

Lucy held a rifle! For a brief second he considered swinging around, poking his head from under the bed, and telling her to fire the weapon. He was certain that one shot would bring the men running from their plowing and planting.

He remained still and silent. He was just as certain the report of a rifle would have all ten warriors inside the cabin within the span of a heartbeat. By the time his father and the others reached the fort, all within would be dead.

Teller clamped his hands over his ears to block the dying screams of those outside. Lucy Parker was right; God rather than man was their only hope now.

Five minutes—five hours, he was not certain of time's passage—before Lucy reached beneath the bed and touched each of those hidden there. "It's quiet outside. I think we can sneak out the back way and make it to the men."

When all the children remained motionless, the woman urged, "Come on out. We have to try and reach the plowing. The savages will be back to search the cabin. God has given us a chance to live, we must take it."

Teller was first to push from beneath the bed. Cynthia Ann

and her brother followed a second later and finally the two small brothers.

Lucy pressed a finger to her lips while she stared into each of the young faces. "When we're outside, move quickly around the house to the stockade's back entrance. Don't make a sound. Just open the latch, duck outside, and run toward the fields as fast as you can. We'll be safe if we can reach the men."

Teller nodded, pressing his lips tightly together to assure not so much as a heavy breath could pass through them. He then followed the woman and her children outside.

His silent prayers that the raiding party had abandoned the fort went unanswered. The Indians now moved on foot from cabin to cabin in search of items to loot, or knelt beside the unmoving bodies of those they had slaughtered. One glance at the bloody head of Billy Tobias's still body amid spilled firewood revealed the gruesome trophies the braves sliced away from the scalps of each of their victims.

A piercing, high-pitched warning cry ripped through the fort's deadly stillness. To Teller's right a Comanche stepped from a cabin and pointed directly at him. Three other warriors swung around and chorused the dog-imitating cry.

"Run!" Lucy ordered as she dropped the rifle and snatched the two small boys into her arms. "Run, children, run!"

Teller needed no further urging. Around the cabin he followed Cynthia Ann. Others must have reached the fort's rear entrance, because the door-sized opening stood wide. With Lucy on his heels, he darted through the passageway and ran toward the low rising hill and the safety that lay on the other side. Ahead he saw a dozen others frantically trying to reach the men, who labored without a hint of the massacre underway within their homes.

"Hurry!" Lucy called in panted desperation. "Run! Oh God, run!"

A stolen glance over a shoulder revealed the source of the woman's desperation. Four Comanche warriors astride their ponies reined around the fort and rode straight for them.

The vision of Billy Tobias's dead, scalped body brought a surge of energy to John Teller's small legs. With all the strength within his body he ran over the uneven ground on a straight line to the hilltop and the men who could save him.

A woman's scream jerked his head around. Behind him Lucy

Parker threw herself and her two young sons to the ground as a warrior thrust a lance aimed for her vulnerably exposed back. The woman's desperate act worked. The lance drove harmlessly through empty air feet above Lucy Parker's back.

The warrior did not rein his pony about to renew the attack on the mother and her two small children. His bare legs rose and slammed moccasined heels into the mustang's side to charge straight toward the six-year-old boy who fled ahead of him.

An image of Billy Tobias's lifeless body, the hair sliced from atop his head by a Comanche hunting knife once again filled John's mind. Death in the form of a black-maned, naked savage carried by thundering hooves swept down on him. The boy's short legs pumped harder, fired by the realization that the lance meant for Lucy Parker was now homed at his own back.

A rock slammed into the back of Teller's head rather than the bite of hand-worked flint and the piercing hardness of a wood shaft. Blackness swallowed the morning's light as he fell toward the ground certain he tumbled into the embrace of death ...

... Not death—realization penetrated his dazed young mind. Although darkness blurred his vision, he felt himself snatched into the air and jerked upward. Hard, he was shoved down atop the solid feel of a moving horse. An arm as tight as a band of steel clamped around the boy's chest. A scream of victory tore into the air to fill the child's ears.

John blinked away the darkness that had tried to suck him down into unconsciousness. Death had not embraced him. Instead he was held atop a mustang by the unyielding arm of a Comanche warrior, pressing him hard against a muscular chest when the brave once again screamed out a victory cry while he tugged the pony's head around.

How or why death had spared him was beyond the comprehension of John's confused brain. That he lived and was enveloped in the gagging smell of sour sweat that surrounded his captor was all his mind could grasp.

He saw the blurred forms of the other attackers as they reined their mounts about and rode northward away from Fort Parker, but their actions meant nothing to the boy. He heard the screams of women and children, but their meaning did not sink through the spinning flight of his mind until a full hour passed and the brave who held him abruptly pulled back on the single-rein hackamore to halt the mustang.

The Comanche leaped to the ground and yanked his young captive to the earth. Before John could scream out his terror, the flat of an open palm smacked sharply against his cheek. The brave's right hand grasped the boy's collar and yanked him forward until the Indian's face loomed a mere inch from the end of John's nose.

The throaty syllables that growled from the savage's lips were incomprehensible, but their tone, the ferocious expression that twisted the Comanche's face, and the brave's upraised fist were more than clear. Pressing his lips tightly together to indicate he would not utter a sound, John nodded his submission.

Immediately the warrior began to strip away the boy's clothing. Shirt, pants, boots, underthings—all were ripped from his body and tossed aside. The boy stood naked as the day he was born when the Comanche grasped him beneath the arms and lifted him back atop the mustang.

A woman's sob drew John's attention to the left. For the first time since the brave had swept down on him, the boy realized that he was not the raiding party's sole captive. Five others had been taken by the band, and like him, all were being stripped of every shred of clothing they wore. He saw Cynthia Ann a few feet away. Tears streamed down cheeks reddened by blows to silence her as her hands and arms tried to cover the pale white of her nakedness. Her brother John stood a stride or two away, crying as a brave tossed him to his back and yanked his pants from his legs.

John's gaze moved to the next two captives. Both were young women from the fort. Rachel Plummer and Elizabeth Kellog stood as naked as Cynthia Ann with arms crossed to cover themselves amid the scattered remnants of their torn dresses and petticoats.

The sixth captive was a mere infant cradled in the arm of a Kiowa who sat atop his mustang grinning as he stared at the two women. The baby was too far away for John to identify; it could have been one of five newborns from the fort. It was not hard for the boy to imagine the fate of the child's mother. From the blood-matted scalps strung from the waists of each of the ten raiders, John doubted that many within the stockade still lived.

Swinging astride the pony behind John, his captor called out to the others. Immediately the remaining warriors grabbed their captives and threw them onto their ponies' backs. No other sound was uttered when the raiding party once more urged their mounts northward following the course of a small stream.

By the time night fell and the raiding party once more halted their mounts, John fully understood the reason he and the others had been stripped of clothing. Not only had their captors etched into their minds how helpless and vulnerable they were, but the Texas sun had burned all their pale skins to bright red. The tormenting pain of being touched by the warrior who claimed him, rather than escape, fully occupied the boy's mind while the brave bound him hand and foot with strips of leather.

In spite of the burning agony of their skin, John, Cynthia Ann, and her brother huddled close together when the Indians placed them on one side of a small campfire they built. The countless tales John had heard of the tortures endured by Indian captives before they were finally allowed to die crowded John's mind while he stared across the low flames to where the ten raiders surrounded the two women. If their captors intended to kill them, it would surely be now.

Although the horrifying flights of his brain prepared him for the worst, a startled gasp of terror escaped his throat when two of the braves suddenly leaped forward and threw Rachel Plummer to her back on the ground. While they held the woman, a third Comanche pushed aside his breechcloth and lowered himself atop the naked woman . . .

. . . John Teller poured the remaining coffee in Dumaine's cup then tossed the grounds from the pot atop the campfire. He took a long slow sip from his own cup before continuing.

"While the three of us watched, every one of them heathens took both them women that night. It wasn't something meant for a growed man's eyes, let alone the eyes of children. It ain't something the years erase. I can still see it as though it had happened a few minutes ago."

Dumaine held his cup in both hands and stared at the campfire's flames for several silent minutes, before asking, "How did you get away?"

Teller glanced overhead. The stars were bright this far away from the town lights of civilized men and women. He wanted just to sit and stare at them, to push old memories back behind the mental locks he had constructed to contain them over the long years since his childhood. Now that his companion had opened those barriers, he knew they would not be contained.

"My pa always said I was a burr under the saddle," Teller eventually said. "I was always gettin' into one thing or another. Didn't make no never mind what the punishment might be if I got caught. I had a mind about me, and the devil take anything that stood in my way. That's the way it was that second night. I didn't care what the braves might do to me. I just wasn't gonna stick around and give 'em a chance at doin' it. After those braves had finished with the women that second night, they fell off to sleep. That's when I slipped away. The brave who claimed me had forgot to check my bonds. I managed to slip them off my wrists and untie my ankles. Buck-assed naked, I ran off into the night. I stuck to a stream the braves had followed as they rode from the fort. Five days later, more dead than alive, I was found by a group of men searchin' for the raiding party."

Teller took a long sip from his cup, washed the coffee around in his mouth as though attempting to remove an indefinable bitterness that coated his tongue, and swallowed. "A week later, Pa and me were in San Antonio. He had decided Fort Parker was no place for a man wantin' to get a new start in life."

The New Orleans reporter downed the last of his coffee then used a handful of sand to scour the tin cup clean. "And the others? What happened to them?"

The older man answered with a shake of his head to shove aside the "might have beens" that edged into his thoughts. "Rachel Plummer was bought from the Comanches by Mexican traders. She ended up writin' a book about all that happened to her while she was a Comanche captive. Found a copy of the book when I was twenty or so and tried to read it. Couldn't get past a few pages or so. Guess I was too close to the subject to appreciate what she had set down."

The niggling doubt that had eaten at Teller since the night he had escaped his captors refused to go away. Despite the fact he had been no more than a frightened six-year-old boy, he had never forgiven himself for fleeing into the night without attempting to help the others escape. Hard, cold logic said he would never have slipped away had he tried to aid the others, that the warriors would have awakened and probably killed them on the spot. Logic did not ease the guilt for what he felt was an act of cowardice as he ran into the safety of the night's darkness.

Above all the raiders had done to him and those in Fort

Parker, he hated the Comanches for that—for planting a seed of self-despise within the breast of a mere child.

"Rachel Plummer was reunited with her son—it was her infant the raiders had taken. He and John Parker were eventually brought to Fort Gibson, thanks to the Army. Elizabeth Kellog was traded to a group of Kitchawas, who passed her on to another band of Indians—can't remember what they were now," Teller said with another shake of his head. "I was still a boy when it happened, but I can remember Pa reading a newspaper article to me. The Indians showed up in Nacogdoches. The folks there paid one hundred and fifty dollars to buy her away from the redskins."

"And Cynthia Ann Parker?" Dumaine asked.

Teller glanced at his young employer and pursed his lips. "She was the only one that didn't get back to her family. She was nine years old when the fort was attacked. No one saw her again until she was a growed woman. By then she was more Comanche than white. She was the squaw of a warrior called Peta Nocona—a bloody bastard every Texan had been trying to kill for years. She had whelped three half-breeds by the time she was returned to civilization. The oldest of them was the one they call Quanah."

Dumaine rubbed a hand over his chin and drew a deep breath. "There is more than a touch of irony in what you have told me, Mr. Teller. A man with white blood running in his veins rising to lead the Comanches against his mother's people—my readers will believe I've penned a wild yarn when my paper prints this story."

"Ain't certain what you mean by 'irony,' Mr. Dumaine, but if you mean it's kind of funny, I guess you're right. In Texas we got a saying 'bout Quanah Parker and the way he's run the army and the rangers ragged these past few years—breedin' will tell," Teller said. "The good Lord knows, he's been every bit as bloody as Peta Nocona—maybe more so. The army's been pressin' the fight since the end of the War between the States."

Dumaine's mouth opened as though to comment, but the younger man kept his thoughts to himself. Teller drained the last of his coffee, then pointed to their mounts. "Best get your sleeping roll. It's getting later by the minute, and we've got a long ride ahead of us tomorrow."

"I thought you said Colonel Mackenzie was near." The newspaperman pushed from the ground and walked to his mount.

"He was, this morning." Teller untied his own sleeping roll from his saddle then checked the hobbles binding the front legs of their mounts and packhorses. "He got another day on us while we was down in Palo Duro."

Certain the leather straps that prevented the horses from wandering away in the night were secure, Teller spread his blankets on one side of the dying fire. "Reckon the place to find Mackenzie will be up at Fort Sill in the Indian Territory. Sooner or later, he'll show up there."

"Won't Mackenzie continue to chase the Comanches who fled the canyon?" Dumaine questioned while he climbed into his sleeping roll.

"For a while I suggest he'll do just that. But he had his chance in the canyon and missed it. If he finds any redskins, they'll be in small bands with little fight in 'em," Teller replied. "With winter comin' on, Fort Sill's the place to be, Mr. Dumaine. If the Comach want to survive, they'll have to go there to surrender. It's either turn themselves in on the reservation or starve to death. I don't see it any other way."

Teller's gaze turned southward to the canyon's rim as he stretched atop the unrolled blankets. He silently cursed Mackenzie. The officer had been given the opportunity to wipe the Comanche from the face of the earth and failed. Texas would be a far safer land were the corpses rotting below those of braves and squaws rather than ponies.

CHAPTER THREE

APRIL 1875

Three braves rode silently through a night hung with a full moon. The gently rolling plains offered no obstacle to the ponies they rode; they had left the rugged span of eroded badlands at the foot of Caprock more than a day behind them. Still they moved with caution, senses alert for a minute warning of attack.

Of more danger than the open flatlands was the moon riding high above the eastern horizon. Once Mother Moon graced the Nermernuh, or the People, as those whom the whites call Comanche named themselves. It was beneath the silvery radiance of her light that warriors rode far and wide to raid the clumsy camps of *Tejanos*, Mexicans, and other Indian tribes who foolishly encroached upon the lands claimed by the People.

Or once rode.

The Nermernuh lands bordered on yesterday, threatened to fade on the morrow to nothing more than memories of glory lost in the vast decay of time. Only a handful of bands remained beyond the boundaries of the reservation and the iron hand of the soldiers stationed to the north in Fort Sill.

The moonlight that once illuminated the ways of

far-ranging raiding parties now left the three braves vulnerably exposed. Should a passing blue-coat patrol glimpse the three, flight would be the only path open to the braves. To run from an enemy did not sit lightly on the shoulders of a Nermernuh. It was shame not to be tolerated.

Still without a sound passing between them, the three reined their mounts down a slight slope. The soft fall of the terrain led to a narrow creek that snaked northward to empty its waters into the Red River, which lay fewer miles away than could be counted on the fingers of a man's hand. Within the cloaking shadows of a copse of black willows that drew precious life from the lazy trickle of water, the braves halted and dismounted.

"This has no wisdom in its heart."

"It is no longer safe for us here."

Two of the braves turned to stare up at the third, who towered over his companions by a full six inches. Among the stocky-built Nermernuh the warrior, who had yet to see thirty comings and goings of winter's ice and snow, was a giant whose height equaled that of the hated *Tejanos*. The dappled moonlight that filtered through the willows' slender leaves revealed other differences when the brave turned to the two. His facial features were aquiline rather than broad and heavy as those who rode with him.

"It is here that I am summoned," the giant answered simply as though no further explanation were necessary.

An unsatisfied grunt burst from the lips of the brave called Forty Buffalo. "Are you certain you have not heard the voice of the *nenuhpee*?"

The tall warrior ignored the question. Like all the People he feared the malicious little people, spirits who delighted in confusing and beguiling those they visited. But it was not the *nenuhpee* who called him here. Since the new moon his dreams had been visited seven times by images of this place. Such medicine could not be ignored.

"Listen to Forty Buffalo, Quanah," Speaks Softly urged in a whispered voice from whence sprang his name. "I can smell the stink of the long knives on the breeze. This place can offer us no shelter."

A hint of smoke did ride in the breeze, Quanah Parker admitted to himself while his eyes scanned the plains. *Wood*, he recognized. A distant fire burned within the hearth of a settler's sod house. A soldier's campfire was fueled with buffalo chips gathered during the day's march.

His gaze centered on three conical forms a quarter of a mile from the creek. To look upon the mounds was to feel their power, to recognize the hands that had shaped them did not belong to mere men. Amid the endless monotony of flat grasslands that rolled from horizon to horizon, they thrust up toward the sky to remind the People of the unseen spirits that walked the earth.

There were those among the Nermernuh, medicine men who garnered great power to themselves, who warned that evil hands had given form to the mounds, and who shied wide of them and the land touched by their shadows. An equal number of the People viewed the mounds as a place woven with magicks where a brave seeking guidance might reach out and touch the forces that molded the lives of mortals.

It was the third mound, the highest of the trio, rising a hundred feet above the prairie, that had filled Quanah's dreams for so many nights. There, atop the mound, he would seek the vision that would lead him to the Path.

"Quanah, we can ride half the journey back to our families by the time the morning sun rises," Speaks Softly's voice edged into thoughts of otherworldly beings. "We can do nothing—"

A rustle in the spring grass swung Quanah around. A long-eared jackrabbit with its powerful hind legs bounded into the moonlight four strides from the muscular brave. Quanah caught himself when he started to swing his rifle to shoulder. He then held out an arm to halt his companions as their rifle barrels rose.

Stomach rumbling in protest, he watched the rabbit lose itself in the high, tangled grass. To remain still and ignore the possibility of fresh meat was an unspeakable torment.

The winter had been long and hard. With so few ponies remaining with his band, it had been difficult to provide meat for the women's great black pots. For those accustomed to eating buffalo and antelope, rabbit had become welcomed fare, when it could be found. Few dogs now guarded the band at night. Taboo though their meat was, one by one their throats had been cut to provide nourishment for the children. Even that often was not enough. He had seen far too many of the young and sick die during the time of ice and snow.

"Quanah, listen to your friends," Forty Buffalo spoke. "Come away from this place. Even the rabbits do not fear us here. They laugh openly in our faces."

"A rabbit scurrying in the night is not the sound of laughter," the tall brave replied while his gaze returned to the alien mounds of earth. He had not come this far from the high plains to turn his back and deny the vision of his dreams.

"No good can come of being here," Speaks Softly added. "The blue coats come and go as they please here. It is not as it once was. Where we once hunted the buffalo, the *Tejanos* now graze their long-horned cows."

Quanah could not deny that. As the black-skinned buffalo soldiers in their blue uniforms pushed back the People from the plains, the Texans had invaded like locusts. Today they had seen five massive herds of cattle where the whites would have feared to walk a year ago.

"Ride back if you fear the blue coats will find you here." Quanah turned to face his friends. His words came not in admonishment, but in the belief that all Nermernuh braves were free to follow the voices of their hearts and souls. The medicine that directed the feet of one often was not meant for others.

Pointing toward the mounds, he said, "I must go there and find the answer. If you ride, leave me but one pony tied to a willow."

He did not wait for an answer. Pivoting, he lifted a buffalo robe from the back of the dappled gray he had ridden, a fine horse he had stolen from the blue-coated soldier Mackenzie. The bundle tucked beneath his left arm, he strode boldly out of the shadows toward the mounds.

"We will wait beside your pony and our own mounts," Forty Buffalo called out behind Quanah.

"Your medicine remains with you. We will—"

Speaks Softly's gentle voice lost itself in the whisper of Quanah's footfalls amid the spring grass. The tall brave's chest expanded while he drew the night air deeply into his lungs. It was good his friends still sensed the presence of medicines and trusted those powers. Since the white colonel called Mackenzie led his black-skinned buffalo soldiers into Palo Duro Canyon before the coming of the snow and ice, there had been little in which the People could find faith.

Yet the belief Forty Buffalo and Speaks Softly displayed in the powerful medicine still surrounding their companion did nothing to lift the weight from the young warrior's heart. Desperation rather than strength had brought him so far into the lands now held by the *Tejanos* with their herds of long-horned cows. Had it not been for the dreams, the only hint of medicine that had touched him throughout the winter, he never would have left the safety of the high plains to risk the lives of friends as well as his own.

Even as he reached the foot of the highest grass-covered mound, Quanah felt a closeness of kin to the jackrabbit he had seen scurry into darkness moments ago. *Brother to the rabbit,* he reflected while delving into himself to reclaim a feel of what he had once been before the soldiers' attack in the canyon.

Young—he had been so very young then. Now he carried the burden of an old man in his breast. And he had been proud. How he had reveled in the sound of his own name when the women and children shouted it out whenever he rode into camp. His chest had felt like it would burst with pride when he saw the approval in faces of the older braves. The young braves' trust and willingness to follow him fed his pride like seasoned wood tossed atop a fire.

An image of his father pushed from Quanah's memories. As a boy he had seen similar expressions on the braves' faces when his father had walked through their camp. Had time not chosen its present path, had Mackenzie not found the miles of tipis raised on the floor of the canyon, the Nermernuh would have sung songs of his deeds as they did of his father's.

None in his camp sang now. Was it the same with the older braves who had deserted their lands and led their bands to Fort Sill? Or had they learned new songs on the white man's reservation? His mind refused the possibility of such songs springing from the lips of the People. Was there coup to be taken when a warrior armed himself with a hoe to work the earth? What bravery was to be found in the planting of corn and beans? How could a man hunt when his ponies had been taken from him?

No, those on the reservation do not sing, he thought while he climbed the steep slope. But did their bellies rumble as his did now? Did their children cry out as starvation pinched their stomachs?

He tried to shove aside the realization that those who had forsaken the old ways for the reservation now feasted daily on the beef brought to Fort Sill. For a full generation Nermernuh bands had camped on the reservation and eaten the white man's beef during the winter. But with the greening of spring they had slipped away during the night to return to their own lands and ways. There was no shame in stealing food from an enemy in such a manner. Among the Nermernuh there was only honor for those who displayed such slyness.

"Cow!" the words came from Quanah's lips in a disgusted curse.

The Kwerhar-rehnuh did not eat cattle. Buffalo and antelope were the hearty fare for the People who claimed the Texas high plains as their own. A cow's meat held no flavor. Better was the rich taste of mule stolen from the blue coats.

Quanah's thoughts stumbled. The Kwerhar-rehnuh did not eat dog or fish or turtle or fowl either. But with the buffalo gone and the antelope staying far from the hunters' arrows during the winter, those in his band had eaten the flesh of all the creatures taboo to the Nermernuh—and still the children and the old died.

Upon reaching the rounded crest, Quanah stood silently and surveyed the plains that seemed to rush out from the base of the mound to swallow the world. For as far as he could see neither night rider nor steer blemished the land. Perhaps some medicine did remain with him. He had no desire to be discovered by soldier or *Tejano* while deep in a medicine vision.

It was for that vision and it alone that he had journeyed to the top of this mound. Time had come to seek guidance from powers greater than himself. He spread the buffalo robe on the ground then settled cross-legged atop it. Without a vision to guide him, he was of no use to his band; he had no idea which was the right road to walk.

As surely as his father's blood flowed within his veins, so did the blood of his mother. It was to her soul and spirit he prayed while he filled the bowl of an ornately carved pipe he had carried within the robe with tobacco from a leather pouch strung about his waist. It was her blood, mingled in his body with the blood of his father, that must direct the vision—must lead him across the vastness of the plains to the white man—must open the eye within and allow him to see into the heart of the enemy. Only then could he foretell the course of the white man and the soldiers and chose a path for his own feet and those in his band.

Fearing a campfire would draw the attention of unseen eyes far out on the prairie, he lit the tobacco with a smoldering tuft of dried grass ignited by a spark from flint struck with the blunt edge of his hunting knife. Carefully he sucked and puffed at the pipe without inhaling until he was certain the tobacco burned smoothly. In the manner passed down for generations upon generations among the People, he lifted the bowl above his head offering the first of the smoke to Mother Moon, who now reigned in the sky. The second rolling cloud of blue smoke was given to Father Sun, whose warmth and light were the givers of life. Lastly he held the pipe to the north, south, east, and west as an offering to the winds.

Tobacco and patience opened the doors to the spirits and the visions they bestowed upon a brave. Thus had the Nermernuh always sought to momentarily bind themselves with the other world. So it was Quanah smoked that first bowl and the second and the tenth. But no veils were lifted from his eyes, no spirit guided his thoughts.

His mind returned to the winter and the cries of the children and the silent pleas read in the faces of his wives. Rather than a mystic mount to carry his soul into the camps of his enemies, he rode the memories of the countless days spent astride his pony hunting for rabbits and quail, while dodging the patrolling soldiers who now crossed the Llano Estacado without impunity from the once-strong Nermernuh.

Another five bowls of tobacco brought only the bitterness of standing on the rim of Palo Duro and staring down at the horror left by Mackenzie and his soldiers. In a battle that had cost the People but two warriors, the longknife colonel had driven a killing blow into the heart of the Nermernuh.

Three more bowls and all he saw were the bands that trudged their way across the grasslands toward Fort Sill to surrender themselves to the soldiers. All he heard were reports of brave warriors confined in meathouses as punishment for warring against the whites—reports brought by the few braves who escaped the reservation.

Quanah freed the ash of his twentieth bowl with the heel of his left hand and stared at the sky above. Mother Moon now rode the western sky; the eastern horizon was tinged with the purples of the coming dawn. Night would soon pass, and he would be denied the vision his dreams had promised.

His gaze dropping to the warm pipe, he traced the intricate carvings and bright paints that decorated it. Tobacco and time had always been the way to medicine vision among the Kwerhar-rehnuh. No more than a bowl or two of the first remained in his pouch, a supply gathered from all the men in his band. Each moment he spent atop the mound increased the danger of being found for himself and Forty Buffalo and Speaks Softly who waited below in the willows.

Reverently he placed the pipe on the buffalo robe beside him. There was another way to bring visions. He dug two fingers and a thumb into another pouch hung from his waist and pulled out a wrinkled, leathery bulb. His first wife, who had not been a wife, had showed him the power held in a simple cactus button. It was with the fruit of the peyote her people, the Mescalero Apache, used to summon the spirits and open the gate to the mystic worlds beyond man.

As though he ate a wild plum, Quanah bit into the peyote button, chewed and swallowed. The pulpy fruit held little flavor; a slight bitter aftertaste remained in his mouth. It took a total of five bites to devour the whole cactus button, then Quanah sat perfectly still, waiting.

A foreknowledge of what came next did not diminish the intensity of the needlelike pain that jabbed deep in his gut.

Quanah closed his eyes and steeled himself as another burning needle flared alive in his stomach. Like living fingers of fire it spread to enclose his belly and squeeze down. He contained a moan that tried to push from his throat.

Even harder to ignore were the waves of nausea that rolled up from his cramping gut. Yet, he struggled to hold down the peyote and the poison it contained in his stomach. To free the medicine locked with the cactus, to give wing to the visions, a brave had to fight past the pain, lift himself above the queasy undulation. If he gave in to the overwhelming urge to clutch his middle and toss forward to empty his stomach like one who had eaten tainted meat, the magic of the peyote would be lost.

Gradually, with what seemed the same slowness with which the seasons proceeds from one to another, the harsh cramping subsided. Instead of wrenching pain, a soothing warmth spread through his gut. As though he had downed several cups of his third wife's strong coffee in a matter of minutes, he felt that warmth burst upward within him to fill his head and flush his cheeks. His heart throbbed in his chest, racing at twice its usual rhythm.

This, too, he expected. Compared to the pain and nausea, the runaway pounding of his heart, the hot rush of blood within his veins were easy to endure. Beyond these earthly physical sensations lay the other world he sought. Soon the medicine he had journeyed so far to find would be—

"Quanah!"

The voice snapped his head straight. His eyes flew open. The drumming of his heart doubled in speed once again. Why would his friends below call to him now? Only approaching danger could force them to break his solemn vigil.

Soldiers! Quanah's mind thrust aside the rushing swirl enveloping it. For Forty Buffalo to shout a warning, a patrol of blue coats must be riding toward the mounds.

His body aquiver with the effects of the peyote, Quanah pushed upward and managed to draw his feet under him until he crouched like some copper-hued cat ready to spring. His gaze shot northward, then to the east, south, and west. Nothing. He saw no advancing column of mounted soldiers; he saw no sign of danger anywhere.

Why did Forty Buffalo call out? A frown darkened his face as he turned toward the willows below where his two companions waited with the ponies.

His eyes widened and a sheen of cold sweat beaded on his broad forehead. The willows—Forty Buffalo and Speaks Softly— the three horses—all were gone! Only the gently rolling prairie stretched before him.

"Quanah."

His head jerked from side to side, but the voice's owner was nowhere to be found!

"Quanah."

Father Sun? Awe and fear set his quivering muscles to trembling when he lifted his eyes to the golden array of light that announced the coming morning. Was it Father Sun who called to him?

Dawn's yellow gold burst into hot white as the round face of the sun thrust above the horizon and pushed into the cloudless blue of the day.

"Quanah."

The brave's wide eyes narrowed. The voice did not belong to the sun. He had heard it before—years before. *Who?*

"Quanah."

"Uncle?" His frown deepened as he recognized the voice of his long-dead uncle. "Uncle, is that you?"

"Quanah, come to my side."

It was his uncle! Fear centered itself in Quanah's heart, threatening to explode it. A Comanche honored only his father above an uncle, for it was the father's brother who was responsible for training a young boy to take his place as a brave among his people. But this was the voice of a ghost!

"Quanah, come to my side."

The sun's light exploded into a maelstrom of colors. Like a shattered rainbow the hues spun outward with maddening speed.

"Quanah, come to my side."

From the center of the swirling colors came his uncle's voice, calling, drawing him. Upward Quanah felt his body lift from the solid earth into the sky. Up, ever up, an invisible hand hurled him into the sky-born maelstrom of spinning color.

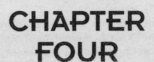

CHAPTER
FOUR

"Quanah, come to my side."

Quanah ignored his uncle's whispered summons. Instead, the boy nocked a cedar-shafted arrow tipped with flint and slowly pulled back the bowstring. His eyes narrowed as he took aim on a young buck's broad shoulder. He and his uncle had found the deer's tracks near the camp just after sunrise and tracked the animal throughout the morning. Now was no time to let tonight's dinner escape.

"Quanah, forget the deer!" The brave's whisper of a second ago was now an echoing command.

Cona Cawb-vey's voice carried not only to Quanah, but to the alert ears of the buck. In the space of a single heartbeat, the deer bounded forward and disappeared into the thick brush of a cedar brake far beyond the range of bow and arrow.

A grunt of disgust burst from Quanah's lips; disappointment knotted within him. Only once before had he brought down a deer. The older boys in the band had taunted him rather than praised his ability. "A child's luck" and "an accident" they had judged the doe it had taken him half a day to drag back to camp. Today with the buck that had just escaped, he would have proven his prowess as a hunter equal to those three years his elder. Now he would once again have to endure—

"Quanah, to my side!"

Cona Cawb-vey's demanding tone cut through the young hunter's thoughts of imagined jeers of humiliation. Quanah slid the unused arrow back into his quiver and turned to his uncle who stood fifty feet behind him holding the reins of their painted ponies. "I come."

With an agitated wave of a hand the brave urged his nephew to hurry. Sullenly Quanah refused to comply. No matter what Fire Face, as his uncle was called because of the brave's love for the red paints he used when he chose the warrior's path, wanted him to see, it could not be important enough to equal the loss of the buck. Today, maybe for several days to come, he would not jump to his feet in instant response to his uncle's every command.

"Quanah, now!" Cona Cawb-vey shouted and thrust a finger toward the south. "Look there!"

Atop a rolling ridge a quarter of a mile away rode seventy-five braves. Quanah recognized the familiar form of Peta Nocona, his father, leading the band. "Where do they go?"

Cona Cawb-vey shook his head when the boy reached his side. "There were no raiding parties planned for today. It is the wrong time of the moon to ride south and raid the *Tejanos.*"

"There are too many braves for a raiding party," Quanah spoke his thoughts aloud. Never would all the able-bodied braves in the band ride off to raid and leave the camp undefended.

"You are right." Cona Cawb-vey tossed his nephew the single horsehair rein to his pony. "Mount. Something is terribly wrong!"

The sweet revenge of ignoring Cona Cawb-vey's commands forgotten, Quanah grasped his pinto's mane and swung to the horse's back. His heels dug into the animal's flanks as he yanked the pony's head around to give chase to his uncle, who rode in a hard run toward the warriors now vanishing on the far side of the ridge.

Halfway to the rise on which he had seen his father, Quanah heard the barking report of rifles. His heels again slammed into his mount's side. The echoing cracks of gunfire came far too frequently to be the two rifles held within his band. Only whites had the number of rifles to equal the gunshots that now continually thundered beyond the ridge. Had a patrol of blue-coated soldiers accidentally ridden this close to the camp?

"Aiieeee!" The wail ripped from Cona Cawb-vey's lips when he reined his mount to a halt atop the hill. "*Tejanos!*"

Quanah's gaze rushed down the ridge's slope toward the broad, muddy band of water that cut through the prairie. A hundred riders, perhaps more, with their heavy leather saddles, had crossed the Red River. Here and there sun glinted silver off the metal stars worn on their chests.

"Rangers!" Cona Cawb-vey said as though cursing. He waved to his nephew. "Follow me."

Again Quanah did not hesitate. He carried a hunting bow and a quiver fat with arrows. If there were need for him to use both, he would do so without question. These invaders from the land in the south they called Texas did not belong here. They came on a blood raid rather than seeking to trade as did the brown-skinned Mexicans who ventured from the west with their wagons filled with coffee, sugar, and blankets.

Instead of a straight path toward the *Tejanos*, Cona Cawb-vey angled his mount down the ridge toward two young braves who stood holding the warriors' now riderless horses. Yanking his paint to an abrupt halt, Cona Cawb-vey leaped to the ground and tossed his rein to the nearest of the young braves, who were no more than boys. He then spun about to face his nephew as Quanah halted his own pony.

"Remain here with these two and guard the horses," Cona Cawb-vey commanded. "Should the *Tejanos* come, use your arrows—and if need be your hunting knife."

"I will do as—"

Cona Cawb-vey gave him no time to finish. Pivoting, the older brave, war lance in hand, ran toward the fighting another quarter of a mile beyond the horses. Quanah's eyes momentarily shifted to the young braves, who glanced at him. The boy's chest swelled with pride. Only the most trusted of the older boys or the youngest braves were given the task of guarding ponies during a battle. He pulled an arrow from its quiver and nocked it. His uncle placed a great honor upon him this day. If need be, he would die fighting to show all that Cona Cawb-vey's trust was not misplaced.

"Look below, child," one of the two said. "Watch and learn. See how Peta Nocona leads our warriors."

Quanah did just that. From his vantage point halfway up the sloping hill the Nermernuh called Antelope because of the game frequently found here, he could see all that happened below without a turn of his head. The *Tejanos* had crossed the river in a spot where its banks had eroded and collapsed.

Although the position offered an easy way across the water, it was obvious the riders had not considered what they faced once on the northern bank. Except for a small semicircle of high-grown weeds, brakes of junipers grew dense and bushy a full hundred strides outward from the water's edge. In spite of the sharp spurs the Rangers wore on the heels of their high boots, their horses would not enter the minor forest of stunted trees.

Watching, Quanah understood why his father and the other warriors had abandoned their mounts. With a circling sweep of an arm, Peta Nocona silently signaled those who followed him to spread out and duck into the brake. Although unseen by the *Tejanos* below, Quanah could see the shifting of green limbs like the movement of wind through the grass as the warriors pushed through the junipers. Within seconds the Kwerhar-rehnuh warriors were positioned just inside the protective cover of the brake all along the perimeter of the clearing.

A cry, imitating the high-pitched bark of the coyote, rose from below. In answer the warriors attacked.

There was no charge as so often employed by the blue coats when they came upon a band of the People. To have run out of the junipers and exposed oneself to the Rangers' rifles would have been sheer madness. While there was honor in dying while defending one's family, there was more glory in living to drive the enemy away and returning to the band's campfires.

To achieve that end the warriors exposed themselves only long enough to release an arrow, then dropped back into the perfect concealment of the juniper brake. To the left a warrior would yell a bloody cry and leap up and quickly send an arrow at the *Tejanos*. When the riders yanked their mounts around to face the now-vanished attacker, two warriors would appear behind them, scream their war cries, then fire their arrows.

So the fighting went. While the Kwerhar-rehnuh arrows rarely found a target, their effect was utter chaos among the Texans. Horses bolted and careened into one another. Riders clung to the broad horns of their saddles to keep their seats atop their mounts. Those Rangers still capable of firing their rifles did so wildly, expending precious bullets into the thick junipers in the desperate hope of hitting a target that was never there.

While the *Tejanos* fought to control their horses, Peta Nocona suddenly broke from the juniper bushes with war lance held before him. Straight at a rider in a red and black shirt he ran. The tip of his lance would have driven deep into the Ranger's exposed side had the man's bay mount not reared. Instead of the Texan, Peta Nocona's lance drove into the horse's belly. The lance's shaft snapped as animal and rider spilled to the ground.

Before the other rider could comprehend what had happened, Peta Nocona spun about and dashed back into cover of the juniper wall.

Quanah stared below as the man who should have died on the end of his father's lance managed to stagger to his feet. One of his companions reined beside him and reached out an arm. In an instant the *Tejano* with his red and black shirt rode behind his companion who reined his mount about and spurred for the river.

The remaining riders saw the wisdom in his action. Tugging the heads of their mounts about, they followed him into the water, across the river, and kept riding southward.

Cries of victory rose from the cedar brake as seventy-five warriors came running from the bushlike trees. Straight up the hill they moved toward their mounts. Peta Nocona was the last to reach the ponies. A grin spread across his face when he saw Quanah waiting with arrow ready in his bow.

"A boy has done the work of a warrior this day," he cried out to the others. Then to his oldest son, he said, "You have honored me. Your task is done for now. Wait here until we return. We must ride after the *Tejanos* and make certain they do not circle back and attack us again."

Quanah merely nodded while his father leaped astride a coal black stallion and rent the air with another war cry. As much as he wanted to follow, the boy sat motionless atop his pony watching the warriors ride toward the river.

He blinked and then blinked again as the realization that the battle was over slowly penetrated his mind. The hint of a smile lifted the corners of his mouth and spread to a wide grin while his chest expanded with pride. Today he witnessed the power of the Kwerhar-rehnuh and shared in the defeat of a hated enemy. His eyes had drunk in the glory of Nermernuh. Seventy-five braves armed with lance and bow had driven away a force twice their number, standing against rifles and pistols.

This is what it meant to be Kwerhar-rehnuh, to be a warrior of the People. This was the heritage that coursed through his veins. One day he would lead warriors into battle as his father had done today. Around the campfires the People would sing of his might and courage.

Quanah blinked again, focusing on the distant forms of the warriors who now rode near the southern horizon. Gradually, he allowed his aching arms to lower the bow and arrow he still held ready to defend against the *Tejanos*. He slowly released an overly held breath.

An undercurrent trembled through the exhilaration that sent his spirit roaring. This day he had seen blood—enemy blood— spilled. The harsh realization that Nermernuh blood might have mixed with that crimson flow was like a slap against a cheek. On more than one occasion during his short life he had seen raiders return with the bodies of dead warriors tied across the backs of their ponies. His ears had heard the keening of the women; his eyes had seen the wives pull hair from their own heads with their hands, slice their breasts with hunting knives in the anguish of their loss.

Quanah's head moved slowly from side to side in denial of this dark possibility. Death claimed only those whose medicine was weak. Warriors protected by powerful medicine stood eye to eye with the enemy and laughed in his face as Peta Nocona had done this day.

Returning an unspent arrow to the quiver for the second time today, Quanah sat straight and proud astride his paint. Strong medicine like that which protected his father also surrounded him. How could it be anything else? Did not the young braves he stood with call him "child"? Yet, though a mere child in the eyes of warriors, he faced battle for the first time this day and still lived. Only the strongest of medicines were his!

"The *Tejanos* were like frightened rabbits before my might!" Peta Nocona lifted a bottle of tequila, traded for from the Mexicans the Texans called Comancheros, to his lips and drank until a thin line of the yellow liquor trickled from the side of his mouth. He belched loudly before continuing. "Their eyes were wide and round with the fear of the Kwerhar-rehnuh. Their horses also felt the shadow of death upon them. So wild were the big *Tejano* ponies that their riders could not control them. They darted first to the left and then to the right. They—"

Quanah reached for the tequila bottle the band passed around the campfire. As his fingers touched the smooth glass his uncle Cona Cawb-vey jerked the prize away and raised the bottle to his own lips before passing it to a brave on his left.

"Time will come when you share the *boisa pah* with the men, my son." Cona Cawb-vey smiled at his nephew and rested a hand on his shoulder. "But this night is not that time."

"But I stood with—" Quanah began in protest.

"Hush." His mother, who sat to his right, shook her head and placed a finger to her lips. "Your father speaks. Honor him by listening as do all in our band this night."

Quanah closed his mouth, seeing the pride in her eyes as they returned to Peta Nocona who stood beside the blazing flames, gesturing wildly as he retold the details of the battle for the tenth time that night. Should he flag in his recounting, a brave or a squaw would call out for him to continue.

Quanah's young chest puffed out with pride while his gaze traveled around the great circle surrounding the fire. Every member of the band was here tonight to share in the celebration of victory, to honor the bravery of his father. Until the dawn broke on a new day men and women alike would demand that Peta Nocona retell and retell how he had led the warriors against the *Tejanos* and driven them away. And they would delight with each new telling as the dangers Peta Nocona faced grew and the courage and strength required to vanquish those dangers swelled.

This was the way of the Nermernuh, to share the greatness of a victory until it belonged to all in the band. There could be no doubt that this was the correct way. The fierce pride the boy saw in the faces of every man, woman, and child bespoke of the rightness of this way. This was what it meant to be born as one of the People.

Quanah's gaze returned to his mother. For the first time, he was struck by the strangeness of the pride he saw reflected in her face. Naduah, she was called more often than the other names, Preloch and Norah, sometimes used by the band. His mother, despite the darkness of her face, was not Nermernuh; she was as white as the breasts she bared when Quanah used to watch her suckle his younger brother.

Yet, the radiant pride he saw in his mother's face was far greater than that Am-a-wau, his father's second wife, displayed. And Am-a-wau, who sat on Naduah's right, was born of both Kwerhar-rehnuh mother and father. How could it be that his mother, who often told her oldest son that her true name was Sintny-Ann-Parker—that his own name was Quanah Parker after the name her father carried, held more pride in Peta Nocona's deeds than one born of Kwerhar-rehnuh blood?

It was beyond the understanding of his young mind. But, he shared that pride. Today his father, long known as a great warrior among the People, had proven himself to be a great leader of the Kwerhar-rehnuh as well!

Above all, Quanah had seen all of it, had witnessed his father's might. How many sons of Nermernuh warriors could claim such an honor? How many sons in all the People could say they stood with their father in the battle that proved him to be a mighty leader?

Quanah could think of none other than himself. Once again he was struck by the magicks that surely must weave about him. Why else had he been so honored this day?

Cona Cawb-vey stirred to his left. His uncle shoved from the ground and eased away from the fire's flickering light. Beside a tipi, he edged his breechclout to one side and relieved himself. Instead of returning to his place in the great circle, Cona Cawb-vey strolled away into the night's darkness.

Quanah eased from his cross-legged position and scooted away from the circle. Standing, he followed the brave. It was not like his uncle to leave amid such joyous celebration.

"You step heavily tonight, Quanah," Cona Cawb-vey said without looking over a shoulder at the boy's approach. "You should be with the others reveling in my brother's deeds this day."

Quanah reached his uncle's side when Cona Cawb-vey paused at the edge of the village of a hundred tipis. "But you no longer celebrate. Is there something wrong? Has the *boisa pah* turned your spirits dark?"

The brave chuckled and shook his head. "There seems to be

no warmth in the fire water for me this night. The chill in the air seems greater than usual."

"Then you should come back and sit by the fire's warmth," Quanah suggested, feeling only warmth in the spring night. "You will be missed."

Another dry chuckle came from his uncle. "Not this night. Tonight belongs to my brother Peta Nocona. This is as it should be. He proved himself to be a war chief today."

Cona Cawb-vey turned to his nephew. "And you, my brother's son, proved that the warrior's blood of our family runs true in your veins. All saw your bravery today. You have made me proud."

Quanah grinned, his chest expanding with each word his uncle spoke. "Then what is it that darkens your spirits, my uncle?"

"The *Tejanos*," Cona Cawb-vey answered simply.

"The *Tejanos*?" Quanah did not understand.

Cona Cawb-vey stood silently, his head tilted back while he stared up at the diamond field of stars that was scattered across the night. Quanah wanted to press his uncle further, but knew better. When the time came for Cona Cawb-vey to answer his question, Cona Cawb-vey would give his answer.

"There is an uneasiness in my bones this night," Cona Cawb-vey eventually said. "The tallest of the *Tejanos* today is known to the People. He is called Sul Ross and wears the Ranger star. I believe it was this Sul Ross who led the *Tejanos* to us today."

"Is he any different from any of the hated whites in the south?" For Quanah, as with all the Nermernuh, the word *Tejano* was considered a curse.

"He is known to the People because we have met him and the men he leads more than once in battle, my brother's son," Cona Cawb-vey replied, still staring at the night sky. "In many ways, he reminds me of a Kwerhar-rehnuh warrior. He fights with a mighty spirit."

"But he fled with the others," Quanah insisted, unable to see the direction his uncle's words led.

"This is so," Cona Cawb-vey conceded. "Yet, never have the *Tejanos* ridden so deep into our lands as they did this day. Always they have remained south of the river, fearing to set foot in Kwerhar-rehnuh lands."

"Perhaps this Sul Ross is a fool for having done so," Quanah answered.

Cona Cawb-vey laughed and reached down to squeeze the boy's shoulder. "Perhaps he is."

"Truly he is," Quanah continued. "He and all the rest were driven away like frightened dogs. Not even their rifles could help them." He paused, looking up at his uncle. "We drove them away without any of our warriors being injured."

"That is also so, which speaks of the strong medicine Peta Nocona carried with him today." Cona Cawb-vey's tone retained the darkness of melancholia. "The *Tejanos* are gone—for now."

Quanah tensed, his eyes peering into the night. "Do you believe they will return tonight?"

"No, not this night, Quanah," Cona Cawb-vey answered. "But they will be back. They always come back. And I fear they will push deeper and deeper into our hunting grounds."

"Then we shall drive them away again as we did this day," the boy replied.

"How does one drive away the wind?" Cona Cawb-vey glanced back toward the campfire and the celebration that continued there. "My father's father, and his father, and his father all made war on the white man. Still they come. Their number is like that of the locusts in times of hunger. And like the locusts, no matter how many the Kwerhar-rehnuh kill, they keep coming."

"But, Uncle—"

"Quanah, this night is not a time for one so young to worry his mind." Cona Cawb-vey pointed back into the village. "Return to the victory celebration. Honor your father as his bravery deserves."

Quanah tried to speak again, "But, Uncle—"

And was once more cut off. "Now go and do as I say. We will talk of such matters again when you are older."

Quanah did as he was told. Turning, he walked back toward the great circle and the laughter that rippled through the band. However, his uncle's words would not leave his mind—*But they will be back. They always come back—they always come back—*

CHAPTER
FIVE

"—They always come back."

Quanah's head snapped around. A rainbow of colors momentarily blinded his eyes. In that instant he remembered the peyote's alkaloids that flowed within his body and brain. He allowed the vision to turn him toward his father's voice. Blinking against a sudden flaring burst of sunlight, he squinted.

Peta Nocona squatted on his heels beside the still body of a fallen stag sporting a massive rack of antlers. "There is nothing to fear, my son. The deer in our lands are like the buffalo. They always come back."

An uneasy sensation twisted in Quanah's belly when he heard Peta Nocona repeat those words. Two *taum*, the coming of winter's ice by which the Nermernuh measured the passing of a year, had gone since Cona Cawb-vey had spoken those same words. Only his uncle had talked of the growing boldness of the *Tejanos*, a divining of the future that had proven true. With each day that passed yet more whites encroached on lands that once only the Nermernuh might ride with impunity.

"But Father, if the People always hunt the antelope and

deer, will we not kill all of them some day?" The question came from Quanah's youngest brother, called Pecos or Peanut, who stood beside his father with the hide of a wolf about his shoulders to hold off the late autumn chill.

"We have always hunted the deer and the antelope as we have hunted the buffalo, little one," Peta Nocona answered with a broad smile while he extracted an arrow from the buck and cleaned its tip in the sand before returning it to his quiver. "For all of time it has been so, and they remain plentiful. They were put into this world by Father Sun and Mother Moon to feed Kwerhar-rehnuh stomachs."

Peanut stared down at the slain stag and shook his head. "But if the Kwerhar-rehnuh grow in numbers and strength, we will hunt all the deer to feed our stomachs."

Although he had seen only eleven *taum* pass in his life, Quanah had found his life governed by the incidents of that day the Rangers attacked at the Red River. Cona Cawb-vey's simple words haunted his waking hours and dreams like a spirit that possessed a man. While others his age played children's games, he watched and studied his elders. His ears always remained open for word from other bands or rumors brought by traders. From these his mind painted a picture of the Nermernuh and all that happened with them.

He saw what Peanut did not see. The Kwerhar-rehnuh did not grow in numbers. Nor did any of the bands who called themselves Nermernuh.

The winters were the worst of times for the People. The cold and the scarcity of game during the long months of ice and snow always claimed the lives of countless infants. Children born in the warmth of spring were far more likely to live to see another spring.

The sickness the winters brought was not easy on those with age and wisdom. Like the infants, their spirits often passed into the Valley of Thousand-fold Longer and Wider when the northern winds howled like a wolf pack in the night.

From one time of ice to the next, a band of Nermernuh was blessed if its numbers remained constant rather than growing smaller. A band swelled in size only when members of other bands abandoned those bands to join another as was often way of the People.

"Quanah, help me lift this buck." His father's voice drew the boy from his reflections.

Quanah threw a leg over the neck of the bay he rode and dropped to the ground. The chill of the earth immediately penetrated the soles of his moccasins to send a shiver of gooseflesh running up his spine. He was grateful they had listened to his mother and worn buckskin breeches and shirts when they left the camp that morning. A line of clouds moving in from the northwest rapidly stole the warmth from the air.

"Will it rain, my son?" Peta Nocona asked, apparently noticing Quanah's glance at the sky.

"The clouds carry rain." He felt the increased moisture in the air and the clouds' bellies were dark. His gaze once more lifted overhead. To the east a flock of birds too distant to identify flew southward, and in the north he saw three buzzards soaring high on wing. "But the birds do not seek shelter from a coming storm. Rain may come, but not until the night."

A pleased smile played across his father's lips when Peta Nocona motioned for his oldest son to lift the hind legs of the buck. As Quanah took his place, together they lifted the animal and swung it to the back of a fourth pony they had brought with them.

"The hunting has been good this day." Peta Nocona stood and admired the four deer their arrows had brought down within the space of an hour. "Every pot in the village will be full tonight. Deer is good."

By his father's tone, Quanah knew Peta Nocona would have preferred to bring a buffalo or even antelope back to the camp. Few antelope had been sighted this fall here near the Pease River. To find these four deer his father had ridden into the Wichita Mountains.

Buffalo were far more difficult to find. Since the whites built the fire-wagon-horse road across the prairie, the herds of buffalo had dwindled. The white men who rode within the belly of the *cona woba-poke* were madmen, firing into the herds with the rifles and pistols. Bulls, cows, and calves fell beneath a hail of lead and were left to rot where they dropped. The white men who journeyed on that road of steel rails killed not to fill the empty stomachs of their families but for the pleasure of killing.

Worse were the white hunters with their heavy wagons and big buffalo rifles who now ventured onto the prairie. Unlike the

Nermernuh who rode into a herd and used bow and arrow to hunt meat needed for life, the whites stood upon hills and fired down upon the buffalo. Whole herds fell beneath their bullets. Nor did they take the precious meat the great shaggy beasts provided. Instead they stripped away the hides, leaving the carcasses to rot beneath the sun.

For the People this was the greatest madness. Every portion of a *cothcho* was used by the Nermernuh. Hide, flesh, bones, horns—even the buffalo's gut was tanned for bowstrings. Such a waste of sustenance was beyond the comprehension of the Kwerhar-rehnuh. Only men driven by evil spirits would kill in that insane manner.

"There will be antelope when we reach our winter camp," Peta Nocona said as he mounted a black and white pinto. He slipped his feet into simple stirrups that dangled from a blanket thrown on the horse's back and nudged the animal forward. "We should have begun our journey sooner. The other bands will have claimed the best spots within the canyon by the time we arrive."

"We came to the canyon after the first ice last year," Quanah answered, swinging to the back of his own pony and reining after his father, "and found good ground for our tipis."

Peta Nocona glanced over a shoulder to make certain his youngest son had mounted and followed. "Good medicine was with us then. This year will be different. There will be more Nawkohnee, Tahneemuh, and even Yampahreekuh among the Kwerhar-rehnuh this winter."

Quanah noted his father made no mention of the Pehnahterkuh or Tehnawa, who were also Nermernuh. Pehnahterkuh and Tehnawa bands were no more. Both once claimed the lands to the south where the Mexicans and then the *Tejanos* settled to dig in the earth and raise their crops. For generation after generation they had raided and battled against the intruders. No matter how many they killed, the whites always returned in greater numbers. Year by year, in a struggle that spanned two hundred *taum*, the Nermernuh fell beneath Texan bullets.

Pehnahterkuh and Tehnawa lands now were held by white farmers. The survivors of those Pehnahterkuh and Tehnawa bands fled north to join the Kwerhar-rehnuh, Tahneemuh, and Nawkohnee.

Quanah drew a heavy breath and released it as he followed his father atop a rise. For as far as he could see, the lands that stretched about him were of the Kwerhar-rehnuh. His people had fought the Kiowa and the Apache for them, had driven away or killed the weaker tribes they found dwelling here, tribes whose names were now forgotten by even the oldest of the Antelope Eaters.

Here there were no whites. Only the Comancheros who came with their trade wagons were permitted on these grasslands— and allowed to live. The white man had no use for these prairies. Water was too scarce, the summer sun too hot, and the winter winds too cold to grow their fields of corn and beans. The plains were good only for the buffalo and antelope that grazed on the lush grass.

The whites will never come this far, he told himself. They could not cultivate the soil so far from the big rivers and the rains of the forestlands. Here the Kwerhar-rehnuh would always dwell safe from the land-hungry white men.

Quanah's thoughts stumbled. Cona Cawb-vey's words returned to his mind—*they always come back.* But why would they come? Why would earth diggers want to dwell here?

That was the dilemma that constantly twisted and knotted his mind until sometimes he felt as though his skull would explode. He sensed more than a kernel of truth in his uncle's words. Yet, he could not see why the whites would ever desire to come so far into the plains where only the Kwerhar-rehnuh dwelled.

At the same time he could not escape another truth. The whites now encroached on Tahneemuh, Nawkohnee, and Kuhtsoo-enkuh hunting lands with their mules and plows. Even the Yampahreekuh, the Yap Eaters in the north, contended with the white buffalo hunters and the blue-coated soldiers. From the south, east, and north, the whites pressed into Nermernuh lands.

Only from the west with its Mexicans and Apaches was there no threat. Although no peace existed between the Nermernuh and them, the battles between those peoples and Kwerhar-rehnuh bands had been fought long ago. A common respect for the lands of each now existed.

"I can see the smoke of our campfires." Pecos sat straight atop his pony and pointed toward the fingers of gray smoke that rose into the sky in the south.

Quanah's eyes shifted to the sight that brought a smile to his brother's face. The ribbon of water that was the Pease River was barely discernable from this distance.

Pecos turned to his father. "Our mother will know us to be great hunters when we return." He glanced at the four deer tied to the pony Peta Nocona led behind his mount.

"The meat we bring will be appreciated more if we return to our village before the sun sets." Peta Nocona gave his pony's sides another solid nudge with his heels. "We should hurry. We have a long distance to travel."

Quanah estimated they would reach the camp long before the sun sank behind the horizon. A sudden shiver worked its way along his spine. He glanced at the clouds overhead as his own heels urged the paint to a quicker pace. The clouds looked darker; it would be good to be in the warmth of their tipi before the rain came.

Peta Nocona threw up a hand to signal his sons to halt. Before either Quanah or Pecos could question his action, he turned to the young boys and placed a finger to his lips. His eyes then returned to scanning the grassland stretching ahead of him.

Quanah watched his father's head tilt from one side to the other. Imitating the gesture, Quanah's head cocked from the left to the right and back again. He listened, but heard only the breath of the wind weaving amid the dry grass. Nor did he see anything except the gray smoke that marked the village's cooking fire—fires that would soon be hung with pots filled with the venison they brought to feed every member of the band.

"Do you hear it?" Peta Nocona asked when he glanced to his oldest son. "I hear the cries of women."

Once more Quanah's head cocked from left to right. His eyes narrowed and a frown creased his young brow. He heard it now. "A keening—someone has died within our village."

His father shook his head. "No. It is more than that for the wailing to be so loud. Come!"

When Peta Nocona's legs rose, it was to drive his heels into his mount's sides. The pony bounded forward with the pack-horse bolting after.

Following their father, Quanah and Pecos did the same. They threw themselves forward on the necks of their ponies and applied the leather quirts carried around their wrists to the animals' rumps to keep up with Peta Nocona as he raced toward the pecan trees growing beside the Pease where the band had camped.

From a quarter of a mile away, Quanah saw no difference in the village of a hundred tipis. It remained as it had been when they had ridden out that morning. But the moment he drew his paint to a halt beside his father at the edge of the village, he sensed a terrible wrong blanketing the village.

Where were the women with their knives and pots ready to claim a share of the meat they brought? Where were the old men with critical eyes to compare today's kill with last week's hunt? Where were the braves with their praise for such a bountiful kill and questions about the hunt? Where was his mother and his infant sister Prairie Flower?

Fear set Quanah's heart to pounding within his young breast. Something was wrong, terribly wrong!

"There." Peta Nocona pointed toward the river's edge.

Quanah saw the members of the band now. Braves, women, and children gathered by the water. The anguished wails came from that direction.

It was the brave Mo-wi who first turned and saw them approaching. When he called out everyone in the village turned. The keening stopped. Mo-wi, named so because of his skill with a rope, stepped forward with his head moving heavily from side to side.

From the corner of an eye Quanah saw that all was not as it had been this morning. Five tipis had fallen, and another two were no more than smoldering mounds of gray and black ash.

"What has happened?" Peta Nocona called to the brave. "Has a windstorm swept through our camp while my sons and I were hunting?"

"A wind on the backs of big *Tejano* horses," Mo-wi answered.

The women's wails awoke anew in a high-pitched chorus behind Mo-wi.

The brave pointed to the north. "*Tejanos* and soldiers led by the one called Sul Ross rode down upon us. They were among the tipis before we knew what was happening. The whole village fought to—"

Peta Nocona jumped from mount and tossed rein and lead to Quanah. "Dead? How many of our people have died?"

Mo-wi turned and gestured toward the other members of the

band, who opened a wide path before their leader. Quanah's gaze moved to the water's edge, to the source of the squaws' cries. Ten bodies lay stretched out on their backs side by side near the sluggishly moving river.

Tears welled in his dark eyes. There was Pena Teja, a boy no older than himself. Two days ago they had hunted rabbits together. Beside his still body was the young woman Not-so-mas, who had so loved to eat the persimmons from which her name stemmed. Cona Mu-a-sh, Fire Moon, the young brave who but two moons ago taken her as a wife, was at her side. And next to him—

No! Quanah caught himself before an unmanly cry could rip from his throat. It could not be, but it was!

Cona Cawb-vey, his body so deadly still lay on the ground. A single purple hole—too small to have robbed a great brave and courageous warrior of life—with a dark trickle of dried blood marked where a single rifle shot had entered his body.

Peta Nocona strode silently to the line of dead. He spoke each of their names aloud as he stared down into their lifeless faces, then knelt to gently close Cona Cawb-vey's wide eyes with two fingers.

When he stood, the Kwerhar-rehnuh leader called out, "Naduah, my wife, my brother must be prepared to met his ancestors."

A hush fell over those gathered and their gazes fell to the ground.

"Naduah."

Quanah heard his father call out again. But his mother did not answer, nor did he see her step forward. His eyes darted over the faces of the band members, searching for her familiar features.

"Naduah!" Peta Nocona's voice rose but could not hide the quaver it contained.

"Friend of my childhood." It was Mo-wi who spoke once again. "Your first wife will not hear your call."

Peta Nocona spun about to face the brave. "Naduah is not among the dead!"

"The *Tejanos* took her, my husband."

Quanah saw Am-a-wau, his father's second wife, push through the villagers.

"She sat in front of our tipi suckling your daughter when the

Tejanos attacked." Am-a-wau stared directly at her husband while tears streamed down her copper-hued cheeks. "Cona Cawb-vey brought a pony for her escape. As they rode away, your brother was shot, and Naduah struck from her mount."

"No!" Peta Nocona's head moved from side to side in denial. "No!"

"My husband, there was nothing I could do—nothing any could do," Am-a-wau continued. "Three of the *Tejanos* snatched her and Prairie Flower from the ground. They threw her atop a horse and rode across the river to the south."

"No!" Peta Nocona muttered a third time before he threw back his head and a howl of pain and anger roared from deep in his chest.

A heartbeat later Quanah's and Pecos's own cries echoed those of their father.

Am-a-wau sat silently on a red-and-black wool blanket while her fingers deftly worked a buffalo bone needle and soft rawhide thread through two pieces of thick, tanned buffalo hide. The rough form of a moccasin gradually took shape under her diligent ministrations.

Wondering why his father's second wife had summoned Pecos and him to the tipi, Quanah kept his questions to himself and his tongue still, out of respect. Twice Am-a-wau had looked up with lips parted as though to speak. But after staring at the two brothers, she had returned to her sewing without uttering a sound. She sought the correct shape of her words in her mind, Quanah realized. When she found what she needed, she would give voice to those words.

Among the Nermernuh, the weight of words could often be judged by the time required to give them birth. When Am-a-wau finally spoke, he would listen carefully, since she usually chattered like a robin with no thought to what she said. Often he had heard his father tease the young woman that she should have been named Bird Tongue rather than Apple.

While Quanah remained quiet and still, his gaze traveled about the tipi's interior. With the rain past, the flap at the top of the simple cone of hide and wooden support poles was drawn back to allow the smoke from a small fire at the center of the tipi to escape. Hung from the poles were pots, tools, strings of shell and glass beads—every possession that belonged to Peta Nocona and his family. On the floor of the conical tent, around its circumference, were rolled bundles of clothing, buffalo robes, and sleeping furs.

The careful arrangement kept the chill of the north wind from entering the lodge. Equally important, the simple storage method allowed for quick movement. In a matter of minutes a squaw could tear down a tipi, tie its poles to a horse, load her family's possessions atop a travois, and be ready to travel should danger threaten the village. Three days ago Am-a-wau had proven her ability to handle that exact task after the Texas Rangers' attack.

Quanah could not find Peta Nocona's shield, bow and arrows, or war lance hung within the tipi. On two occasions did a Nermernuh brave remove his weapons from his tipi—when he rode on a raid against his enemies, or during a woman's time of blood. During the time of the latter, the medicine held in a weapon could be destroyed should a woman touch it.

Since Quanah had been at his father's side when Am-a-wau called Pecos and him to her side, he knew Peta Nocona's lance and shield were now carefully hidden away to protect their powerful magicks. Where his father concealed them, he did not know. Before the *Tejano* raid, Peta Nocona had kept his weapons in Cona Cawb-vey's tipi.

Quanah closed his eyes to hide the moisture that welled within them to blur his vision. A brave did not openly weep as did a woman, no matter how heavy his loss. Silently he prayed for Father Sun to open the years before him and place him at the time of *tao-yo-vises*, when the band would declare him a brave. Then he could raise his own tipi and not have to live within his father's lodge and be constantly reminded that his mother no longer dwelled here.

When he felt his tears subside, he opened his eyes once more. How empty all this seemed without Naduah. Nothing is missed until it is gone—he felt the full bitter sting of the ancient Nermernuh adage. For life to continue without his mother and the comfort she always gave was impossible to conceive.

Yet, life would continue; this he knew. To accept that fact in the manner of the Kwerhar-rehnuh, however, seemed beyond the ability of his tortured heart. That Cona Cawb-vey had ridden to the Valley of Ten Thousand-fold Longer and Wider brought pain to the center of his soul. His uncle's death was a loss that could never be replaced. But being Nermernuh, Quanah understood and accepted death. Cona Cawb-vey died defending his family and band. No warrior could ask for a more honorable way to end his life.

Naduah and his sister Prairie Flower were not dead. They still lived, captured by the *Tejanos*. They lived as prisoners in the hands of the Kwerhar-rehnuh's greatest enemies. Death itself could not be worse for a Nermernuh to face.

"Quanah, Pecos," Am-a-wau's voice came softly.

Both boys lifted their head and looked at the woman, who smiled sweetly at them.

"The time of burials and funeral songs has been put behind us." Am-a-wau placed her sewing aside and folded her hands in her lap. "All within the village carry heavy hearts at our loss. Yet, I feel your hearts are burdened by a far greater weight. For children, even those so close to the time of manhood, there is no more painful loss than the loss of a mother."

She paused as though still searching for her words. Her gaze shifted about the tipi like the eyes of one hoping to find an answer in the air. "What you must realize is that Naduah is not dead. She is now with the people who gave her birth. She still lives and cradles Prairie Flower in her arms—"

Returned to her people! What Am-a-wau suggested was like a slap in Quanah's face. How could this woman believe his mother was anything but Kwerhar-rehnuh! Did she not see the pain in Pecos's face? Could she not feel the rending of his own heart? Was Am-a-wau without a shred—

Quanah clamped his eyes closed again when a fresh wave of tears threatened to flow. As hard as it was for him to admit, there was truth in what Am-a-wau said. His mother was not of Nermernuh blood, but *Tejano*. She had been taken captive as a child no older than Pecos. She had not been born to the ways of the People; she had been taught to be one of the band.

For the first time in his life Quanah sensed a closeness to Naduah that transcended the flesh-and-blood ties of mother and son. Some of the anguish he now felt must have been hers when the warriors had torn her away from the lodge of her mother and father. How frightening and strange the ways of the Kwerhar-rehnuh must have appeared to a girl who understood not one word of the Nermernuh.

Still, Quanah found no comfort in the thought that his mother was once again with the white *Tejanos*. As Naduah grew toward womanhood, she had become one of the People. She had become wife to the great Peta Nocona and bore him sons and a daughter. Pale and white though her skin might have remained, she was Nermernuh. There was no other way it could be seen.

"—We must hope that Naduah is returned to us one day," Am-a-wau's soft voice wove into Quanah's mind, returning his thoughts to the tipi. "Until that day, I will be your mother, as will Cona Cawb-vey's wife, who will join this family when we reach our winter camp. You will never truly be able to see me in Naduah's place, this I know. But my love for you is the same as though you had been born of my body. Know that I say this with a heart as open to you as my arms now are."

With that Am-a-wau's arms rose and opened wide. She smiled and nodded her head.

Quanah pushed to his feet with Pecos right behind him. Together the brothers entered Am-a-wau's embrace and returned her affection with hugs of their own. As welcome as the warmth of her arms was, Quanah's mind could not push aside thoughts of his mother and the terror she surely felt having been torn away from her family once again.

The crisp chill of the night could not mask the heaviness of the air. Quanah felt the weight of the moment on his shoulders as he settled cross-legged to the ground a full stride behind his father. Am-a-wau held Pecos's hands when she took her place beside the oldest of her adopted sons. From the solemn expression on her face, Quanah knew she too felt the importance of this night.

Turning his attention to the circle of men seated about the blazing fire, the boy read all their faces and saw them as mirrors of his own soul. No hint of joy danced in those dark eyes; no trace of mirth touched the drawn lines of their mouth. Every member of the village carried the burden of this night equally.

Quanah lost count of the number of pipes the braves passed among their inner circle, while the women and children sat watching in the outer circle. None spoke; all silently pondered the full measure of what must be decided before dawn announced a new day. Answers found this night would determine whether the band remained together, or whether each brave would take his family and make a home among those of another band.

"A council of braves is the most solemn of times among the Nermernuh," Mo-wi broke the silence, and all eyes shifted to him. His own gaze focused on the yellow and orange flames of the fire. "All men gathered in this circle of council must speak the truth they carry in their hearts. To do less would be the way of fools."

The men nodded and grunted their agreement. Quanah also added his own tilt of the head. Unlike other tribes such as the Apaches, the Nermernuh bands were not led by a chief whose voice ruled his people. Bands of the People came and went like the movement of the wind, held together by a common belief that the strength of a band would best serve an individual. In each village certain braves were recognized as peace leaders. Except for the wisdom of their visions, their words held no more weight than that of any other man.

It was the same of war leaders. When a brave felt the time was right to ride south and raid either *Tejanos* or Mexicans, he would announce his intentions to all in the band. If others felt his medicine was strong and his plan true then they would ride with him when the moon grew to its full face.

Any brave within a band might prove to be a leader in peace or war, thus all gathered were open to the words that would be spoken this night. What would be said by one would be weighed against that which was spoken by another.

When the final decision of the council was reached, those who could not abide by that judgment were free to gather their tipis and possessions and join another band. No animosity was harbored against those who did so. That was the Nermernuh way; a brave must seek the life he felt best for himself and his family. To do less was to be less than a man.

"We should wait until we reach our winter camp and council with the braves of the other bands." This came from an aging brave known as Chocufpe Kas-kai because his heart grew as old as the wrinkles deeply lining his face. "We should give ourselves more time to consider this thing from all sides. To move with haste is also the way of fools."

Old Heart's comment drew another round of approving nods. However, Cab boon Pa-arch-quee, whose dreams were said to see into tomorrow, answered, "When we reach the canyon we will council with the other bands as we always have. But to step wide of what is our duty is also the way of fools. We should not place our decisions on the backs of others as though they were horses carrying our burdens."

Before the inner circle could complete another nod, Mo-wi spoke again. "Since the *Tejanos* rode against us beside the Red River, Peta Nocona has led us well in the time of peace and the time of raiding. I would hear Peta Nocona's heart."

A murmur of agreement rose from the circle of men while gazes moved over the fire-illuminated faces to find Peta Nocona. Quanah's heart doubled its pounding in anticipation of his father's words. However, Peta Nocona did not speak immediately. Instead he sat staring at the flames glancing to neither left nor right, as though he gathered the strength held in the fire.

When he finally spoke, the words lacked the blaze Quanah expected to echo throughout the village. Peta Nocona's voice was low and steady. "When we drove the Rangers from the Red River, I listened to the council of my brother Cona Cawb-vey. He warned that unless we constantly raided the farms of the *Tejanos*, they would soon sweep over our lands like the waters of a flash flood. Unlike the waters of a flood, the white man would not recede from the land, but would drown the Kwerhar-rehnuh in his numbers until no Nermernuh of the Antelope Eaters' bands walked this earth."

"Cona Cawb-vey saw with the eyes of wisdom," a brave whose face was hidden from Quanah said. Another added, "Cona Cawb-vey was always ready to raid against the *Tejanos.*"

When the nods and words of agreement died away, Peta Nocona's voice rose once more. "I believed as Cona Cawb-vey believed. For two *taum* I have led raiding parties against the white men whenever the moon rose full in the sky. As all gathered here know, I have gathered many scalps to number the whites whose lives I have ended. Those who ride with me have been protected by my medicine. In those two years only three braves have not returned to our village—"

"All were young and inexperienced warriors," Mo-wi interrupted. "Even strong medicine can not protect the foolish."

"No one doubts Peta Nocona's courage and strength," added a brave called Three Horses, called so because his weight required he take three ponies on a raid rather than the two most warriors used. "Even warriors from other bands seek out Peta Nocona so that they may ride with him against the *Tejanos*. The name Peta Nocona is known among all the Nermernuh as greatest of war leaders."

"More than being known to the People, Peta Nocona's name is feared by our enemies." Powder Wind, a young brave who had ridden on but two raids, called out with enthusiasm. "There can be no greater praise for a warrior."

"What I have done is not enough."

Quanah's father's pronouncement brought a sudden silence over the council. Again all heads turned to him.

"Three days ago, *Tejano* Rangers once again rode into Kwerhar-rehnuh lands. Never have white men so boldly pushed into the prairie. I can not say what devils possessed their minds to drive them to do such. But we were like a man who comes upon a snake hidden in the grass. We were taken by surprise."

Quanah saw the disguised power of his father's words. The Nermernuh were called snakes in the grass by their enemies in the cold northern country. To the People this was an honor that openly bespoke of their ability to conceal themselves where others stood vulnerable and exposed. Those who could hide among the blades of grass could ambush any seeking to harm them.

"So little was what I did that ten of our number died with *Tejano* bullets in their bodies," Peta Nocona continued in his slow, determined voice. "And while they died, the *Tejanos* stole my wife Naduah and my infant daughter. This is something I can not live with."

When his father paused and let his gaze move over the inner circle of braves, Quanah heard no voice lift in comment or question. All the faces of the men remained on Peta Nocona.

"No matter what choice others make this night, I make a blood vow." Pushing from the ground, Peta Nocona pulled his hunting knife from its sheath to press the blade to the palm of his left hand and draw it across his flesh. A trickle of crimson welled in his hand and fell to the ground. "When we reach our winter camp, I shall ride out and seek the Mexican traders. From them I will buy rifles, powder, and lead. And when I have no more ponies for rifles, I will ride south and steal the pistols and rifles of the *Tejanos*. Every warrior who rides with me will carry a rifle to face the whites. We shall drive them from Nermernuh lands—kill them as they have killed our people. There can be no true peace while they live."

Quanah thrust from the ground, his heart beating like a runaway drum within his chest. Though his legs trembled, he stepped forward to stand at his father's side—a boy facing the council of braves.

Swallowing hard, he drew a deep breath and found his voice. "No longer will I be called a child. I am *tao-yo-vises.* I am a warrior. Where my father rides, I will ride."

Rather than the jeers and heckling Quanah expected, the braves simply sat and stared at him. He drew another breath, his courage growing. "As my father vows, so vow I. One day I shall bring my mother back to the People and her family."

Pride gleamed in Peta Nocona's eyes when he turned and stared down at his oldest son. Warm and moist was the feel of his father's blood on Quanah's right cheek when Peta Nocona lovingly cradled his face in his hands.

"You are blood of my blood, my son. You are a true Nermernuh. May your feet always walk the way of the People."

CHAPTER SIX

John Teller clucked his tongue against the roof of his mouth, between a series of sharp whistles. With reins, knees, and heels he worked the buckskin gelding he rode while herding twenty horses into a cedar post corral.

"They're all yours, boys." The Texan wheeled the buckskin around to allow a private in a dusty blue uniform to swing the gate closed on the horses. "Or they will be as soon as I get the money the government promised for 'em."

"Cap'n said you was to pick up your pay at his office in the mornin'." The soldier tied the gate closed before turning to face the lone rider. "Said you could pick whatever spot that felt right to bed down for the night—long as you didn't get underfoot."

Teller grinned and shook his head while he stepped from the saddle and wrapped the buckskin's reins around one of the corral's posts. "That's what I like about the army—always hospitable—always know how to make a man feel welcome."

"Not much to welcome a man to here at Sill." The private walked to a small fire and squatted beside it. "If I had my druthers, I'd be stationed down at Bliss. At least a man's got a chance of gettin' himself into some trouble in El Paso on a Saturday night."

"Reckon there ain't much for you soldier boys to do here in the middle of nowhere." Teller's gaze surveyed the herd of twenty saddle-broke horses in the corral while he loosened the girth to let the buckskin breathe easy. The animals represented three months of backbreaking work, but at sixty dollars a head it would be all worth it when he collected from the captain in the morning.

"You can say that again, Mr. Teller. If a man's got a thirst, he's got the choice of poisonin' hisself with the rotgut the sutler peddles or downin' some of that rattlesnake-head firewater we confiscate from the heathens. Either one's liable to blind ya or leave you up and dead after a couple of healthy swigs." The soldier tilted his head toward the penned horses when Teller approached the fire. "They broke or wild?"

"Ready for bridle and saddle." Teller lowered himself to the ground, trying to ignore the nagging aches that plagued every portion of his body. Bronc busting was a young man's work; he had stopped feeling young a lifetime or two ago. "That coffee I smell in that pot?"

The private grunted and handed the Texan a brown-stained cup sitting in the sand beside the low flames. "Officer mounts. Enlisted men got to break their own, you know. No wonder they stuck me out here for the night. If a guard wasn't posted, your horses wouldn't be here come sunup."

"Trouble with horse thieves?" Teller considered scouring the cup clean with a handful of sand, and decided not even a bar of lye soap and a tub of steaming water would accomplish the task. He lifted the pot and poured half a cup of the thick black liquid it contained, realizing the strength of the coffee would kill anything dangerous to human health that might be lurking in the cup.

"Of the red-skinned variety." The private nodded. "Never seen anything like these heathens when it comes to horses. If a man rides to the sutler's for some stogies, like as not he's goin' to find himself afoot when he comes back outside."

Teller's gaze lifted to the horses in the corral. "Not that I don't trust your abilities, Private, but if it's just the same with you, I'll bed down right here tonight. I've got a lot ridin' on those mounts and would like to make damned sure they're still here when I visit the captain in the mornin'."

"Makes no never mind to me," the soldier answered. "I'd appreciate the company."

Taking a sip from the cup and barely concealing the sour look that tried to climb to his face when the bitter taste flooded his mouth, Teller surveyed the corral's location. Built in the open, it would be difficult for would-be horse thieves to approach without calling attention to themselves.

Although he had never considered horse thefts being a problem here at Fort Sill, it did not surprise him. The army post was situated in the western portion of the Indian Territory where all the plains tribes were gathered to begin their lives on the reservation. To the grasslands bands there was nothing of greater value than a horse. The Comanches measured a man's fortune by the ponies he claimed.

"Where'd you come from this time, Mr. Teller?" the private asked while pulling a cigar from a pocket and lighting it with a twig he stuck into the campfire.

"Austin, San Angelo, mostly from around Forth Worth," the Texan answered, aware of every kink the long ride had knotted in his body.

"Fort Worth—a long way for a man to ride by his lonesome. See any redskins?"

"Nary a one." The Texan shook his head. "Not so much as any Indian sign. Reckon most of the bands have made their way up here."

"Most, I suppose." The private gave his head a tilt in agreement. "Grierson's fit in Mackenzie's shoes like they was cobbled for him. He's kept the 10th Cavalry and Shafter's foot soldiers out on patrol since he took command. Post duty's the best of the draw here at Sill."

Teller had kept up with the reports in the Fort Worth papers. As he had expected after seeing what Mackenzie had done at Palo Duro Canyon, the winter had starved out most of the Comanche bands. One by one they had made their way to Fort Sill to surrender themselves. Lone Wolf, Woman's Heart, and Owl Prophet had been among the long list of Comanche war chiefs who found prison sentences waiting for them when they reached the fort. Teller had been surprised to read that the army, usually known for discarding anything that resembled common sense, had grasped the present situation enough to send many of the Indian leaders to the swamps of Florida where they were kept under armed guard. To confine Comanche, Kiowa, and Cheyenne war leaders together on a reservation would have been like igniting a powder keg.

"Still a few diehards out there, though," the soldier continued. "But I reckon it won't be long 'til Grierson and Shafter either run 'em in—or run 'em down—"

Teller pursed his lips atop another mouthful of the bitter coffee. He swallowed, wishing it was a stiff slug of whiskey he drank. Two or three fingers of corn mash—or even rotgut—would help him forget the nagging protests of his back and legs and allow him to get some needed sleep. As soon as he saw the captain in the morning, he planned to ride back across the Red River.

If luck rode with him, he would be carrying another government requisition for twenty horses tucked into his coat pocket. While the horse business was guaranteed to send a man to an early grave, he figured he could survive one or two more trips to Fort Sill.

After that—his mind's eye drifted to a parcel of land he had ridden through two days ago. With plentiful water supplied by the Red River and miles of lush grass, he had never seen a spot more perfect for a man who had a few head of cattle he wanted to turn into a profitable herd. The War between the States had left the nation with a taste for beefsteak that had grown more demanding in the past decade. More than one enterprising Texan had made a fortune on the hoof; Teller saw no reason why he should not join their ranks. With the railroads pushing their way into Texas, it would be far easier to get a herd to market than having to drive stubborn steers up into Kansas.

"—Them that's come here ain't been all that much trouble, I reckon. Give each other more trouble than they give us," the private's voice wiggled inside Teller's daydream.

Tossing the last few swallows of coffee aside, the Texan shook his head. "If it's all the same with you, I'll feel a damned sight safer when I've placed about two days between me and here. And if I was in your boots, Private, I wouldn't turn my back on any of your wards for more than a second or two. If you do, you're liable to find some red-skinned buck took a mind to relieve you of your hair."

"You still hold no love for the red man, do you, Mr. Teller?"

Startled by the voice that came from behind him, Teller twisted around. For uncertain seconds, he peered up at the bearded man who stood above him. Slowly his mind and his eye put a name to the vaguely familiar features hidden behind the neatly trimmed patch of facial hair.

"Dumaine?" Teller shoved from the ground, wiped his right hand on the thigh of his breeches, and stuck his paw out to the man. "I don't believe it, but that does look like Mr. Charles Dumaine behind that face full of whiskers!"

The Louisianan grinned widely when he accepted the extended hand and pumped it vigorously. "I'm surprised to see you here, John Teller. After you delivered me to the fort last fall, I suspected you'd ride as far from the Indian Territory as your hundred dollars' pay would take you."

"I fully intended to do just that." Teller shrugged and smiled sheepishly. "But a Captain Jason Bowden made me an offer of twenty-five dollars a head for every horse I could bring up from Texas. With your hundred and a lot of quick talkin', I managed to wrangle together a hundred head of the greenest cayuses you ever laid eye on. When Bowden paid off, he gave me another order for those saddle brokes over yonder."

Dumaine looked at the corralled animals and nodded. "It appears you've found yourself a profitable career as an army supplier."

"I'm doing all right for myself." Teller was unable to get over the changes in the man that had occurred since leaving him at Fort Sill last October. All traces of the citified dude he had led into the plains were gone. The sun had burned Dumaine's face a deep nut brown and turned his hair a shade or two lighter. Gone were the man's fancy duds, replaced by an army-issue wool coat, worn buckskin breeches, and a coarsely woven cotton shirt of indeterminate color. "And you? What keeps you here in the Indian Territory?"

"I haven't remained in the Indian Territory," Dumaine answered when he squatted on his heels to warm his hands over the fire. "I accompanied Colonel Mackenzie on his patrols, and then have ridden with Grierson. Whenever we got close enough to a telegraph office, I managed to wire my stories back to the *Picayune* in New Orleans. The fact is I just rode in no more than an hour ago. I heard a corporal mention a John Teller had driven some horses up from Texas and decided to see if it was the John Teller I knew." Dumaine glanced at the Texan.

"Reckon I'm a mite like unwanted in-laws. I keep showin' up when I'm least expected." Teller grinned. "How long you plannin' to stay in these parts?"

"Until the army declares its campaign completed," the journalist answered. "Although the way things are proceeding, I should be on my way back home soon. That is, if your old friend Quanah Parker ever surrenders."

"Old friend?" Teller spat into the fire with vehemence.

Dumaine frowned. "You truly carry no love for our red-skinned brothers, do you, John?"

"Brothers? In a pig's eye!"

The reporter hiked both his eyebrows and shrugged. "That's what the government now calls hostiles who have accepted reservation life."

"Does a man call a mad dog his brother? Not if he's got an ounce of sense, he doesn't. He takes his rifle and kills it before it can bite him." Teller had also read of all the aid Congress had approved to educate the Indian tribes in the ways of civilized men. Teaching a Comanche or a Kiowa brave to plant beans was like trying to teach a polecat not to stink, as far as he was concerned. For all the good it would do, the legislators should have used that money as kindling for their fireplaces. At least it would have served some purpose.

"Gentlemen," the private said as he rose, "if you'll excuse me, I have to go through the motions of guarding this corral." He pointed to a knapsack on the ground beside the fire. "There's a couple canteens of water and a bag of coffee inside, if you want to make up some fresh brew."

Nodding to the soldier, Dumaine and Teller watched as the man began to make a circuit of the corral. It was Dumaine who eventually spoke:

"You do truly surprise me, John. You carry a lot of hate around inside you for a man who was only six years old when Fort Parker was attacked. After all, you *did* escape your captors."

Teller felt his chest tighten. Dumaine may have been a changed man on the outside, but his seven months with the army had not taught him about the Comanches. Then, how could it? The reporter had witnessed only army triumphs. He had not lived in Texas when the Army paid little heed to Indian depredations within the nation's youngest state.

"When we were camped at Palo Duro, I remember telling you my pa was a farmer," Teller answered. "After the raid on Fort Parker, me and him headed down to San Antonio as he had originally planned. It was a matter of luck he heard about a man called Vardeman—a Swede he was—who had given up trying to make a go of it and had his farm up for sale."

Teller recounted how his father purchased fifty acres, twenty miles to the northeast of San Antonio, along the river. He recalled how a father and son's new home had been little more than a lean-to of cedar branches and a few flatboards.

"But Pa dug in and by fall had harvested a crop of corn as well as 'taters and beans. It was enough to get us through the winter and provide seed for the spring," Teller said. "It wasn't easy livin', but it was good. It took five years to put a real roof over our heads. But by the time I was seventeen and met Samantha Elizabeth Burnett at a circuit meeting, Pa and me had socked away enough money to start adding two extra rooms onto the house. Six months later when the circuit preacher came by again, Samantha and I was married."

Words. The thought edged into Teller's mind with disgust. Even as he spoke he found it hard to accept. How could mere words convey all the love he had felt for Samantha, or all they had shared when they had stood before the preacher and spoken the vows that united them as man and wife in the eyes of God, their families, and friends? Words were no more than empty utterances when compared to all that had filled his heart and soul when his gaze met Samantha's deep blue eyes.

"Until death do you part—those were the words the parson said. We were both seventeen, and those words didn't mean much to either of us. All we heard was 'I now pronounce you man and wife.' " When the private was on the far side of the corral, Teller rose, poured the dark sludge from the coffeepot, and made use of the coffee and water in the knapsack to prepare a fresh pot.

A smile slipped over the Texan's lips as he recalled the warmest of memories. "Another six months went by before Samantha announced she was with child. Except for the day she said she would have me as a husband, that was the proudest day in my life. It was one of those unexpected warm December days we get in Texas when little Patrick came a-bawlin' and a-squallin' into the world. My chest was stuck out three feet when I picked up my son and held him in my arms."

Teller found a stick and poked at the fire to hide the moisture that filled his eyes from his friend. Even now, even after all these years, he recalled every detail of his son's face, felt the smoothness of his tiny hands within his own rough paws, smelled the sweetness of his body when he was fresh from a bath.

God, Teller silently prayed to be spared the deluge of memories that spilled forth from the recesses of his mind, memories he had refused to recognize for more than half his life. His prayer went unanswered. His mind embraced and caressed each of those precious moments. How many lifetimes had he dreamed for Patrick and himself during those gentle evenings by the fireplace while he watched Samantha in her rocker nursing their son? Why did such memories remain so vivid when time turned all else dust with its passage?

"John, are you all right?" Dumaine's question parted the dreams Teller once held so dear.

"Just caught up in old memories," the Texan answered, still refusing to let the newspaperman see the tears misting his eyes. "It was in early October I rode toward San Antonio to help a neighbor bring in the last of his corn crop. We worked from early mornin' to sundown gettin' those ears safely stored in his crib. After supper and a swallow from his jug, I started home. I was five miles from the farm when I saw the flames comin' from our house."

The panic he had felt those long years ago once more set his heart slamming against his ribs. He drew a deep breath to steady himself, but the action did nothing to stop the knots that twisted his gut.

"I almost killed the mare I rode, spurring her with every stride she took to cover that five miles. It didn't help. There was nothing left of the house when I got there, except smoke and embers. I found my father near a corral. There were five Comanche arrows in his body. He had been scalped," Teller slowly related the horrors of that night. "From the overturned bucket near his body, it appeared he had been watering a mare and a foal we were keeping in the corral when the attack came. Death, as ugly as it had been, had come easy for him."

Teller paused and swallowed in an attempt to remove the lump that filled his throat. "I found Samantha's body staked to the ground about a quarter of a mile from the house. Patrick's still body was a few feet away. His tiny head had been bashed against a rock."

No tears moistened the Texan's narrowed eyes when he looked at Dumaine. "Samantha was a Christian woman, loving and gentle. Only Satan's own demons could have made her suffer the way the Comanches did before they finally slit her throat. I buried her, my son, and my father that night. When morning came, I rode into San Antonio. I was a Texas Ranger before the sun went down that day. It was the only thing I saw to do. Texas would not be safe for a God-fearing man, woman, or child until the bloody savages who had murdered my wife and son were wiped off the face of this earth."

In the days before the Civil War, Teller explained to the reporter, Rangers had but one task, to protect the frontier from Indian attack. "Even when Texas was admitted to the Union, the Rangers remained the first line of defense. The army was too busy protectin' the Butterfield stages to be concerned with massacred farmers."

The sound of boiling water drew the Texan's attention to the pot on the fire. He poured a portion of the brew into the cup to test its color. Finding it suitable to the eye, he filled the cup and passed it to his friend. "By the time Texas seceded from the union, I had reached the rank of captain. Not that it meant much. A Ranger was a Ranger. The pay was low and a man still rode after Comanche and Apache no matter his rank."

Dumaine sipped from the cup and nodded his approval. "It was the Rangers that eventually found Cynthia Ann Parker, wasn't it?"

"Yep." Teller settled to the ground and scrounged through the sack for another cup, with no success. "Seems like the Maker likes to tie things up in neat bundles on occasion. I was there when the Comach snatched her away from her family, and I was there when she was brought back. Kind of funny if you think about it."

Ranger Captain Sul Ross was not a man to have on one's trail, Teller told his companion. And in early December 1860, Ross

was on the trail of Comanche war chief Peta Nocona, who
had led countless successful raids against the frontier for
years.

"I was a sergeant under Ross then. That day we had a few soldiers from the Second Cavalry riding with us, as well as a dozen
or so farmers out of Bosque County. Peta Nocona's raiding had
been hard and heavy around then." Teller hiked the collar of his
coat high when a gust of wind rose from the north. "It was early
in December. You could see dark clouds hanging on the
horizon—a blue norther about to blow in."

A broken trail of Indian sign that came and went from mile
to mile brought them to the Pease River, Teller outlined. There
the trail picked up again. While allowing his men to rest their
horses, Ross set two scouts ahead to reconnoiter a series of
low rising hills to the west. The men returned to report they
had located a large Indian camp a mile beyond the first of the
hills.

"Ross swung us wide so that we came down on the village
from out of the north. I reckon he figured no Comanche would
ever expect an attack from that direction so deep in redskin
lands," Teller said. "It was a big village, and from the looks of it
they were preparing to move when we came ridin' in."

Teller paused to take the empty cup Dumaine passed to him.
He refilled it and took a sip of the steaming coffee. "If there was
ever a day I felt like God rode with us, it was that day. Just as we
made our charge, a strong wind running in front of the norther
hit. Sand and dust was blowing everywhere. The Comanches
didn't know we were there until we were in the village."

Teller described how the Indians scattered in all directions
when the first rifle shot rang out. The sandstorm that had
worked to the Rangers' advantage moments ago abruptly gave its
allegiance to the Kwerhar-rehnuh band. Swirling sand blinded
the mounted men while providing the Comanches cover in
which to escape.

"I ain't sure how they did it, but Captain Ross and Tom
Killiheir got sight of Peta Nocona trying to make a getaway on
a mustang. They rode him down and killed him," Teller added.
"There was a squaw ridin' a pony beside him. They would have
shot her dead, too, except for the whiteness of her teats. She
must've been nursing the baby she had in her arms when we
rode down on the village."

The Texan's account followed the official Ranger report of the raid in which he had participated. Rumors garnered from Indian scouts and captured Comanches over the months that followed had left the waters muddied a mite as to whether Peta Nocona had actually been killed that day. Many claimed the Rangers had shot a warrior who resembled the war chief, not Peta Nocona himself. Teller had never given much credence to those claims. After all, he had ridden beside Ross and Killheir—those spreading the rumors had not been there.

Teller shook his head and sucked at his teeth. "I tried talkin' with her on the way back to Camp Cooper, and then again while she was waiting to be transported to some Parkers we had located in Birdville down by Fort Worth. I told her who I was, but it didn't mean nothing to her. She didn't remember me. Hell, I didn't think she even remembered how to talk white. She looked to be Comach through and through."

"A sad story." Dumaine's gaze lifted to follow the private as the soldier began another circuit of the corral. "Torn from her family as a mere girl, then torn from her family again as an adult."

A frown creased Teller's forehead as he stared at the journalist. The Louisianan still had no idea about how things were. "We didn't tear her away from nothin'! We saved her from savages and brought her back to her own people. There ain't a damned thing sad about that."

Dumaine turned back to the Texan. "I'm sorry, I had assumed the child she nursed was her own, that she had taken a husband while with the Comanches."

Teller shook his head. "No Comanche buck is a fit husband, except maybe for a coyote bitch. It did turn out the babe was the offspring of Peta Nocona hisself. She called it Topsannah, which means Flower On The Plains or some such. Also turned out she had two sons by Peta Nocona. That was the first time anybody in Texas ever heard of Quanah Parker."

A shadow of melancholy passed over Dumaine's expression while he sat and stared at Teller. "And today? Where are Miss Parker and her daughter today?"

"Dead," Teller answered curtly. "I read some articles about her in the newspapers that said she was passed around among her relatives for a while. But after the War between the States broke out, I didn't have much time to keep up with her. In '63 when

I was stationed down at Fort Davis, I saw an old paper that mentioned Topsannah had caught a fever and died. About a year later I saw another notice saying where Cynthia Ann herself had died."

Dumaine nodded and asked no further questions. Teller downed the last of the coffee. He did not like the expression on his friend's face. It was if the reporter had gotten something out of all the Texan had related that Teller could not see himself.

"The sun'll be down soon." Dumaine tilted his head toward the west. "I have a tent of my own down beside Grierson's. You're welcome to its shelter for the night."

Teller pushed to his feet as the reporter rose. "Reckon how I'd better bed down right here tonight. The private said there's been trouble with Comach bucks stealin' horses. Wouldn't want them to get their hands on my stock until I've gotten paid for 'em."

"If you change your mind, ask the private for directions. It does get cold here at night," Dumaine added.

"I'll keep your offer in mind," Teller assured him, with no intention of doing more than he planned. Since he had buried his family at age eighteen, he had spent more nights under the stars than with a roof over his head.

Dumaine held out his hand. "In case I don't see you in the morning, John, I want to wish you well."

Accepting the reporter's hand, Teller shook it. "And the same to you."

With that Dumaine turned and walked toward the fort's buildings and the rows of tents beyond. Teller watched him for several minutes. He liked the young man well enough. It was just that he had never lived in Texas. Seven months of riding with the army had not been enough to teach him about Comanches. It took a lifetime of living in fear of the next full moon, when the raiding parties would once again sweep down out of the plains, to get that kind of education. It took losing a loved one to their savagery to understand that a Comanche was not a man but a wild animal.

Walking to the buckskin, Teller unlaced the bedroll tied behind the saddle. Rather than pulling saddle and blanket from the animal's back, he left both in place. His long years as a Ranger and then five years as an army scout after the war had taught him to remain prepared to ride at the first sign of danger whenever in Comanche country. Reservation or not, it made no difference to him. No matter how many soldiers were stationed at Fort Sill, he was still in the heart of Comanche land. He would feel a damned sight more comfortable when he crossed the Red River back into Texas.

CHAPTER
SEVEN

You are blood of my blood, my son. You are a true Nermernuh. May your feet always walk the way of the People.

Quanah blinked against the harsh flare of the small campfire that blurred his vision in a shattered spectrum of glaring colors. Somewhere within his brain he realized the peyote continued to weave its vision within him. That realization was not strong enough to break away from the old pain it awoke—pain that came not from the glare of the campfire's flames but was born in the echo of his father's words which had sounded within his skull throughout the day.

Cona Cawb-vey had once stood at his side to assure his feet were on the right path, but he had joined the warriors in the Valley of Ten Thousand-fold Longer and Wider three *taum* ago. His mother and Am-a-wau's love once were like a guiding hand that held him to the way. Now Naduah and his sister Topsannah were captives somewhere in the south among the *Tejanos*. And Am-a-wau, too, had joined all her Nermernuh ancestors who awaited her in the Valley of Ten Thousand-fold Longer and Wider. During the time of ice after the Rangers had taken Naduah and Topsannah, the coughing sickness had slowly drained her spirit and eventually her life.

Quanah mentally named all those who had been among his family. Now there were none except Pecos, who sat across the fire from him. Even Cona Cawb-vey's wife was gone. Before Am-a-wau's death she had found a new husband and left with him to live among the Yap Eaters in the north.

The two wives Peta Nocona had brought to his tipi after Am-a-wau died were no more than young girls, barely older than Quanah's fourteen years. Both lacked the wisdom and caring of Naduah and Am-a-wau. Although they seemed to comfort his father, their giggles were a constant irritation to Quanah.

You are blood of my blood, my son. You are a true Nermernuh. May your feet always walk the way of the People.

Who would guide him now? Who would train his brother in the ways of the People? Like a steeled fist, desperation closed around Quanah's heart. Even when he had stood against the whites beside his father, he had never felt the fear that now settled into his breast. How did one walk the road of the Nermernuh when there were none to show the path?

"Quanah?" Pecos's voice came like a frightened whisper into his dark reflections.

Quanah looked up. His brother's face was a mirror of his own soul. Pecos appeared lost and small, cowered as though the whole world rose against him.

"We have sung the songs of mourning," Pecos said, his gaze locked to his brother for guidance. "What do we do now?"

"Back to the camp." Quanah knew nothing else to say. Pecos and he had completed the rituals, sung the songs required, to send Peta Nocona on his journey to the Valley of Ten Thousand-fold Longer and Wider. They had done all that a living Nermernuh could do for their father's spirit. "Our father's tipi is now ours."

Rising from the ground, Quanah waited until his brother circled the fire before he turned and began the walk back to the village with Pecos at his side. To the west the sun drifted toward the horizon to set the sky ablaze with brilliant hues of reds and fiery oranges. Quanah looked away. Today the world should be blanketed by clouds that wept for the great loss suffered by the People.

You are blood of my blood, my son. You are a true Nermernuh. May your feet always walk the way of the People.

Quanah closed his eyes and clamped his hands over his ears. Peta Nocona's voice persisted. Time and again it repeated those same words. Why? Why did his father's pronouncement haunt him so? Did Peta Nocona's spirit linger in the world of flesh and blood, refusing to pass into the other world where his ancestors waited with ponies to lead him to the evergreen hunting grounds where buffalo always abounded? What reason could be so strong to keep his father's ghost among the living?

With a shake of his head, Quanah opened his eyes and let his arms drop to his sides. Peta Nocona no longer had reason to touch the lives of those who lived. No ghost hovered beside him. It was merely Quanah's own memories that plagued him. Now remembrances of his father mingled with those of his mother.

"Quanah?" Pecos's voice drew his attention. "Did our father die as a warrior?"

He understood Pecos's concern. Peta Nocona's death seemed a senseless waste. All of the Nermernuh knew of his valor. While the white men warred among themselves, his father had strengthened the People. He brought promised rifles and bullets to the warriors who followed him. Braves from across the Nermernuh lands left their bands to raise their tipis beside his. Even the Kiowas, who had always allied themselves with the People, recognized the power of Peta Nocona's great medicine. They rode for days to join the raids he led against the *Tejanos*.

And those raids! How they lifted the spirits of all the bands! Quanah's chest swelled with pride. Peta Nocona had driven the whites back. No longer did their farms encroach into Nermernuh hunting grounds, but were abandoned as the *Tejanos* fled southward to the safety of their cities or hid in the pine forests of the east.

Only the Rangers, with their stars carved from silver coins and their pistols that spat ceaseless bullets, still braved their way into the lands of the People. But these incursions grew so rare they no longer worried the minds of the warriors.

With his power so strong, with the band having grown to more than two hundred tipis, Quanah struggled to find meaning in his father's sudden death. No bullet claimed his life while he charged screaming his defiance into the face of his enemies. No lance or arrow pierced his body.

Yesterday morning while the band's women and children took baskets to gather plump, ripe blackberries in the dense patches that grew near a creek, Peta Nocona and four other braves had ridden guard. A rattlesnake hidden in high grass startled the paint his father rode. The pony reared high to throw the great warrior to the ground. Peta Nocona did not rise to throw himself astride his mount again. His head had struck a rock half buried in the earth. By the time the sun rode high in the sky, life had slipped from his body.

"Our father did not die at an enemy's hand," Quanah gave voice to the conclusion he had reached after pondering Peta Nocona's death throughout the day. "Yet, he died a warrior's death with war lance in hand. Death took our father while he protected those of our band from danger. There is no greater honor than for a warrior to give his life for the People. Those who proceeded him to the Valley of Ten Thousand-fold Longer and Wider will welcome him as befits one of such courage."

Pecos stared ahead for several moments before nodding solemnly. "It is good for a great man to die in such a manner. Our father will be long remembered in the songs of the People."

Evening's shadows grew long and stretched into the blackness of a moonless night by the time the two boys entered the darkness of an empty tipi. A cold chill worked along Quanah's spine when he ordered his brother to light a fire. Something was terribly wrong. Their father's two young widows should be waiting with supper prepared for them.

The flickering flames of Pecos's small blaze revealed that neither of the girl-women were within the tipi. Nor were any of their possessions evident among the things of Peta Nocona that still hung from the lodge poles.

"Where are our mothers?" Pecos's expression could not hide the fear he shared with his older brother. "They should be here. How will we eat without the food they prepare?"

Quanah's head moved slowly from side to side. His gaze raced over the interior of the buffalo hide tent. Only the women's possessions were gone. He found nothing else missing or out of place. This made no sense. What could have happened to cause the girl-women to leave their home without so much as a word for Pecos and him?

"Quanah and Pecos, it is I, Mo-wi."

The unexpected voice outside the tipi spun Quanah around,

leaving his heart pounding. Even though the boy heard Mo-wi utter his name, the brave's voice sounded unfamiliar, distant and changed from that of the man Quanah had known all his life.

"I would council with the sons of Peta Nocona," Mo-wi said.

"Add sticks to the fire," Quanah urged his brother while he hastened to the far side of the tipi and found his father's tobacco pouch and pipe neatly wrapped in a bundle of soft doeskin.

He then snatched a wide leather bag filled with pemmican from a nearby pole before arranging himself cross-legged by the fire. He motioned Pecos to sit by the fire, then stuffed a handful of the mixture of fat, berries, nuts, and grains into his mouth. He passed the pemmican to his brother.

"Mo-wi is a welcomed visitor to our tipi," Quanah finally called out around the pemmican. While he did not know where his father's young wives had gone, he saw no reason for Mo-wi to believe anything except that all was as it should be. "Please enter and share our evening meal with us."

An arm pushed aside the leather flap covering the tipi's oval entrance. Ducking into the opening, Mo-wi stepped inside. Silently he stood above the two boys until Quanah waved an arm wide and motioned for him to sit by the small fire. Without a sound, the brave lowered himself to the ground and crossed his legs.

Pecos held out the pemmican pouch. "Mo-wi is an old friend and is welcome to share our meal."

Quanah slowly released the breath he had held since Mo-wi had entered the tipi. Without an explanation, Pecos apparently sensed what his older brother required and played the role needed.

Mo-wi reached into the pouch to bring forth a handful of the nourishing mixture usually reserved for times of travel or days when there was no game to fill the village's pots. Quanah considered this night to be one of the latter, since his father's widows had vanished without preparing an evening meal.

The brave quickly ate the pemmican and waved away a second helping when Pecos held up the pouch again. Mo-wi's gaze shifted between Quanah and Pecos as though studying each carefully. Although Quanah tried to read a glimmer of the reason for the brave's visit, Mo-wi's expression betrayed no hint of purpose.

"Would you share a pipe with us?" Quanah gathered pipe and tobacco from beside him.

Mo-wi's eyes widened slightly as though the offer was unexpected, but the brave merely nodded and said, "It is good to smoke before a council. It assures that those gathered together will speak the truth in their hearts."

Quanah tried to ignore the ominous ring of the brave's words while he filled the bowl, lit the tobacco, and puffed before passing the pipe to the brave. Mo-wi placed the pipe to his lips and inhaled deeply. When he released the blue smoke from his lungs, he handed the pipe to Pecos.

Again Quanah watched with relief when his younger brother assumed the role of a fully grown man. Pecos accepted the pipe and drew from it. The ease by which he inhaled and exhaled revealed that Pecos, like most Nermernuh boys, had managed to sneak a pinch or two of tobacco from his father's pouch to sample on more than one occasion.

The pipe made several circles about the fire before Quanah tapped the ash from the bowl. When he reached for the tobacco pouch again, Mo-wi finally spoke:

"Though I still ride to raid with the younger men, I have become a peace leader among the people of our band."

"A wise brave whose council our father often sought," Quanah said, noting a hint of relief flutter across the man's face.

"It is as peace leader I come this night," Mo-wi continued. "Peta Nocona was a great warrior and a wise brave. While he led this band, its numbers swelled and our strength grew like that of a bear. Your father was the heart of this band—a heart protected by the most powerful of magicks."

Mo-wi paused and glanced at the two boys as though giving them a chance to speak before he went on. "His death stilled that heart. In a single day change has swept through the village. You returned from your burial songs after the sun set or you would have seen these changes. Twenty-five braves and their wives have torn down their tipis and chosen to walk another path."

"This has always been the way of the Nermernuh," Quanah said. "A brave must follow the call of his heart."

"In this there is truth," Mo-wi acquiesced with a nod. "But others speak of leaving and finding other bands. By the time the raiding moon shows her face in the night sky, the number of tipis in our village will be half of what they are this night—"

Quanah's gaze shifted to his brother. Pecos's expression said he had no greater understanding of why the brave told them this than did Quanah.

"—Look around you, sons of Naduah. Where are the wives of Peta Nocona? Why do you eat pemmican for your supper when the fresh haunch of an antelope hangs from a pole outside this home?"

Sons of Naduah? Quanah frowned. Why did the brave evoke their mother's name?

"Though pride holds your tongues, I will answer the questions you will not speak." Mo-wi paused again as though making certain he held the boys' attention. "While you mourned your father this day, two young braves spoke for Peta Nocona's widows. They left this tipi and now sleep beside new husbands. When I asked the members of our band who would speak for the sons of Peta Nocona, no one answered my question."

A shiver that was not born of the night wiggled its way up Quanah's spine. Try as he did, he could not ignore the undercurrent in the brave's words.

"Am I one who needs others to speak for me?" Quanah asked. "Have I not ridden beside my father against the *Tejanos*? Do I not carry a war lance that has been blooded with the lives of two white men? Am I an orphaned child who needs to be spoken for?"

Mo-wi's face darkened, but no edge sharpened his voice when he replied, "You rode beside Peta Nocona because his medicine protected you, son of Naduah. The blood of the white *Tejanos* that flows in your veins has given you the body of a man before the years of manhood. Because of this and our warriors' love of Peta Nocona, it was easy for them to forget that you are not yet *tao-yo-vises*, but still a *tao-yo*."

"I am not child," Quanah answered firmly, fully realizing that he had never performed the band's rites of manhood. A manchild had to see fifteen *taum* before the time of *tao-yo-vises*.

"You are *tao-yo*, as is Pecos," Mo-wi asserted again. "There is no one in our band who will offer the shelter of their lodge to you, even though the wealth of Peta Nocona's fifty ponies now belongs to you—"

The brave's pronouncement drove like a knife straight to Quanah's heart. He had forgotten about the legacy of horses his father had left his sons. For Nermernuh to refuse their tipis to ones with so great an inheritance spoke louder than any words Mo-wi could utter.

"—during this time of change in our band, there may be wisdom for you to also consider change." Mo-wi's eyes locked on Quanah. "You and Pecos have no family here, but Naduah dwells in the south with the whites who gave her birth. The whites would welcome two boys who came to them with fifty horses. You would surely find a home among the *Tejanos* when there is none to be found for you here among the true People."

Quanah's mouth drew into a thin tight line. He gritted his teeth to hold back the curses that struggled to spit themselves in the brave's face. Although Mo-wi did not exile them from the band, he made it more than clear they were no longer welcomed here.

"I go now, sons of Naduah. Consider well all I have said. No others will come to this home this night. There is nothing else to be said." Mo-wi untangled his legs and pushed from the ground. He stared at Pecos and then at Quanah. "That is all."

Containing the rage that now boiled within him, Quanah sat perfectly still and watched the brave who had called himself Peta Nocona's friend disappear into the night. The boy then turned to his brother. "Tie the flap against the wind."

Pecos did as ordered, staring at his brother when he returned to a fire that had lost its warmth.

"Do you understand all Mo-wi said?" Quanah asked.

"Mo-wi spoke for all our people," Pecos said slowly. "We are no longer wanted. The band sees us as white men because we carry our mother's blood."

"But we also carry the blood of Peta Nocona in our veins," Quanah said over the bitterness that coated his tongue.

"If we travel south, the *Tejanos* will surely know that, no matter how many ponies we bring with us. They will kill us. It will make no difference that Naduah is our mother." Fear widened Pecos's eyes.

Quanah Parker—until this moment he had never realized the full meaning of his name. He was—as was Pecos—half Nermernuh and half white man by birth. Both the People and the *Tejanos* were blind to all but the half that they hated.

"I do not want to ride south, Quanah—even to see our mother. I know nothing of the white man's way." A tone of pleading filled Pecos's voice. "The Nermernuh way is all that I know."

You are blood of my blood, my son. You are a true Nermernuh. May your feet always walk the way of the People.

His father's voice rang in Quanah's ears as clearly as if Peta Nocona had stood at his side. In the blinking of an eye, his anger faded, replaced by quiet resolve. Now he understood why his father's spirit lingered in the world of the living. Peta Nocona remained to guide the feet of his sons.

"We will not ride south, my brother, that I promise you."

While Quanah pronounced the words he felt a warmth surround him. Then it was gone. As surely as he had known his father stood beside him a moment ago, he now knew Peta Nocona had departed to take his place among the warriors in the Valley of Ten Thousand-fold Longer and Wider. A smile touched the corners of the boy's mouth. All was as it should be.

"We are not welcomed here, Quanah," Pecos said. "How can we live among those who do not want us?"

"Are we any different than the others? We must prove ourselves to be braves and warriors as all male children born of the People must do," Quanah answered.

"But we can not cook and sew. How shall we live?"

"If we must learn the work of women to survive, then we shall learn the work of women." Quanah sat straight and proud. "We have no need of others to speak for us, my brother. We are not children. We are the sons of Peta Nocona."

"And Naduah," Pecos added, sitting straight and tall in imitation of his older brother.

That the braves of the band did not recognize his manhood meant nothing, Quanah told himself. He had ridden at his father's side. He had watched and listened—and learned. He knew the secrets of the lands as well as those twice his years. He understood the ways of the antelope and the deer. He could read the signs of birds on wing. He could find the small water holes that stood between a man and death on the prairie where creeks and streams were as rare as rain falling from the sky.

His eyes lifted to the lance and war shield that hung from a lodge pole. Yesterday morning his father's lance and shield had been there beside his; now they were with Peta Nocona so that they might serve him well as he hunted in the Valley of Ten Thousand-fold Longer and Wider.

That his father was gone did not mean the strength of his medicine had abandoned his sons. Peta Nocona's hands had shaped and tempered the lance. The same hands had stretched the buffalo hide over the shield's wooden frame and hardened it like a turtle's shell with water and fire.

Quanah clearly saw the answer to the question that had plagued him throughout the day. Lance and shield—and bow and arrow—would guide his feet. All had been touched by his father. They would guide him and Pecos; they would keep their feet upon the Nermernuh way. Young warriors could ask for no greater mentor.

"This is our home, Pecos. We belong here, and the others will see and accept that one day. But what they see now or in the future does not matter. The true weight rests with you and me. You are my family, and I am yours. That is all that has meaning." Quanah's eyes shifted back to his brother. "It is all we need."

"It is all we need," his brother repeated the words as though they were a vow.

"We are blood of our father and mother's blood, my brother. We are true Nermernuh. Our feet will always walk the way of the People." Quanah's head turned back to the walls of the tipi and his gaze once more lifted to the war lance and shield.

CHAPTER EIGHT

The sun broke through the flat, gray clouds. A world lost too long in winter's shadowless monotony exploded in light that splintered against ice and snow in a blinding kaleidoscope of brilliance.

Quanah clamped his eyes shut to ward off the painful assault of sunlight. The numb fingers of his right hand clamped around the lance, uncertain whether he felt its firm shaft or the bitter cold played tricks on his senses like a hungry coyote attempting to beguile its prey. Icy needles stabbed into his flesh when a wind howled out of the north, caught his shield, and attempted to rip it from his left arm.

The cry of an infant rose above the wind's whine.

Quanah opened his eyes to narrow slits, then widened them. The clouds once more devoured the sun and swallowed the world in constant twilight.

The child's cry ended in a sudden high-pitched yelp like that of an injured dog.

Twisting to his left, Quanah saw a newborn babe two strides from where he stood. Naked it lay in the blowing snow. No plump, red-faced child was this with arms and legs a-wiggle in the air. Still it lay, its gray skin stretched tautly over a skeletal frame. Motionless, unseeing, its eyes stared blankly at an uncaring sky.

A girl-child, he saw while watching crystals of ice form on the infant's open fingers. Like a chrysalis spun by a phantom insect, the ice flowed down those emaciated arms to cover the baby's body. In an instant wind-whipped snow blanketed the icy cocoon, burying it beneath a deep drift.

A horse screamed.

Quanah spun to the right. A thin sheet of ice that had encased his body in the seconds he had stared at the dead child shattered like delicate glass. Shards flew into the air to spin away in the wind.

A pinto stallion stood no farther away from him than the child. Like the infant, its matted hide was stretched as tight as the skin of a drum over its bones. While its muzzle dug into the snow searching for grass hidden beneath the carpet of white, its body trembled and collapsed. Ice crystals enshrouded it a moment before the blowing snow swept over it like a white wave.

Atop that wave, Quanah rode. The wind carried him through the air as though he were no more than a flake of snow. Southward he flew, while the featureless whiteness raced beneath.

In the space of a dozen heartbeats the gray clouds melted away to reveal a blue sky warmed by a golden sun. Below, Quanah saw the high plains fall away to be replaced by the gentle grasslands of his birth. The perfume of the profuse wildflowers that painted this land each spring had awakened his name within his mother's mind. She called him Quanah or Sweet Aroma.

Beyond those plains he rode the wind. He saw the deer on the banks of the Colorado River. Beyond, bucks and does ran with pronghorn antelope all the way to the mountain ranges and grasslands of the south that fringed the Chihuahuan Desert.

Quanah's eyes opened wider.

He stared at the interior of his tipi.

He blinked, unable to comprehend the sudden transition. The wind howled outside, its bitter bite burrowing beneath the edge of the lodge and nipping at his bare skin. In his hands, he held a cool pipe. At his side lay the open tobacco pouch that had belonged to his father.

Gradually his mind accepted. He stood not naked in the snow, nor did he ride the fierce winter winds that blew outside. Day no longer cast its dim light as it had that morning when he first settled atop the buffalo blanket. Night now reigned outside to bring an end to the fifteenth passing of the day of his birth.

A medicine vision. He remembered his reason for sitting beside a fire that now was no more than glowing embers. Fifteen *taum* marked the passage of child to man among the People. On this day a boy, carrying tobacco and pipe, was to seek a sacred place and wait until the spirits revealed the magicks that would guide his way throughout life. From this he would gather the items of power for the *wannup*, a small leather pouch to be tied beside his testicles.

With snow covering all for the full time of a moon, the sacred places had been denied him. Instead he sought a vision of manhood within the tipi. For one shunned by the People, Quanah could conceive of no place he held more sacred than this lodge that once sheltered his father and his mother. Their memories were like his lance and shield, his father providing strength to endure and his mother's love comforting him when no member of the band would utter his name.

Quanah's eyes shut. He drew a steadying breath to fortify himself against the morass of self-pity that seeped up from deep in his core. He tried to herd his thoughts away from the months that had passed since Peta Nocona's death. During the days it was easy; survival, hunting for what little food could be found, tending the horses, mending clothes and tipi—all kept his mind busy.

But at night, when the day's work was completed and the time for sleep came, the doubts pushed free to rob him of rest. He felt the sting of each moment of life. The band totally abandoned Pecos and him. Should they do so little as to offer a greeting to those they had known all their lives, they were shunned. Rather than a friendly reply and smile, they found themselves staring at the backs of men and women. To the People they did not exist, no better than the black-skinned white men who the Nermernuh believed walked without a soul.

Quanah opened his eyes and let them slowly take in the interior of the tipi. He felt no bitterness, only a knifing pain that jabbed at his heart. He and Pecos carried the blood of the *Tejanos*! He, too, would have shunned those such as they. It was the way of the People, the way by which he lived.

He had sought the medicine of a man in the hope of discovering the means to reveal to the band that it was the Nermernuh blood in his veins that ruled his soul. But where was the magic in his vision? Quanah tried again to sort the rush of images that had come to him. No animals of power had appeared. No buffalo, wolf, eagle, or coyote spoke a pledge of power. Instead the vision had been populated with a dead infant and a pony. And what did flight upon a changing wind portend? Where was meaning in soaring over the lands of the south? And the mountains, what was their secret? Bands of Nermernuh and Lipan and Mescalero Apaches once claimed the mountains as their own, but now they belonged to the *Tejanos.*

Quanah rubbed a hand over his face and unfolded his aching legs. Nothing in his vision made sense. If magicks that could guide a man lay within those tumbled images, he could not discern them.

The wail of an infant rose above the howl of the wind that blew outside.

Pushing to his feet, Quanah quietly stepped to the tipi's flap, careful not to disturb Pecos, who slept bundled in a buffalo robe at the rear of their home. Poking his head outside, he listened. The cry came from the lodge of the young brave Tah-hah-let. His wife had given birth to a daughter three days ago.

Nermernuh children were taught to contain their cries, which might alert an enemy to their position, at an early age. A baby knowing only three days could not hold back its tears of hunger. The hard months of a fall barren of game, except for occasional rabbit, had left the child's mother with milkless teats. The infant would soon follow old Te-naw into the dead. Starvation gave little heed to age when it claimed its victims.

Quanah's gaze moved among the camp's twelve tipis. How the band had dwindled since Peta Nocona's death. If more than half the tents still stood when spring came, it would be a simple matter of luck rather than ability.

The band had been unable to reach the other bands who gathered in Palo Duro Canyon before winter's first snows. They had taken shelter in a small canyon that sliced into the Caprock. While it offered some protection from a wind that constantly blew from the north, hunters found it lacking game. For one moon they rode out each day and returned each night empty-handed. Even rabbits eluded their bows. The stores of pemmican made during an abundant summer now ran low. Soon it, too, would be gone.

A horse whinnied farther up the canyon, where the band's ponies were gathered. Like their masters, they slowly died, unable to reach the dried winter grass beneath the blanket of snow covering the ground.

The flesh of the horse, like that of the dog, was taboo to the Nermernuh. But like dog, the People would eat horse to stave off starvation. When that time came, death would soon follow. Kwerhar-rehnuh without mounts to take them across the plains were no better than the dead.

Quanah pulled back inside the tipi. Legs still weak from endless hours of sitting beside the fire went liquid beneath him. He fell, a shoulder striking the side of the tipi. His lance and shield spilled from their pole and fell across his legs.

A shiver shot along his spine when he reached down to lift the weapons. Icy snowflakes fell from his arms like the veneer of ice that had coated his naked body in the vision. The shiver became a tremor that raced through his body.

The vision! He saw its meaning. The war lance was his father and the shield his mother. Their spirits dwelled within his heart and were his guides! Their wisdom and teaching had brought him to manhood.

And the skeletal infant and dying horse—they were the band. The winter slowly destroyed them.

The wind? He frowned, then saw the disguised truth. He was the wind that ran across the land that had given him birth.

What of the deer and antelope in the south lands?

He needed no insight into the other world to understand what was obvious. The game had fled to the warmer lands of the south to escape the snows. His vision had not been one of manhood; his parents had given him that. The vision brought by the tobacco was an answer, a way to save the band.

Carefully lifting lance and shield, he hung them back on their pole. He then crossed the tipi to gently nudge Pecos's arm. When his brother's eyes opened sleepily, he said, "Rise and dress warmly. I know where the deer hides from our arrows. We will ride to them this night."

Although Pecos's eyes questioned his older brother's sanity, he made no protest while he followed Quanah's lead and dressed in three layers of clothing. Together, buffalo robes wrapped about them and the weapons they carried, the brothers slipped from the tipi into the night.

"Can we not rest here the night and savor our meal?" Pecos asked while he watched his brother slice the roasted venison backstrap and drop the hot meat into his pemmican pouch. "Have we not earned a full night's sleep with our bellies full?"

Quanah tossed Pecos a slice of the meat. "Eat while I work. This should be enough to quiet our stomachs while we return to the village."

"We have not had more than stolen naps since we left our tipi." The boy bit into the grease-dripping meat and devoured it like a wolf. The second and third slices Quanah handed him disappeared as quickly.

"There will be time for sleep once we have returned to our home." Quanah glanced at the six deer tied to the backs of the packhorses they had brought with them to the Colorado River. The meat would fill the village's pots for a full week. By then—

"But it's two days back to the band." Pecos wiped the grease from his mouth on the sleeve of his buckskin shirt.

"We'll ride day and night, pausing only to let our horses rest." Quanah placed the last slice of backstrap in his mouth while he closed the pouch and looped its strap over shoulder and head. "Cover the fire. The sooner we begin, the sooner we will silence the hunger of our people."

Scooping double handfuls of sand from the ground, Pecos did as he was told. His gaze scanned the grasslands, and a smile lifted the corners of his mouth. "You were wise to ride here, my brother. The deer are plentiful. Why did the other braves not think of this?"

Quanah swung to the back of his mount and shook his head. "Their visions did not show them the deer or the antelope that graze farther south. My medicine pointed the way."

He untied the shield from his pony's neck and slipped it onto his left arm, and then hefted the lance to point its tip toward the north. "Come, we have growling bellies to still."

Pecos nodded and mounted his pony. Each brother led a packhorse behind him weighted with three deer, as they reined toward the dark clouds on the horizon.

A hand nudged Quanah's shoulder, bringing him from the depths of sleep. Blinking past the veils of sleep cotton, he saw Mo-wi squatted beside his sleeping pallet.

"Quanah," the brave said, "I have brought you and your brother hot food to chase the cold from your bodies. My wife has spiced the stew with peppers traded from the Mexicans."

Pushing to his elbows, the young brave saw the two steaming bowls Mo-wi held. His heart jumped to his chest, hammering with hope. Containing any outward sign of his excitement, Quanah called to Pecos, who twisted and groaned, but eventually sat up and blinked at Mo-wi. Quanah saw a flash of surprise on his brother's face, which was quickly replaced by a mask of disinterest. Pecos, too, understood the importance of Mo-wi's unannounced visit, Quanah realized.

Quanah accepted the bowl the older man passed to him and used his fingers to fish a chunk of the venison from the dark, rich broth in which it floated. The spicy flavor satisfied his mouth and pleased his stomach.

He had not realized how hungry he was. When Pecos and he had ridden into camp with the rising sun, they had barely had the strength to leave the horses with the deer at the center of the village, then stumble into the tipi and collapse atop their buffalo robes.

"All in our camp have feasted throughout the day because of your gift." Mo-wi sat on his heels watching the two brothers eat.

Through the wind-rustled door flap, Quanah saw night reigned outside. A campfire burned at the center of the tipi. He could not remember lighting it before sleep took his mind and body. Had Mo-wi set the fire? "It is the way of Kwerhar-rehnuh hunters to share their kill with all in the village. Are we not all one?"

Mo-wi stared down as though examining the floor of the tipi, but said nothing.

Quanah frowned, uncertain of himself. Had his reply been too haughty for one who had been shunned by the band for months? That Mo-wi sat here within a tipi he had once said no one would enter again meant the man had swallowed his pride and admitted he had been wrong. To rub his nose in dung would accomplish nothing.

"Please tell your wife the meal is excellent. Pecos and I have grown weary of our own cooking," Quanah said, sensing Mo-wi struggled to find words that did not come easy.

"She will be pleased. She had saved the peppers for such a feast. She honors those who have provided when others failed."

Again Quanah's heart raced. That Mo-wi gave voice to the obvious signaled he was making doubly certain that Pecos and Quanah understood that they were no longer ostracized from the band. The cold months of exile ended this night.

"I am shamed that I have no tobacco to offer Mo-wi." Quanah nodded to the empty pouch tossed to the side of the tipi. "I am afraid I smoked all that remained to open my medicine vision that led Pecos and me to the deer."

"It was a good vision." Mo-wi looked up at the young brave. "There will be tobacco enough for all. I have called a council for this night. You will sit among the braves. We will hear of this vision."

Quanah nodded while he scooped another portion of meat from the bowl and popped it in his mouth. He felt his brother's eyes on him and could feel Pecos's soaring spirits.

"When you have filled your stomach, join us by the council fire." Mo-wi stood, turned, and walked into the night.

"We are Nermernuh again," Pecos said with a broad grin stretching across his face from ear to ear.

"We have always been Nermernuh. The others were too blind to see that until we opened their eyes," Quanah answered with a shake of his head.

Hiding his own grin behind the venison he stuffed into his mouth, the young warrior hastily wolfed down the meat, then drained the bowl of its peppery soup. He wiped his hands on the thighs of his buckskin breeches and stood.

"Finish quickly," Quanah ordered his brother. "I must speak in council this night."

Pecos's grin widened. Quanah barely noticed. His mind raced while he gathered the words he would say this night. They must be few, and as true as the arrows that had brought down the deer by the Colorado River. If he were to hold true to his vision, he must convince Mo-wi and the other braves that the band's ways must be changed. To camp in one location at the base of the Caprock throughout the winter as they had always done meant death.

Quanah sucked in a deep breath and slowly exhaled it. The weight of this night sat heavily on his shoulders. If his words rang true in the other braves' ears, with the rising of tomorrow's sun a man who had barely seen his fifteenth *taum* would lead the band to the bounty to be found in the south. If his words failed, then—

Quanah shoved the thought away. He would not fail this night—could not!

CHAPTER
NINE

Sunlight glinted off the rifle barrel to momentarily blind Quanah with the brilliance of the spectrum. He jerked back behind the granite boulder and blinked to clear his eyes. A splotch of fading yellow superimposed itself over the mountains the whites called Davis when he glanced about once again.

"How many ride toward us?" Sawne Wea whispered behind the young warrior.

"One gray-coated rider who carries a rifle." Quanah eased forward and risked another peek around the boulder. "Two ride within the shadow of the wagon's black cover. I can't see more than that, Grass Rope."

A slight crunch of stone beneath moccasin came when the older warrior shifted his weight from one foot to the other. Quanah continued to study the approaching gray-coat *Tejano* and the one-horse buggy. He had no want to see Sawne Wea's expression. He could well imagine the doubt that lined the face of the brave five years his elder.

Since leading the band from the killing snows of the plains to the game-rich mountains, the braves had grown to respect the medicine that surrounded one so young. Yet, only Sawne

Wea trusted that medicine enough to ride beside the fifteen-year-old warrior when Quanah suggested a raid on the gray coats' horses at Fort Davis.

Although Quanah had scouted the fort with its adobe buildings for a full two weeks, the other braves thought the *Tejanos'* numbers too great when their own were so small. Sawne Wea, however, was poor, with only three ponies to his name. The twenty-year-old warrior needed at least half a dozen horses to buy the hand of the young maid he sought for a bride. The lure of soldiers' ponies rather than belief in his companion's ability as a warrior was the determining factor in his decision to ride this day, Quanah realized.

Sawne Wea's reasons did not matter. That he rode with him was all that was important to Quanah—and that they succeeded. To return with *Tejanos* horses would prove the power of the magicks he commanded to all in the band. When he called his next raid, others would follow him as they once did his father.

Quanah's gaze lifted to the cliffs of red-brown granite that formed the faces of the two hogbacks, between which ran the narrow trail thirty feet below. These great hump-backed mountains that thrust from the prairie were not unknown to the Kwerhar-rehnuh, but they were not the open plains of the north, Quanah thought. A brave could not see for miles on end here. There were too many places danger might lurk among the massive boulders that lay strewn at the foot of each mountain. Closed in and cramped, this land was better suited to the Lipan and Mescalero Apaches, who often raised their camps among the mountains.

On the open plains a brave could flee in all directions should danger suddenly rise up. Here the mountain passes limited the path one could take. Although, he silently admitted, there were more ways to be taken than seen in one glance. While studying the numerous deer paths that crisscrossed each mountain, he had discovered a narrow pass that lay directly behind the *Tejanos'* fort. No soldier guarded that path. Through it, he would reach the gray coats' corral when darkness shrouded the mountains.

"We should let them pass," Grass Rope eventually said. "We came for the gray coats' horses."

Quanah silently watched the unsuspecting soldier. The young warrior's attention centered on the man's rifle. To ride back carrying such a weapon would show all the strength of the medicine he possessed. More, he would bring firearms to the band as Peta Nocona had once done.

"Two horses walk straight to us," Quanah said. "We can not slip into the corral at the fort until it grows dark. We can take these two while the sun still shines. Miles lie between us and the fort. What we do here will not alert them to what we will do this night."

"But the gray coat's rifle," Sawne Wea began.

Quanah cut him off. "I do not fear the *Tejanos'* bullets. If you do, remain here. I will face the gray coat by myself."

The young warrior cast out the worm of doubt that squirmed in his brain when he turned and mounted a pony tied to the branch of a live oak growing behind the boulder. He would have preferred knowing who rode within the buggy, but they were of no concern. Today he carried father lance and mother shield; they would protect him. He needed nothing else, not even Sawne Wea.

Without waiting for the older warrior to announce his decision, Quanah dug his heels into the horse's sides. The pony lunged forward, stone and sand flying as its hooves bit into the earth. Down the gentle incline to the trail below, the young warrior rode. He swung the pony's head to north, slammed heels to flanks, and charged straight toward the lone rider.

Whether the man drifted in the saddle or merely daydreamed of another place or time, Quanah did not know. But the gray-coated soldier's head did not snap up until the young warrior screamed a war cry from chest and throat. Nor did the shock of the sudden attack vanish from the soldier's face when Quanah's lance shafted into his chest to drive through his body and send him tumbling over the rump of his mount.

A woman's scream, echoed by that of a frightened child, drew Quanah's attention while his pony carried him past the fallen gray coat. As he yanked his pony's head around, he glimpsed a young mother, bundled in a dark blue coat and bonnet, holding the buggy's long reins while her daughter clutched at her side. In spite of the hindering child, the woman sharply popped the reins on the back of the bay hitched to the buggy. The horse responded, breaking into a full run.

Quanah ignored the buggy and the soldier's escaping mount when he drew his pony to a halt beside the gray coat and leaped to the ground. Skewered with lance protruding from chest and

back, the man still lived. He fought to get his feet under him
while his right hand fumbled spasmodically to free a pistol from
the holster on his hip.

The razored edge of a hunting knife drawn across the soldier's
throat from ear to ear ended the last struggles of his rapidly fading life. The same blade opened his forehead at the hairline and
sliced back to cleanly separate scalp from skull.

Quanah tucked the bloody trophy beneath a rawhide band
tied about the waist of his buckskin breeches. With foot planted
on the dead man's chest he used both arms to tug his lance free
before stripping the soldier of pistol, holster, and cartridge belt.
He rummaged through the gray coat's pockets to discover two
fully loaded pistol cylinders and a small cloth bag of tobacco.
These he dropped into a pouch hung at his side.

Although a rifle could kill an enemy at a great distance, a pistol was a prize to be coveted. The weapon's ability to fire round
after round gave a man the power of six rifles at close range. The
Tejanos Rangers had taught the Kwerhar-rehnuh that lesson time
and again.

Lastly Quanah snatched up the rifle the soldier had dropped
into the sand. A victory cry tore from his throat when he threw
back his head and held the weapon high.

A yipping yowl like that of a coyote answered him. Sawne
Wea atop a white and brown paint bolted from behind the boulder. The warrior's heels repeatedly dug into his mount's flanks as
he reined after the escaping buggy.

A thin smile slipped across Quanah's lips. With danger past,
Grass Rope entered the fight. Although the warrior's courage was
questionable, today Sawne Wea was his only follower. The young
brave would not confront him. Around the campfire tonight he
would tell the others in the band of this fight. When Quanah
raided again, other braves would answer his call.

The power of the rifle coursing through his arm, Quanah
swung to his pony's back and reined after the riderless horse that
now galloped after the racing buggy and the warrior who chased
after it. With ease the young warrior reached the horse's side and
leaned forward to grasp one of its dangling reins. As important
as the horse was to a Nermernuh, Quanah was more concerned
with the leather bags tied behind the saddle. Within the broad
pouches he was certain to find cartridges for his new rifle.

A woman's scream snapped his head up. A quarter mile down

the trail, Sawne Wea had managed to grab the bay's bit and drew up his paint. As the the buggy rolled to a halt, the mother and daughter jumped to the ground and ran toward a pile of talus. Sawne Wea cried out in delight.

He released the bay and nudged his pony after the two. Like a white man might herd a cow and calf, he worked mother and child into a wide crack formed by two green lichen-mottled boulders. Sawne Wea tossed aside his lance and slipped to the ground. With hunting knife drawn, he advanced toward the young woman.

"Ka!" Quanah shouted a denial before he knew what he did. "No! Sawne Wea, no!"

The older warrior stumbled to a stop and stared up at his young companion. "No? But it is our right to take this woman. We have captured her. She is ours to use."

"We came for horses, not women and children." Quanah shook his head. "They are of no use to us."

"Then I will kill them."

"No." Quanah swung the rifle toward the older warrior and thumbed back its hammer as he threw a leg over the pony's neck and dropped to the ground. "We will take the two horses and let them go."

Sawne Wea's eyes narrowed when a dark shadow passed across his face. For a moment his gaze shifted to the woman and child. Then he looked back at his young companion. "They are not your mother and sister."

Grass Rope's words took Quanah off guard. Were his reasons so obvious that even one such as Sawne Wea could read them? "It does not matter. They shall not be harmed."

Sawne Wea's mouth opened as though intent at further protest, but he merely nodded. "I ride with you. It is your medicine that protects us. I will do as you say."

Quanah eased the rifle's hammer down and lowered the weapon. He turned toward the woman and her daughter before releasing an overly held breath. His bluff had succeeded. It was not the way of the Kwerkar-rehnuh to kill each other. Had Grass Rope ignored his wishes and taken this woman as was his right, the young warrior would have turned his back and walked away.

"Ein mea-dro," he ordered the young mother to go.

The woman, blue eyes round with fear, stood trembling with

her daughter clutched in her arms. Tears streamed down both their faces.

"*Ein mea-dro,*" he said again, and still the woman and girl remained frozen in place like the boulders that pressed into their backs.

Stupid, he realized. The woman was ignorant of the Nermernuh tongue. Of all the peoples who had encroached upon the prairies over the long generations—the Spanish and Mexicans, the French, the British, and the other red-skinned tribes— only the *Tejanos* were so arrogant. Only they refused to learn the language of the People.

"*Vaya!*" This time Quanah used the little Spanish he had learned from the Mexican traders.

The woman's remained frozen with fear.

Quanah's arm snaked out, and his hand roughly grasped the woman's shoulder. He yanked her forward and shoved her toward the trail that led to the gray-coated soldiers' fort. "*Vaya! Vaya!*"

When the mother and child stumbled a few strides and froze in place once again, Quanah stooped and gathered a handful of stones from the ground. Shouting for the two to run, he threw the first of the small missiles to strike the woman in her side. The second rock was hurled with greater force and hit her in the shoulder. The third and fourth struck her back as she and the child turned and began to run south.

Sawne Wea chuckled while he imitated his companion by tossing a half dozen rocks at the fleeing pair, all of which missed their mark.

Quanah glanced at the sun riding in the western sky. He then turned to the soldier's horse and pulled off the saddlebags before handing Grass Rope the animal. "Free the other horse from the wagon." He looked at the woman and child and watched them disappear behind a sheer face of granite that marked a sharp turn in the trail. "By the time they reach the fort, it will be dark. It will be a good night to steal *Tejano* horses. All the gray coats' attention will be held by the story she will tell of her escape from the Kwerhar-rehnuh. The soldiers will never notice the two warriors who empty their corral."

Sawne Wea turned to Quanah and grinned slyly. "I misjudged you, my friend. I thought you weakened by memories of your mother and sister. Instead you use the woman and girl-child to aid us. There is much wisdom in your plan. You are surely the son of Peta Nocona."

While the older man cut the bay from the buggy's harness, Quanah mounted his pony and sat there with lance and rifle resting in the crook of an arm. Sawne Wea could believe what he wished. In truth he had seen Naduah and Topsannah in the faces of the mother and daughter. The pain his mother carried in her heart rang in sympathy with the ache in his own breast. Unlike the whites who had stolen her from his family, he would not be the one to create such sorrow in the heart of another woman, whether she be white, red, or brown.

"Come," Quanah said when Sawne Wea climbed atop his paint. "We have a long ride before we reach the gray coats' fort."

Nudging his heels against his pony's sides, Quanah continued along the deer path he had followed when he had first seen the soldier and the buggy. He gave the rifle a slight heft, savoring the weight of it in his hand. The raid was already a good one; when they returned to the camp with stolen horses, their triumph would weave a dozen new songs.

The rifle barrels rent the sunlight into a shattered array of color when Quanah placed the weapons beside the small fire over which two rabbits roasted. The heads of the ten braves lifted and stared up at him.

"Our raid has been bountiful." He deposited six pistols beside the rifles. "We fired five of the *Tejanos'* homes, stole their horses, and their weapons."

"And took the scalps of seven," a Kiowa brave added while he turned the rabbits above the flame. "I chose right to ride south and join my Kwerhar-rehnuh brothers."

"You were wise to ride with Quanah." Mo-wi grinned at their single Kiowa confederate. "The white men flee before his power."

Quanah did not mind the old warrior's exaggeration. It was the Nermernuh way to boast of one's own exploits. But it was better when other warriors voiced praise. Through such words a brave's stature grew, and with that came the warriors willing to follow him.

In the two years since Sawne Wea and he had returned from Fort Davis with twenty of the gray coats' ponies, word of the young warrior's powerful medicine had spread through the bands of the Nermernuh. Each passing of the moon's faces brought new tipis to the band, and with them warriors desiring to share in the glory Quanah brought to those who followed him.

Even the defeat of the gray coats and the return of the blue-coated soldiers had not hindered the raiding, Quanah considered. The blue coats seemed more concerned with the *Tejanos* than with the raiding parties that swept down from the high plains. With each rising of the new moon, Quanah grew more daring in his attacks. He drove deeper and deeper into the lands the whites considered safe and secure. In turn, the raiders from other bands imitated his methods.

Whites abandoned their plowed fields and retreated back to their cities, and Nermernuh lands once more swelled. After this day, Quanah thought proudly, the farmers will flee farther south along the Brazos River to escape Kwerhar-rehnuh raiders. Their flight was futile; he would only push deeper when the Blood Moon next rose.

"When do we ride to our homes?" a voice broke his reflections.

"We wait here for the others to join us," Quanah answered. "Then you may divide the rifles and pistols among you before we ride west."

A full twenty warriors had ridden beside Quanah on this raid. As often was the way of large war parties, they had divided to attack from two directions at once. If all went well, it had been decided, they would rejoin here among the pecan trees along the river. Once, before the white men came, this had been a favorite spot for fall camps among the People, who gathered the plentiful nuts to mix in their pemmican.

"The others should have joined us by now," Mo-wi said. "Perhaps they are being followed by soldiers?"

Quanah glanced at the fire. "We shall eat. If they have not arrived by then, we shall ride west."

Although the blue coats posed a danger, it was small. While fast over short distances, their ponies tired quickly. The mustangs ridden by the People easily outdistanced them. Unlike the Ranger patrols, it was child's play to lose the soldiers on the vastness of the prairie. Their ignorance of the lands, their inability to find the hidden water holes, made it impossible for them to push deep into Nermernuh lands.

Quanah smiled to himself. Those foolish enough to attempt to patrol the grasslands were constantly harassed by warriors who struck out of nowhere and then vanished into nothingness. No battles with armies amassed were needed when the People could hit and run, killing the black-skinned soldiers one by one.

"The others!" The Kiowa brave pushed from the ground and pointed to the south.

Quanah turned. He counted ten mounted warriors. This was good; all returned safe. From the black smoke he saw snaking toward the sky, they had been as successful as had the ten who followed him.

The young warrior's eyes narrowed. His lips pulled back in a tight line. As the raiders reined closer, he saw they were not alone. Four of the warriors carried women. Why? Why did they defy him so?

Before the riders could draw their mounts up, Quanah stood facing them with an accusing finger pointed at the captives. "Do you hold the power of my medicine in contempt? Do you seek to shatter the power that protects us?"

For two years Quanah had cultivated the stories Sawne Wea had begun after their return from the raid on Fort Davis. He openly added to those tales by suggesting that his magicks were garnered in part from a refusal to take white women while raiding. It was well known to all who rode with him that no captives were to be taken, that to do such might weaken or destroy the strong medicine needed to protect a war party from enemy bullets.

In those two years, Quanah had come to believe the same. Never had he taken a captive or allowed one to be returned with his raiding parties. In that time little evil befell those who followed him. Only once had a warrior died, and this when his pony stepped into a prairie dog hole and he broke his neck in the fall.

"They are young, Quanah." This from Twenty Horses, once called Grass Rope. "They took the women without considering what they did."

"They are stupid." Mo-wi stepped to Quanah's side. The warrior's words brought a rumble of agreement from those at the fire. Mo-wi jabbed a finger at each of the four warriors. "Only fools would allow their genitals to lead them and leave those they raid with unprotected by the shield of medicine."

If the four had thought to protest, Quanah saw it evaporate from their faces. Instead of defiance, their expressions were those of whipped dogs wanting to slink off with their tails tucked between their legs.

"Down," Quanah ordered the four. "Sit the women upright on your ponies. There is a way to sew together what you sought to rend apart."

Without question the warriors dismounted and seated their captives atop their mounts. There was a glimmer of hope in their faces when they turned back to Quanah. However, the faces of the four women, none of which appeared to have seen twenty *taum*, were filled with fear and despair, certain the warriors surrounding them were death incarnate.

"I will return these four to the *Tejanos*," Quanah announced.

"You can not." Twenty Horses shook his head and stared at his friend. "The whites will kill you."

"Better one die than all." Quanah's gaze shifted over all gathered about him. "It is my medicine that has been tainted. Only I may right this wrong. Until this task is completed, it is better that you ride to our village and remain far from me. If I return to my tipi, then all will know my magicks have been restored."

Mo-wi, the oldest of the warriors, frowned but acquiesced with a nod. "There is wisdom in your words. We will ride home and await your return. Should you not return, these four warriors will not be welcomed in any village of the People. They will live out their lives as outcasts."

Quanah offered no comment, but mounted a roan pony, then gathered the reins of the captives' horses. Without a glance at those behind him, he reined the horse southward and led the four women through the pecan trees.

The sun rode overhead when the young warrior topped a treeless bluff overlooking a wide stretch of bottomlands. Below, near the banks of the Brazos, stood a *Tejano*'s sod house. Smoke rose from a chimney protruding from the grass roof.

Uncertainty clouded the four women's faces when Quanah turned and ordered them from the ponies. Where words failed to convey his meaning, a series of exaggerated arm and hand gestures succeeded. One by one the women dismounted. Quanah pointed to the house below and motioned the four forward. Hesitating at first, then moving faster and faster, they ran down the hill toward freedom.

Quanah watched them until they were halfway down the bluff, then he turn and nudged his roan and the four ponies he led into an easy gallop. He told himself that he returned the women to maintain the might of his medicine, trying to avoid the truth that rolled deep within him—the hope that one day a *Tejano* might do the same for his mother and sister.

CHAPTER
TEN

The sunlight broke into miniature rainbows while it danced atop the ripples of the stream flowing through the canyon. So brilliant were the colors that Quanah's eyes ached from the beauty.

"I have talked with all the traders," Pecos said from his brother's side. "None of them have any word of Naduah or Topsannah."

Quanah felt his heart sink. He expected as much, but with each arrival of the Mexican traders his hope mounted. It was through them the Kwerhar-rehnuh learned bits and pieces of what occurred in the world of the whites. Although he and Pecos constantly sought any information about their mother and sister from each and every trader who traveled the Llano Estacado, none brought the slightest inkling of Naduah's and Topsannah's fate.

"What of guns and ammunition?" Quanah pushed aside personal concerns and moved on to matters that affected the whole band.

"The rifles are old." Pecos shook his head. "There are none of the ones that shoot many times. The wagons carry more sugar and coffee than cartridges. It is as always. Our Mexican friends provide us with what they deem is safe."

Quanah pursed his lips. Nothing changed. The Comancheros from New Mexico were the Nermernuh's only source of goods produced by the whites. They willingly brought these deep into the lands of the People in exchange for hides and horses, mules, and cattle taken during raids. Yet, in their hearts, the brown-skinned men were no different from the *Tejanos* and the blue coats. Although they profited from Nermernuh raiding, they feared the strength of the People.

Without weapons—steel-bladed hunting knives, metal for arrowheads, rifles, pistols, and ammunition—the traders knew the Nermernuh would never allow their wagons onto the plains So they brought ancient one-shot rifles and ball-and-cap pistols, frightened the People would turn to raiding their lands should warriors arm themselves with newer weapons. With no other firearms available, except for those taken in raids, the People traded for what was offered.

Despite proclaimed friendship for the Nermernuh, often there seemed to be little difference between *Tejanos* and Comancheros in Quanah's mind. Though the latter used the People, often it seemed to him that they would prefer to see the Nermernuh wiped from the face of the earth, as would the Texans.

"What of the cowherders that have been seen driving their steers from the south up into the white cities in Pawnee land?" Quanah asked his younger brother.

"I have heard the whites far to the east have acquired a taste for cow—"

Quanah spat to the ground in contempt. Cow was a bland, tasteless meat. Why would anyone choose it over the rich flavor of antelope and buffalo? Of all the white man's animals, the young brave delighted in the taste of mule, as did most of the People.

"—The *Tejano* ranchers amass great herds and push them north to the fire-wagon-horse-road. From there they are carried all the way to the great waters in the east," Pecos concluded.

Although Quanah concealed any outward sign of the cold finger that tapped at the base of his spine, the words of his long-dead uncle Cona Cawb-vey whispered from deep in his mind. The white men always returned. Now there was a reason for their great land hunger. Prairie grass could feed more cattle than ten men could count in their lifetimes. In spite of the years spent successfully driving the farmers back during the great war of white men against white men, Quanah could not escape the feeling of the *Tejanos*' shadows spreading over the plains once again.

"There is tobacco, coffee, sugar, and flour in the wagons," Pecos's voice drew his thoughts back to the Comancheros' wagons. "Should I barter for the supplies we need?"

"Barter carefully," Quanah warned. "We are not poor, but we are no longer rich. We have only twenty ponies."

Pecos nodded and smiled. "My brother's generosity is known to all the People. He gives away our ponies to any brave who shows him moccasins with holes in their soles. I will make do with deer hides to trade for the provisions we need. One of us must show common sense in such matters and keep us from poverty."

Quanah laughed and gave Pecos a playful shove to send him on his way, while he continued to slowly wander through the goods the traders had spread on the ground to attract the eye. Although his brother exaggerated, his words struck close to the truth. It was the way of the Kwerhar-rehnuh, of all the People, to generously share the bounty of their raids and hunts with those in need.

Quanah's wealth in ponies swelled after raids on the *Tejanos*. That number dwindled within days, often to the point where Quanah and Pecos possessed only the horses they rode. The older men openly called the easy manner in which he freely gave away his possessions foolish. When there were those who needed more than he, Quanah could do nothing but give.

Those now in need were the Yampahreekuh bands to the north. The blue coats in Texas still offered no more than token opposition to the Kwerhar-rehnuh. But the soldiers in Kansas openly warred on the People. Daily, Yampahreekuh bands fled their lands seeking shelter among the Kwerhar-rehnuh. If the braves still rode horses at all, they were animals that hovered near death. It was to the Yampahreekuh braves Quanah gave his ponies. The People could not survive without mounts from which to hunt. The white men could not be driven back without warriors mounted astride fleet horses.

Quanah abruptly stopped amid a wealth of wool blankets spread beside the stream. It was not the colorful weave that caught his eye. Nor did his attention center on the copper pans or iron skillets the traders arrayed on pegged poles firmly driven into the sandy soil. Not even the gleaming steel of finely honed hunting knives called to him.

Had Pecos or any of his friends asked, he would have been unable to explain the hot sensation that flushed his face or the sudden race of his heart or the hollow emptiness that contracted within his belly. Yet, all those things and more beset the young warrior in a befuddling rush when his gaze fell upon the doeskin-clad woman who unloaded white cloth bags filled with coffee from the back of a wagon.

Mescalero. Quanah recognized the cut of the young woman's clothing, while he tried to sort through the confused feelings she awakened within him. She was beautiful to be certain, but he had seen beautiful women before, and never had he been so unsettled by their faces. Not even Weckeah, daughter of Yellow Bear, whom he had silently vowed to marry since they played together as children, stirred the desire that now coursed through his veins.

Her dark eyes remained downcast while she moved between wagon and the semicircle of Nermernuh women who haggled with a rotund Mexican over the price of the coffee. Nor did the Apache woman's oval face lift when she retrieved the required bags at the trader's command. Despite that fact, with her sleek black hair tied back in long twin braids, Quanah easily studied the straight, narrow line of her nose and the gentle curve of her cheeks and chin. Her mouth was full with lips that appeared kissed by the juice of spring's red berries.

"My little To-ha-yea is a good worker, no?"

Quanah glanced to his right and found a young Mexican grinning at him from beneath a moustache that dangled below the corners of his mouth. The trader was dressed in tight black breeches and a white shirt. A wide-brimmed sombrero as dirty as his mud-splattered boots shaded his face from the sun. "She is young and strong and would make the right brave a good squaw. She has yet to see sixteen summers."

"She is Mescalero," Quanah replied. "What is she doing so far from Apache lands?"

"She was taken in a raid on her tribe a month ago," the man answered. "I bought her from a band of Kiowas not more than a week past. Paid four horses for her."

What Quanah had thought to be shyness, he now recognized

as fear. This To-ha-yea was frightened of all the strangeness that surrounded her. Nermernuh and Comanchero ways were not those of the Mescalero. She kept her eyes downcast and her face turned from all in the hope none would notice her, and all would let her be.

"I am a married man with three children," the Comanchero continued. "I can not take her with me when I return home tomorrow. Unlike the People, a man such as me can not have more than one wife. I would sell her for what I paid for her."

Four horses, Quanah thought with contempt. He well knew the Kiowa and the low value they placed on captives. The Mexican had paid no more than a single pony for the young woman.

"I have no need for a wife at this time." Quanah glanced at the girl, turned, and walked back to his tipi, leaving the Mexican staring after him.

Need—the word echoed in his mind as he settled to the ground to think of the coming full moon and the raid he would lead against the *Tejanos*. There was no escape from the gentle image of To-ha-yea that fluttered within his head like a phantasma come to haunt his soul.

He forced images of Kwerhar-rehnuh women into his mind's eye—and they were edged away by the downcast gaze of a Mescalero girl. Even the love he had held for Weckeah could not hold her vision against the memory of the delicate Apache woman he had seen but for a few moments.

Need—he had no need for a woman within this tipi, he told himself when Pecos returned from his bartering and prepared the evening meal. He was still young, and there would be time enough to take a wife after he was fully established as a leader of his people. His life was ruled by shield, war lance, and rifle. There was no time for him to be a husband or a father.

The last thought sent a nervous shiver up his spine. How could he think of bringing a child into the world when he was still considered a young warrior by most of the older braves? To be certain, word of his deeds spread among the Nermernuh, but he had yet to see twenty *taum*.

"The name of Quanah Parker is known by the *Tejanos*," Pecos said as he passed his brother a bowl of steaming antelope stew spiced with fresh green chiles traded from the Comancheros that day. "I know because the white beard among the Mexicans asked me to point you out. He chuckled when I did. He said the Texans believe you to be at least twice your age. The Rangers can not accept one so young can be such a fierce warrior."

Quanah smiled, barely hearing his brother's words. While Pecos and he shared the day's gossip, the Mescalero To-ha-yea walked at the periphery of his thoughts. He imagined her among the Mexicans while she prepared their meal of tortillas and beans. As they ate, she quietly slipped into the shadows and trembled while she prayed none of the men would remember her and seek her out that night.

Need—what need did he, a Kwerhar-rehnuh, have of an Apache wife, Quanah asked himself while he covered himself with a buffalo hide and closed his eyes. Not only was she Mescalero, not even one of the People, but she was a captive taken during a raid.

He tossed from one side to the other imagining how To-ha-yea had been used by the Kiowa warriors who stole her from her parents' wickiup. The first night they had held her spread-eagle on the ground while each of them had sated their lusts with her young body—not once but time and again. When the raiders returned to their village, they had passed her among themselves, using her for their pleasure until they tired of her and sold her to the traders.

And the Mexicans—the light of predawn seeped beneath the edges of the tipi when Quanah considered To-ha-yea's treatment in the hands of the Comanchero band for the past week. Had she been white, they would have considered her valuable merchandise. After all, the families of white captives paid in gold to have their loved ones returned to them.

To-ha-yea was not white. She was Mescalero, and her family had no gold to buy her freedom. The Mexicans used her as the Kiowas had. To them she was no more or less than the painted whores they bought for pleasure in the cantinas of Santa Fe.

While Pecos prepared the morning meal, Quanah stood outside the tipi and watched the traders' two wagons slowly move along the steep trail that led up the wall of the canyon. Although he refused to admit it to himself, he hoped for a glimpse of the Apache girl. However, To-ha-yea remained hidden to him. She huddled among the remaining bags of coffee trying to make herself as small as possible, he imagined.

Need—he needed no wife, especially one who was Mescalero and had been captive to both Kiowa and Mexican, he told himself when he ducked back into the tipi. That the traders' wagons disappeared high above on the Staked Plains was for the best. He would never see To-ha-yea again, and that was good.

When the time was right, he would approach Yellow Bear and seek Weckeah's hand in marriage. It was to her that he had secretly pledged his love throughout his life. And though she had never spoken sweet promises in his ear, he was certain she carried the same vows in her heart as he.

After their meal, Pecos announced his intent to ride with friends on a hunt that day. Quanah merely shook his head when his brother asked if he wished to accompany the party. With a questioning eyebrow hiked high, Pecos left his older brother seated cross-legged by the fire.

The midday sun rose high in the sky when Quanah finally stepped outside with shield and lance in hand. Without a word to those he passed in the village, he followed the stream up the canyon to where the band's older boys guarded the horses. There he bridled a black-and-white paint and slipped ropes around the necks of three other horses. Swinging astride the paint, he reined toward the path that led up the canyon's wall.

Need, he considered the weight of what he did, *and want are two different things in a man*.

Marriage among other plains people was a ceremonious occasion where the new husband and wife stood at the center of prescribed rituals and joyous celebrations meant to bestow the new couple with a life of happiness, wealth, and children. To the Nermernuh the joining of man and woman was a part of life requiring no special note.

As natural as it was for the sun to shine or the rain to fall, it was natural for a brave to choose a woman to share his tipi and for a woman to select a man who would provide for her and the sons and daughters she would bear him. Should such a joining prove unsuitable to man or woman, it was just as natural for them to go their separate ways and seek happiness elsewhere. Marriage and separation were conducted in the same manner among the Nermernuh; brave and woman stood in the middle of the village and announced their intentions.

So it was when Quanah returned to the camp at sunset with To-ha-yea riding behind him. If he expected surprise among the braves and women, there was none. Not even Weckeah batted an eye when he proclaimed that the Mescalero girl he had purchased from the traders for *two* ponies, rather than the four first demanded, was his wife and he her husband. Only Pecos reacted, rushing into the tipi and running out with his arms filled with his sleeping blankets. He then took the reins of Quanah's and To-ha-yea's mounts, saying he would find another place to sleep until his brother once more summoned him back to their lodge.

While Pecos led the ponies away to care for them, Quanah reached out and took To-ha-yea's hand in his own. Holding himself straight and proud with his new wife at his side, he walked through the village to his tipi and held open the flap while To-ha-yea entered before him.

During their ride from the Comancheros' wagons, To-ha-yea had not spoken a word. That same silence held her tongue within the tipi. Without a glance at her groom, she found the chunks of antelope and peppers Pecos had left in bowls for the evening meal. Mixing both with salt and water, she placed the stew on a small fire she lit in the ring of stones at the center of the hide lodge.

Quanah settled atop a blanket near the flames. Since Peta Nocona's death had left Pecos and him orphaned, he had forgotten the beauty in a woman's movements while she went about the simple things. The slight rustle of his young wife's doeskin dress was like the gentle song of a morning breeze.

In his heart he would have been contented just to sit and watch her. That was, had her eyes ever lifted and danced his way, or had the hint of a smile touched those berry-hued lips. He wished for both; neither was granted him. To-ha-yea went about her cooking in the same manner she had unloaded the bags of coffee from the Mexicans' wagon. Her neck remained bowed and her eyes downcast.

More than anything he had ever desired in his life, Quanah wanted to reach out, to let his fingertips gently brush the softness of his new wife's cheeks. And when her dark brown eyes rose to gaze into his face, he would take her shoulders in his hands and tenderly ease her diminutive form close. With soft whispers of reassurance and the tender caresses of his palms, he would soothe away the tremblings of uncertainty and doubt that coursed through her body.

When, at last, her eyes once again rose to met his, this time lit with acceptance, he would lower her to the softness of their buffalo blankets. Slowly, careful not to reignite her fears, his fingers would free the leather laces of her doeskins. While her own fingertips explored the hairless contours of his chest and back, he would lay back her clothing to reveal the ripe forms of her young breasts, the mysterious dark triangle bushed between her legs. Their coupling would not be accompanied by the screams and struggles he had known from captive women brought into the camp by other braves. When he came to her it would be with the same tenderness which had first guided . . .

To-ha-yea dipped a bowl into the pot that now boiled over the small fire. She handed the stew to Quanah, breaking the daydream of their first night of lovemaking. Accepting the offered meal, the warrior blew across the steaming bowl while he watched his wife fill a bowl for herself and sit back on the ground with legs crossed.

Quanah tested the stew with the tip of a finger when the last thread of steam dissipated in the air. Assured he would not burn himself, he scooped three fingers into the mélange of meat and peppers and lifted the portion to his mouth. After chewing an appropriate time to display that he was not some wild beast who wolfed down food without appreciation, he swallowed and once more looked to the young Mescalero woman.

"The meal is good," he pronounced. "It pleases my tongue and warms my stomach."

To-ha-yea offered no answer, but kept her head downcast while she used her own fingers to dip two chunks of antelope from the bowl in her left hand.

"We are fortunate," Quanah continued, hoping to draw her from the silence. "My brother Pecos hunted this day and provided us with fresh meat."

To-ha-yea remained silent while she continued to eat. Nor did her head so much as nod to show the brave that she even heard his words.

Quanah pursed his lips as he searched for the correct words that would reach out and touch the woman. He drew a heavy breath and softly exhaled it. The words that formed in his mind felt as awkward as the moment surrounding him. His was the way of spear, shield, and rifle—the way of a warrior. The words that would win a woman were not his, nor had he ever had use for them before this night.

Returning his attention to the meal, he quickly emptied the bowl and placed it on the ground beside his crossed legs. Only then did To-ha-yea react. In a fleeting glimpse, her gaze lifted to Quanah, then darted to the empty bowl.

"I will get you more of the stew." The words sounded awkward as they stumbled from a tongue unaccustomed to Kwerharrehnuh expressions.

As she reached for the bowl, Quanah's own hand lifted to take her wrist. "This is not a night meant for filling our bellies until they are fat and bloated."

Still she did not look at him.

"It is the night of our marriage," he continued, trying to ignore his heart that pounded like that of a frightened child. "It is a night for wedding—for the sharing of a man and woman. This night we become husband and wife."

The Mescalero woman's head jerked up. For an instant, Quanah thought he saw the flare of hate and defiance burn in her dark eyes. In the next instant, her head bowed once again. With the slightest of tugs, she freed her wrist from his hand, then laid her bowl aside and rose.

"When I dwelled with my people among the mountains to the west," she said, her fingers unlacing her doeskin dress, "I was a maiden. Then Kiowa dogs raided our village when our men were away hunting. The Kiowa robbed me of my maidenhood. Comanche, the wife you have purchased has known more Kiowa pigs than you can count on your fingers and toes. And to the Mexicans who bought me from the Kiowa, I was no better than the whores among their own kind to be used to pleasure them."

Her doeskins fell about her ankles. She stood before Quanah unashamed of her nakedness. The defiance the brave had glimpsed a moment ago once more fired deep within her dark eyes.

"I stand here," she said, "to show you what you have purchased with your two ponies."

Quanah swallowed while his gaze caressed the sleek, lithe form of her body. Her breasts were fuller than he had imagined. Conical in shape, they pushed from her chest with upthrusting dark nipples. The flatness of her stomach led his eyes downward to her womanhood. Fires of desire burned within his groin.

"You have bought this body with your ponies. It is the way of your people and mine that captive women are to be used." She turned, stepped to the waiting pile of buffalo blankets, and knelt atop the bed of furs. Her dark eyes still refusing to met Quanah's, she stretched out on her back with her thighs spread wide.

Quanah rose, his fingers dipped beneath the leather thong which bound a leather breechclout about his waist. As he began to shove it downward, To-ha-yea spoke again:

"Know this, Comanche. This body you may have. You may share me with your brother as is the custom of your people. I will even do the work required of a wife. But I will never be your wife, should you live until the time of man comes to an end."

Quanah halted and blinked down at the naked beauty stretched atop his bed. The openness of the young woman's legs was not an invitation to share the pleasures of a man and woman, but a flaunted defiance meant to taunt him. The fires of his groin fizzled in the cloud of confusion that filled his mind.

"I am Mescalero. This village is not the village of my people. My heart will never find a home here," To-ha-yea said in a broken mixture of Comanche and Spanish. "So use me for your lusts as did the Kiowa and Mexican pigs, but I will be no wife to you, Comanche. And when the time comes and you are not looking, I will run from you and find my way back to my people."

Quanah's hands fell to his side and dangled there, as limp as his once-aroused passion. He stared at the naked woman, trying to remember the daydream of their lovemaking that had filled his thoughts but moments before. Now, all he could summon within his head were images of his mother and sister.

Had his mother felt as To-ha-yea when she had been first torn from her white family? Did she feel so now, having been stolen away from the People by the *Tejano* Rangers?

"Cover yourself." Quanah sank back to the ground, his breechclout still tied about his waist.

This was not what he wanted. He had bought To-ha-yea so that they might share love between them. Now he saw the lies in his actions. The love, the desire, all belonged to him. To-ha-yea felt nothing except the contempt she held for the Kiowa and Mexicans who had taken her body time and again.

While he saw himself as buying her freedom, to the Mescalero woman, she had moved from one captivity into another. It mattered not that Quanah had taken her as a wife or had done so out of love.

His eyes traveled over the interior of the tipi. In spite of the fire within, the tanned hides that surrounded him provided no shelter from the night's chill. This was not how it was meant to be between husband and wife.

His head moved slowly from side to side as though in denial, but in his breast there was no escape from the truth. What he did not understand was what he must do next. He was uninitiated in the ways of a man and woman.

He could not seek advice from the older men of the band, not without all knowing there was a weakness in the magic surrounding him. Among a Comanche band there were no secrets. To go to even one brave for guidance would mean every squaw in the band would laugh behind his back when he stepped from his lodge in the morning. Cona Cawb-vey and Peta Nocona had taught him well in the ways of the hunter and warrior, but left him ignorant in the ways of the heart. He yearned to have them by his side this night so he might learn from their now-lost experience.

His gaze fell on an ornate, hand-carved wooden pipe and tobacco pouch hanging from one of the tipi's poles. For answers not carried in a man's head, a brave must seek the wisdom of the spirits. Pushing to his feet again, he saw To-ha-yea cringe and gather a buffalo robe closer about her nakedness.

He turned to her. "I am Comanche, not Mexican or Kiowa. I will not take you as did those who held you captive. You have nothing to fear from me." He glanced back to the pipe and tobacco. "Still my thoughts are muddy. We are husband and wife, but not husband and wife. I will leave you here to sleep while I seek a vision to show me the way. I know not what must be done with you."

To-ha-yea's eyes shifted to the left, following Quanah's gaze to the pipe before she looked up at the brave. "Among my people there is a better way to find the magicks held in a vision."

As though unaware of the effects of her nakedness on him, she shoved back the robe, and stretched out to snatch up a small pouch amid the pile of her clothing. From within she withdrew a half-withered cactus button and held it out to the brave. "For my people, the fruit of peyote cactus is the most powerful path to the spirit world."

Quanah lifted the leathery fruit and studied its dried form with a questioning eye. To-ha-yea had carried the cactus long enough that it had turned brown with age and was as wrinkled as an old squaw's face.

"Have no fear, brave Comanche." An undercurrent of sarcasm ran in the woman's voice. "I am not fool enough to try to poison you while in the middle of your own village. Although the peyote contains poison that must be conquered before it can un-lock magicks. Eat it and hold it in your belly until the visions come."

Quanah eyed the button again, then looked back at the Mes-calero woman. "What do you expect to gain from this?"

There was no defiance in her expression or sarcasm in her voice when she answered. "My freedom—a return to my home. The spirits that guide this world will show you that, Comanche. Of that I am certain. I sense a gentleness in your heart. The spir-its will show you that you must follow the way of your heart."

Quanah snorted. No vision he had experienced had ever led him over a gentle path. He looked back at the cactus button in the palm of his hand, then closed his fist around it.

"Eat it, Comanche," To-ha-yea urged in a voice no more than a whisper. "Taste the magic of my people."

Lifting the peyote button, Quanah bit into it as though eating a wild plum. The taste was slight and not unpleasant. Like the apple harvested from a prickly pear, the button's flesh held a slight earthy flavor similar to the sands in which it had grown. After chewing, Quanah swallowed, waited a moment, then when he felt nothing, he took another bite and carefully chewed it and swallowed again. It was as he chewed the seventh bite his head abruptly jerked back to see a light as bright as the sun radiating at the peak of the tipi—

CHAPTER ELEVEN

—Quanah blinked against the harsh light that seared his eyes. His hand closed around the peyote button and held it tightly.

Quanah's fingers slid across the wrinkled surface of the peyote button strung on a leather thong about his neck. Every time he touched the cactus fruit he wore as a sign of his magic, his memories skirted back to the Mescalero woman who had been a wife but not a wife. He had been right in riding the long journey to the desert mountains in the west and returning To-ha-yea to her family.

Comanche he might be and they Apache, but his act planted a strong friendship between To-ha-yea's band and himself. A friendship that provided open trade for a supply of the peyote he now used when seeking the guidance of a medicine vision. What took tobacco hours, perhaps days to bring, the peyote opened to the mind within minutes.

"There, atop that hill." Quanah pointed to a low rolling hogback that rose a mile from his position. "Eckitoacup rides toward the hill. When he enters the draw below, he will find us waiting for him—mounted and ready for battle."

Quanah glanced back to the dust that rose like a storm

cloud on the northern horizon. He tried to ignore the sense of dread that crept up his spine, but could not. For Comanche to fight Comanche was wrong. His hope was that Eckitoacup's eyes were open enough to see that. If not—

"What of Weckeah?" one of warriors behind him asked.

"Have her and two braves remain with the herd," Quanah answered. "Tell the rest to gather their weapons and join me atop the rise. It is there I will greet Eckitoacup when he rounds the mesa."

Without looking at the five men who accompanied him to scout the approaching war band, Quanah grasped the mane of a chestnut mustang and swung to its back. His heels nudged the animal's flanks, and his left hand slightly tugged the single rein to move the horse toward the hogback.

The approaching warriors were at least an hour's ride away, Quanah judged by the column of dust their horses stirred high in the sky. There was no need to push his pony now. Later, if Eckitoacup did not see the wisdom of laying aside his desire for personal revenge, all the animal's strength would be needed—as well as that of the mustang's rider.

Quanah allowed the gentle rocking rhythm of the pony's strides to work the tension from his body. What would be would be. The time he had hoped would never come now stared him in the face. In truth, he now realized, he always had recognized that he and Eckitoacup would one day have to face each other and put this matter behind them, whether with words or with blood. Had Quanah stood in Eckitoacup's place, he would do as the young warrior did. Weckeah was a woman worth dying for.

Quanah's mind eased back through the days and months. Over a year ago, he had discovered Eckitoacup entering Yellow Bear's tipi to seek the hand of the warrior's daughter. Yellow Bear refused the ten ponies Eckitoacup offered, but made it more than clear that Weckeah would become a bride the day Eckitoacup brought twenty horses with him.

Except for To-ha-yea, Quanah had never loved another than Weckeah. As children they had played together, been friends. In both of their minds had always been the certainty that one day Weckeah would be one of Quanah's wives. Not even declaring To-ha-yea his wife had changed that for Weckeah, who saw Quanah's marriage to the Mescalero as merely a way of returning the woman to her people. It was not the way of the Nermernuh, but when it came to captive women, Quanah was not like the others of the People.

Even with the five horses Pecos gave to his brother, Quanah could raise but ten mounts. To double those ponies within the week Eckitoacup promised to return was impossible. Quanah took the only course opened to him: He stole Weckeah away from her father's tipi and with twenty-two warriors beside him rode south to the Concho River deep into Texas.

A smile of pride touched Quanah's lips. During that year, he and his band had raided the white man time and again. Hundreds of ponies now stood in the band's herd. Word of their success spread through the Nermernuh bands, and young warriors rode south to join those who followed him. The Comanchero traders whose paths he crossed told tales of the blue coats who scoured the Texas drylands for the young warrior they all knew by name.

The soldiers could not find Quanah and his band. Nor could Eckitoacup, although the brave rode into Texas time upon time in search of the warrior who had stolen a bride from him.

Today I will end Eckitoacup's search, Quanah thought as he stopped atop the rise's crest and turned to the north. Eckitoacup had not found Quanah, but Quanah had decided to reveal himself. His band grew too large, and the horses they traveled with swelled in number. With each raid it grew harder and harder to shake the soldiers and the Rangers from their trail. Unless he moved his band northward again, away from the white men and their towns, it would be only a matter of time before the soldiers discovered his band.

Worse perhaps than facing the soldiers in open battle was the growing scarcity of game. No longer did the buffalo herds wander this far south; the white buffalo hunters had killed all that migrated into Texas except for the herds that grazed the high plains. The heat of a long dry summer and equally dry winter drove the deer and antelope far from the three branches of the Concho River. The meat that filled the bellies of Quanah's band was mule taken in raids on the white men's farms. After a full *taum* of raiding, even the mules grew less in number.

Cona Cawb-vey's now ancient words pushed into Quanah's thoughts—*They always come back—they always come back.* A year of endless raids had not driven the whites back, the warrior realized, but only increased the patrols they sent out to track

down the Nermernuh. That the soldiers rarely found those they
hunted did not diminish the *Tejanos'* tenacity. When others
would have fled, abandoning their farms and towns, the whites
remained dug in like prairie dogs. Worse, more came from the
eastern lands to plow the earth and plant their crops.

In the end, their labors will be like dust in the wind, Quanah
thought. When the din of the last battle died, the Nermernuh
would once more ride freely over all the lands they claimed as
theirs. It could end no other way; he had pledged that.

Five warriors urged their mounts up the hogback and took a
position beside the young war chief they followed. Another five
came, and then ten. Soon a full seventy-five braves armed with
lances and bows and rifles formed a line along the sloping crest
of the long hill. No man spoke, but all stared to the north,
watching the cloud of dust grow closer and closer.

Their wait was not long. As the sun climbed its way to the ze-
nith, Eckitoacup and a full hundred braves rounded the mesa
and drew to a halt when they entered the two-mile draw that
stretched toward the hogback.

Quanah's heart pounded. This was the moment; either
Eckitoacup opened his eyes and saw, or he closed himself to all
but his need for revenge. Motionless, Quanah stared down on
the band of warriors who appeared to be no more than like ants
in the distance. If an attack came, it would be in a single charge,
all hundred warriors riding to meet the seventy-five who awaited
them.

No charge came. Quanah allowed an overly held breath to escape his lips. His peyote vision held. Eckitoacup had not expected to find so many warriors waiting for him. To lead his
hundred warriors into battle would result in more deaths than
he wanted to bear on his shoulders. Now was the time to offer
him another path that would assure his honor remained un-
blemished in the eyes of all who rode with him.

Quanah turned to the brave to his right. "Ride down and tell
Eckitoacup I have no desire to cross my lance with his unless
that is his wish. If he is willing to palaver, I too am willing to
talk."

The brave nodded, then reined his pony down the hill.

Quanah watched as did the others who rode with him. None
of Eckitoacup's warriors rode out to challenge the approaching
rider. Instead the brave reached the war band and halted without

incident. Try as he did, Quanah could not make out what happened then; he could only hope.

A full hour passed before a single rider separated from the distant band. Halfway across the draw, Quanah recognized the brave. He allowed himself a smile. Eckitoacup still did not charge.

"He is willing to speak," the brave said when he returned to Quanah's side. "He will send four braves to the middle of the draw. They will meet with four of our braves to decide what should be done."

Glancing down the line of warriors at his side, he called out four names and watched the men ride toward the four who moved to the center of the draw. "Now we wait."

The sun sat near the western horizon before the eight who counciled summoned Quanah and Eckitoacup to join them. When they did, it was Yellow Bear, Weckeah's father, who spoke:

"For Nermernuh to shed the blood of Nermernuh is the way of fools when our enemies are so close. Yet there are wrongs that must be made right. First is the matter of a daughter taken from my lodge. Twenty horses had been set as the gift to be given to her father for her hand."

"I shall give twenty-five," Quanah answered, his chest swelling in pride.

Yellow Bear nodded and looked at Eckitoacup. "This brave, too, has been wronged. It has been decided that he should receive nineteen ponies to lay aside his grievance. Those ponies he shall hand pick from Quanah's finest mounts."

Quanah's gaze moved to the other warrior. "Pick your nineteen. I know of ranches mere miles away with horses just as fine to replace those you take."

If Eckitoacup even noticed Quanah's boast, his facial expression revealed nothing. "Take me to your ponies. I will make my pick and begin home this night."

Quanah remounted and led the brave toward the waiting herd. The day had gone well. To be certain, Quanah would be poor once again when Yellow Bear and Eckitoacup took their payment, but it didn't matter. Weckeah was truly his wife, and he could once more lead his band northward away from the Texas soldiers.

A good day, Quanah's heart sang as he turned to the west, the rays of a setting sun filling the sky—

CHAPTER
TWELVE

—*Sunrise!* The purpled grays on the eastern horizon that softened the blackness of night surprised Quanah. Time passed so quickly. It seemed like mere moments since he and Naube had shared their passion beneath the buffalo roles.

He glanced back at the four women within the tipi before ducking outside. Weckeah, his first wife, with their daughter snuggled safely in her arms. His three other wives now lay beside each other on the opposite side of a now-cold campfire. Rather than uplifted in a smile, Quanah's lips drew back in a tight line. No brave could complain of the pleasures four wives afforded. Yet, it was the manner in which his wives had come to his tipi that troubled him.

His gaze climbed to the predawn sky to search for the first twinges of pinks and golds that signaled the sun's imminent arrival. Only a thin line of gray hung above the earth.

Gray, the word tumbled in his mind. The coming dawn colored itself like the mood that had sat within his breast since he had returned to the village yesterday.

His eyes shifted from side to side. Conical silhouettes, black atop the black of night, rose about him. A full hundred tipis, he considered. The number of the band normally swelled his chest with pride. Those who were here chose to be so because of him. This morning that pride eluded him.

In the distance he heard the soft lowing of cattle mingled with the snort of horses. Again a sense of pride escaped him. For a full week he and his warriors had raided the *Tejanos*. Horses and mules were the bounty taken with ease. The cattle, too, came from the ranchers and farmers—trade goods on the hoof to be used to purchase rifles and bullets from the Comancheros who would come from New Mexico.

By all measures of importance to the Nermernuh, the week-long raid was the sturdy thread from which songs were woven. Yet, even such treasures could not shake the grayness that hung about the warrior's heart.

He studied the tipis again while he relieved himself on the ground. A village of one hundred lodges—beside the *Tejano* towns he had seen, the tipis seemed so few. With a soldiers' fort built to protect it, the town of San Angelo now spread along the banks of the three branches of the Concho River, like the open sore blowflies dig into the back of a horse.

Far worse were the farmers with their earth-rending plows and the ranchers with their ever-growing herds of cattle. Where Quanah and his braves once hid from Eckitoacup three years ago, white men now built their dwellings of sod and stone. Vast prairies meant for grazing buffalo and antelope now provided grass to swell the bellies of long-horned steers.

Time after time, year after year, Quanah's band and those of other Nermernuh constantly raided the men who dared to transgress upon the lands of the People. No matter how many scalps were taken, how many bodies were left rotting in the sun, the whites remained, forever pushing outward, spreading like locusts during a drought.

The blue-coated, black-skinned soldiers grew bolder, too. Quanah drew a heavy breath and slowly released it as he walked quietly through the sleeping village. As the farmers and ranchers spread across the lands, the soldiers pushed deeper and deeper into the domain of the People.

To be certain, the warrior thought, he and his braves still eluded their pursuers, but with each successive raid it took greater skills to shake those uniformed hounds that snapped at their heels. A full day was needed to lose the soldiers before returning to this camp on the Brazos. Never had it taken so long, nor required so many false trails to assure they traveled far from the raiding party's true destination.

Beneath the low branches of a mesquite tree near the end of the village, Quanah lowered himself to the ground with legs crossed beneath him. The week-long raid had not come without a price. Five of the fifty warriors who had ridden with him had not returned. The wives of two of those dead braves now slept in Quanah's tipi. In time they would find other husbands to care for them, but for now he claimed them as wives to assure they had food to fill their stomachs and blankets to keep the chill of the night from them while they slept.

Five warriors killed. The number bent Quanah's shoulders like the weight of a great limestone boulder. He tried to convince himself it was their lack of strong medicine that cost them their lives. He recognized the lie. The whites grew stronger with each passing day. The Nermernuh—

His thoughts stumbled. How the People had changed in a few short years. Once only the Kiowa claimed friendship with the powerful Nermernuh. This day the Cheyenne, the Pawnee, the Sioux—all the races that rode the plains forgot the differences that once set them warring against each other. Openly the tribes talked and aided each other in the fight against the ever-encroaching sea of whites.

Had his uncle Cona Cawb-vey been cursed with the gift of long sight? Did the brave have the power to see far into the future? Were these the times he had tried to warn Quanah about so many years ago?

The grayness tightened like a band of steel around Quanah's heart. Images of his uncle and father deluged his mind. How much easier it was to keep his feet on the path of the People when they were at his side, showing the way. How much they had left untaught, unspoken.

To the east, gentle fingers of pink suffused into the gray and black. Even the first color of a new day did not loosen the hold the gray had within the warrior's chest.

He turned from the coming dawn and stared to the south. Lost, too, were his mother and sister. Where were they at this moment? Did they still pray to the dawn for the day he would deliver them from the white men? Did they hold dear to the hope that soon they would sit together with their lost sons and brothers?

Closing his eyes, Quanah leaned back to let the mesquite's trunk share the weight of his burdens. That one day he would be reunited with his mother and sister remained a certainty in his mind. How he would find them amid the lands of the *Tejanos*, he did not know. But he would.

Or did he merely deceive himself? Over the years he had lost count of the times he had asked of this mother and sister among those who traveled freely among the *Tejanos*. Comancheros, white traders, and warriors who rode deep into the white land—none could provide even the slightest hint of his mother's and sister's fate.

Nor, Quanah admitted, would he be able to recognize his sister were she standing before him at this very moment. She had been a babe in arms when the Texas Rangers stole her away. Now—he could only imagine how she grew toward womanhood.

He would never mistake another for his mother. Her image was burned into his mind. Even though her hair might flow white with the passing years, he would know her. And she would know him. As surely as he knew the seasons changed with the passing of a *taum*, he knew this to be the truth.

Quanah's eyes flew open. His head jerked from side to side, searching but finding nothing. He cocked his head to the left and then the right, listening for any sound that did not belong to the rosy glow of morning. Still there was nothing.

His heart a-pound in his chest, he sank back to the tree trunk, uncertain what had startled him. Perhaps he had drifted into half sleep and caught himself before he fell fully into the arms of unconsciousness. Perhaps—

He sat up abruptly again, then leaned back against the mesquite.

No, he had not imagined sensing approaching danger. He felt it in the wood. The pound of hooves ran through the earth and vibrated within the tree.

Jumping to his feet he ran into the village. "Awake! Riders come! Awake!"

Here and there he saw braves push from their tipis in answer to the warning as he reached his own lodge. Weckeah's open eyes met his gaze when his head poked inside. "Wake the others and break camp. Move to the west as quickly as you can."

His first wife didn't question, but threw aside her buffalo robes and rose with child tucked beneath one arm.

When Quanah returned to the center of the village, rifle clutched in hand, the braves stood waiting, their own weapons ready.

"The soldiers have found us," he said, knowing no other enemy would threaten the village here by the banks of the Brazos River. He swept an arm over half the braves. "Stay with the women and children. See that they remain safe."

To the rest gathered he ordered, "Mount your ponies. We will stand against the soldiers until our families have fled."

Less than a quarter of an hour passed before Quanah and his defenders sat astride their mounts to await the approaching soldiers, but that was enough time to bring up the full face of the sun and reveal a column of dust that rose to the north.

Quanah spat to the ground and signaled a brave to his right. "It's not the *Tejanos*, but soldiers from the reservations. Warn the others to hurry west along the river."

The brave wheeled his mount about and rode back toward the collapsing tipis.

For a moment Quanah watched the efficiency with which the women worked. The majority of the tipis were down, and the women lashed lodge poles together and tied them to the backs of ponies. As quickly as they worked, it was not fast enough.

"The soldiers see us!" a cry came from the warrior's left.

Quanah's head jerked back to the north. A curse escaped his lips like the hiss of an angry snake. He recognized the dapple-gray mount that stood at the head of the column of blue-coated soldiers. It was the one called Mackenzie. The Cheyenne told of his ability. While others might give up and fall from a trail, this Mackenzie was like a snapping turtle, refusing to release its prey once its traplike jaws closed.

Quanah also recognized the futility of facing the troop of over two hundred soldiers in an open fight. The blue coats' carbines would cut through the fifty braves who stood with him in a matter of minutes. Once they had fallen, the soldiers would swoop down on the fleeing women and children.

That Mackenzie still led his soldiers in long columns said the army officer had not expected to find the village, but had stumbled upon it by accident. If Quanah intended to strike, he had to do so before Mackenzie formed his men into their battle lines.

Glancing over a shoulder, the warrior saw the women and children hurrying westward with the remaining braves following

at their heels to protect their flank. Only the herd of grazing ponies and cattle remained to mark where the village had stood but
moments ago. No Nermernuh willingly left such wealth behind.
But wealth meant nothing to the dead. Better to fill the lungs
with life-giving breath than to possess all the horses in the world.

Quanah's eyes snapped to the soldiers who now scurried to
each side of Mackenzie in answer to his barked orders. Immediately the warrior's head jerked back to the horses and cattle.

His band had already lost this vast wealth. Perhaps there was
still a way he could use it to snatch his people from the closing
maw of death.

"The herd!" Quanah called out. "Drive the herd into the soldiers! Quickly! Before the blue coats charge."

Fifty warriors answered the cry. Wrenching the heads of their
ponies around, they circled behind the grazing herd. A chorus of
yipping cries and gunshots awoke the animals. In the single beat
of his heart, Quanah watched the horses and cattle bolt away
from the unexpected din. Straight toward the soldiers the herd
raced, stampeding out of control.

Lifting his right arm high with rifle in hand, Quanah let it
fall. Another coyote-imitating chorus of war cries rent the morning as fifty warriors responded to the signal and charged.

Through the cloud of dust stirred by pounding hooves,
Quanah saw Mackenzie and his soldiers scatter before the stampeding herd. Not all the blue coats were fast enough. Their
screams of terror rose and died abruptly as they fell beneath the
onslaught of horse and steer.

Sighting on a mounted officer, Quanah squeezed his rifle's
trigger. He did not wait to see if the bullet found its mark, but
swung the weapon to a black-skinned foot soldier and fired.

Around him the bark of his warriors' rifles resounded and
were answered by the soldiers' carbines. Like angry wasps, lead
buzzed through the air. Yet, Quanah saw not one warrior fall
from his mount.

If Mackenzie expected the Nermernuh band to swing about
for another attack once they had broken through the soldiers'
line, that tactic was the furthest thing from Quanah's mind.
When the herd lost the momentum of its original flight, the warrior urged his band through the animals and rode northward.

A glance over a shoulder brought a grim smile of approval to
Quanah's lips. Mackenzie reacted as he hoped. Rather than

following the river west after the women and children, he rallied his troops and rode on the heels of the fleeing warriors.

Quanah lightly tugged on the rein to slow his pony. He did not want to outdistance the soldiers too quickly. For an hour he would provide an easy chase to assure the women were far to the west. Then he would order his warriors to split, each going his own way, leaving Mackenzie with far too many trails to follow.

Moonlight lit the faces of the warriors. Silently, Quanah counted their number while Yellow Bear spoke:

"My daughter's husband led us wisely this day. With the ability of the coyote he tricked the blue-coated soldiers. His medicine remains powerful."

Fifty! Quanah completed his mental tally. All fifty warriors survived the day. It was far more than he had hoped. Fortune had ridden with his band this day.

"What now, Quanah?" Yellow Bear asked. "Do we wait here beside the river for the soldiers to come, and then attack them? Or do we ride west to rejoin our families?"

For an instant Quanah recalled the Yellow Bear he had once known, war chief who would have gladly taken the scalp of a young brave who had stolen his daughter. In the years since Quanah had paid him twenty-five horses for Weckeah's hand, Yellow Bear had become the closest of friends. Even the disgruntled Eckitoacup numbered himself among Quanah's supporters, although Eckitoacup never rode beside the warrior.

Quanah's gaze moved from the older war chief toward the east, where Mackenzie and his command had camped for the night. A mere two miles of the Brazos River's crooked path separated Nermernuh from the soldiers.

"We can not risk riding west to rejoin our families." Quanah shook his head. "The braves who accompany them will see to their safety."

"Then we wait and attack the soldiers when they come in the morning?" Yellow Bear asked.

The question brought another shake of Quanah's head. "The blue-coated Mackenzie would expect such an attack. He long fought against the Cheyenne in the north. Even though we hid ourselves well, he would be prepared for us."

His frown lit by a moon three days shy of full, Yellow Bear

stared at his son-in-law for a long, silent moment, then acquiesced with a nod.

Quanah noted the disappointment in the faces of his companions. They, like him, wanted revenge on the soldiers who had so boldly ridden upon their camp. Quanah sensed a power he had never felt before. At this moment, he realized that these men would follow him no matter what he suggested. Rather than elation, that knowledge brought an unexpected weight. He gave a name to that burden—responsibility. Not only was his own life in his hands, but those of the warriors who chose to follow his path. Had his father felt the weight?

Drawing a deep breath and slowly exhaling it, Quanah once again looked into the faces that stared at him. "Yellow Bear has said I was gifted with the wisdom of the coyote this day, but I do not feel this wisdom in my heart or head. A wise man would council to ride fast and far from this place—to flee before the greater numbers of Mackenzie's soldiers."

Quanah paused to allow his words to sink in. In truth, the wise course would be travel northward, leaving an easy trail for Mackenzie to follow for a day, then once more vanishing into the prairie.

"But I am not wise like the coyote. This night I feel like the wolf is my brother," Quanah continued. "Like the wolf, I hunger."

No face turned from the young warrior.

"Unlike the wolf, I am not rich. The soldiers robbed me of all my riches this day." That the ponies and cattle he spoke of had been stolen from farmers and ranchers to the south never entered Quanah's mind. Raiding and taking from those weaker than oneself was the way of the Nermernuh. It was not a matter of right or wrong, it simply was. "I feel less than a man this night."

He saw the heads of his companions nod in agreement. Though no man spoke, he knew their hearts held the same weight as his.

"I will not be a man again until I reclaim what is mine. So this night, when the soldiers sleep, never expecting me to ride upon them, I shall sweep out of the night and take what rightfully belongs to me."

Yellow Bear's smile slowly slid across his face. "And perhaps increase that wealth with a few of the soldiers' horses?"

"If they are foolish enough to leave them where I can take them," Quanah replied with a firm tilt of his head. "Is that not the way of the People?"

"It is the way of the Nermernuh!" an unseen warrior answered. "It has always been our way."

"Then we ride east to take back what is ours," Quanah concluded.

"We ride," Yellow Bear confirmed.

Without further discussion, fifty warriors mounted their ponies and quietly rode eastward. A quarter of a mile from the soldiers' camp, Quanah signaled a halt. With his hands, he ordered all but five of the fifty to circle northward and wait. As he watched his companions depart, he motioned for the remaining five to dismount.

Leading their ponies behind them, the six warriors moved through the night. Two arrows eliminated the guards posted on the outer fringe of the herd Mackenzie had ordered gathered in a wide clearing near the river's banks. With ease Quanah and his companions slipped among the horses and cattle. Like shadows they moved toward three guards who stood as sentinels over a remuda of army horses and mules.

An unexpected prize caught Quanah's eye. The dapple gray he had seen Mackenzie ride that morning stood no more than ten strides from his position.

Another quick signal sent three more arrows whistling through the night and the three guards fell to the ground.

Quanah darted forward with hunting knife in hand. One slash and he freed the gray from the rope that bound the remuda. Another snake of the warrior's arm severed the rope itself loosing horse and mule.

In the next instant Quanah swung onto the back of his pony. The five braves who followed him did likewise, waited for his signal, then let blood-curdling cries rip from their chests and throats.

As surely as the herd had stampeded that morning, the animals responded in kind that night. Snatching the gray's halter in his right hand, Quanah urged his mount after the fleeing horses and cattle. He and the five warriors were far beyond rifle range when they heard the first shot ring out behind them.

A mile to the north, Yellow Bear and the remaining braves

greeted them, falling in beside the reclaimed herd and driving it northward.

Quanah rode silently now, laying plans for their escape. Until daybreak, they would continue together. Once the sun rose, half his braves would drive the herd westward toward the Caprock where they would rejoin the rest of the band. The others would ride northward for another day to lay a false trail for Mackenzie and his men—that was, if the soldiers had enough mounts left to follow.

He glanced at the dapple-gray stallion he led and smiled. It had been a good night. Mackenzie would long remember this night and think twice before pushing so deep into Nermernuh lands again.

As it was born, Quanah's smile faded. Cona Cawb-vey's warning echoed in his mind:

. . . *They will come back. They always come back.*

CHAPTER THIRTEEN

Quanah accepted the rabbit leg Pecos passed to him. He tore away a bite with his teeth and pulled the blanket close about his shoulders. The hunting party had ridden far from Palo Duro Canyon to find the ten antelope tied to the backs of their ponies. Rather than travel on a moonless night, the party decided a campfire and three jackrabbits for their evening meal would be the safest path to follow. When dawn broke, they would return to their families with the bounty of fresh meat they had found.

". . . he is a man of great medicine, this Eeshatai," a brave called Mahapea because of the white man's shoes he wore said, while he warmed his hands over the small fire. "He says that all braves are of the same blood. He says all the races should put aside their wars against each other and unite against the white man."

"Eeshatai? What kind of name is that?" Pecos tore himself a leg from one of the roasted rabbits and gave the rest of the meat to the others.

"It is Cheyenne." Mahapea accepted the portion of rabbit passed to him. "His name means Coyote Droppings. He speaks of the Sun Dance and how all the tribes should be united in its medicine."

Quanah caught himself before he snorted aloud. Although he openly palavered with the likes of Cheyennes, he could never consider them equals to the Nermernuh. They were not the true People.

"Eeshatai says all the tribes must come together as one. Only then may the white man be defeated and driven from our lands. The tribes must become an army, like the army of blue coats," Mahapea went on.

An army of all the plains people. Something about the sound of it struck a chord within Quanah. On first hearing, it sounded ridiculous that Cheyenne, Arapaho, Kiowa, and Nermernuh could join together and fight as one against the whites. Yet, if it were possible, if the countless years of warring against each other could be laid aside, it would mean an army no white could stand against.

"I think you have spent too long on the whites' reservation," Pecos commented. "No man could ever unite Arapaho with Kiowa."

Mahapea frowned. Like many of the People he often weathered the long winters on the reservation, filling his belly with the white man's beef. As the buffalo hunters killed off the vast herds, more and more of the Nermernuh became "tame Indians" each winter. When spring came, they slipped away from the reservation to rejoin the free bands.

"Eeshatai is no white man," Mahapea finally answered. "I hear wisdom in his words."

"I hear smoke dreams." Pecos shook his head. "And what is this Sun Dance? Cheyenne medicine?"

Quanah paid no attention to Mahapea's answer. He needed no Cheyenne's magic; his medicine had always been strong. It was the idea of an army bred of all the nations that held his mind—an army to stand against the whites' blue coats. He admitted to himself that this Eeshatai was a dreamer or a madman, or both. Yet, the shaman's dream was woven with a vast thread. No Kwerhar-rehnuh had ever considered the possibility. If this Eeshatai's dream found the breath of life—

"The night is not for talk," the brave Sawne Wea interrupted when Mahapea paused. "My belly no longer rumbles, and the time has come for sleep."

A smile lifted the corners of Quanah's mouth while Grass Rope stretched out by the fire and pulled a blanket over his shoulders. For an instant Quanah's mind traveled back to the day when only Sawne Wea followed him on his first raid against the gray-coated *Tejano* soldiers. Though years had passed since that day, it seemed a mere blink of an eye in the warrior's mind.

Quanah's gaze moved over the twelve braves in the hunting party while they followed Sawne Wea's lead and prepared for sleep. Except for his brother Pecos, Grass Rope had supported him and ridden with him longer than any other. Although Sawne Wea was never sought for council, he was always at Quanah's side whether it be for a raid or a hunting party. Few could be trusted as Sawne Wea or were as loyal.

Quanah's smile grew while he lay on the ground and covered himself with a buffalo robe. Remembering the nervousness and uncertainty that had plagued Grass Rope when they rode as a raiding party of two against the confederate soldiers, he was grateful for the strong friendship time had woven.

Closing his eyes, Quanah pushed thought from his mind. The dawn would come early, and their families waited back in the village with empty cooking pots. The ten—

Metal clinked against metal.

Quanah bolted upright. His right hand shot out and snatched his rifle from the ground. His eyes narrowed in attempt to cut through the veil of darkness beyond the glow of the campfire. He saw nothing. Nor did he hear—

"Take 'em, boys!" The voice of a white man sounded out of nowhere.

In the next instant the thunder of pounding hooves rent the night asunder. Riders—soldiers in blue coats—charged out of the darkness straight down on the hunting party.

Across the campfire from him, Quanah saw Grass Rope jerk up. In the next instant a flower of orange and yellow blossomed. A dark hole appeared in the middle of the brave's forehead as his body was thrown back to the ground.

Quanah was not certain whether he heard the report of the rifle that left his friend's body twitching in death throes. He was sure of only one thing—to remain where he sat meant certain death. A black-skinned buffalo soldier astride a bay mount rode toward him.

Rolling to the side, the warrior avoided the hooves meant to crush the life from his body. In the next instant, Quanah leaped to his feet. Before he could hike rifle to shoulder, another soldier with silver-bladed saber held high charged down on him.

Quanah threw himself to the ground again and rolled to escape the descending longknife that would have severed his head from his body. When he regained his feet, the soldiers were gone—lost in the night's blackness. Gone, too, were the hunting party's ponies, scattered by the charge.

The sound of snorting horses, the creaking of leather, and the grunts of men reining their mounts about for another attack came from the darkness.

"Away from the light!" Quanah shouted. "Get away from the fire's light. Hide yourselves!"

Another rifle barked. The warrior followed his own command and threw himself from the circle of light cast by the campfire. Behind him, he heard the death cries of his companions when the soldiers charged again and opened up with a full volley.

Quanah cautiously lifted from the grass, scanned the night on all sides, and saw nothing. A glance at the stars overhead revealed a full hour had passed since the soldiers had given up their search for the hunting party.

His mouth drawn in a tight line, the warrior turned and began the walk back to the glowing embers that marked where he and the others had camped for the night. In spite of the time that had passed since the surprise attack, his mind still held no answers. Where had the blue coats come from? How had they ridden onto the high plains without being seen?

"Quanah?" Pecos's voice called in a forced whisper to the right.

The warrior saw his brother kneeling in the grass. "Are you injured?"

"I am well." Pecos walked to his brother's side. "But I saw Rabbit Running and Walks Alone fall."

"Grass Rope also fell."

A rustle of dry grass to the left and right accompanied four other braves when they pushed from the ground.

Quanah's heart pounded; cold fear ran like ice in his veins. One by one he called out the names of the missing. No voice answered his call.

He found the reason for the silence beside the cherry-red embers of the campfire. Six braves lay dead, cut down by the soldiers' bullets or trampled under the hooves of the charging horses.

"Is no place safe for the Kwerhar-rehnuh in this world?" a brave whispered behind Quanah.

The same question echoed in the warrior's mind. Never had the soldiers been so bold as to ride into the very heart of Nermernuh lands. Nor did Quanah believe that the blue coats who had found them were all of the force that rode this night.

"Pecos, you and the others find the ponies and return to the village and warn them. We were found by a scouting party. The main body of soldiers is nearby."

"And you?"

Quanah looked at his brother. "I will take Mahapea with me. I go to speak with this Cheyenne Eeshatai. The time has come to wipe the white man from the face of this earth."

"You go on foot?"

"If need be," Quanah answered as he motioned to Mahapea and walked into the night. "But if there are soldiers nearby, they will have horses enough for me."

Silently the warrior vowed at least six of the blue coats would not live to see the sun rise. The blade of the hunting knife he carried would extract retribution for his six fallen companions.

And when he found Eeshatai, he would help breathe life into the medicine man's dream. The nations of the plains would unite into a single army of warriors greater than any ever seen by the whites!

CHAPTER
FOURTEEN

Fire coursed through Quanah's veins. Like searing lightning that can set the prairie grasses ablaze, it boiled within his body, setting his heart and head pounding at a runaway speed. Never had the young war chief experienced such devouring flames, not even in the heat of passion between man and woman.

Before this day ends, the fire will leap from my hands and burn the white man from these lands! Like a brave drunk on whiskey, the power of the moment consumed him, drove him like a pony beneath the bite of a quirt.

With Quanah rode seven hundred warriors adorned in feathers and war paints. The same blazing fire ran molten within their veins. The same fire roiled higher and higher ready to leap forth and strike the faces of their enemies.

Nermernuh, Kiowa, Cheyenne, and Arapaho sat astride their mounts. Today they were one—a single army united by the Sun Dance. Today the white man would face their might, and the whites would die. As certain of that as was Quanah, so were the seven hundred who rode with him.

And they do ride with me, my father, Peta Nocona! Quanah called out within his skull. The warrior's chest swelled barrel-wide with pride. *I am named war chief this day! Lone Wolf and Woman's Heart of the Kiowa—Stone Calf and White Shield of the Cheyenne—they called me to lead—named me war chief of all the war chiefs! I have remained faithful to the ways of the People as you wished, my father. It has brought me to this day when our enemies shall fall before me like blades of grass caught in the inferno of a wildfire!*

Quanah's gaze shifted to Eeshatai. The shaman sat above the flat of the plains on a humpbacked hill. Naked except for the yellow paint that covered every inch of his body, he would watch the power of his medicine spread across the prairie from the back of his pony.

And Quanah would be the spearhead of that medicine. It was the young warrior who had brought Eeshatai among the Kwerhar-rehnuh. Only the Kwerhar-rehnuh of the People, among all the nations of the plains, remained unbroken and strong against the whites with their blue-coated soldiers.

That the Sun Dance was alien to the People was of no consequence, Eeshatai told the bands of Kwerhar-rehnuh. That the *taime* dolls and the sacred bundles of the ritual were totally unknown among the People did not matter. That the People placed their faith in the Sun Dance's medicine and shared in the ritual was all that mattered, Eeshatai explained. After all, his magicks made him immune to bullets.

The few who questioned the Sun Dance and its inability to protect Cheyenne, Sioux, and Kiowa against the whites, found their protests met by ears of stone. Did not Eeshatai ascend into the clouds to speak with a great spirit? Did he not predict the coming of the comet and the drought that followed? And there were the rumors of his miracles—how he belched forth a wagon-load of cartridges for his people's rifles, and how his hands had brought the dead back to life.

It was Eeshatai's words that summoned all but a few of the Nermernuh bands together in one camp. And it was his teachings that ignited the Sun Dance that had continued four days and nights—and finally brought seven hundred warriors to face the most hated of all the whites—the buffalo hunters!

Quanah's head turned from Eeshatai to the old fort the whites once called Bent that stood before him. Abandoned by the soldiers years ago, the buildings, now called Adobe Walls, were used by the buffalo hunters who worked to kill every one of the great bisons that wandered the plains. Today the old fort and the evil that dwelled within would die—the first blaze of a fire that would devour all white men before its hunger was finally quenched.

Gaze shifting back to Eeshatai, Quanah watched the Cheyenne medicine man lift a yellow-painted arm. He pointed toward the old sod fort.

A yipping cry of the coyote burst from deep in Quanah's chest and rose from his lips to greet the morning. A chorused answer of similar war cries rose from the Kwerhar-rehnuh warriors who followed their young war chief this day.

Slamming his heels into the flanks of his pony, Quanah signaled the charge. The Kwerhar-rehnuh responded and drove their mounts toward the decaying adobe buildings. Another war cry ripped from Quanah's lips. Today the dream lived, it breathed life—an army of the plains nations struck back at those who would rob them of all that was theirs.

Before the screaming horde of painted warriors covered half the distance to the old fort, thunder split the morning—the roar of firing rifles.

A brave called Heard the Owl yelped as a bullet slammed into his chest and sent him careening over the rump of his sorrel pony. Three warriors to Quanah's left fell, claimed by the hunters' bullets or lost as the hunters shot their ponies out from beneath them.

How? For the first time since he had met Eeshatai, doubt shadowed the war chief's mind. The old fort still lay beyond the range of his warriors' rifles and carbines, yet the whites' guns struck with deadly accuracy. *How can this be?*

Another volley opened from the adobe-walled fort, and more warriors fell beneath the barrage.

Buffalo rifles! Quanah recognized the weapons his army faced. The hunters used the same rifles on the attackers that they used to kill the buffalo at such great distances.

It would not matter. Quanah bolstered himself against the doubt that gnawed within his chest. Not even the whites' big rifles would matter this day.

A hundred strides from the fort, Quanah saw the bloody, butchered carcasses of bison strewn outside the cedar-post corrals that surrounded most of the buildings. For this atrocity and all the horrors they had brought to the plains, the hunters would die.

Fifty yards from the adobe walls, the Kwerhar-rehnuh war chief discerned the windows of the old fort and the barrels of the rifles that poked out and belched blue fire. His eyes narrowed, and doubt once more ate deep with his breast. He counted no more than twenty rifles! Were only twenty men within?

A mere two strides from the cedar fence another volley blasted from those windows. Instantly Quanah went flying over the head of the black mustang he rode. The horse fell beneath a bullet that tore into its broad chest. That the warrior's momentum carried him over the ground in a head-over-heels tumble saved him from the angry hornets of hot lead that slammed into the ground around him.

His disjointed escape came to an abrupt end when he careened into one of the butchered carcasses. Three of the hunters' shots pounded into the rotting meat that stood between him and certain death.

The charging warriors surrounded him as they urged their mounts toward the fort. Pushing to his knees, he saw two Cheyenne braves throw themselves from their ponies in an attempt to breach the fort's windows. He then saw them die—buffalo rifles exploding death into their howling faces.

A brand of white hot fire sliced into the side of Quanah's head. An unseen hand spun him about and hurled him to the ground.

He groaned, not in death, but in pain. His fingers lifted to his left temple and came away red with blood. One of the hunters' shots had grazed his head! He who had never been wounded in countless raids had barely avoided having his head blown away by one of the buffalo rifles. For the first time in his life Quanah Parker felt a fear of death. While the hunters loosed another volley, he scrambled back behind the bloody carcass and crouched there.

Where was Eeshatai's medicine? Quanah's head spun, sending his thoughts flying in a hundred directions at once. Where were the magicks of the Sun Dance that were supposed to protect all who rode against the whites on this day?

And his own medicine? Had it abandoned him because he had placed faith in a medicine that was not of the Nermernuh?

Silence!

Quanah's head snapped from one side then to the other. Except for the pounding within his bleeding head, he heard nothing—no war cries, no bark of rifles.

Risking a glance over the hide-stripped haunch of the bison, he saw why. The charge of warriors had split around the fort. Instead of a direct attack on the adobe structures, the horde of howling riders had ridden past. Although they had emptied their rifles at those within, the shots had slammed into the fort's mud walls.

Before Quanah could consider how to escape from beneath the very nose of his enemy, another chorus of war cries came from the north. Eeshatai sent a second wave of warriors against the old fort.

Quanah watched in horror as the buffalo hunters' rifles found their marks time and time again. Riders and horses fell beneath the hail of lead the twenty rifles continually fired into the attackers.

Among those leading the charge, the young war chief recognized Mo-wi, his father's old friend. That moment of recognition was the last instant of Mo-wi's life. A buffalo rifle thundered to send death directly into the aging warrior's heart. He spilled from his pony with an expression of shocked surprise on his face.

Mo-wi's mount offered Quanah an avenue of escape. As the riderless horse raced by, the war chief entangled both his hands in its mane and swung atop the animal's back. Following the second wave of warriors as they split around the old fort, Quanah rode to safety. When he judged himself beyond the range of the powerful rifles, he reined toward the hill on which Eeshatai still sat.

The shaman was not alone when he signaled a third charge on the fort. Both Kiowa and Cheyenne war chiefs had reined their ponies beside the naked medicine man by the time Quanah reached the crest of the low hill.

"My medicines remain strong." Eeshatai stared below, watching the warriors in the third assault fall beneath the hunters' rifles. "Find the brave who killed the skunk this morning and you will find the cause of all these deaths. All know killing a skunk brings misfortune."

Stone Calf, who stood closest to the yellow-painted Eeshatai, struck out with his quirt, lashing it across the medicine man's right cheek. "We should have known the foolishness of placing ourselves in the hands of one untried in battle."

Untried in battle? Quanah's spinning head whirled anew like a maelstrom. Eeshatai had never faced battle?

"The only thing killing a skunk brings is a stink!" Stone Calf spat to the ground. "Call back our warriors before they all are killed. There is no medicine to be found in this madman."

As the brave the chief commanded reined his pony about to carry out the order, a shot rang out from the fort below. A thud like the sound of a fist striking a man's belly sounded. The side of the brave's head exploded in a shower of red and gray.

"Away!" Stone Calf cried out to those around him. "Call your warriors to you and ride far. The white hunters' rifles can find us at any distance."

In spite of the splitting pain within his head, Quanah managed to signal the Kwerhar-rehnuh below to gather beside him. When they came, he turned his back on Eeshatai and rode northward to where the bands had camped.

The fire he had envisioned sweeping across the plains this day drowned in a rain of Nermernuh blood. The dream he had helped breathe life into had been transformed into a nightmare.

CHAPTER
FIFTEEN

... They will be back. They always come back ...

Quanah's left hand lifted, and he traced the scar ridge hidden by the hairline on his left temple. He fingered the remainder of his brush with death at Adobe Walls while studying the early morning stars of the newly arrived autumn.

Surely his uncle Cona Cawb-vey *did* have the long sight. How else would he have known that the white men and the blue-coated soldiers would never stop coming no matter what the Kwerhar-rehnuh did?

Quanah shook his head. He had yet to see the coming and going of thirty *taum*, but he felt as ancient as the oldest gray-haired brave camped within the secure walls of Palo Duro Canyon. What had once been an excellent location for the bands to gather for the winter now had become the last refuge of the People. The soldiers and *Tejano* Rangers freely patrolled all the lands the Nermernuh claimed. Here was the final stronghold, the one place the whites had not penetrated.

Quanah took a measure of comfort in that fact. Something in a world of constant turmoil should remain unchanged.

His gaze lowered and traced along the western rim of the canyon barely discernible in the early morning darkness. He had been uncertain of Palo Duro and ridden ahead of his band to ascertain the canyon remained secure. Today he would ride back to the village and lead the band to their winter camp.

Winter, the thought of the coming season slowly turned in the war chief's mind. In spite of the howling winds and ice and snow, he welcomed winter's return. The blue-coated soldiers were less likely to press deeply into Kwerhar-rehnuh lands when snows covered the ground. With the soldier hounds off his heels, there would be time to ponder the future. He needed that opportunity. When spring once more coaxed the bright green shoots of grass from the ground, he had to be ready for a new attack on the whites—one that would drive them back to their cities in the south or the forests in the east.

Peta Nocona had done that when the soldiers in blue and gray had fought each other. Quanah's mind wandered back over a decade when his father was the greatest of all the warriors among the People. With tobacco and peyote, he would seek visions throughout the winter. He would ask his father's spirit to guide him, to reveal the path that would defeat the whites once and for all.

For an instant the disastrous defeat at Adobe Walls wiggled into his mind. He pushed it aside. His mistake during the spring had been to abandon the spirit of the shield and lance that had served him since Peta Nocona's death. The medicines of the Cheyenne, Kiowa, and Arapaho were not for the Nermernuh. He should have known that, but desperation blinded him like fear blinds a frightened rabbit. The winter would give him time to cleanse himself and—

"Blue coats!"

A single cry echoed through the canyon.

Temples a-pound, Quanah twisted, his gaze probing the darkness, as the warning cry abruptly died in a strangled gurgle.

"The soldiers come!"

The second alert came from the east where the bands grazed their herds of horses and cattle.

There! Quanah saw them, black silhouettes against the grays of the predawn twilight. They pushed to the canyon's rim and worked their way down a narrow path that led to Palo Duro's floor. That they hastened downward in single file hampered the soldiers, but it did not stop them.

"No!" Shock that Palo Duro Canyon had been violated pushed from Quanah's trembling lips. His head shifted from side to side in denial. Then, in a cry that held pain in its core, he screamed, "Noooooooo—"

—*No.* The seated brave's body quaked as though caught in the throes of a fever.

No!

He would not relive the horrors of that morning in Palo Duro. His ears would not contain the screams of the women and the children as they fled the onslaught of buffalo soldiers who scrambled down from the heights. He would not stand against the blue coats again to buy time for the People to claw their way up the face of the canyon walls and escape.

No!

Above all he would not gaze down from the canyon's rim and watch Mackenzie's troopers slaughter a thousand ponies beneath a relentless fusillade of carbines.

"No," the brave said aloud with a shake of his head in denial.

The action was a mistake. The peyote's poison he had held in his belly for so long refused to be contained. It twisted his gut into knots upon knots. He doubled over violently and vomited. Again and again, he emptied his stomach until only thin, yellow bile came as spittle from his lips.

Leaning back, tension easing into the muscles of his body, Quanah slowly drew in a deep breath and released it. Twice more he sucked down the cool air to help clear his head.

The peyote button had brought the vision he had traveled so far to see, but what was its meaning? All that had opened to him was his past. He had seen the days of his life walk before his eyes as though he lived them once again. Where was the road to tomorrow hidden in those vivid memories?

Quanah opened his eyes. The warm yellow hue of a newly dawned day bathed the rolling plains that stretched before the medicine mound on which he sat. He blinked, remembering the rising sun that poked its head above the horizon when the peyote awoke. Had he gazed into the vision for the going and coming of the sun, or had the progression of his life occurred in mere moments? He knew not. Visions, especially those brought by the sacred cactus of the Mescalero, distorted time when they swept a man into the mystical realms of the other world.

Gradually Quanah uncrossed his legs and stretched. No

muscles cramped in either legs or arms. The slight stiffness within his limbs would soon fade. That was good; he and his companions below had a long ride before they rejoined their families atop the Caprock.

The brave eased his feet beneath him and stood. His balance held, and his legs supported his weight without the slightest quiver. This too was good. Weakness would hamper a quick return to the high plains, and he had endangered the lives of his friends far too long as it was.

"Quanah!"

The young war chief's body went rail rigid at the sound. "Uncle?"

"Quanah, come to my side."

A sense of dread flowed like ice in a winter's stream within Quanah's veins. Still, he turned.

"Quanah, come to my side."

Cona Cawb-vey stood before him. The awakening morning sun rose behind the warrior's straight and proud body to bathe him in a radiance that seared Quanah's eyes. Was this a residual effect of the peyote, or had the long-dead brave come to haunt him?

"I am here, Uncle. I am here."

Even through the blinding glare of the sun, Quanah saw Cona Cawb-vey's dark eyes. So full of life they were, not glazed with the dullness of death. And those eyes stared directly at him, unmoving and unblinking as though their sight pierced to the very soul.

"How does one drive away the wind?" Cona Cawb-vey's arms lifted with palms open to the cloudless blue of the sky. "My father's father, and his father, and his father all made war of the white man. Still they come. Their number is like that of the locusts in times of hunger. And like the locusts, no matter how many the Kwerhar-rehnuh kill, they keep coming . . ."

Quanah recognized the words his uncle had spoken to a child on a night many long years ago.

". . . They will be back. They will always come back."

Before Quanah could release an overly held breath and ask all the questions that packed into his head, Cona Cawb-vey vanished.

. . . They will be back. They will always come back.

The words echoed within his mind as they had throughout

the peyote vision. The weight Quanah hoped would be lifted from his shoulders by visiting this sacred place only pressed down with increased burden. The way to which Cona Cawb-vey pointed was not the road he wanted to travel. It was not the Nermernuh way.

The cries of starving children touched his ears. The images of the bodies of old, gauntlike skeletons, paraded before him. Quanah clamped his eyes closed tightly and swallowed hard. He did not try to deny the truth of those horror-filled images; he had seen the toll in the lives of children and the old the winter had brought. That was the Nermernuh road.

"All roads come to an end." The bitterness of the whispered words that slid from his tongue did not lessen their harsh reality. The People had walked as far as their path would take them.

Quanah bent and gathered the buffalo robe, pipe, and tobacco pouch that lay at his feet. Tucking them under an arm, he walked down from the mound's crest and crossed the quarter mile to where Forty Buffalo and Speaks Softly waited by the ponies.

Neither pressed him to speak when Quanah mounted the dapple gray he had once stolen from under the nose of the blue-coated Colonel Mackenzie. But he could feel their tension and see the questions that puzzled their copper-hued faces.

"I have talked long with my uncle Cona Cawb-vey." Quanah eased the gray stallion's head to the west and tapped the animal's sides with his heels.

He now recognized that it was Cona Cawb-vey who had greeted him when the vision began, and that it had been his uncle who had directed the progression of images. Cona Cawb-vey had used Quanah's own life to show him what must be done.

Forty Buffalo and Speaks Softly reined beside their friend. Quanah turned to one and then the other as they positioned themselves to each side of his pony. "The People have traveled on a long and proud journey since they first came to the prairie lands. But the road the Nermernuh has trod is now worn to dust from the passing of many feet. For the Kwerhar-rehnuh—for the Nermernuh—to continue their journey, they must turn their feet to a new path."

From the corners of his eyes, he saw new questions darken his companions' faces. He expected this. It was the same reaction he would awake in the braves back at the village. It would not be easy, but he now knew the task that lay ahead of him. In time he would lead his band to the new road they must take if the Nermernuh were to survive.

Quanah's gaze lifted to the western horizons. For several moments he allowed his eyes to drink in the richness of the land that once had belonged to the Kwerhar-rehnuh. The road that stretched into the future led away from the freedom of the plains. It would be a hard path for reluctant feet. But it was a path that must be taken.

Quanah's hands tightened to balled fists around the lance and shield he carried. He forced himself to relax his grip on the weapons. They had been part of the old path. They would have no place on the new. He must clear his mind of all that had been and what might have been and focus on what would be. There would be time enough on the long ride home to prepare the words he must speak before the band's council fire.

CHAPTER
SIXTEEN

John Teller pulled a sweat-stained hat from his head and ducked into the tent. Colonel Mackenzie stood behind a field desk, leafing through sheets of yellowed paper.

The man was smaller than the Texan remembered him. Perhaps it was the stature of the man's deeds that had added to the officer's height in Teller's mind. Although the civilian world had never recognized the immensity of Mackenzie's accomplishments at Palo Duro Canyon, those within the military realized that his actions last September had led to the Comanches slowly surrendering themselves to reservation life.

Mackenzie smoothed a salt-and-pepper temple with the palm of a hand then looked up at the horse trader. "Mr. Teller—"

A spike of dread wedged itself at the base of the Texan's spine. He did not like it when the colonel called him "Mr. Teller." During his brief time as a scout for the officer, he had learned that the more formal Mackenzie became the more likely it was that the colonel was about to reveal a piece of bad news.

"... it seems we have a bit of a problem with the horses you brought into Fort Sill yesterday."

"Problem?" Teller's eyes widened, then narrowed. "What kind of problem? Never been a problem with the three other orders I've filled. The Army was pleased enough to keep givin' me work."

"We never had a reason to believe you were dealing in stolen horses until now, Mr. Teller." Mackenzie answered without so much as the bat of his dark eyes.

"Stolen horses?" Teller could not believe what he heard. "Bought every one of the hundred horses outside in the corral free and clear. I've got the bill of sale to prove it."

The Texan dug a hand into a back pocket, but before he could produce the paper to support his claim, Mackenzie waved it away. "Bills of sale can be forged—just as surely as brands can be changed."

Mackenzie passed the papers he held to the horse trader. "I think you'd better read this, Mr. Teller. Read it real carefully."

Teller did, and each line of the missive only stoked the head of steam that was building under his collar. "This has nothing to do with me. Those horses were taken from a Mexican ranch below the Rio Grande out El Paso way. I ain't traveled that far west in five years or more. My horses all came from around Fort Worth."

"Careful horse thieves would sell the ill-begotten bounties of their labors far from the place of their crime," Mackenzie replied without hesitation. "The brands on three of the mounts you brought here to Sill suspiciously resemble the Mexican brand described in that dispatch."

"That brand is the Bar Double-T. Colonel, every man in Texas knows the Bar ..."

Teller's words trailed off. The more he thought about it, everything Mackenzie had uttered since he had entered the tent had come too quickly from the colonel's mouth. It was as though the officer had prepared and rehearsed his words long before the Texan's arrival.

"This ain't about stolen horses, is it, Colonel?" Teller stared the officer directly in the eye. "You got something hidden up your sleeve, ain't you? What's goin' on here? Lay it out on the table."

Mackenzie rubbed a hand over chin and throat. "As long as there is a question about the ownership of those horses, Mr. Teller, the army will have to keep them as evidence should criminal charges develop. This would by necessity, of course, require that any monetary amounts owed you be held until which time it was determined whether or not the horses in question are or are not stolen."

"Damnation! I should have known better than to ever do business with the army!" Teller needed the promised payment to cover the section of prairie he had just bought through a bank in Fort Worth. Banks had only come to Texas after the end of the War between the States. The scalawags who ran them were quick to foreclose on a man who was late with a loan payment.

"In light of your former service as a military scout, I believe there are arrangements that can be made to free the money presently due you in exchange for certain service to be rendered for the United States Army," Mackenzie said, barely concealing a smile of victory that rode at the corners of his mouth. "You will, of course, be compensated for those services."

"Now it comes." Disgust welled within the Texan. "What do you want me do, ride scout for you again?"

"Not me, but Mr. Sturm—"

"J. J. Sturm? He's an Indian Agent, not a soldier. Why would he need a scout?" Teller stared at the officer uncertain of what churned in the man's mind.

"Sturm no longer serves in the capacity of an agent. Instead he has been assigned to accompany the Comanche chief Wild Horse onto the plains to locate the few remaining hostile bands and convince them to surrender here at Fort Sill."

Each sentence the colonel uttered made less sense. "You're cutting Coby loose from the reservation? Why don't you just stick your hand down a rattlesnake hole and see how long it takes for you to get bit?"

"Wild Horse, or Coby, as you call him, has been instrumental in bringing in several of the wild bands. And Mr. Sturm has long held the respect of the Comanche leaders," Mackenzie said. "It is felt that working together, they will be able to bring in the last of the Kwerhar-rehnuh bands with less effort and expense than will armed soldiers."

"Quanah Parker! It's him you're after." The pieces fell into place and stood out clearly in Teller's mind. "He's the only one that matters who's still runnin' free. Sturm is goin' after Quanah Parker, ain't he?"

"I require a man to accompany Sturm and Wild Horse who

is familiar with the high plains," Mackenzie continued without acknowledging the Texan's question. "I also need a man with a head on his shoulders, who will provide me with a clear evaluation of the situation. Will you accept the job, Mr. Teller, or would you prefer to have the money due you entangled in a morass of legal details for the next year or two?"

The colonel had Teller over a barrel, and he knew it. The Texan could not risk losing the small fortune he had already given to the bank. Worse, he could not risk losing his future, and that's what the parcel of land he bought was—the only shot at a good future that he saw on the horizon. Saddle tramping was not a life for a man who had passed forty.

Yet, Teller pondered, there might be a way to add some honey to the bitter tonic Mackenzie tried to force down his throat.

"It's a mite easier to catch flies with sugar than it is with salt, Colonel," Teller eventually answered.

Mackenzie hiked an eyebrow high. "What's on your mind, Mr. Teller?"

"I just want to sweeten the pot a bit." Teller drew a breath and crossed his fingers behind his back. "You want a man, call him a scout if you want, to spy on Sturm for you—to make double-damned certain he don't go gettin' the wool pulled over his eyes by Quanah Parker or any other of the Comach still runnin' wild. You must think I'm the man for that job or else you wouldn't be tryin' to put me between a rock and a hard place."

"I wouldn't put it in those words—"

Teller did not let him finish. It was the Texan's turn to play his hand, and he would not be stopped until his cards were on the table. "I want more than just the money that's already legally mine. And I want a mite more than a few dollars a month scout's pay if we bring Quanah Parker into the reservation. After all, you're asking me to risk a permanent haircut goin' out with Coby."

"What is it you suggest, Mr. Teller?" Mackenzie's eyebrow arched sharply once more.

"A contract with the army—a five-year contract to be the sole supplier of horses here at Fort Sill. You might throw in a few phrases about occasionally buying a few head of cattle, too." Teller spread his hand before the colonel.

Mackenzie pursed his lips and looked past Teller to the open flap of his tent. When his gaze returned to the Texan, he said, "A two-year contract for the horses with the clause that should additional beef be required over the amount contracted with our present supplier, you will be the first contacted."

"A three-year contract," Teller pressed.

"Two," Mackenzie countered with finality firm in his voice. "Take it, Mr. Teller."

"Taken—if you see that the money owed for them horses outside is wired to my banker in Fort Worth by the end of this week."

"Agreed."

"Agreed." Teller stuck out his hand, which the colonel took and shook firmly.

"You made a wise decision, John. Your nation thanks you."

Now it's John! Teller shook his head. "Ain't nothin' but foolishness to go traipsin' off all over the Llano Estacado lookin' for red-skinned trouble."

Taking a cigar from a box on the desk, Mackenzie bit off the end and spat it aside while he settled into a chair. He struck a match, lit the cigar, and exhaled a thin stream of smoke into the air above his head. "In truth, I don't think you'll run into trouble. If the Comanches who have come straggling in here the past few months are any indication, you'll be damned lucky if you find Quanah Parker and his band still alive. This has been a hard winter."

Teller could well imagine. Comanches without horses were little match for fleet-footed antelope and deer. The cooking pots in Comanche villages had gone empty more often than not. "What about sign? Have your patrols found sign?"

"Here and there," Mackenzie admitted. "A few times they followed the trail of what appeared to be quite a large band. The trail never went that far."

"It's Quanah Parker as sure as the world," Teller said. "Ain't no one else it could be. All the other war chiefs have come in, if what I've been readin' in the papers is right."

"He's the last holdout." Mackenzie drew another puff from the cigar. "From the sign the patrols have seen, I suspect he's been moving around all winter, afraid to stay in one spot too long."

"And you got reason to believe Coby just might know where he'll be and when?" Teller asked.

"The Comanche on the reservation seem to stay in close

contact with those still wandering free. Coby has been very cooperative since his release," Mackenzie answered. "I suspect he'll lead you straight to Quanah Parker's band."

A hundred other questions fluttered in the Texan's mind, but he let them pass; they were of no consequence. Either he found Quanah Parker or he did not. It was that simple. "When do we leave?"

Mackenzie looked up at his newest scout. "As soon as you collect the supplies that have been waiting for you for the past week at the sutler's. Coby and Sturm are both waiting here at the fort."

Teller swallowed back the curses that rode on his tongue when he realized the colonel had been planning to rope him into this bit of "scouting" for quite some time. "Then, I'm on my way to the sutler. Have that contract ready to sign after I pick up my supplies. Just to keep everything on the up-and-up and all legal like, you understand."

The officer chuckled when the Texan turned and started from the tent. "I understand, John."

CHAPTER
SEVENTEEN

Weckeah's drawn face greeted Quanah as he slid from the back of the pony in front of his lodge. Without asking the warrior sensed another black cloud had settled over the village during his three-day absence.

"You and the other hunters have returned with meat for our pots, my husband. This is good." Weckeah's head nodded to two horses bearing two antelope and ten jackrabbits slung across their backs. "All will be grateful."

Quanah's own gaze slowly took in the conical shapes of the tipis. He saw no new lodges, nor did he note there were less than when he and the other hunters left. He looked back at his wife, searching for the brightness that had once filled her eyes during their youth. He saw only sorrow.

"Ten braves rode with me. For three days and nights we rode from the camp in sweeping circles that grew larger and larger," he finally said with a shake of his head. "Two antelopes and a few rabbits were all we found. There is no buffalo, and the deer have deserted this land. How can we feed more than two hundred bellies with so little?"

"We will make grass stew, my husband. It will fill our stomachs as it has for these many passings of the moon."

Quanah heard his wife attempt to force hope into her voice. It could not disguise her disappointment at the paltry game the hunting party had brought back to the camp. Her disappointment was no greater than the warrior's. The meat would do no more than flavor the stew pots. To be certain, grass would fill bellies, but men and women and children could not live on grass.

"Windsinger's daughter and Red Clover's son died while you were gone," Weckeah said in a tone she might have used to describe the coming and going of an afternoon rain shower. "Their mothers could no longer produce milk. They could not feed their babies."

Quanah said nothing, afraid that should he speak his words would be transformed into a high-pitched wail of keening. Did all the Kwerhar-rehnuh's sons and daughters have to die before the men of the village saw the truth of his vision?

Weckeah reached up and touched his shoulder. "Husband, a council has been called. The men gather at the center of our village."

"A council?" Quanah frowned. "In the middle of the day? Who has done this thing?"

"Twisted Foot," his wife replied. "The morning the hunting party left, he said all would council upon your return. He has said no more."

The warrior's frown deepened. Twisted Foot was the oldest and wisest of all the men in the village. He had been old even when Peta Nocona had been a child. When his ankle had been broken during a buffalo hunt, the brave had turned to the ways of healing. No other understood the medicines to be found in the plants that grew on plain and in wood more than Twisted Foot.

"Find our daughter and bring her to the council," Quanah ordered. "I will take the antelope and rabbits there so all may share in the meat."

When Weckeah nodded, he turned to the ten warriors, who remained on their ponies. He signaled them to follow him. At the center of the camp the band's members had begun to gather. While the women dressed and divided the game, the men built a small fire and seated themselves about its flames. Once pipes filled with tobacco would have been shared, but months had passed since Quanah had used the last of the tobacco to help summon his dream.

When at last the two rings of the council sat about the fire, men circled within and women and children without, Twisted Foot walked from his tipi to the flames. Beneath his arm was a small bundle wrapped in doeskin. Rather than taking his place among the other braves, he slowly turned and stared into the faces of all those around him.

"I have heard Quanah speak of his vision these long months," the ancient brave eventually spoke. "Of all in our band, it was I who stood against this new road he would set Kwerhar-rehnuh feet upon. I have been a fool."

The healer paused to draw a heavy breath. "I thought my years brought wisdom, but they only blinded me to all I did not want to see. It was here on the prairie that my mother brought me into this life, and it was here that I wanted to die. Because of this I have spoken against any who might wish to follow Quanah down the new path. Because of this many have died with bellies empty. I now see the foolishness of all I have done."

"Twisted Foot, all among this band may speak their hearts. It has always . . ."

The brave with his long mane of silver gray waved Quanah to silence. "Today I will no longer be a fallen log across the path of the People. All the friends of my childhood have journeyed to the Valley of Ten Thousand-fold Longer and Wider. My eyes have seen the children of these friends go to join their parents. These eyes can no longer bear the burden of watching the young go where the old should journey."

For a second time Twisted Foot paused. He lifted a hand and made the sign of farewell. "I go now to seek my friends in the Valley of Ten Thousand-fold Longer and Wider."

With that, the old man strode proudly from the council circle. Quanah and the others watched silently as Twisted Foot made his way through the village and disappeared far out upon the plain.

"A great brave has passed from the People this day." It was Speaks Softly who addressed the council. "We should return to our tipis and mourn his passing. When evening grays the sky, all should return to talk of this new road we face."

No one else spoke. The two circles broke when the villagers rose and quietly returned to their lodges.

• • •

"Will the council listen to my husband this night?"

Quanah glanced at his wife while he scooped a mixture of antelope, grasshoppers, and grass from a bowl and lifted it to his
mouth. He chewed and swallowed. The stew lacked flavor, but it
silenced the rumbling of his stomach. "The council always lis-
tens, but they do not hear. Perhaps the time has come for us to
leave and seek the reservation on our own."

"No," Weckeah answered firmly. "We have talked of this before. You have led our band in times of warring. It is your place
to lead them in the time of peace. There is no honor in doing
less."

In spite of the hunger-stretched features of Weckeah's once
rounded face, a fire of strength still burned in her breast. His
chest swelled; he had chosen well when he had stolen her from
Yellow Bear's lodge.

"And you, my daughter? How would you council your father?" Quanah turned to the seven-year-old Nahmukuh. "Do the
other children still whisper that their parents believe I wish to
travel to the reservation because white blood flows in my veins?"

The girl's head moved from side to side, although she refused
to let her eyes meet her father's.

Quanah smiled. Nahmukuh would not lie, but because she
did not speak, he knew she did not reveal the whole truth. An
old pain lanced through the warrior's heart. Even after all these
years, there were those who questioned his love of the
Nermernuh. Would that always be the way?

"Those who call the father of my daughter a white man are
fools—greater fools than old Twisted Foot."

This came from Cho-ny, Quanah's second wife who sat with
their three-year-old daughter in her lap. Cho-ny carefully fed the
child with her fingers, making certain not so much as a drop of
the precious stew dribbled wasted down the girl's chin.

"Twisted Foot was no fool," Quanah replied. "He was a great
brave whose power with plants healed many of the People. He
will be—"

"Riders!"

The cry from outside drowned the remainder of Quanah's
comments.

"Riders come toward the village!"

Laying his bowl aside, the war chief pushed to his feet. "Wait here until I know what is happening." He snatched up his rifle and ducked from the tipi.

"Riders come!" A boy still two years from the time of manhood sat astride a pinto pony.

"Is it the blue coats who come?" Quanah called as he and the other village braves gathered around the messenger.

The boy shook his head. "Five riders approach. Two are white, but the other three appear to be of the People."

"Nermernuh lead whites to our camp!" a brave shouted behind Quanah. "We should ride out and greet them!"

"No!" Quanah's voice came loud and firm. "They do not bring soldiers with them. They come in peace. We should allow them to enter our village and hear their words."

The rifles and lances that were raised high above heads gradually lowered. Forty Buffalo stepped toward his friend. "Could this be the one we've heard of? The one that Coby has brought to other bands? The one called Sturm who talks of the reservation."

"We shall see when they reach our camp," Quanah answered. "If the one called Sturm is among them, the council should listen to him this night."

Quanah heard a low rumble of disapproval move through the men, but no one openly voiced a protest. Quietly the warrior released his breath. That the braves did not rush to collect the scalps of the riders was a beginning. For now, he could ask for no more.

"... land to grow crops and build a home to raise your families," Coby translated Sturm's words into the tongue of the People for the council. "Beef to fill your kettles, and clothing and blankets all await you to the east. There will be schools to teach your children new ways to live. All that was promised in the Medicine Lodge Treaty of 1867, which was signed by your chiefs, waits for you if you return with me to Fort Sill. The decision is yours to make. The fighting is over. The time of peace is upon you."

When Sturm's voice fell silent so did Coby's. Quanah studied the short white man in his coat of black. Although the war chief had never stepped foot on the reservation in all the years of his life, he had heard of this bearded Sturm. The man had served as reservation agent and was known for fairness—or so said the Nermernuh who often wintered on the reservation. The other white man, who had sat silently throughout the council, Quanah had never seen before.

Of Coby he knew much. Wild Horse was a great warrior whose courage was beyond question. Only after Mackenzie's bloody raid on Palo Duro Canyon did Coby lead his band east to Fort Sill and surrender to the soldiers. The two braves who now rode with Wild Horse on this mission of peace had once ridden beside him on countless raids into the lands of the *Tejanos*.

"We have smoked your gift of tobacco and listened to all you have said." Yellow Bear stood and faced Sturm. "What you ask of us can not be decided in one night. We must think long and hard upon your words."

"Think hard," Sturm answered, with Coby once again translating his sentences. "But do not take too long to come to your decision. Patrols of soldiers sweep across the high plains and have orders to treat all Nermernuh bands as hostiles. With peace so close at hand it would be a disaster to have war fall upon this village."

Quanah sensed no threat in Sturm's words. He only voiced the fact that all within the village were aware of. Mackenzie's blue-coated buffalo soldiers scoured the plains to find this village. Because of that, Quanah had moved the band constantly throughout the summer.

"We will meet as council again when the sun rises tomorrow," Yellow Bear answered. "At that time we shall talk again and give you our decision."

Sturm nodded and rose. He signaled to the other white man, and they walked to the edge of the village where their bedrolls waited. Coby and the two braves remained by the fire.

"Tell us of the reservation," Forty Buffalo urged the former war chief.

"It is small." Coby shrugged. "The whites expect all to become diggers of dirt and our children to go to their schools to learn to be white."

Grunts of disapproval rumbled around the circle of men.

"What of the buffalo?" another brave asked.

Coby looked up and shook his head. "There is no more buffalo, except in Nermernuh dreams. The whites have killed the great herds whose hooves once shook the earth."

Only silence answered Wild Horse's words. All gathered knew the bison were gone, but to hear it voiced was a harsh truth for ears that did not want to hear.

"If all this is so, why should we surrender to the soldiers at Fort Sill?" Pecos asked from Quanah's right.

"To live," Coby answered simply. "Like this village, my band was dying. I led them to the reservation so that they might live. The white men now claim the vastness of the prairie. There is no place for the People here any longer. On the reservation, the Nermernuh can live."

"What kind of life is it to be bound by a small spot of land?" Pecos pressed. "The Nermernuh have ridden with the wind across all of the plains."

"The children of my band still live." Coby's gaze met Pecos's eyes squarely. "Can you say that of the children in this village?"

Pecos fell silent. His own newborn son had fallen sick and died before the spring grass had pushed from the earth.

"Many have escaped the reservation and ridden to ours and other bands," Yellow Bear spoke again.

"More have ridden to the reservation," Coby answered. "Many of those who chose to return to the old ways have ridden back to Fort Sill. The great bands are no longer. You who are gathered here are the only band still wandering the plains. I have ridden with the man Sturm for two months. All the others we have found have been traveling alone or with camps of no more than three tipis. That is the way of it."

Coby paused and turned his gaze to Quanah. "Sturm is a man of peace. He was sent by whites who believe like him. But there are those who would prefer that the Nermernuh were wiped from the face of the world forever. Do not give them reason to destroy the People.

"We have thought the whites to be like us," Wild Horse continued. "But their numbers are more vast than the stars that fill the night sky. The time of change has come. As surely as the Nermernuh drove the other tribes from the plains when they first came here, the whites now drive us from the prairies. When we were the stronger, we took what we wanted and killed those who stood against us. That was the time of the People. Now it is the time of the whites. That, too, is the way of it."

. . . They will come back. They always come back.

Quanah closed his eyes. Wild Horse's voice might have been the voice of Cona Cawb-vey. His mind could not grasp the numbers of whites Coby described. Yet, it must be true. How else could there still be whites after all that the Nermernuh had killed?

"What of the soldiers' prison?" Quanah opened his eyes to stare at Wild Horse. "We heard that all warriors who led raids against the whites were placed in prisons in chains."

Coby nodded. "I was among those they locked in their great icehouse. All those whose names they knew were imprisoned. It is a place I had no wish to be. But my wives and children no longer suffered. They had blankets to warm them from the cold and food to fill their bellies."

A cold as powerful as the ice that trapped the springs in winter froze Quanah's spine. *To be locked within the four walls of a white man's prison!*

Across the flames of the council fire, he saw the haggard faces of his wives and daughters, read the hunger that drew their flesh taut atop the bones of their skeletons. He understood clearly all that Coby had said.

"The night grows late." Yellow Bear rose and spoke again. "We should return to our lodges and consider all that has been said. When the morning light comes, we shall light the council fire anew and speak on these matters."

Quanah waited until all who desired to speak said their words. The old ways of the Nermernuh remained strong within the braves of the village, but he sensed a willingness to seek the new road Cona Cawb-vey's vision had revealed. All they needed was for one among them to stand and say he would lead them on that road.

"I know nothing of treaties made with other warriors. Such treaties mean nothing to the People. Each brave must decide what is right for him and his family. That is the way it has always been." Quanah slowly turned so that all saw his face when he spoke. "These treaties were made in the past and today is not the past. What we must seek is the future."

Several of the braves gathered in the council circle grunted and nodded their approval.

"Were it within the power of a single warrior, I would drive the whites from the prairies and return the plains to the bands of the Nermernuh. Such power is not to be," Quanah continued, choosing his words with certain deliberation. "This is my home. Were I alone like the great healer Twisted Foot, I would choose to stay and walk a path that leads to the Valley of Ten Thousand-fold Longer and Wider. There I could hunt the buffalo every day and feast on rich meat every night.

"But I do not walk alone. My family hungers and grows weaker with each day that passes. I do not wish my wives and daughters and the children of my children to pass from this earth forever. The Nermernuh must be more than memories of a nation that once walked this earth."

Quanah paused again, his gaze finding his wives and daughters before he continued. "Because of this, I will ride east this day and surrender myself to Mackenzie and his soldiers. I will tell them that my family follows me so that a place will be made ready for them on the reservation. That is the road that I will travel. If it is the wish of the braves of this village, I will carry the same message to the soldiers for them. For me there is no more to be said."

As Quanah returned to the ground, Speaks Softly rose. "My friend Quanah may carry my voice in his words. My family and I have followed him across the plains. We will now follow him to Fort Sill."

One by one the braves stood and announced they would travel the long road to the reservation. Even those who had first spoken in favor of remaining on the prairie and dying in a final fight against the blue coats rescinded and pronounced they would take their families eastward to the reservation. Quanah felt no pride in their decision, merely relief. The white man's road would not be an easy one to follow for those accustomed to the vast reaches of the plains.

"Since all here say that I may speak for them, know that my words shall be like words from their own lips and shall bind a man as surely as though he spoke them himself." Quanah pushed to his feet again and waited to see if any protested his pronouncement.

None did.

"Then the time for me to leave has come. I wish three braves to ride with me. Make the choice among yourselves. You will find me with my family when you are ready."

Quanah stepped from the council circle, gathered his wives and daughters, and returned to his lodge.

"Ride with eyes wide, my husband." Weckeah kissed Quanah's cheek. "Know that I see the bravery in what you do this day."

The last of the Nermernuh warrior chiefs returned his first wife's kiss then walked from the tipi where Sturm waited with his white companion and the three braves the village had chosen to accompany their leader to Fort Sill.

"I will remain with your people and journey with them to the reservation," Sturm said with Coby translating. "If we should run into a soldier patrol, my presence will assure that there is no attack. Wild Horse and Mr. Teller will ride with you and your braves to see to your personal safety."

"The day is half through, and we have many miles to cover." Quanah swung to the back of a black stallion and took a lead Pecos handed him. The braided horsehair rope was looped around the neck of a dapple gray.

Quanah nudged the black pony with his heels and reined to the east. He held back the urge to free a war cry that grew within his chest and drive the pony ahead at a full run. Instead he allowed the animal to find its own pace, while his eyes drank in the flat grasslands that spread out in all directions. Once he reached Fort Sill, he would no longer ride these lands. There was no need to hasten this last journey.

CHAPTER EIGHTEEN

May 19, 1875, John Teller repeated the date in his mind. He had no intention of ever forgetting it, nor did he doubt would any Texan. On this day, this *very* day, he thought as he escorted the five braves through the lines of white tents toward Colonel Mackenzie's personal tent, the war with the Comanches was over.

And he had brought in the last warrior holdout—Quanah Parker!

That his action would be rewarded with a two-year contract to supply horses to Fort Sill never entered his mind. All that mattered was that the long years of bloody butchery by Comanche raiders was over. Texas was safe for every farmer and rancher who wanted to build a life for himself and his family!

At least twenty armed soldiers surrounded the five warriors when Teller drew his buckskin to a halt outside Mackenzie's tent. He looked at Parker and signaled with his hands as he spoke, "You wait here. I will get the colonel. You wait here."

Teller stepped from the saddle and pivoted toward the tent

just as Colonel Mackenzie shoved aside a flap and walked outside. A broad grin split the Texan's face.

"You wanted Quanah Parker"—he swept an arm toward the Comanche warrior mounted on the black mustang—"I brought him to you."

Rather than the stern, granite expression Teller had grown accustomed to during his time as the officer's scout, he saw a smile uplift the corners of Mackenzie's mouth while he walked forward and extended a hand as though he welcomed a visitor to his home.

"Parker," the officer said. "You have given me and the U.S. Army one long chase. It is my hope that we can place those times behind us and begin a new era of peace between our people."

The Comanche stared at the proffered hand then looked questioningly at Wild Horse. Coby repeated Mackenzie's words in the tongue of the Kwerhar-rehnuh and explained the hand was an offering of friendship. Quanah swung a leg over the neck of his mount, slid to the ground, and accepted the hand with an overvigorous shake.

"I am Quanah Parker," he said in slow, uncertain syllables. "You are Mackenzie, greatest of those who fought my people."

The English obviously had been practiced during the long ride from the Llano Estacado, Teller realized. But try as he did, he could not recall the warrior speaking a word other than Comanche during the two weeks it had taken to reach Fort Sill. Parker had seemed more interested in hunting down any game that happened to cross their path. On more than one occasion Teller had felt as though he were on some sportsman's holiday rather than escorting a dangerous war chief to the army.

"The path of war," Quanah continued in a tongue awkward to him, "I put behind me. I will ride that road no more. I will now walk the white man's road. On this I give my word."

The sentiment contained in the Comanche's speech did not surprise Teller. What else could he say? He was surrendering himself to Mackenzie. A man did not expect a savage in such a position to spit in the soldiers' eyes and openly vow to take their scalps and stake them atop an anthill the first time he got the chance.

What did shock the Texan was the colonel's reaction. Mackenzie's smile stretched to a pleased grin, and he said:

"Your words are admirable. The fighting ability of yourself and all the Quahadas bands is known to every soldier here. It is my hope that you will now direct the vigor you displayed in war to settling here and living a good peaceful life."

Good peaceful life? Teller frowned. Mackenzie was acting like he admired the brave, as though he faced some general amid a formal surrender of civilized armies. Why wasn't he locking Parker away in the icehouse as he had done when the other Comanche chiefs had come to Fort Sill? It made no sense; this was the bloody butcher who had raided the Texas frontier for at least a decade. Didn't the colonel realize how many good men and women he had left scalped behind him? If Mackenzie didn't, he should be aware of the number of soldiers who had died beneath Comanche bullets and arrows.

Apparently Parker's English had run to the end of the line, because Coby once more translated for the young war chief when he assured the officer that his words were those of all the braves in the band he led. Parker then explained that Sturm now traveled with that band as it made its way to the army fort.

"Sturm feared your buffalo soldiers might attack my people, thinking them to be hostile," Quanah said in the words of the Nermernuh while Wild Horse conveyed his meaning to Mackenzie. "This, too, is a fear with me."

"Assure Parker that I will immediately send out gallopers with dispatches to all my officers in the field to tell them they are to allow Sturm and the Indians with him safe passage to Fort Sill," the colonel replied. "No harm will come to his band now that they have turned from the ways of war."

Teller saw relief flash across Parker's face. Then, in the blink of an eye, the Comanche's features returned to an unreadable mask.

"There is a gift that I bring to the soldier Mackenzie." Quanah tugged on the horsehair rope held in his right hand.

"A gift?" The officer's face brightened with obvious anticipation. "No gifts are necessary."

"This strong stallion has served both Mackenzie and me well." Quanah stepped to one side so that the colonel could see the dapple gray he brought as an offering to the officer.

Teller coughed back a laugh that jumped up his throat when he caught the expression on the colonel's face. Mackenzie's eyes went as round as saucers and seemed to bulge from their sockets.

An embarrassed crimson appeared just above the starched collar of his blouse and flushed upward to cover his face. There was no doubt the officer recognized the prized horse he had once ridden—a horse Parker had stolen from Mackenzie's own remuda.

"The gift is generous," the colonel managed to sputter. "But it is not necessary. My horses are supplied by the U.S. Army. The gray would better serve you here on the reservation. It is only fitting you should have such a magnificent animal to ride."

Teller's mind reeled. First, he remembered how much the gray had meant to Mackenzie. The colonel had cussed for at least a week straight after the horse had been stolen. Second, no Comanche who had surrendered at Sill had been allowed to keep any of the ponies they brought with them. A Comanche astride a horse was too dangerous a combination for white men to abide—and keep their hair intact.

"He is to keep the gray pony?" Shock filled Coby's voice as he stared at the army officer. "You will not take the pony away?"

"And the mount he now rides." Mackenzie nodded and smiled at Parker. "The men of his band will be allowed to keep their favorite ponies when they arrive here."

While Teller's brain did another confused cartwheel, Quanah spoke. "I will keep the gray and always consider it to be the best of my horses because Mackenzie has given it to me. Now I am ready to go to the white man's prison."

"Prison?" Both of Mackenzie's eyebrows jumped high. "I have made no mention of prison."

"Others of the Nermernuh who rode against the white soldiers were placed in prison when they came to this fort," Quanah answered. "I am ready to take my place among those warriors."

Mackenzie's shook his head and grinned. "The others were not Quahadas as you are . . ."

I'll be damned and damned again! The colonel does admire the half-breed devil! Teller gave up on trying to understand the officer. What he saw and heard was without rhyme or reason.

". . . of all the Comanche bands, only the Quahadas refused to come to this fort during the winters and eat government beef, then ride off when the spring came to raid far and wide. The Quahadas did not attempt to deceive the army. If Quanah Parker tells me that he and the braves of his band come to the reservation to learn the white man's ways, then I will believe him—until the contrary is proven. And until that day, I will personally see that he and his braves get what assistance they need in settling in here."

Teller again saw relief spread across the war chief's face when Wild Horse repeated Mackenzie's words. More confusion clouded the Texan's mind. It was apparent that Parker knew the other war chiefs had been imprisoned when they surrendered. Knowing this, why had he given himself up?

"I feel the soldier Mackenzie's offer to aid me and my braves is given from his heart," Quanah eventually said. "Because of this there is something I would ask of him today."

The colonel listened carefully to Coby's less than perfect English, then asked. "What is it you wish?"

For a long moment Teller watched Parker stand silently, gathering the words for his thoughts as was the way of an Indian. When he spoke it was with one sentence at a time, making certain Wild Horse conveyed his meaning before proceeding:

"In the days before my manhood, a party of Texas Rangers raided the village of my father Peta Nocona. In this raid several of our band were killed, including my uncle Cona Cawb-vey, who taught me the ways of the bow and lance. But it is not of the dead I speak. It is of my mother, who was of white blood, and my sister Prairie Flower. The *Tejanos* stole my mother and sister away from their people. I would know of them again, if the soldier Mackenzie can do this. I would know if they are safe and happy."

Parker's first request had been to see to the safety of those who followed him, and now he asked about his mother and sister? What kind of heart beat within that naked chest? Teller's eyes narrowed while he studied the warrior he had brought to the army. How could one responsible for the bloody deaths of so many care about another human being?

"I will write letters to the authorities in Texas and inquire as to the health and whereabouts of your mother and sister." Mackenzie motioned a lieutenant to his side. "Now, Lieutenant Powell will escort you to the land you and your band will occupy here on the reservation. I think it's time you saw your new home."

Parker nodded, leaped to the back of his pony, and reined after the lieutenant when the man swung to the saddle and rode though the small city of tents. Mackenzie stood watching the warrior depart. "It's a fine day. The Comanche wars are over. To be certain, there are still a few renegades running wild, but they represent only a minor danger."

"I thought you told me Cynthia Ann Parker and her daughter had died, John Teller?"

The Texan twisted around to find the New Orleans reporter Charles Dumaine standing on the right side of Mackenzie's tent. "You still writing about redskins, Mr. Dumaine?"

"Still writing, Mr. Teller, although I believe the ink is about to dry up on this story. After today, I doubt the *Picayune* will have a need to keep me here any longer."

"What was that you mentioned about Parker's mother?" Mackenzie asked the newsman.

Dumaine tilted his head toward his old friend. "I was just recalling that Mr. Teller once mentioned that Mrs. Parker and her daughter died shortly after they were returned to the woman's family in Texas."

Mackenzie's gaze shifted to Teller. "Is that true?"

The Texan shrugged. "It's what I read in an old newspaper years ago, during the war."

"Hmmmm." Mackenzie thoughtfully ran a hand over his chin and throat. "Then I shall write my letters to confirm that fact. It's the least Parker deserves."

"Deserves?" The question broke across Teller's lips as a startled grunt. "Hell, Colonel, the way you been actin', it's like that redskin is some West Point classmate or somethin.'"

The officer cocked his head to one side, gaze returning to the departing Indians. "In a way, I suppose you're right, John. Quanah Parker and I have known nothing but the school of war for all our lives. A man who doesn't have respect for his enemy is a fool. And I don't know of any enemy that fought longer, harder, or better than that half-naked savage riding there. Even the rebs I faced in the war would be hard-pressed to put up the fight he did. This country might never notice it, but today it lost something that was here yesterday."

Teller spat to the ground. "Now you're soundin' like some of those bleedin' hearts in Congress back east, that are always tellin' us we have to protect the Indians."

"No, I would never do that." The hint of a forlorn smile flitted across the colonel's lips while he continued to watch Quanah Parker depart. "We and the red man are too different for both to exist together. One had to dominate the other. It's like an Englishman named Darwin wrote about back before the war—the fittest of a species survives, the weaker dies."

Teller had no idea who this "Darwin" was, but Dumaine commented, "Darwin wrote about animals, Colonel."

Mackenzie turned to the reporter. "As much as we like to deny it to ourselves and surround our actions with lofty motivations, Mr. Dumaine, men are still animals. The hard, cold fact is that the stronger devour the weak. When the Comanches first came to these plains, they killed other tribes to claim the land as their own. Now we come along and do the same thing to them. Survival of the fittest—plain and simple with no frills attached."

Mackenzie paused to let his gaze trace over the plains that surrounded the fort. "If there is a difference between us and the Comanche, it is the fact that on this reservation we will give them the opportunity to become like the enemy they fought against for so long. And that, Mr. Dumaine, is what we call being civilized."

Teller could no longer hold his tongue. The colonel babbled nonsense. "We ain't like them. Quanah Parker and all his bucks are heathens—nothing more than savages who killed women and children. You got no right to go comparin' white men to bloody devils like that."

"The Quahadas," Mackenzie used the common term for the Kwerhar-rehnuh bands of the Nermernuh, "or their deeds were no more bloody than what you Texans or the men under my command have done, John. You were a Texas Ranger once, weren't you?"

"Good Christian men, defending the homes and lives of good Christian men and women," Teller answered with an affirmative tilt of his head. "If it hadn't been for the Rangers, the Comanches would have burnt every farm and ranch in Texas."

Mackenzie looked back at the Texan. "I'll grant you that. But with all the Christian trappings you carried with you, all the words of brotherly love, can you tell me that Rangers didn't ride down Comanche women and kill Comanche children?"

"Mongrel pups that came at us with huntin' knives and bows strung with arrows," Teller answered. "They'd kill you just as sure as a buck if you gave 'em the chance."

Mackenzie's lips parted as though to answer, but he waved the Texan away. "We'll find no grand answers here today, John, and

I have work waiting for me. Besides, you've completed your service to the United States Army. Where will you be heading now?"

Teller stepped into a stirrup and swung into the saddle. "I got me a section of good grasslands just below the Red River. Reckon it's time I put some horses and cattle on it. Might even build myself a big fancy house with all the money the army's goin' to pay for the livestock they'll be buyin' off me."

"A noble enough pursuit." Mackenzie smiled. "I wish you well in your endeavors, John."

"Thank you, Colonel." Teller reined his buckskin to the reporter. "And you, Mr. Dumaine, in case we don't see each other again, I hope life has nothing but good things waitin' for you back in New Orleans."

Dumaine offered his friend a hand of parting, which Teller took and shook before he turned his mount's head southward toward the Red River which separated Texas from the Indian Territory. He had no doubt that Dumaine would continue writing his newspaper articles once he returned home. But what about Mackenzie? What would the colonel do, now that the Indians had been swept from this part of the country? Of what use was a fighting man when there were no more wars to be fought?

CHAPTER NINETEEN

June second in the year eighteen and seventy-five. Quanah tried to hold tight to the white man's name for the day. Like all the new things he had faced since his arrival at Fort Sill, the concept that each day carried its own name was alien to him.

For the whites it was not enough to know that the day was hot and dry and that no clouds moved across the blue sky above. For the Nermernuh a day was to be remembered by what events occurred that day—this is the day my first daughter breathes life—this is the day my first buffalo fell— this is the day that the great rains swelled the river until it swam out of its banks. Naming each day seemed foolish. Did the whites not have better things to do . . .

Quanah caught himself. This was not the way to think. It was the Nermernuh way. He had given his word to Mackenzie that he would follow the white man's road. To do that he must learn to think and speak as did the white man. Both would be hard. The white man's thinking had no center, and his words tangled the tongue in knots.

Quanah's eyes lifted and traced down the avenue of soldiers who opened to allow his band to approach. Their horses confiscated by Mackenzie's men, although the colonel promised each would be given the pick of his favorite pony before being located on their new land, the braves came first in a long line. Few looked at the soldiers with their rifles, but walked with eyes staring at the dusty ground.

Quanah sensed the shame they felt this day. The Kwerhar-rehnuh were the proudest of the Nermernuh bands. To deliver themselves into the hands of their enemies weighed heavily in their hearts. *But they will live. For now that is enough. In time there will be more.*

Behind the braves came the women and children. During the two weeks Quanah had been on the reservation, his eyes had grown accustomed to the faces of those who fell asleep each night with full bellies. He had forgotten how harsh the long winter had been to his people. Now he saw it in their faces and eyes. No woman spoke; no child smiled.

He sensed the shadow of death hovering above their heads. In spite of all he had learned to hate about the reservation in his short stay, seeing his band this way confirmed that his decision had been the right one. The plains no longer could feed the Nermernuh. Only here would they once more grow strong and live to bring other generations into this world.

Near the head of the line of women, Quanah saw his wives and daughters. Wedging his way between two soldiers with rifles ready, he moved to them in long, quick strides.

"Walk tall and straight as befits the family of Quanah Parker," he greeted his family. "My name is known here among the whites. Show them that you are proud, and not like some whipped dogs with their tails between their legs. You are Nermernuh."

Weckeah shot a glance at her husband, and shook her head. "There is no pride in walking. Our ponies have been taken."

"I have ponies waiting for you. Two fine bay mares I traded my black stallion for," he answered. "Come quickly. It is a long ride to our new home."

"But our tipi and belongings?" Weckeah protested. "I will not leave them. They are all we have now."

Quanah pointed to a soldier who approached leading a pony that dragged lodge poles with his family's possessions atop. "See, I said my name was known here. The soldier colonel Mackenzie has helped us this day. We will be home safe in our own lodge this night while the others still talk with the soldiers. Now walk straight and proud."

Weckeah straightened when she took the handwoven lead from the soldier and followed her husband toward the waiting ponies.

Weckeah shook her head as she studied the drawing Quanah had traced in the dirt beside the campfire. "I understand this squiggly line is the river the whites call the Red, and this square is the reservation, but where will our village be?"

"Here there will be no village. Each family will live apart from the others on land they will farm." Quanah pointed to a spot near the stones he had placed on his makeshift map to represent the Wichita Mountains. "Here is the land on which we will live. One of Mackenzie's officers helped me select it. There is none better to be had by any in our band."

He swept an arm about him to indicate all the land about them would be where they built a new life. For a moment he considered telling his wives that three million acres composed the reservation. But in truth he was uncertain exactly what an acre was. He told himself that he must understand this measure of land white men set so much store by. If an acre was important to the whites, it must become important to red men.

Weckeah looked around. "These oaks are good. They will shade our tipi from the summer sun. But why will there be no village?"

"The whites are still frightened of us," he answered.

"But you told them we now walk the white man's road," Cho-ny said.

"Telling them is not the same as their believing my words." Quanah settled to the ground beside his map and studied it. "They fear that should our people come together in one spot, they will return to the old ways of raiding. So the white soldiers keep our lodges separated."

"Are we expected to plant beans and corn on this land?" Weckeah asked. "I have never planted corn and beans."

"Mackenzie has told me there will be those who will give us tools and teach us to dig in the ground." Quanah saw the disgust on his wives' faces. It equalled the disgust he felt in his own breast. This would be the hardest of the white man's ways to learn.

"We may raise ponies and cattle on this land," he added almost as an afterthought and pointed back to the map. "Here is land owned by all the People, where all may graze the animals they own."

"The days will be long without other women to talk and work with." Cho-ny's eyes traveled to the canopy of oak limbs that overhung their tipi.

Quanah was uncertain his wives heard anything he said. They seemed uninterested in the land that now belonged to the People. For him, too, it was difficult to grasp that men might own the land. The earth belonged to no one. Yet, the owning of land was the way of the white man and he must learn to think and act as a white man. Land to the whites was like ponies to the Nermernuh. If owning land was a sign of wealth among the whites, then he would own land. To do else would be foolish.

"Others among our band and all the other bands may come and visit our lodge, and we may travel and visit their lodges whenever we wish. The soldiers will not bother us as long as we remain here." He used a finger to point to the boundaries of the reservation.

"Why would we want to go there, there, and there?" Weckeah asked, her own finger pointing to the portions of the reservation that had been parceled to the Kiowa, and Kiowa-Apache. "They are no friends of the Nermernuh."

With that Quanah agreed. During his short stay among those on the reservation, he had already sensed unspoken undercurrents of friction that developed between the different nations. There were even those among the other bands of the People who complained that Mackenzie treated him better than he had treated the leaders of their bands.

"We will have no need to go into those places," Quanah assured his wife. "But we can visit among our people."

"It would be better if all lived in a village," Cho-ny said. "Then we would not have to travel long distances to see those who are friends."

With a disgusted shake of his head Quanah shoved to his feet and walked from the campfire. He paused beside the bole of one of the oaks and stared out to the deepening shadows of evening that crept over the Wichita Mountains. There was a sense of comfort here, a feeling of familiarity. He had known this land and these mountains for as long as he could remember. It was here that he once hunted deer with his father. It was good land.

It was the life Mackenzie and the other whites expected of him that awoke the violent storm within his head. Questions, as many as there were raindrops when the thunder rolled and the lightning seared the sky, bombarded his mind. He had attempted to speak with his wives, but the ways of women bore no fruit for a man. Their worries were of the lodge and children. They could not be expected to give council on all the puzzles that packed inside his skull.

Who was there among all the People who might council him? His mind raced through the names of the great Nermernuh warriors from all the bands that now resided on the reservation. In the two weeks, as the whites measured the passage of time, he had sought out those he had once ridden beside. Although their time here was greater than his own, their thoughts were as confused as his own; they held no answers. They lived within their tipis and filled their bellies with the white man's beef. Beyond that, they had no life.

Quanah was not yet ready to become like some ancient gray hair who sat outside his lodge watching the days slip by before his eyes. Nor was he willing to become a "good Injun" like those braves he had seen around Fort Sill who scurried about like slaves to perform every demeaning task the soldiers demanded of them. To be certain, these braves received payment for all they did, but the ones they labored for despised them and saw them as creatures no better than the ants that crawled across the sands.

For one who had forsaken the old ways of his people to walk the white man's road, there was no one to turn to for council. Even the spirits of his father and uncle could not guide him. What did Peta Nocona and Cona Cawb-vey know of living within the confines of the reservation? Like their son, the freedom of the rolling plains had been theirs.

He told himself that the blood of the whites as well as that of the Nermernuh flowed in his veins. His lineage offered little comfort. His mother had never taught him white ways or even spoken of her people, except to make certain he understood that he carried a white man's name.

Had his pouch still contained a cactus button, he would have found a place at the center of the field that opened before the oaks and let the peyote awake his spiritual eyes so that they might gaze upon the future. His source for the powerful cactus lay in the distant mountains of New Mexico. No longer could he ride westward to gather fresh supplies of peyote from the Mescalero Apaches.

Quanah closed his eyes. Was this all he could expect from the reservation? Had he severed himself from the life he had known only to drift on the winds like some dried blade of grass?

No. His head moved from side to side in denial.

He could not accept that fate for himself or the Nermernuh. Life had thrown rock upon rock beneath his feet, and he had trod across each of the sharp stones to rise as a leader of the People. All that came before were merely trials for this moment; life had tested him as t¹   aves of a village test a young boy as the time of manhood .   ɔaches. Every moment of his life had been nothing more than a wetted rock honing him. Like a carefully shaped arrowhead, he had been molded to lead his people, to set their feet on a path that would allow them to prosper in a world that seemed wretched from its very roots.

"My husband!" Weckeah's fingers grasped his shoulder, her nails biting into his flesh. "Soldiers! Soldiers come!"

The soft evening light could not hide the panic that twisted her face, nor the fear that tightened her voice. Quanah reacted as he had throughout his life. He pivoted and in long, quick strides shot for the tipi and the rifle that stood beside the entrance.

He covered half the ground to the lodge before he skidded to a halt. No rifle waited inside the tipi; he had surrendered rifle and pistol to the soldiers upon his arrival at Fort Sill. He blinked. This was not the high plains, this was the reservation. If soldiers came, it was not to raid.

"Coffee." Quanah turned back to Weckeah and directed her back to the campfire with a wave of his hand. "Make coffee. If the soldiers come, it is to visit. We must greet them as welcomed guests to our lodge."

Confident though his words were, Quanah felt far from certain when he faced the three riders who reined their mounts at a brisk pace across the grassy field. He had heard of the soldiers who visited the tipis of those they suspected of stealing or concealing whiskey within their lodges.

"Quanah!" Colonel Mackenzie's voice called in a greeting as the officer spurred his horse into an easy lope.

The brave's doubts doubled. Was there trouble back at the fort? Had those who followed him to the reservation forgotten their promise of peace and fought with the soldiers? Did Mackenzie now come to carry him to the icehouse prison?

Quanah buried his doubts and raised a hand in greeting. "Ay, Mackenzie. Drink coffee among friends."

"Coffee would be welcome after the ride," the officer answered, and Wild Horse, who had ridden unnoticed behind the three soldiers, translated while the Mackenzie dismounted.

"Sit beside my fire and rest yourself," Quanah offered, signaling Weckeah to gather cups for the soldiers and Coby.

Mackenzie shook his head. "I'm afraid there isn't time for polite amenities. Please apologize to your family for me. But a mail sack came into the fort after you had left today. A letter came that I thought you should see."

Quanah hastened his wife to him with cups of steaming coffee, which she gave to their guests while her husband listened to his fellow Nermernuh give voice to the colonel's words in their own tongue.

Mackenzie handed Quanah a folded piece of paper when Coby finished. "I know you can't read the words on this paper, but I thought you might want to have this."

Quanah unfolded the paper. He frowned in puzzlement when he saw the dark symbols scratched upon it. "What does this mean?"

"It's an answer to my inquiry about your mother and sister," Mackenzie replied. "It seems your desire to locate your mother and the fact that she was white has stirred up a lot of interest in you down in Texas. The folks there seem to view you as one of their own. A lot of people wrote into the Dallas newspapers that printed my letter—"

"My mother?" Quanah's head snapped up, his gaze locking to the colonel's eyes. "Have you found my mother and sister?"

Mackenzie drew a deep breath. "I'm afraid so, Quanah. Both of them have passed on. The letter is sketchy, but it tells how your sister fell sick and ..."

The officer's voice transformed to a meaningless buzz like that of an annoying insect in Quanah's ears. *Dead!* His mother and sister were dead! Agony as great as any he had ever felt ripped at his heart and gut like the talons of a mountain lion. All the years he had sought news of them, all the hope held had been for naught. His mother and sister were dead!

"I'm sorry to be the one to bring you such bad news, but I thought you'd want to know," Mackenzie said. "You have my condolences in this time of sorrow."

Quanah nodded, unable to speak, afraid the scream that grew within his throat would burst forth.

"I don't wish to intrude at a time like this." The officer motioned his men back to their mounts. "If there is anything that I can do, please let me know."

Again all the brave could do was tilt his head while he watched Wild Horse and the soldiers ride back in the direction they had come.

"My husband?" Weckeah asked. "What is it the soldiers wanted?"

He did not answer. Instead he walked out into the shadows of the night toward the center of the field. As the last glow of twilight faded from the sky, a lone voice lifted in a song of mourning that carried into the nearby mountains.

CHAPTER TWENTY

Quanah raised an arm high to halt the ten armed braves who rode with him. Speaking with his hands rather than voice, he ordered the men to sniff the hot Texas air.

"Fire!" the brave No Saddle signed back when he inhaled.

Quanah nodded. The bite of burning wood carried on the southwest wind filled his own nostrils.

To the Nermernuh leader's left Speaks Softly's hands added "Cedar" to indicate he recognized the distinctive odor. The brave then questioned, "Kiowas? The ones we seek?"

Quanah's sweat-glistening bare shoulders shrugged while his hands spoke, "Maybe. Maybe whites. Be careful. No trouble."

Standing in the rope stirrups, Quanah scanned the sandy terrain that stretched before the hunting party. Stunted mesquite trees and creosote bushes with their needlelike briers dotted the land. In the distance, perhaps two miles to the south, he sighted a dark green patch of vegetation that ran for miles toward the southeast. He pointed to the cedar brake then used his hands to indicate, "The Pecos River."

The nods that answered him spoke of agreement. The prey they had sought for nearly six weeks was somewhere ahead along the banks of the narrow river. Nor was it four-legged game the party hunted, but renegade Kiowas who had escaped from Fort Sill with twenty-one army horses.

During the long days that had stretched into a month and half, Quanah had followed the Kiowas' broken trail deep into Texas. Since the Nermernuh had surrendered at Fort Sill, it had become doubly dangerous for any of the People to be in the land of the *Tejan*—

Quanah caught himself and corrected his mental words— *Texans.* If he were to live with the whites, he had to speak their language, although the sounds of their words still left his tongue tangled in knots. He told himself that three months among the whites was not enough time, and with practice he would conquer the new language. Yet, in his heart he doubted he would ever master the white man's English. Others among the Kwerhar-rehnuh who had been on the reservation less time than he already spoke with ease among the soldiers.

Again, Quanah caught himself. *Tejanos* or Texans did not matter. What did was the fact that the Texas lawmakers had made it illegal for any man of Indian blood to hunt within the confines of their lands. Should a rancher or cowhand discover them this deep within Texas, they would be mistaken for a party searching for meat to fill stew pots. That would mean a fight. Quanah had no wish to confront the whites again; he had given his promise to walk the white man's road.

With another sign to emphasize the need of caution, the Kwerhar-rehnuh leader motioned his braves to spread out in a long line and slowly move forward. The Kiowas did not expect to be found this far into the land of the Texans, or they would have never risked a fire. Surprise was on his side, Quanah realized. Surprise was always a welcomed ally.

A series of metallic clicks sounded among the braves as each cocked the repeating rifles Colonel Mackenzie had issued them before leaving Fort Sill. Moccasined heels tapped ponies' sides to edge mounts forward in a steady walk.

Quanah's heart pounded. He wanted no fight, but feared the renegades would not surrender without bloodshed. If there would be blood this day, the brave-turned-manhunter offered a silent prayer to Father Sun overhead that it would be Kiowa blood that flowed and not that of his men.

To return the renegades and their stolen horses was an important task. Although there were those who rode with him simply to be free of the reservation once again, for Quanah this duty represented the first act of open trust Mackenzie and the Indian agent James Haworth had extended to the Kwerhar-rehnuh.

Such responsibility could not be taken lightly. After all, Haworth had refused to recognize the Kwerhar-rehnuh as a separate band of the People when they surrendered at Fort Sill and had placed them under authority of the Naconi leader Horse Back, whom Quanah had never heard of before coming to the reservation. It rubbed the Kwerhar-rehnuh the wrong way to be placed under the leadership of a "chief" they did not know. For Quanah, a proven leader among his people, the agent's action had been like a slap in the face that stung the pride rather than the cheek.

A quarter of a mile from the river, Quanah once more halted his men. Tilting his head to a side he listened. The wind carried voices—Kiowa voices. From the loudness of their tones, it was easy to read that the renegades felt safe beneath the blazing August sun.

"The ones we seek," Quanah again used his hands to speak to the braves.

He recalled the river at this point. The ground dropped down ten feet of steep bank to the river's bed. A narrow shelf of limestone lined each side of the Pecos. The Kiowas could be camped on either side; by the time he and the others knew exactly where the renegades made the fire, they would ride in plain sight of those they followed.

Quanah scanned the terrain up and down the river. He could split his men, sending one group southward and riding north with the other. Together the two groups could then ride down on the Kiowas from both directions. He pushed away the plan. Ten braves were too little a number to divide. It would take a show of force to convince the Kiowas to surrender—that required all his men appearing suddenly out of nowhere.

"Follow me." Quanah's hands spoke. "Do not fire until my rifle speaks."

In a tactic uncharacteristic of the Kwerhar-rehnuh, Quanah slammed his heels into the dapple gray's flanks. In a full charge, he rode straight toward the river without a war cry tearing from his throat. The ten behind him drove their mounts at his heels without a sound passing their own lips.

As quietly as they rode, it was not enough. The instant Quanah's gaze alighted on the twenty Kiowa camped on the southern side of the river, a brave below sighted the charging Kwerhar-rehnuh. Before he raised a warning cry, the Kiowa jerked a stolen carbine to his shoulder and fired.

The shot went high, but it was all that was needed to bring the remaining renegades to their feet, swinging weapons on the charging riders.

Quanah threw himself low to the neck of his horse as the Kiowas opened up with a thundering volley that sent buzzing hornets of lead flying through the air. The startled cry of a horse rived through the echoing reports of carbines. Speak Softly's mount reared, crimson flowing from its broad chest, and spilled its rider atop a creosote bush.

Rather than pulling back the bolts of their carbines and shoving fresh cartridges into chambers, the Kiowas ran for the herd of horses a hundred strides from where they had sat about their campfire.

"The horses!" Quanah shouted while he lifted his rifle. "Don't let them reach the horses!"

Forefinger around trigger, Quanah squeezed off a shot meant to bring down the runner heading the column of panicked Kiowas. Weapons fired from the back of a bounding horse rarely found their mark. This shot was no exception. Hot lead bit into the limestone ten feet ahead of the man and ricocheted off the white rock with an angry whine.

Nor did the marksmanship of the braves with him prove to be more accurate. Nine rifles barked and nine bullets slammed harmlessly into the rock, sending a shower of limestone into the air.

The barrage, however, was enough to make the Kiowas abruptly skid to a halt and swing about. No longer did they run toward their stolen horses, but scrambled up the banks of the river to disappear into the dense cedar brake.

"Sonofabitch," a curse learned from the fort's soldiers broke from Quanah's lips as he threw up a hand to signal another halt.

Since the white men first began to give chase to Nermernuh raiders, the People had used the impenetrable density of cedar brakes to escape their pursuers. Quanah knew there was no way he would ever drive the Kiowas from the minor forest of stunted juniper trees. Even with a party five times the size of the one he led, it would be senseless to follow the renegades into the brake. Like it or not, the men had escaped him. He would have to be satisfied with returning the horses to Mackenzie and Haworth. It was not what he wanted, but it would have to be.

"Move the horses across the river and a mile to the north." He called out of the names of the braves assigned the task. "We'll check the camp for supplies and ammunition."

"Aayyiiee!" A cry of victory rolled around the river.

Quanah's head jerked to the right. There by the Kiowas' fire stood Speaks Softly, his body dripping water from a swim across the Pecos. "I have caught one of them, Quanah! This one did not get away!"

The brave threw back his head, which sent a spray of water flying from his long black mane. Laughter rolled from his belly when he lifted a bundle of kicking legs and swinging arms from the ground.

Quanah's laughter and that of the other braves echoed Speaks Softly's mirth. The captured Kiowa was a boy—a mere boy!

"Mackenzie and his soldiers will have their hands full when they try to deal with this one," Speaks Softly shouted as he dodged a small, balled fist meant to smash his nose.

"That they will, my friend, as it seems you have," Quanah answered as he reined the gray into the water to collect the unexpected captive. Reaching the campfire, he held a hand out to the boy. "I am called Quanah Parker. No one here will hurt you. That I promise."

Quanah saw recognition flicker on the young face. The boy then reached out and clasped his hand. Quanah swung him high and deposited the boy behind him on the gray. "Hold tight, boy. We have a long ride back to Fort Sill."

• • •

"You wish to adopt the boy, this Herman Lehman?" Surprise rounded Colonel Mackenzie's eyes.

"The boy is small for his age, but he will make a good son in a lodge that has only daughters and wives. It is not good for a brave to be surrounded by only women," Quanah answered. During the two-week ride back to Sill, he had learned that Herman was in fact thirteen years old and had been taken captive by the Kiowas in 1870. "It would not be a good thing to return the boy to the Kiowas. Have they not shown themselves to be bad, using a boy to help steal soldiers' horses? I will raise him as a son and see that his feet are placed on the white man's road—if Mackenzie and Haworth will allow it."

James Haworth leaned back in his chair with a wink and a grin at the army officer who sat beside the desk within his office. "I think he speaks sense, Colonel. The boy should not be returned to the Kiowas."

Mackenzie pursed his lips and stared at Quanah, finally acquiescing to the Comanche's request with a nod. "You may take him into your lodge, but I will also write letters to see if I can locate his real family. Is that understood?"

"I understand." Quanah felt a kinship to the boy; both of them had their feet planted in both the white and the red man's worlds. "It is right to try and find his mother and father. I know what it is like to lose both."

Again, Mackenzie nodded. "I'm sorry to learn the renegades you were after got away, but you did well in returning all the horses to the fort. And, of course, returning the boy."

Quanah's gaze shifted between the officer and the reservation's agent. He tried to shape the English words he knew. "It saddened my heart that I did not capture the Kiowas. Some of my men might have died in that brake. It was better to return to the fort."

He gave voice to only half of what he held in his heart. Though he would have brought the renegades back had the opportunity presented itself, a part of the Nermernuh within him was glad the Kiowas had managed to flee. They were afoot amid the lands of the hostile Texans, but they were free. They had not had to surrender their rifles as Quanah had done when he returned to Fort Sill.

"As far as I'm concerned, thou did a fine job," Haworth said. "I am pleased with the way thee and thy braves handled the situation. So much so I have another task—if thou are willing to give it a try?"

Quanah turned to the man. He walked on shifting sands. What he said could determine how the white leaders saw him. He wanted their trust, but he would not be a "good Injun."

"Dost thou know what a 'beef chief' is?" Haworth asked.

While the term "chief" was not one used by the Nermernuh, Quanah had come to realize it was a badge of authority to the whites. It meant a man called chief was a leader. "It is one who distributes rations to his people."

Haworth tilted his head in affirmation. "While thou were gone, I have reorganized the division of Indians on this reservation. There are too many people for the existing beef chiefs to handle. I have created a new division that will encompass all those who came to Sill with thee. The job of beef chief is open, if thou want it."

Like a bird on wing, Quanah's heart soared. This was more than he had expected. Once again he would lead the Nermernuh band that had followed him on the plains. No longer would they—or he—answer to the wishes of Horse Back.

"It will be good to serve Mackenzie and Haworth in this manner. My feet are firmly on the white man's road," Quanah accepted the position offered him. "May I return to my family now? It has been two months since I slept within my lodge."

Mackenzie cleared his throat and shot a glance at Haworth. The agent leaned forward in his chair and shuffled through a stack of papers before looking up at the new beef chief who stood before his desk. "Quanah, there is another matter that must be addressed—that is of the situation in thy lodge."

"My lodge has no problems," Quanah replied, uncertain what the agent meant.

"It's the matter of thy wives. Thou has two of them," Haworth continued. "As thou knows, a white man takes only one wife. There are many who consider it bad for a man to have more than one wife among the whites."

"It is not so among the People," Quanah answered simply.

"Still, I want thee to consider having but one wife," Haworth said. "Will thou do that?"

"I will consider it."

Quanah did not lie. He considered it for the ten-mile ride to where his tipi stood beneath the oak trees. When Weckeah and Cho-ny and his daughters ran from the lodge to greet him and his new son, he knew the white men were wrong to have but one wife.

CHAPTER
TWENTY-ONE

Quanah hugged the buffalo robe tightly about his chest to hold back the February wind when he reined the dapple gray to a halt atop a gentle rise. Below, a wagon rolled westward toward the broad plains of the Llano Estacado.

A pleased smile touched the brave's lips as a hand within the robe rested on a leather pouch with seams strained from the peyote buttons stuffed within. The traders, as the New Mexicans called themselves rather than Comancheros, had not forgotten the vision-inducing cactus that were so important to him. Although he lacked the buffalo robes he once traded for the peyote, the men seemed pleased to accept a government-issued shovel and hoe instead of the hides.

The trade had been good. What need did he have of the two hoes and shovels the Quaker Haworth had given to him? For that matter what use did he have for the remaining hoe and shovel that leaned against an oak back at his lodge? He was no farmer who dug in the dirt to plant corn and beans. He was Nermernuh—a hunter.

Like the majority of the People, he used the farming implements and tools Haworth issued either to sell to whites near the fort or to trade with the New Mexicans who found their way to the reservation. It was the best use for the tools; this land was not meant for farming.

There were those among the bands who attempted to raise the crops Haworth desired. They dug into the earth and planted their seeds. But the rain needed for corn and beans never came. The young sprouts that pushed from the ground burned to a dry brown beneath an unyielding summer sun.

The crops that did mature belonged to those who planted along the streams and creeks. Despite the high plants that rose and flourished, the harvest had been no more than a few pitiful ears of corn or a handful or two of beans. Like plants, insects preferred moisture, which creeks and streams offered. The crops raised by the would-be farmers provided a bountiful feast for those six-legged invaders throughout the summer.

The grasslands were meant for grazing. Haworth seemed unable to grasp that simple fact, Quanah reflected. Colonel Mackenzie, however, did appear to understand, at least in part. Recognizing the dream of lush green Indian farms spreading throughout the reservation was doomed, he had personally arranged for the purchase of livestock to be distributed among the bands on the Comanche and Kiowa Reservation.

Quanah shook his head. Well-meaning as was the officer's gesture, he had no greater understanding of the People than did Haworth. Mackenzie purchased thirty-five hundred sheep to initiate his program to transform Indians into stockmen. What the colonel failed to recognize was the Comanche and Kiowa hatred of sheep. The creatures were smelly, and their meat lay foul on the tongue.

As with Haworth's beans and corn, there were those of the Kwerhar-rehnuh who attempted to tend their sheep. Because of the Nermernuh distaste for mutton, they had no market for the slaughtered animals. And the wool they sheared was too little to sell to the whites. Mackenzie's sheep now ran wild in the fields, easy targets for coyotes and wolves. Few would live to see the green grass of spring, Quanah realized.

Although his band had pledged to walk the white man's road, the whites opened no avenue for that journey. If a path was to be found, Quanah pondered, the red man would have to find it on his own. It was that way that the brave sought.

Quanah's hand eased from the pouch of peyote. His meeting with the traders had brought more than cactus buttons from

New Mexico. There was word of a small buffalo herd wintering
north of the reservation. Such news set his heart pounding. He
must find a way to fill the stew pots of his people with rich buffalo meat.

Swinging the gray's head to the southeast, he nudged the
horse forward with his heels and immediately pulled the animal
to a dead stop. Less than ten strides ahead of the brave sat a jackrabbit behind a tuft of winter-brown grass.

Slowly, Quanah edged back his buffalo robe and lifted bow
and quiver that had been hidden behind him beneath the hide.
He nocked an arrow, took aim, and released a bowstring drawn
tight. Straight and true the missile flew. The long-eared rabbit
gave a startled leap when the shaft drove into its body then
flopped to the ground, dead.

The flesh of a rabbit is not buffalo meat, Quanah thought when
he dismounted to claim the unexpected prize. But the jackrabbit
would assure meat for his family this night.

The United States government allotted each Comanche and
Kiowa on the reservation one and a half pounds of beef a day to
be cooked over their lodge fires. Once a week this beef was ra-
tioned to the members of Haworth's "beef bands." To facilitate
distribution of the meat, Haworth selected "chiefs" for these
bands. To fulfill his duties as beef chief of his band, Quanah and
his family rode the long ten miles from their lodge to Fort Sill.

Nor were they alone on the road to the soldier's fort.

The brave's gaze surveyed the band that traveled toward their
weekly dole of meat. The pride once so clear in these familiar
faces no longer ruled their features. Instead he saw a solemn res-
ignation to a life that was little better than imprisonment. He
had led his people to the reservation so that they might live. This
was not life, but a slow death that would take years before demanding its final toll.

Although the braves of his band had been allowed to keep
one pony, their wives and children had not. For some of the
band the journey to the fort was twenty miles—a long walk for
moccasins that grew thin without fresh buffalo hides to replace
them.

Quanah pursed his lips. Even if Haworth's farming or
Mackenzie's sheep had been accepted by the Kwerhar-rehnuh,

both methods meant to provide Nermernuh independence would have failed. For most of the band the weekly trek to Fort Sill consumed three full days—a day's journey to the fort, a day collecting the beef, and a day to return to faraway lodges. Three days out of each week devoted to meat rationing left little time to care for crops or stock.

Those three days did assure whites that the bands on the reservation remained dependent on the United States government, Quanah realized. Despite what the whites declared, they did not want their red-skinned wards to gain new lives too quickly. They were too frightened the People would grow strong and ride the road of war again.

Reaching the fort, Quanah left his wives with the task of raising their tipi while he walked among the campfires of his band. He listened to the words of both men and women. Since winter had descended like an icy wolf pack running from the north, they all spoke the same thing—their bellies growled. Most found their stew pots empty three days before each rationing day.

"You have the ears of the agent Haworth and the soldier Mackenzie," Forty Buffalo spoke as the men gathered around a large blaze when darkness fell over the fort. "Speak to them for us again. It was the promise of food for our children that swayed us to come to the reservation. Are we to starve here after giving up our old ways as the white man wished?"

"I will not allow that. That I promise. Tomorrow, I will talk with Mackenzie and Haworth once again." Quanah wanted to tell his friends of the buffalo to the north, but he held his tongue. Should they learn of the meat so nearby, many would turn renegade and ride from the reservation. Then he and the others whom Mackenzie trusted would have to ride after them and return them to the fort as prisoners. "When the morning sun comes, I will talk with Mackenzie and Haworth."

Quanah then fell silent, his mind returning to the words he had pondered throughout the day.

The Indian agent and army colonel followed Quanah from the fort to a field where the Nermernuh slaughtered the steers the soldiers herded to them. They watched as three braves deftly opened the belly of one of the animals and began to dress it.

"I do not lie." Quanah pointed to the scrawny steer. "The

winter grass is not enough to keep meat on the cows. See—what meat there is must be scraped from the bone. One cow doesn't give enough meat to feed a child for a week. How can a brave and his family be expected to live on so little meat?"

While the white men who now ruled the lives of the People moved from steer to steer to confirm the lack of meat each steer provided, Quanah thought of the braves who secretly made bows and shaped arrows within their lodges. Although such weapons were disdained by the whites, they did offer a man a chance at bringing down the few deer and antelope that still wandered the reservation.

Or jackrabbits, Quanah considered the game he had brought to his family two days ago.

When agent and colonel had seen enough, Haworth waved them back to an office built adjacent to the fort. Once inside a room warmed by a metal stove, the agent turned to his self-named beef chief. "Thou must realize that I have written letter upon letter to my superiors in Leavenworth. They can promise nothing. The Congress will not authorize more funds for additional supplies. There are more Indians on this reservation this year than ever before, but the funding remains the same."

Quanah again listened, as he had for week upon week, while Haworth explained that the roadwagons which brought flour, sugar, bacon, coffee, and sugar from the railhead a hundred and sixty-five miles to the east had once again been delayed by snows and rains. The agent made no mention of the rocks often stuffed in the bags of flour or the lumps of coal contained in pork barrels instead of the full weight in foodstuffs the government had purchased to feed its wards.

When Haworth looked at Mackenzie, the officer shook his head. "My cupboard is all but bare. I've barely got enough supplies to feed my men. I can't give you any more."

Quanah knew Mackenzie had raided the army supplies on more than one occasion to feed the bands. Like the agent, he had written letters to those commanding him, requesting more supplies. He had received the same answers.

"I have arranged from my own funds to have a herd of four hundred beeves to be driven up from Texas and to be divided among the bands." Mackenzie's gaze moved to the Nermernuh brave. "I hope these will be used to start herds that belong to both Comanche and Kiowa, when they arrive in a month or so."

"Herds will not grow when the stomachs of children are empty." Quanah knew a large portion of the herd would find their way into his band's stew pots.

Mackenzie wearily nodded his head as a heavy sigh escaped his lips. "I was afraid of that. But it was all I could think of. There is nothing else I can do. Both Mr. Haworth's and my hands are tied."

This was the answer that Quanah expected. While he knew both men did fight a thing they called "bureaucracy" to provide more food, their efforts bore no fruits that could still hunger-cramped bellies.

"Allow the men of the People to feed their families in the way they have always fed them," Quanah answered, using the words he had chosen over a day and a night. "Once Mackenzie let braves ride from the reservation and hunt the buffalo. Allow the braves to do so now. Send your soldiers with them, but let them hunt."

"You know of the buffalo herd in the north?" A frown creased the officer's forehead when Quanah nodded. "Do all the men know?"

"Only a few. Did all know, they would not be here today," the brave replied. "Even those without ponies would be running on foot to find the herd."

Mackenzie found a chair and dropped heavily into it. "That is what I have feared."

Haworth's head turned to the colonel. "Two years ago thou allowed bands to ride from the reservation to hunt. Would there not be wisdom in letting Quanah and trusted braves do so now? The meat could be divided equally back here at the fort."

Mackenzie rubbed a hand over his face and then stared outside at the braves who used knife blades to whittle stringy meat from the carcasses of butchered steers.

"Braves of my band would be willing to ride with those of other bands, even the Kiowa and Kiowa-Apache," Quanah added.

Mackenzie drew another heavy breath and released it in a loud hiss. He relented with a nod. "Select three braves from your band, and I will tell the other beef chiefs to do the same. In two days, you'll ride north accompanied by three patrols of my soldiers. I will also have wagons ready to bring your kills back to the fort."

"One hunt will not be enough to fill our pots for all of the time of snow and ice." Having achieved his goal, Quanah pressed the moment.

"I know," Mackenzie said, obviously uncomfortable with his decision. "We will discuss further hunts when the need arises."

Quanah let the matter drop. He had pushed as far as was safe. "You are a good man, Mackenzie."

When the beef chief left the agent's office, it was to find Pecos and his friends Speaks Softly and Forty Buffalo and tell them of the hunt and the buffalo meat that would soon silence their families' growling stomachs. While an open path to bring his people fully onto the white man's road still evaded him, Quanah had found a way to keep the Kwerhar-rehnuh from starving to death their first winter on the reservation.

For today, that was enough, Quanah told himself. A hunt would lift the spirits of the People, give them hope. Tomorrow—

Quanah shoved aside thoughts of tomorrow. Today he had secured rich meat for his people. And that was good.

CHAPTER
TWENTY-TWO

"Boss, we got company comin'!"

John Teller looked up from a plate of beans and sow belly as a cowhand rode beside the chuck wagon and drew to a halt beside Charles Goodnight, who leaned against a wheel while he ate his own meal.

"Indians?" the prosperous Texas rancher asked his hand.

"They ain't buffalo gals come to keep us company to-night," the rider said. "Look to be Comanche. 'Bout ten of 'em ridin' in from the east."

"Better Comanche than Kiowa." Goodnight scanned the area to which the cowhand pointed.

Teller saw the riders. There was no way to mistake the ten braves for Kiowa; they were Comanche. "Better Comanche than Kiowa? What the hell do you mean?"

"This is your first trip up the Western Trail, John. There's still a few things you've got to learn," Goodnight answered his fellow rancher while he went back to his meal without another glance at the approaching braves. "The Comach are almost gentlemen when it comes to collecting their tolls. That is, compared to the Kiowa. Last summer about a dozen Kiowa bucks nearly beat one of my hands to death before I rode up and gave them a few head."

"Gave them a few head?" Teller blinked at the man in disbelief. Goodnight was known as a no-nonsense rancher throughout all of Texas. Yet, he stood there talking about giving away cattle to Indians—Comanches at that.

Teller stood and walked to a buckskin tied to a stunted mesquite a few feet from the chuck wagon. "I'll feel a damn site safer with a rifle to—"

"Let your rifle lay where it is," Goodnight said sternly. "You're a cattleman now, John. The days of Indian fighting are over. Let me handle this, and everything will go without a hitch. Trust me on this one, John. You didn't ask to drive your herd with mine because I didn't know what I was doing."

Teller slowly relented and shoved the rifle back into its saddle holster. Goodnight was right. He had joined his two hundred and fifty longhorns to the rancher's three thousand because he wanted to get them to Dodge City. Goodnight had proven his ability to take a herd to the Kansas railhead since Texans had first moved their cattle up the Chisholm Trail.

"That's Quanah Parker!" Teller's eyes went round when he recognized the warrior who rode at the head of the braves.

"Getting to be a bit of a celebrity, ain't he?" Goodnight grinned. "Saw in the paper last time I was down in Fort Worth where Sul Ross had sent him a daguerreotype when he wrote to Austin trying to get a picture of Cynthia Ann Parker."

Teller blinked in confusion again. His old Ranger captain was sending photographs to an Indian he would have gladly killed a few years ago?

The hollow sound of approaching hooves drew his attention to the Comanche riders who drew up a dozen strides from the chuck wagon.

"Ayeeee, it is my old friend Charlie Goodnight!" Quanah grinned at the rancher. "These eyes are glad to see you are still healthy."

Goodnight placed his plate aside and walked to the brave, offering him a hand. "You're glad to see me so I can increase the size of your herd. Hell, in a year or two, you'll be running more head than I do."

"Not for me." Quanah shook his head. "Have many mouths

to feed, and the buffalo are all gone. Cattle is the white man's way. All Nermernuh are on the white man's road."

Goodnight chuckled. "If you ask me, you Comanches are learning too good from the government boys. You'll be as big a bunch of thieves as them that's in Washington 'fore too long."

Quanah shook his head. "Not thieves. We have right and authority."

With that the beef chief reached inside the buckskin shirt he wore and pulled out a folded piece of paper. This he handed to the rancher. While Goodnight read the letter, Quanah's gaze moved to the left. "John Teller? Do you remember me? Do you now work for Charlie Goodnight?"

Surprised the Comanche recalled his face and name, Teller walked forward to shake the hand Quanah extended. "I'm running a little spread of my own south of the Red. Some of these cattle are mine."

"That is good." Quanah nodded. "A man should have something that belongs to him alone. We try to do the same here. It is the white man's way."

"Take a gander at this." Goodnight passed the letter to his fellow rancher. "Last year the Kiowa who jumped my hand ended up behind bars for cattle rustlin'. Now, Quanah here has this."

Teller scanned the letter. The words were plain and simple, and beneath them was scrawled the signature of James Haworth, agent for the Comanche and Kiowa Reservation. The letter gave Quanah Parker the right to demand cattle in payment for the passage of herds across Indian land. "This legal?"

"Don't make no nevermind whether it's legal or not. You don't see no courts or judges out here, do you?" Goodnight answered. He then motioned to two of his cowhands, who nursed cups of coffee while they studied the braves. "You boys saddle up and cut out twelve head for Quanah and his men."

"Only lame cows," Quanah added. "Those that will not live to see Dodge City. We do not want good cows that will make you money."

The two cowboys looked at their boss, who nodded. "You heard him. Pick cows too sore to make the rest of the drive. Throw in any dogie that looks in bad shape. I'd rather Quanah here added it to his herd than leave it for the buzzards on the trail."

"You are a good man, Charlie Goodnight." The Comanche

brave smiled at the rancher. "I will leave four braves with you to make certain no Kiowas bother you or your herd."

"Maybe not good, but smart enough to know some of these 'cows' are gonna end up among your herd whether I give 'em to you or not." Goodnight grinned widely and winked at Teller. "You and your boys like a cup of coffee while my men cut out the stock for you?"

"Coffee would be good." Quanah slipped from his gray and walked toward the pot that sat on the side of the campfire.

John Teller shook his head while he watched a man he would have once killed in the blink of an eye stir six spoonfuls of sugar into a tin cup of steaming coffee. Goodnight was right; he still had things to learn. The Comanches still raided Texas cattle herds, but now they did it with a piece of paper.

Teller smiled to himself. Maybe they were becoming civilized. What they did here was not that different from what bankers did every day with their legal papers.

Quanah and the braves released eleven head of cattle and five calves onto the common pasture shared by all the People. One cow and one calf had been left behind in a field near Quanah's lodge, along with forty other cows and five ponies.

"Two hundred cows," Speaks Softly said in a voice barely louder than a whisper beside his friend. "Soon we will have a herd as big as the Texans."

"We make certain our families have food."

Quanah's mind returned to the harsh winter that had passed but two months ago. Although Mackenzie allowed hunting parties to scour the prairies around the reservation for buffalo, no bison had been found. The colonel had sent out wagons laden with supplies to rescue the hunters before starvation robbed them of their lives. The humiliation of that moment still burned in the brave's breast.

"Where do you go from here?" Speaks Softly questioned when his old friend tugged the gray's head toward the north.

"I must talk with White Eagle and other chiefs this day," Quanah answered. "Haworth wished to move our agency to Anadarko. The new agent Hunt desires the same. We must consider how to stop this."

Speaks Softly pursed his lips and nodded. "I will visit your lodge tomorrow."

Quanah bid his friend farewell and moved the gray into a lope with a tap of his heels. The reservation forged strange alliances. The brave's mind moved to the council that waited near the Kiowa lands. White Eagle had once claimed to be Cheyenne and had been called Coyote Droppings when he united the nations in the attack against Adobe Walls. Today White Eagle swore to be Nermernuh and had risen to prominence on the reservation with the support of Agent Haworth.

It was with the former shaman's aid and that of the other beef chiefs that Quanah hoped to prevent the combination of the Comanche and Kiowa Reservation Agency with that of the Wichita Agency. The merger of the two would save money, the whites claimed. However, for Quanah and all on the reservation, it would move their agency headquarters from Fort Sill to the Washita River, fifty-five miles away.

There were other matters to be considered. Quanah tallied the problems in his mind. Despite two years on the reservation, many braves still slipped away to raid the white settlements that steadily pushed closer to the boundary of Indian lands. While Colonel J.W. Davidson, Fort Sill's new commander, set his troops after these renegades, rustlers from Texas brazenly rode north of the Red River to steal the ponies and the cows of the Nermernuh.

And there are the ranchers. Quanah's thoughts returned to the foremost problem that had occupied his mind throughout the day. Of all the vast lands once once ridden by Nermernuh and Kiowa, the whites had given the bands but three million acres for their reservation. Even this appeared to be too much for the cattlemen in Texas.

The western portion of the reservation represented lush pastures the white government persuaded the bands from occupying. To Quanah the reasons for this were as plain as the nose on his face. Texas ranchers wished to use these rich grasslands.

Last summer five massive herds had been driven northward along the West Trail on their way to Dodge City. The Texan ranchers allowed each of the herds to linger on the reservation pastures to fatten their stock before continuing toward market. No fee was levied against the ranchers; thus, Quanah convinced

Haworth the ranchers should provide "gifts" to those whose lands they crossed.

Worse were the ranchers who blatantly allowed their cattle to cross the Red River and graze on Indian grass as though they owned the land. That the white man's law prohibited this meant nothing to them, nor did it appear to have meaning to the army which refused to drive the cattle back below the river. Braves who raided the herds at night, however, were caught and punished.

Quanah shook his head. White men weighted the scales against those with red skin as they did against the blacks who served in their army. While the brave had been unable to convince Mackenzie that men who took steers to feed their families were not criminals, he had persuaded the officer to imprison such braves at Fort Sill rather than send them far from their families in Leavenworth, Kansas. Not even Haworth's favorite White Eagle had been able to accomplish that.

Have you ever thought about leasing these pastures?

Charles Goodnight's question that morning rolled back into Quanah's mind. He knew others of the chiefs had been approached by ranchers, but never had one broached the matter with him. Quanah had waved off the question, telling the Texan that the ranchers had all the land and grass they needed, that these lands belonged to the Nermernuh and Kiowa; it was all that was left to them. Goodnight acceded for the moment, but said he would talk with Quanah and the others about it again.

Quanah smiled. For once the chiefs moved ahead of the whites. They had already counciled and stood firm against the ranchers using the pastures, even if they paid to do so. Now they must convince the soldiers to drive the unwanted cows away.

Beef chief, Quanah mentally hefted the title the Quaker Haworth had bestowed upon him. To the agent it had meant a trustworthy brave to aid him in the weekly distribution of beef among Haworth's self-delineated bands of Indians residing on the reservation.

For Quanah the title had come to mean so much more. Foremost, it meant feeding his people by whatever means he could and still walk the white man's way. It also opened opportunities to aid his people Haworth had never considered.

Wearing the title beef chief, Quanah openly moved through the reservation to council with the other chiefs, as well as with the braves who had ridden in his band. Although the People no longer warred against the whites, at Quanah's urging they once again wore knives on their belts and carried bows and quivers filled with arrows. Colonel Davidson viewed this as open defiance of his authority, but did nothing to stop it. To the Nermernuh the weapons were pride regained.

The white man used words and laws to maneuver against each other, so Quanah learned the white way. With each minor victory, his influence grew. Once the People spread word of the powerful medicine that surrounded a young warrior in battle; now they spoke of his ability to aid the People when they were in need.

Quanah dismissed the few who labeled him a white man's Indian; he worked with the whites, and in return increased the power of the People. Had not the new agent Hunt called him the most influential chief among all the Comanche and Kiowa? Peta Nocona and Cona Cawb-vey would have understood; new ways were needed to lead the People onto their new road.

For those who accused him of using his power to garner cattle and horses for himself and friends, he turned a deaf ear. Had it not always been the Nermernuh way, for the one who led to select from bounties before the others of the band? And did he not freely share with those in need who came to his lodge as had always been his manner?

Brave or squaw who visited him with empty bellies were fed and given food for their families. To those who walked, he saw that they rode away on the back of a pony. Did those who criticized him not see the constantly changing tipis of those with need that stood beside his own lodge? Was that not proof of how he served the People?

Quanah allowed the gray to drop to a steady walk. Such bickering had never been the way while the People dwelled on the open plains. Then a brave would take his family and move to another band should he feel it better suited his needs. On the reservation, a brave was denied that, so he complained like an ancient one with soreness in his joints—even when there was no truth in his complaints.

"Quanah! Quanah!" His name carried on the south wind.

Tugging on the gray's rein, he shifted his weight in the saddle and glanced over a shoulder. Speaks Softly drove his pony in a full run down the gentle slope of a rolling hill.

"White horse thieves!" the brave called when he halted beside the beef chief. "Yellow Bear's ponies have been stolen as have Bareback's and those of five other braves. Yellow Bear asks for you to come to his lodge."

Quanah's eyes darted toward the north and the council that waited with White Eagle and the others. As important as the words that would be spoken there were, he could not abandon the needs of his father-in-law and friends. "Will you ride to White Eagle and tell him I will come when I can?"

Speaks Softly frowned. "I would ride with you as I always have."

"I need you to ride *for* me," Quanah answered. "If needed, speak to the other chiefs. You know my words and my feelings."

The brave's chest swelled. "I will ride for you. And I will speak—only if what is said is different from what you believe."

"You are a good friend." Quanah reached out and squeezed Speaks Softly's shoulder. "Ride swiftly, but not too swiftly. White Eagle must not be made to believe that Quanah Parker comes running whenever he calls."

Speaks Softly grinned widely, then slammed his heels into his pony's flanks. While the brave rode northward, the beef chief of the Kwerhar-rehnuh reined the gray about and drove the animal toward Yellow Bear's lodge.

"You judged the whites right." Yellow Bear leaned close to whisper in his son-in-law's ear. "They intend to cross the river here as you said they would."

Quanah glanced at the six men hidden among the black willows and underbrush that lined the banks of the Red River to each side of the narrow path leading to the water. A month ago, he had discovered the route while numbering the cattle that grazed on the western portion of the reservation. The grass was as worn as a frequented deer path, a testimony to the number of hooves that had passed over it as rustlers drove Nermernuh horses and cattle into Texas.

Today, the four riders who casually herded twenty-one stolen ponies toward the river would find a surprise waiting for them.

In sign language Quanah repeated his earlier command that the white thieves were not to be killed but taken captive. He then watched each of the braves acknowledge his unspoken words.

With an approving tilt of his head, his attention returned to the four riders. Heart a-pound in his chest, racing as it had when he had led war parties across the plain, he waited patiently, letting the men in their wide-brimmed hats draw closer and closer.

Only when the first two riders passed his position did he release the war cry that ripped from deep in his chest and spring from behind the trunk of a drooping-limbed willow.

He saw the two forward riders' hands drop for the pistols holstered on their waists. In the next instant, the weapons were totally forgotten as six warriors threw themselves from the bushes and charged with blood-freezing yowls tearing from their throats.

The fight he expected did not come. Startled by the Nermernuh attack, the horses went wild. The riders at the lead found themselves abruptly unseated when their mounts reared high. Both men spilled into the deep red clay mud of the river's bank.

Quanah turned and found that the two whites who rode behind the stolen horses fared no better. His braves' cries sent the ponies wheeling about and charging straight into the men who sought to steal them. Both thieves tumbled from heavy leather saddles when their mounts suddenly wheeled about to escape the ponies' stampede.

"Yellow Bear, Forty Buffalo!" Quanah pointed to the fallen thieves. "Take them!"

When he spun around to the first riders, he found the two men had managed to scramble into the water and swim to the safety of the opposite bank. Their horses, however, now were in Nermernuh hands.

A loud groan returned the beef chief's attention to the two thieves Yellow Bear and Forty Buffalo had apprehended. The Texan the older brave wrenched to his feet clutched his nose in an attempt to stem the blood that flowed from both nostrils. Though he said nothing, Quanah realized Yellow Bear had administered a touch of his own justice to the horse thief. Whether the brave had used foot or fist, Quanah did not know.

"Will we ride the other two down?" a brave who brought the parties' mounts from their hiding place asked. "They can not get far afoot."

As much as he wanted the two thieves who climbed from the water on the southern bank, Quanah shook his head. Should the army hear even a hint of the possibility he had led braves into

Texas to track white men, all they did this day would be twisted about and turned against him and the braves with him. "We will gather the ponies and ride to Fort Sill. It is Colonel Davidson's job to punish these two."

In spite of grunting disapproval, the braves mounted their ponies and started after the scattered horses. Quanah and Yellow Bear also took to the backs of their horses, but instead of herding horses, they herded two thieves, now afoot, toward the distant buildings of Fort Sill.

Disapproval shadowed Colonel Davidson's face as he ordered two guards to take the horse thieves to the stockade. He drew a long breath before looking at Quanah and Yellow Bear. "Wish you had come to me before taking the law into your own hands. I'm certain to hear about this from some official down in Texas."

Unlike Mackenzie, who had traveled west to Apache lands, Davidson was what the soldiers called "by-the-book army." If he held any respect for the Nermernuh as had Mackenzie, he did not show it. Quanah knew the new colonel had also called him a threat to army authority, when the agent Hunt had once commented that the Kwerhar-rehnuh beef chief was the most progressive of the Comanches on the reservation.

Rather than say that he had come to Davidson on several occasions to report the thefts of horses and cattle and nothing had been done, Quanah replied, "There was not time. The horse thieves would have crossed the river before I could have ridden here."

"There's still going to be a stir when the Texans learn Indians are riding down white men." Disgust twisted the colonel's mouth.

"They were thieves. We only did what your soldiers would have done."

"Just the same, it's a good thing I've got a prison wagon scheduled for Fort Smith in the morning," Davidson answered. "I'll put those two in with the four Kiowas scheduled to pay a visit to Fort Smith—"

Quanah reminded himself to speak with Hunt again soon. The Kiowa braves the officer spoke of had done nothing against white men, but had fought among themselves. To determine their crimes should not be left to the white judge in faraway Arkansas, but should be placed in the hands of a judge chosen from the bands on the reservation. The transgressions of red men should be judged by red men.

"—Getting those two out of here might defuse the situation," Davidson continued. "But other than give them a long ride to think about what they did, the trip to Fort Smith won't make a difference to them or the other Texans who ride up here."

Apparently the officer noticed the puzzled expression that worked across Quanah's face because he gave a disgusted shake of his head. "You don't understand, do you?"

"They are thieves," Quanah replied. "I understand that well enough. They stole horses. Men are hanged for that."

"They weren't stealing, not under the law," Davidson said curtly. "It isn't against the law to take an Indian's horse or the cattle he claims to own. The law was put on the books when there was war between our people, and it's never been changed. Legally, those two men out there, no matter how many horses they were riding away with, weren't doing anything wrong. Do you understand now?"

Quanah stiffened at the pronouncement. He then turned and walked from the colonel's office without a word. He understood—understood more than Davidson could ever understand. There would be no justice for men with red skin until they sat in courts of their own. One day, he vowed, he would bring such courts to the People.

CHAPTER
TWENTY-THREE

"She is called A-er-wuth-takum." Quanah stood beside a blazing fire hung with a full side of beef that lazily rotated on a spit. "For my white friends, her name means She Fell With A Wound. Though she was once married, her husband fell sick with the winter snows and died of a fever. She is now the wife of Quanah Parker. Her children are my children."

Together, man and woman, husband and wife, slowly turned so that all might see them. As with all marriages among the Nermernuh, there the ceremony ended. Quanah now shared his lodge with three wives and seven children.

For one who now walked the white man's road, the old way of taking a wife was not enough. Quanah waved an arm to three white men who stood beside an oak trunk, and immediately the strands of fiddle, banjo, and guitar filled the air in a lively rendition of a song whose words had no meaning for ninety of the guests gathered at Quanah's lodge. In an imitation of the dances he had seen the whites perform during their celebrations, Quanah led his newest wife around the fire, stopping only when A-er-wuth-takum whispered into an ear that his action embarrassed her.

The three musicians continued to play while the chief and

bride moved among the guests to welcome them to their home and the feast that sizzled above the fire. As was wont among the People, the men and women soon separated to congregate on opposite sides of the fire, talking among themselves. It was then that Indian Agent Hunt motioned the brave to one side.

"It is good that you came, my friend." Quanah held up his tin cup. "And the apple cider you brought is good."

"Do you think this prudent?" Hunt swept an arm about him to indicate the gathering.

"Do not the white men celebrate their weddings?"

"But white men don't have three wives. You know there are very powerful men in Washington that look down on Indians who practice polygamy. To take a third wife and then celebrate it so boldly will surely draw attention. There will be articles in the newspapers," Hunt continued.

Quanah smiled and gave a shake of his head. "There were stories in the newspapers when they named a Texas town after me."

"You know this is not the same thing."

"Do these men in Washington wish a widow and her children to go without care and food?" Quanah looked the agent directly in the eyes. "It is the way of the People to take in many wives so that all women and children are cared for. I will go to Washington to tell these men this, if you will allow it."

Hunt sipped from the cup he held. "And will you tell them of the peyote? Will you tell them how you encourage the other men on the reservation to use this narcotic?"

"We eat cactus. The Nermernuh have always eaten cactus," the brave answered. "Do white women not make sweet jellies from the apples of the prickly pear? Is that not a cactus?"

Quanah expected Hunt to once again say, "That isn't the same thing." Instead the agent said, "I am simply warning you that everything you do attracts attention. You claim to walk the white man's road, yet you still live in a hide tent and wear buckskins. Nor do you cut your hair, but wear it long and braided. There are those who say that Quanah Parker has not changed, but merely tries to pull the wool over the eyes of white men."

"When needed, I wear a white man's black suit. But I will not live in the wooden houses with their leaky chimneys." Quanah contained a shiver; the thought of the two-room houses the government had built for other beef chiefs was like a black vision from some dark nightmare. A prison cell could be no worse. "I wear my hair and clothing in the style of the People so that all may know no matter that I walk the white man's road, I remain Nermernuh."

Hunt fell silent while he took a pipe and pouch from a pocket. He carefully packed the bowl with shredded tobacco and lit it with a match. He blew several streams of blue smoke into the air.

Quanah looked away. Unlike the men of the People, the whites did not share tobacco. Quanah ignored this rudeness. Hunt, like Haworth before him, tried to aid the beef chief. Hunt had written to Texas lawmakers in an attempt to secure for Quanah a portion of the land Texans had granted his mother while she lived. No land was granted; Texas legislators ruled the land had been given to Cynthia Ann Parker while the state was in illegal rebellion against the United States of America, and because of this all actions of the state during the Civil War were illegal.

"There is a more important matter we need to speak of," Hunt eventually said. "I have been approached by a group of ranchers in Texas, wishing to lease Comanche lands for their cattle."

"I have talked of this many times with Charlie Goodnight and others." Quanah's attention returned to the Indian agent. "They know where I stand. The white man's law says a dollar per head must be paid for cattle crossing the reservation. No one collects this fee. Why is this so?"

Whites did not hesitate to throw the law into his face whenever Quanah suggested changes on the reservation they viewed contrary to their interests. He learned from them—and learned the law.

Hunt blew another cloud of smoke into the air. "The colonel and I have told you many times that there are not enough soldiers to enforce the fee. Not only do the cattle have to be caught on the reservation, but the owners also must be there. Then the claims have to be taken to the attorney general of this whole country. He has to file charges. The process takes years."

Quanah said nothing. He always knew when the ranchers' cows crossed the reservation, and which white men were with them. Why did this elude Hunt and the soldiers? Did Hunt believe Quanah and the other chiefs were fools? All were aware that

the agent had applied to the secretary of the interior for the right
to run cattle on Indian lands and been refused.

Legally, only the white men who married red women, men
their white brothers called "squaw men," could graze cattle on
reservation land. Quanah saw nothing wrong with this. The
cattle fed the families of these men. Although, Quanah admitted
to himself, some of these whites abused their privilege by grazing
the cattle of other men and claiming them as their own.

"This isn't talk anymore. I have received a formal, written request to lease the land," Hunt continued. "I feel it would benefit
every Indian on the reservation were it agreed to. There would
be a large sum of money involved."

"This is not the time to speak of grass money. It is my marriage day." Quanah admired to his new bride, who walked toward the roasting beef with a butcher knife in her hand. "The
time has come for us to eat."

As Quanah took a step to join A-er-wuth-takum, Hunt
reached out and grabbed his arm. "I want you to talk to the others about this, Quanah. It's important. The others will listen to
what you have to say. You must explain what this lease would
mean for your people."

That the others would listen to what he said was exactly what
Quanah hoped for. The Texan ranchers already controlled all the
lands that the Nermernuh once roamed. They had no need for
the pastures of the reservation.

"I will talk to the others about the grass money as you have
asked," Quanah finally answered, choosing his words carefully so
that Hunt believed him to support the agent's wishes. "Let us
eat. Today is a day to celebrate."

"When the soldiers turn their backs or glance away, I will escape." Herman Lehman glared at the man whom he had come to
accept as his father. "I will return here and live in the lodge of
my real family."

Quanah's gaze shifted from his adopted son to the soldiers
who approached, then returned to the boy. Since he had found
Herman on the banks of the Pecos River, abandoned by Kiowa
renegades, the boy had grown tall and strong. He had adapted to
Nermernuh ways quickly and brought pride to his father. It was
not an easy thing to give him up.

"I am your father, and you are my son. These are not empty words. What has grown in our hearts during our years together has made it so," Quanah said. "Nothing can change that."

"Then why must I go?" Herman refused to accept the inevitable. "I do not know these people who claim to be my mother and father—and they do not know me."

"But you are their son—son of their blood. They, too, have a love in their hearts. Why else have they sought you for so many years?" Quanah tried not to think of his own mother, and the loss he knew had rent her heart. "It is right you should return to them. It is right for a son to be with his mother and father."

"Do you want me to go?" Herman demanded.

Quanah could not lie, nor would he stand between the boy's reunion with his blood parents. "I want what is right."

Herman looked away, his gaze falling to the ground. "Then I will go. But I will return, if only to visit the lodge of my true father."

Grasping his adopted son's shoulders, Quanah squeezed firmly. "I would like that. It will not be easy when you leave. My lodge will seem empty. You have brought great joy to my heart."

Quanah glanced back at the soldiers, who were less than a quarter of a mile away. "Now hold yourself like a brave of the People. Mount your pony and sit tall. You are the son of Quanah Parker. Do not let the soldiers see your sorrow. Ride out and meet them."

Herman's eyes lifted to the brave. "I *am* the son of Quanah Parker. I will always be that no matter where my steps take me."

"You are my son," Quanah repeated, then watched the boy mount his horse and ride from beneath the oaks to meet the soldier escort that would return him to his family in Texas.

As the blue coats reined their mounts about, Herman looked back at his father, his hands signing a wish for a long life. Quanah's hands echoed the boy's words. It was better this way, the brave thought. It was better his son did not see the tears that welled in his eyes.

CHAPTER TWENTY-FOUR

John Teller cast a sideways glance at his seven-year-old son, who sat beside him in the buggy. A smile touched the Texan's lips. Jeff's eyes were as round and wide as dinner plates. The boy's head twisted from side to side. He was oblivious to all except the terrain they traveled through.

"Pa?" Jeff's small arm jerked up, and he thrust a finger to the left. "Is that an Indian?"

"Yep." Teller popped the reins atop the hump of the chestnut mare hitched to the rig.

"I mean a *real for sure* Indian?" the seven-year-old pressed.

"Yep." Teller's smile grew. "That a real for sure Indian."

"Bet he's a Sioux or an Apache, like the army's fightin'," Jeff said with a decided relish.

"You'd be wrong, son. He's a Comanche, just like the man we're goin' to meet." Teller tilted his head in reply to the brave's uplifted hand of greeting as the buggy rolled by a tipi made from army canvas.

Seeing the material stretched over the lodge poles surprised the rancher. Comanche tipis were supposed to be made of buffalo hide. With the bison gone and the Comanches eight years on the reservation, he supposed the hides once used for the conical tents had rotted and fallen away. Those who still chose to dwell as they had on the plains were now forced to use the inadequate substitute. The thought bothered him, although he was uncertain why.

"Comanche?" Jeff turned to look at his father, his blue eyes, his mother's eyes, narrowed in question. "What kind of Indian is that?"

" 'Bout the meanest kind a man could hope to come up against." Teller edged the chestnut to the right when the worn dirt path he followed divided in a Y. "Least they were when they rode the warpath. Now they've made peace. The fight's all out of them."

"Oh."

Another smile moved across the father's lips when he detected the disappointment in his son's voice. Once gooseflesh born of real fear would have crawled across his son's skin with the simple mention of "Comanche." Now the name only elicited a disinterested "oh."

Times have changed, the rancher reflected. *Have changed fast.* Where once newspaper headlines were filled with the horrors of Comanche raids, an occasional headline told of the wars against the Apache tribes in the west or the Sioux bands in the north. Both Sioux and Apache ranged far from Texas's borders, so news stories concerning them were usually buried in a paper's back pages. Teller rarely saw mention of Comanches, except for an occasional few paragraphs that reported the apprehension of braves who had gotten drunk and wandered off the reservation.

"Who is this we're goin' to meet again?" Jeff's voice slipped into his father's thoughts.

"Quanah Parker," Teller told his son for the hundredth time since they had left their home at sunrise that morning.

"Parker ain't no Indian name!"

"Isn't," the father corrected. "Don't say 'ain't.' Me and the others ain't payin' good money for that school and teacher so you grow up actin' and talkin' as ignorant as your father."

"Parker *isn't* no Indian name," the boy said.

"His mother was white. She was taken captive when she was a little girl—not much older than you are."

Teller had never told his son about the Comanche raid that had swept Cynthia Ann and him from Fort Parker. Once when he started the tale, Tess had placed a finger to her lips and shook her head. She had leaned to his ear and whispered, "Don't go giving our son nightmares. He's too young to be hearing your bloody stories. Wait until he's older."

"A *half-breed*!" Jeff exclaimed with increased enthusiasm. "Is his skin red? Red as that Indian we just passed?"

"Yep." Teller gave his head a tilt. "And he was a warrior among his people. Everyone in Texas knew and feared his name back when the Comanches roamed free. Today he's considered a chief."

"A chief!" The boy's interest definitely grew. "What do I call him when I meet him?"

Teller arched a reprimanding eyebrow when he turned to his son. "You call him 'mister,' just like you'd call any growed man that's your elder. Just 'cause he's an Indian ain't no reason to forget your manners. If you do, you'll feel my hand on your backside. Understand?"

"Yes, Pa," Jeff answered. "I wasn't wanting to be impolite, that's why I asked."

"Good." Teller's attention returned to the path.

Ahead he saw a copse of oaks under which six tipis stood. From Indian Agent Hunt's description, this was what he was looking for. Two campfires burned among the tipis. While women stirred smoke-blackened pots, children of various ages played among the tents. The scene was reminiscent of the Comanche villages that once rose on the plains. That there were only six tipis brought the same rootless feeling the rancher had felt when he noticed the canvas tipi earlier.

Drawing the mare to a halt, Teller stood in the buggy, removed his hat, and called to three women by one of the fires, "I'm lookin' for Quanah Parker. Can you tell me where to find him?"

A woman who appeared a few years older than the others raised her head and turned a rounded face to him. She pointed toward a field to Teller's left. "Out there. Think he cowboy."

Thanking the woman, the rancher firmly replaced his hat atop his head and stared in the direction she indicated. About a mile from the camp, he saw a lone rider atop a hill. Teller picked up the reins and clucked to the mare when he took his seat again.

Jeff craned his neck to stare back at the children who now

stood looking at their unexpected visitors. "I didn't know Indians had kids. Those two boys and that girl look my age."

"Reckon they could be." Teller saw the rider turn his mount so that he watched their approach. "Suspect those were Quanah's wives and young'uns."

"Wives?" The boy's eyes rolled to his father.

"Or maybe they was just friends come to visit," Teller corrected hastily, deciding Tess would not appreciate his choosing this moment to enlighten their oldest son about the facts of life. Meeting his first Comanches would be enough for Jeff today.

"It is a good day, John Teller," Quanah called when the rancher maneuvered the rig within shouting range.

"Quanah," Teller answered with a slight wave of a hand.

In spite of all the times he had seen the Comanche chief and paid Quanah's beef tolls, the rancher admitted he still felt more than a little uncomfortable with this meeting, no matter how important it was to his stock. Reservation or not, this was Comanche land. He had lived as long as he had by staying out of Comanche land as best he could.

Quanah dismounted a dapple gray when Teller tied off the reins and began to climb from the buggy. With hand extended, the chief walked to the Texan. "It is good you would come this far to talk with me."

As he gave Teller's hand a shake, his attention shifted to Jeff, who scrambled from the rig and hastened to his father's side. "This boy yours, John Teller?"

"My oldest son, Jeff."

"How do you do, Mr. Parker." Jeff offered a hand to the Comanche chief.

"I do good, Jeff Teller." Quanah accepted the hand and squatted on his heels so he could look directly into the boy's eyes. "And do you do good, Jeff Teller?"

If the Comanche's slightly mangled English bothered Jeff, Teller could not discern it. The boy immediately launched into a description of the way his backside felt after the long ride from the ranch. What surprised the rancher more than his son's lack of a shy bone in his body was how the Indian listened with what appeared to be genuine concern.

"It is the wagon that makes you hurt here." Quanah reached around and grabbed the seat of his buckskin breeches. "Men are not made to ride in wagons. They should sit on horses."

"Wish Pa would listen to you," Jeff replied without a blink of hesitation. "I been wanting a horse of my own since I can remember. But he says I have to wait until my next birthday. But I can ride. Been riding for two years."

Quanah grinned and tilted his head to the gray. "Do you want to ride an Indian pony? He is a good horse. I stole him from a soldier many years ago."

"A stolen horse!" Jeff's eyes went round again, obviously impressed by the Indian's pronouncement. "Can I, Pa? Never rode a stolen horse before."

Quanah pushed to his feet. "It is Mackenzie's horse. He has lost most of his spirit with the years. He will not harm the boy."

Teller glanced at the animal and then his son. "I reckon it won't hurt anything. Just don't go ridin' off and get lost, son."

With a grin splitting his face, Jeff let the chief lift him to the makeshift Indian saddle, nudged the animal's side with his boots, and rode off toward a herd of about two hundred and fifty cows grazing in the distance.

The rancher noticed at least twenty-five horses among the cattle. Apparently Quanah had not forsaken all the Comanche ways. He still wore buckskins and kept his hair in long braids. Rumor had it he kept four or five wives, and apparently lived with them in a tipi while other chiefs chose to live in wooden houses. And it was more than apparent Quanah still measured his wealth, at least in part, by the number of horses he called his own.

"If you do not have enough ponies to give your son one," Quanah said with a sweep of an arm to the livestock, "I will give him one of mine."

A flush of embarrassed red suffused the rancher's cheeks as he managed to stammer, "No . . . no, I have horses enough for Jeff. It's just that his mother and me don't think he's ready for one of his own."

"He is ready. See how he sits. Jeff Teller should have a pony of his own."

"It wasn't horseflesh you wanted to talk about when you told Hunt you wanted to meet with me, was it?"

Quanah turned from the boy and faced the Texan. "Of all the white men, I have known John Teller the longest. But we are not friends, are we, John Teller?"

The Texan was uncertain what the chief wanted to hear, but he had no intention of lying. "I don't reckon we ever will be."

Quanah frowned. "Is it because Comanche braves took you the day they captured my mother?"

Teller felt his head snap back in a startled reaction to the question before he could control himself. "You know 'bout that?"

"And that my people killed your wife and son," Quanah answered. "A man called Dumaine told me of you after I came to the reservation."

Dumaine! Damn his eyes! Teller had not thought of the newspaperman from New Orleans for years. Apparently his old friend had interviewed Quanah before returning to Louisiana those long years ago.

"We are alike, John Teller," Quanah continued. "White men robbed me of my family. Did you not ride with Sul Ross, the day my mother was stolen from her lodge?"

The rancher pursed his lips, but did not know what to say. Dumaine had left him in a very uncomfortable position.

"That is why I ask to talk with you, John Teller. I trust what is in your heart more than I do the lies that fill the hearts of men like Hunt. He would use me and my people."

Still uncertain about the ground he stood on, Teller kept quiet while the Comanche turned and gestured to the cattle. "The cows you see belong to Quanah Parker. The man who rides among them is the husband of my oldest daughter. He is white. We have talked long about the grassland the ranchers wish to lease."

Quanah looked back at Teller. "You tell me why I should let *Tejano* cows on Comanche land."

With one word—*Tejano*—the chief let Teller know that, despite the trappings of civilization, Quanah Parker had not forgotten the old hate.

"Plain and simple—you're stupid if you don't," Teller answered. "How long have you and the other chiefs tried to stop the cattle from grazing north of the Red? Has it done any good?"

It was now Quanah's turn to fall silent. A shadow darkened the chief's face.

"Ain't nothing you can do to stop men from using land the Comanche and Kiowa are just lettin' go to waste. Since you ain't usin' the land, you should let those who have a need for it use it. There's nothin' wrong with makin' a lot of money in the process. It's been three years since a formal request was made to lease your land. Think about all the money you threw away by turnin' that offer down. Instead of honest men runnin' cattle on the land, you've got a lot of squaw men cheatin' you out of what should be yours."

Quanah's gaze left the rancher and returned to the herd of cattle. "Is there anything else?"

"I could talk all day 'til I went blue in the face, but I'd be saying the same thing again and again," Teller replied. "What I said is the way it is. There are honest men who'll pay a fair cash value to lease the land. I think it would be to your advantage and for the good of your people to listen to them. The fact is, I reckon they'd be willin' to make some kind of arrangement with you personally, if you were to talk for them."

After another long silence, Quanah's head turned back to the Texan. "I hear truth in your words, John Teller. It is the same truth I hear in my daughter's husband's words. But my mind is still undecided. I must think on this and speak with others before I decide."

Teller nodded. "Nobody's askin' for more than that." The rancher pointed to the buggy. "Meanwhile, you might want to try a bite of some of the food my Tess bundled up for Jeff's and my ride. Got some fried chicken, brisket sandwiches, biscuits and butter, and a three-layer cake with strawberry icin'."

"There is another thing I would ask of you, John Teller."

The rancher hauled a heavily laden picnic basket from behind the rig's seat. "I'm listenin'."

"I wish for you to help me find the grave of my mother."

The request so startled the rancher that the basket almost slipped from his hands and spilled to the ground. "You want what?"

"I want to find the grave of my mother," Quanah repeated. "You were her friend when you were children. As her friend, I ask you to help find her grave. I wish to bring her body here so that she may rest at peace with her family."

Teller never expected this. Yet, he sensed that this was more important to the Comanche chief than were the grasslands. Teller slowly nodded his head. "I ain't sure what I can do, 'cept maybe write a few letters and ask around. But I would be willin' to do that for you."

"I would be pleased for you to do that. Sometimes old enemies understand a man better than do newfound friends," Quanah answered. "Now I would like a piece of the cake you mentioned—a big piece."

Quanah watched the buggy safely cross the Red River and roll up the clay bank on the Texas side. A smile brushed his lips when a leggy weanling colt stopped for a moment to shake the water from its dapple gray coat. He saw the head of Jeff Teller poke out of the buggy and proudly gaze back at the prize he led home.

Reaching down, the chief stroked a palm over the neck of the gray he rode. "Your son has made the son of an old enemy smile this day. I think Mackenzie would be pleased by what you have done, as am I."

As the horse shifted its weight from one leg to the other, Quanah edged the animal's head to the west and tapped its side with his heels. When his body fell into the gray's gentle rhythm, he opened a pouch hung at his waist. He tossed the cold chicken within aside without looking where it fell.

The food John Teller had given him, as well as the cigars, was generous, but the People had no taste for bird or fish. He selected a sandwich made of roasted beef brisket stuffed between two thick slices of bread that still smelled of yeast. Teller's wife had covered the beef with a tangy red sauce that tasted of tomatoes and red pepper. It pleased Quanah's tongue.

Beneath another sandwich inside the pouch were three thick slices of cake. This he decided to save for the long ride home that night. Of all Teller's food, he liked the cake the best. It was sugar sweet and tasted of strawberries.

The sun set and a full moon, a raiding moon as the Nermernuh once called it, sat halfway in the sky before Quanah reached his destination. It was not raiding, but counting that filled his mind this night. Teller and his daughter's husband were right as he knew they would be. The white man's cattle roamed across the western pastures of the reservation for as far as he could see. Thousands of cows ate Indian grass—thousands of Texan cows.

No matter how many words he spoke or the countless letters he had found others to write for him, the cows kept coming. All battles were meant to be fought, but some were not meant to be won. He saw that now.

Teller spoke the truth. No matter what he and the other chiefs did, it would not stop the whites' cattle from eating reservation grass. Rather than nothing, the People should receive something for what was theirs. If that something was grass money, so be it. Money would buy cattle and horses. Money would help feed empty bellies.

Quanah was uncertain what Teller had meant by arrangements being made for him personally, but if it meant more money, then that was good. The whites should pay all that was possible for use of the pasture lands.

Having seen what he needed, the Kwerhar-rehnuh chief reined the gray toward the east. In the morning he would speak with Hunt and tell him he was ready to talk with the ranchers and do what was needed to help them obtain the lease they wanted.

That will be easy to do, he told himself. It was the others he would have to speak before that would be hard.

Twice he had stood before the great council of Nermernuh and Kiowa leaders and spoken loudly against leasing the land. Now he must stand again and tell all that he had been wrong, that to oppose the white ranchers only robbed the People of their just due.

Those he numbered as friends would see what he saw, of that he was certain. However there were those, powerful men, such as White Eagle, Horse Back, Shaking Hands, and White Wolf, who would oppose what must be done. They would not see the truth, but would openly call him a traitor to the red man.

If it is to be, it will be, Quanah thought with firm resolution.

CHAPTER
TWENTY-FIVE

"That's him." A half-whispered male voice came from Quanah's right when the Nermernuh chief stepped into the hotel lobby from the misty spring night.

Another voice, this one female, added, "He's taller than I thought. The paper didn't say anything about him being so tall."

"It's his white blood," the whispering man replied. "His mother was a white woman, you know. She was kidnapped by the heathens when she was two years old—or something."

"Well, no matter what the newspapers said," another woman's voice broke in, "I don't think he looks like he could have killed all those people they said he did. He looks like a Mexican, except for those braids. I wonder why he wears his hair . . ."

An amused smile touched the corners of Quanah's lips when he started up the stairs to the third-floor room which the Texas cattlemen had paid for. The reaction to his presence in Fort Worth had been the same throughout the day. Whispers and stares followed him, whether he strolled down the street or traveled within a carriage, as he had done for hours this night to see this city of white men with his own eyes.

Tomorrow, when he once more rode within a train car as he returned home, he would sort through all he had seen this night. His wives and children would want to hear the details time and again. The buildings, the houses, the food, the clothing, the people, the sounds, and the smells—all would stir their minds with wonder. For weeks on end they would question him about this and about that. He had to be certain he remembered everything.

But that would be tomorrow when the railroad tracks sang their clack-a-da-clack song in his ears. Tonight he was too weary to examine the bombardment to his senses the Texas cattle town had provided. When he turned to a room located at the end of the hall, he forced his thoughts back to the reason for journeying from the reservation—the grasslands.

Throughout the morning and late into the afternoon, Yellow Bear and he sat and listened to the cattlemen who wished to lease Indian pastures. Although it was Yellow Bear who had not yet decided whether to support the whites or continue his opposition to leasing, the ranchers' main attention focused on Quanah.

"Gentlemen, Quanah Parker," Agent Hunt had introduced him. "None is more progressive or has more influence on the Comanche and Kiowa Reservation than Texas's own Quanah Parker. He will listen with an open ear to all you have to say."

Quanah did that. Offer atop of offer was presented to him. Even now his mind still swirled around like a coyote pup chasing its own tail. Tomorrow, he told himself again while he dug into a pocket of the black suit he wore to find the key to the room, he would try to sort through all he had heard. Perhaps when he could present a solid offer to the council, those chiefs who opposed leasing would open their eyes and see that the grass money would benefit their people.

Unlocking the hotel room's door, Quanah stepped inside. Yellow Bear lay sprawled in the sheets and blankets of the lone bed within the room. The flames of lights still flickered from the metal pipes that curved outward from the wall.

Quanah closed the door and blew out the two lights before he settled on the floor. If nothing else, he considered while he tucked an arm beneath his head, Yellow Bear now was convinced grass money would help the People. Before they had parted for the evening, the older chief had pledged to stand with Quanah.

Not even the hardness of the hotel's wooden floor could stave away sleep. Quanah closed his eyes and let his weariness carry him into the realm of dreams.

"Can you hear me?"

A voice as sluggish as a pony with its hooves mired in the deep mud of a river bank rolled within Quanah's aching head.

"Mr. Parker, can you hear me?"

Quanah groaned. He tried to open his eyes, but lead weights sat upon their lids.

"Mr. Parker? Mr. Parker? Open your eyes. If you can hear me, open your eyes."

It took Quanah three attempts to accomplish what was asked of him. Having done so, he recognized the action as a mistake. Light stabbed into his eyes, setting them afire. His head throbbed and pounded, as though a demon dwelled within and fought to escape by shattering his skull.

"That's good."

The voice came from a round-faced white man with spectacles pinched on the bridge of his nose. When he spoke, the man revealed a front tooth rimmed in gold.

"Sit up if you can." The man slipped an arm beneath Quanah's shoulders and helped him to rise. He then held a glass under the chief's nose. "Drink this. It will help clear your head."

Quanah did. He had downed three small swallows before he realized the amber liquid was whiskey. "Whiskey makes head hurt worse."

"Not in medicinal doses, Mr. Parker. That will make you feel better," the man assured him. "You know, you're a very lucky man to still be alive."

"Lucky?" Quanah downed the last of the whiskey that burned from tongue to stomach.

"You went to sleep close to the door. The draft coming in beneath it kept you alive, or that's my best bet," the man continued. "Your friend in the bed wasn't as fortunate. His heart had stopped hours before you were found."

"Yellow Bear?" Renewed waves of pain exploded within Quanah's skull when his head snapped up. "My wife's father is dead?"

"It was the gaslights. They had been extinguished, but not

turned off. It didn't take long before the room was filled with gas."

"Gas?" Quanah blinked. "I blew the candles out before I slept."

The man pursed his lips and studied the chief for a long moment. "You thought the gaslights in your hotel room were candles?"

"Candles hung on the wall." Quanah nodded. "I have seen the candles white men use in their houses."

The man rubbed at his throat. "Your friend's death was from asphyxiation. He died from breathing gas that was released into the room when you blew out the flames. It was obviously an accident, and I will note it so in my report. After all, you almost killed yourself, too."

Yellow Bear was dead! Quanah's pounding head reeled. And he had killed him by blowing out the lights! It made no sense. How could this be?

"When the gentlemen outside found you and detected a heartbeat, they brought you straight away to my office. It took me two days to revive you. Like I said, you are a lucky man."

Quanah looked up when he heard a door open. Four of the Texas ranchers entered the small room in which he sat. He knew only John Teller by name. "John Teller, you almost lost an old enemy."

"That's what the doc here said," Teller answered. "I told him you were too tough a buzzard to be goin' and dyin' on us."

"You are a medicine man?" Quanah looked at the man in spectacles. For the first time he noticed the shelves of colored bottles filled with powders and liquids that lined one wall of the room.

"Yes, I am a physician." The man pointed to a framed piece of paper hung on the wall to his left that meant nothing to Quanah. He then spoke to the ranchers, "The best thing for Mr. Parker at the moment is fresh air. You may take him with you, if you wish."

Quanah offered no protest when Teller and one of his companions helped him from the table on which he sat. He needed their support while he taught his legs to walk. Still his mind could not comprehend how Yellow Bear had died. This "gas" was unknown to him. How could it kill a man while he slept?

"In another hour or two, Mr. Parker should be feeling his old self," the doctor said while the two ranchers assisted the chief through the office door.

If he could not understand how this "gas" killed a man, those back at the reservation would not understand either. What if the soldiers thought he had killed Yellow Bear? If not the soldiers, then surely those who aligned themselves against the grass money would accuse him of murdering his father-in-law because Yellow Bear would not support leasing the pastures.

Quanah stumbled to a shaky halt. With a firm grip on Teller's shoulder, he managed to half turn and look back to the physician. "You said you wrote a report?"

"The report that accompanies your friend's death certificate," the doctor said. "As I mentioned earlier, the cause will be listed as accidental."

Quanah's eyes shifted to Teller. "I need the report. The soldiers and other chiefs will need to see the report to know that Quanah Parker did not kill his friend Yellow Bear."

Teller blinked as though he missed Quanah's meaning, then his eyes opened wider with understanding. He glanced at the doctor. "Could Quanah here get a copy of that report? It would help clear things up when he returns to the reservation. There are those who might think he killed Yellow Bear and try to use it to see he's given a rope necktie."

"I understand," the doctor assured the rancher. "I will make two copies of my report. You can pick one up in an hour or so."

"Much obliged, Doc." Teller tipped his hat toward the physician, then once more helped Quanah walk into the fresh air outside.

The mourning songs were sung and the women's keening had died away when Quanah led twenty chiefs and braves along a narrow footpath that wound through the oaks to a clearing a mile east of his lodge. After the burial, he had promised to provide for Yellow Bear's wife as was the Nermernuh custom. He offered to let his mother-in-law erect her tipi beside his own so that she might be close to her daughter Weckeah. The widow had declined, saying she would now live with her third daughter and her white husband in a three-room house they had just built. His obligation complete, Quanah and the others had ridden from the funeral. They had done all that could be done to honor the passing of a friend and warrior.

The time came to seek a vision to guide the way. Although there were those who questioned Yellow Bear's untimely death, the report Quanah had brought from Fort Worth silenced their outrage before it could be voiced. It was not his would-be accusers for which he opened the flap of an isolated tipi and allowed the twenty to enter. It was for men who supported him. They required a vision to assure them that Yellow Bear's death was not an omen warning against the grass money the whites offered.

Inside the chiefs and braves seated themselves on cushions filled with sage. Each took a place then scooted to the left to make room for the next who entered until they progressed around the lodge's interior circumference. Dressed in his finest buckskins, adorned with colorful beadwork, his hair braided in strips of fur, and his face streaked with paint, Quanah finally ducked inside and stood before an open altar in the shape of horseshoe. Within the altar he lit a fire of cedar branches. Aromatic smoke curled upward to fill the tipi with a thick haze of blue.

"I am the Road Man," Quanah began to chant as he placed a large peyote button atop the altar. "I come to lead the way to father peyote. The peyote chief will open our eyes. The peyote mother will show the way to renewed life. It is the road we seek so that our feet may travel without stumbling ..."

The chant changed with each recital, although its sentiment remained the same. It was a prayer for wisdom, strength, and guidance. Quanah called upon father peyote to bequest those gathered with peace and prosperity. He asked that all might find love in their hearts rather than hate, which led to a road of warring.

To-ha-yea had simply bid him to eat the first peyote button she had given him; Quanah found the ritual he structured about the sacred cactus increased the importance of the moment. It reminded all who participated of the ceremony required to invoke the visions contained in tobacco. So it was Quanah introduced peyote to the People, training others to serve in the place of Road Man.

When the rattle Quanah held fell silent, and the Drum Man stopped his rhythmic pounding on the hide drum between his knees, pipes of tobacco were shared by those in the circle. Only then did Quanah distribute a pouch of peyote to his followers. Each man would now offer his own chant, and more peyote would be eaten. Only when the morning sun broke on the horizon would the tipi's flap again be opened and the men come forth.

Quanah slowly ate from a bowl containing an ear of boiled sweet corn, berries, and beef heavily flavored with green and red chilies. Rather than drink coffee, he washed the meal down with cool water he dipped from a bucket Weckeah carried among the men who lay on the grass outside the tipi.

One by one, chief and brave shared the visions the peyote had opened in their heads. Not one had seen Yellow Bear's ghost warning them away from the ranchers.

"Our visions are woven as one," Quanah finally said, "for I saw nothing but good for our people. I will continue talking with the whites and seek grass money for the use of our land."

"White Eagle and the other chiefs will oppose the grass money," Forty Buffalo spoke.

"Let those who would follow White Eagle follow a fool who led the People to defeat at Adobe Walls," Quanah replied. "We can not change the minds of fools. Our task is to show those whose minds are still uncertain that this new road is the way to strengthen all."

As those gathered nodded agreement, Quanah saw the invisible line they drew in the sand that would divide all the bands within the reservation. The angers he awoke this day would not quickly cool.

CHAPTER TWENTY-SIX

Quanah sat straight and motionless in the government-issued, black woolen suit, with a matching derby perched upon his head. He washed all emotion from his face so that none might read the feelings in his heart or the thoughts that filled his head. This was the way of a chief of the People. Today he carried the honor of all who remained back on the reservation, as well as his own, on his shoulders.

The carriage, drawn by a matched team of sorrels, rocked from side to side atop a street paved with red bricks. Quanah's eyes remained straight ahead as though he found no interest in his surroundings. The truth was the exact opposite.

Since the locomotive engine with its bowl-like, metal stack belching black smoke and red embers had carried him across the frighteningly wide waters of the Mississippi River, his eyes had been unable to drink in all that passed before him. Had Cona Cawb-vey with his long sight glimpsed this in a dream?

Here, east of the Mississippi, there were no plains that rolled on from horizon to horizon. Where dense forests did not cover the earth, the white man had built his farms with endless rows of plowed dirt and crops growing green.

And the towns! He had stopped trying to count their number after the first day. They melted into a blur outside the window of the railroad car he had ridden in.

Between those towns were more farms, and roads connecting all. In his heart he had known, when Cona Cawb-vey first warned him of the ceaseless numbers of whites, that the white men were more than the stars in the night sky. But to see this, for his own eyes to be unable to comprehend the countless number of whites, was more than his brain could accept.

As amazing as the towns with their whitewashed houses were, the cities were beyond anything he had ever imagined. Although the train on which he rode had stopped within these cities, there had been no time for him to walk among the streets. But from the window he had seen the towering buildings of brick and wood; he had glimpsed the massive factories with chimneys as tall as buildings pouring dark smoke into the sky.

Not even the views outside his railroad car had prepared him for this moment. Memories of his single visit to Fort Worth paled like worn, threadbare cloth compared to the vision that spread before his unblinking eyes.

Nor did the fact that this was the second time in as many years that he traveled to this city of cities diminish the impact on his senses. There were white men who never had gazed upon the grandeur that now surrounded him. Yet he, a red man, had come not once, but twice to these revered avenues. Neither the light flurries of snow that fell from the slate gray February sky nor the bone-chilling wind that whistled off the river basin lessened the excited pounding of his heart and temples.

The carriage he rode within, an interpreter at his side and a driver in the seat before him, rolled down the streets of Washington, D.C. It was here the white leaders came from across the whole country. Here dwelled the Congress who the reservation agents had told him were responsible for the laws that ruled the People. And here lived the leader of white leaders, the one called the President.

So overwhelming were Washington's massive buildings and never-ceasing traffic that his mind had been unable to retain the rushing blur of images that assailed his eyes during his first journey eastward. This day he carefully memorized all he saw and felt. This day Washington would not leave him like some awestruck child unable to speak with the voice of those he represented.

In truth, he admitted to himself, he had not lost his tongue during the first visit. However, Washington itself had intimidated him, leaving his mind a-churn and fear corded tightly around his heart. Today he felt no fear, only the confidence he could speak the words those in Washington needed to hear to make their decision. Seven years had passed since the ranchers first proposed to lease the reservation's grasslands. The time had come for the People to harvest the benefits that had been denied them for so long. Today, he would correct what his own blindness, in part, had kept from those who followed him.

The steady clip of shod hooves on brick died when the driver edged the sorrel team to the street's curb and eased the horses to a halt. Quanah's head turned to an imposing marble building with lofty columns.

"We're here." Horace Jones, the Kwerhar-rehnuh chief's interpreter, pointed to the building. "Secretary Teller is expecting us."

Secretary Teller? Quanah did a mental double take. For a moment the image of the Texan John Teller flitted in his mind. He brushed aside the rancher's face. White men and their names based on familial relations were often confusing. The Teller he met with this day was not the Texan, but the present Secretary of the Interior Henry M. Teller.

Quanah laid aside the plaid blanket with which he had covered his legs during the drive and stepped into wind-whipped flurries. Two carriages joined the one by the curb. From the first came the Nermernuh chiefs Saddy-teth-ka and Permamsu with the Kiowa called Loud Talker. The white ranchers George Fox and E. C. Suggs exited the last carriage.

Quanah pushed thoughts of Washington's sights from his mind as the delegation climbed a mountain of steps and entered the building through a pair of ornately decorated wooden doors. A month earlier other chiefs, led by the Nermernuh Tabananaka, visited the Secretary of the Interior Henry M. Teller. Tabananaka, with White Eagle, led those opposing the lease of reservation pastures. Fox and Suggs, and the ranchers they represented, had paid to bring Quanah and the others to the nation's capitol to insure those who fought against the lease had not swayed the leaders who would finally decide the matter.

Down a wide hall that echoed the delegation's footsteps,

Quanah followed Jones to a flight of marble stairs that climbed to a second floor, and another wide hall lined with glass-paneled doors. James M. Haworth stood near the end of the corridor. The Quaker who had served as the reservation's agent when Quanah brought the last of the Kwerhar-rehnuh to Fort Sill waved the men toward an open door on his right.

"The Secretary is waiting for thee inside," Haworth said, then greeted each member of the delegation individually.

"Haworth, my eyes are glad to see you after all these years." Quanah shook the hand of his old friend. "I did not expect you would be here."

Haworth explained he now served as superintendent of Indian schools. "I was in Washington on other business. Secretary Teller asked me sit in on the meeting when he learned I was in town."

"This is a good thing. Your ears know the truth when they hear it." Quanah tilted his head in approval as the former agent escorted him through a reception area into the office of the Secretary of the Interior.

Henry Teller, although he greeted all with handshakes and smiles, went directly to the point. "Gentlemen, as you are aware, there seems to be some discrepancy as to the sentiments of the Indians on the Comanche and Kiowa Reservation concerning the leasing of Indian lands for the purpose of grazing cattle belonging to non-Indians. I sent a special agent, a Paris Folsom, to Fort Sill last fall to study the question and report back to me."

Teller lifted a folder thick with papers and letters from a dark-stained wooden desk while he motioned the delegation to seat themselves. Opening the folder, he selected a page from the top. "Agent Folsom seems to be quite decided that the Indians on the reservation are being forced into accepting something they neither want nor perceive is in their best interest. Let me read from this report, 'For ways that are dark and tricks that are vain, the white man beats the Indian.'"

Secretary Teller paused and looked up. "Folsom does not refer to the physical act of flogging Indians, but to his impression the cattlemen are attempting to defraud the Comanches and Kiowas out of land that this government has designated for their personal use."

It was Loud Talker who spoke after Jones had translated the Secretary's concerns. "The land the white men wish to pay our people to graze their cattle upon has never been used by our bands. Our cows and ponies are not of great enough number to need this land. It is to increase our own herds we wish the ranchers' money."

Teller listened, nodded, and drew another paper from the folder. "And what of this? Agent Folsom interviewed nearly seven hundred Comanche and Kiowa men in November. He concluded by a margin of four hundred and two to two hundred ninety-two that those on the reservation were staunchly opposed to the leasing of any Indian-held grasslands. How do you explain this?"

"I'm uncertain who Folsom talked with," George Fox answered while he slipped a hand into his coat and brought out papers of his own, "but Folsom was presented with this lease agreement on December twenty-third. It contains the signatures of four hundred and four Comanches, Kiowas, and Kiowa-Apaches. You'll also find the signatures of four white men at the bottom who swear that none of the Indians who signed were coerced to do so, and that all the terms of the lease were thoroughly explained to these men before they signed."

The Secretary of the Interior accepted the lease agreement and carefully scanned through its pages. He read aloud the names of the four witnesses at the bottom. There was no mention of the fact that all four were employed by one of the nine individuals or cattle companies who sought the lease. Nor did Secretary Teller question the white men's background, Quanah noticed.

Teller pursed his lips when he refolded the agreement and handed it back to Fox. "Impressive, gentlemen, impressive." His gaze then shifted to the three red men seated in his office. "Last month I listened to a delegation from your reservation explain why they felt this lease would harm your people. I would like for you to explain why you feel that it is beneficial, if you would."

Saddy-teth-ka and Permamsu each took the opportunity to detail the poverty that held their followers in its grip. The money the lease would bring would help make the bands self-sufficient and able to compete in the white man's world. Loud Talker echoed these sentiments.

These were the words the white leaders wanted to hear, Quanah knew, but they were not the words he had carefully arranged in his mind during the long trip from the reservation.

"All that these chiefs has said is truth," he began. "But there is more. Agent Folsom is right, in part, in his reports. The white men are hungry for land. Because of this hunger, the Comanches and the other nations of the plains fought the whites and their black-skinned soldiers and were driven to the reservation. That was in the past. Now we try to walk the white man's road.

"Still the white men hunger for our lands. They see our pastures go fallow, and they say among themselves that the red man is stupid for not using this land. We are not stupid. We are new to the ways of the white men and must have time to learn."

Quanah outlined the farming and shepherding failures the People had faced during their first days on the reservation. With cattle bought by Mackenzie and with the help of Haworth, the Nermernuh began to run cattle close to their lodges, he said while the Secretary listened.

"Seeing the grasslands were more than our small number of cows needed, the white men brought their herds onto our lands. We were not allowed to drive them away, nor did these men pay to use our pastures. When we left the reservation, more than five thousand cows belonging to white ranchers grazed on grass belonging to the red man," Quanah continued, noting he had opposed leasing the land at first. "Then my eyes opened. The white man was right and the red man was right. Today we do not use these grasslands, and the white man can. Someday our herds will grow, and we will need this land given us. Until then we should be paid for the use of our land the same as white men are paid by those who use their land. This is right."

Quanah did not stop there, he pressed forward, detailing that in November, with Agent Folsom present, the bands had gathered in council and determined that grass money from any lease should not be paid into the United States Treasury to be doled out like beef rations when the government saw fit, but be paid directly to those on the reservation. "This, too, is right. For the red man to walk the white man's road, he must first be able to stand on his feet."

While the Secretary pondered what he had heard, he opened a canister of cigars on his desk, selected one of them and passed the container to the men seated before him. "I believe it is the custom of your peoples to share tobacco when you discuss matters of importance. It is a custom of which I wholeheartedly approve."

While every man in the office selected a cigar from the

canister, except for Haworth, Teller lit his smoke and puffed on it thoughtfully. He stared at Quanah when he finally asked, "Can you tell me why Tabananaka and the other chiefs who visited me last month are so opposed to this leasing?"

Quanah allowed himself three deep puffs from his own cigar before he replied, "I cannot say what objections they have to it, unless they have lost their sense. They are old in their thinking, on the wild road yet. That or they haven't brains enough to understand the advantages the lease will bring to our people."

"And why were these men and companies granted the lease?" Secretary Teller asked.

Quanah explained that their ranches bordered the reservation, and that he had known all for several years. "They are good men who do not want to cheat the red men out of money that is rightfully theirs."

Secretary Teller asked to see the lease again and read it over another time. "Six cents an acre each year for six years. The price seems fair enough. And I approve of this clause stating the ranchers will employ fifty-four Indians. I don't know about these wages of thirty-five dollars a month."

"That's about what a good cowhand makes," George Cox asked. "The thirty-five is what we'll pay chiefs. Any other brave will get twenty dollars."

The Secretary of the Interior's eyes moved to Quanah again. "You haven't been paid anything to sign this lease, have you?"

The Kwerhar-rehnuh chief shook his head. He did not consider the forty dollars a month the ranchers paid him to have been in exchange for his signature. The money was paid for his help in convincing the men of the reservation to sign and for the right to use his name on the letters the ranchers had written to garner support for the lease during the past two years.

That the Texas ranchers also promised to deliver five hundred head of cattle to Quanah's lodge when the lease was approved also seemed of little consequence to the chief. The promised cows had not bought his signature on the lease. The cattle were the spoils of battle—this battle one of words and laws. They differed in no way from spoils taken when raiding parties fought against white settlers. As was the way of the People, Quanah would take his rightful share and see that those who followed him received what was due them. It had always been that way among the Nermernuh.

Tilting his head back Secretary Teller slowly exhaled a thin stream of smoke, watching as the tendrils curled upon themselves within the sunlight filtering into the room. Eventually, he looked back at the delegation. "There is still one matter that weighs heavily on me. While I agree that a man, red or white, should receive a fair value for land that is leased, I am bothered by the possibility that those on the reservation will not have enough land for their own use."

"There is enough land left for all horses and cattle," Quanah assured him. "We were very particular in making the lease not to lease any land that came within the neighborhood of any of our farm settlements."

The Secretary drew another puff from the cigar and finally said, "As you are probably aware, the final decision on the lease does not rest in my hands, but with the Congress. But as for me, I believe this to be a very good lease as long as the Indians have reserved enough acreage for their own cattle and farming purposes. And I will say so in my report to the President and Congress."

"Gentlemen." Haworth rose and offered the delegation his hand to signify the meeting had ended.

After another round of handshaking, Haworth walked the group outside to the hall. He held Quanah back while the others started toward the stairs. "Thou has come a long way in the ten years since we first met. There are a lot of white men who could never become the politician thou has become."

"I walk the white man's road," Quanah answered simply. "When on the plains I used bow and lance. Now I use words like the white man."

The chief thought he saw a flicker of sadness cross his old friend's face as the man glanced to each side, then said, "I think there is a matter thou should be made aware of. There are those within Congress who talk against the reservation. They speak of enacting a clause of the Medicine Lodge Treaty of 1867, that will allow the President to divide the lands the Comanches and Kiowas now hold jointly."

Quanah frowned. He had never heard of the clause, which Haworth explained would dissolve the reservation and give each man three hundred and twenty acres of land, with lesser amounts for his wife and children.

"Many men in Congress feel the burden of feeding those on

the reservations grows too expensive. They wish for the Comanche and Kiowa to become self-sufficient. To divide the land would force this, they believe," Haworth concluded.

"I have heard no word of this," Quanah replied, his mind immediately seeing the disaster such action would wreak upon the People. "I thank you, Haworth, for telling me this. I will turn my thoughts to it."

"Thou do that, Quanah. Thou do that." Haworth took the red man's hand and shook it once again, then nodded his head toward the rest of the delegation that waited by the stairs.

"I think you can safely say that you accomplished what you intended in coming here." Horace Jones placed aside the copy of Secretary Teller's official transcript of the meeting. "The lease has the Secretary's support. I don't believe there are any in Congress who will seriously oppose its passage."

While those around the dinner table congratulated each other over their success, Quanah leaned to the interpreter and asked, "Would you read the words Secretary Teller used to name me again?"

Jones leafed through the report and read, " 'Quanah Parker, Chief of the Comanches'—is that what you mean?"

Quanah nodded. No man had ever called him by the title. That it came from a white leader gave it weight. Nor did he find the sound of "Chief of the Comanches" sour in his ear.

"I would like to have letter paper with those words on it," Quanah said.

"Letter paper? Oh, you mean stationery!" Jones said. "I think that can be arranged. In fact we probably can get stationery printed for you before we leave Washington. I will try to find a printer who can do the job tomorrow, if you wish."

"Stationery would be good," Quanah answered, letting Secretary Teller's phrase roll around in his head—Quanah Parker, Chief of the Comanches. "It would be very good."

CHAPTER
TWENTY-SEVEN

Quanah turned the small cloth-bound volume over in his hands. The feel of the book was unfamiliar to a man who could not read. "This is a white man's story about my mother?"

"By a man named DeShields, James T. DeShields." John Teller opened the book to the title page. "See, he put his John Hancock right there. And back here is a picture of you." He leafed toward the back of the thin tome to find the page with Quanah's photograph.

"Why would a white man write about my mother?" Quanah studied the photograph. The pictures white men took of him with their black boxes never looked like the man he saw in his own mirrors.

"Reckon Cynthia Ann is famous among us Texans. Not many lived through what she did." Teller shrugged. "You're makin' quite a name for yourself, too, you know. Especially after you helped prevent a Kiowa uprisin'. I know that made all the papers down home. Heard they carried the story as far away as New York City."

"I did nothing except write Agent Lee Hall a letter saying I and my people have quit fighting long ago."

Quanah tried not to think of the Kiowa medicine man Pa-ingya, whose words had threatened to destroy the life he and the People had made for themselves on the reservation. The self-proclaimed Kiowa prophet had fired the blood of his people as they prepared for their annual Sun Dance. He declared he would bring down a great wildfire that would sweep across the plains to destroy all the whites and their buildings on the reservation. The red men who hoped to escape this catastrophe were ordered to cast aside all that was white and flee the reservation with their families.

Quanah had revealed to the Indian agent a plan for a Kiowa attack on Fort Sill. Prompt troop movements and the aid of a Kiowa leader called Joshua Givens had defused the would-be uprising before it was fully born.

"Principal Chief of the Comanches is what DeShields calls you." Teller's pointing finger drew Quanah's attention back to the book. "Says here that 'Quanah speaks English, is considerably advanced in civilization, and owns a ranch with considerable livestock and a small farm; wears a citizen's suit and conforms to the customs of civilization . . .'"

"This DeShields never came to meet with me," Quanah said with a broad grin. "If he did, he would know I have no liking of the white man's suits. I prefer buckskin."

"Well, when Tess read about this DeShields being in Dallas, I thought you might like a copy of his book. I wrote a letter and ordered one from a bookstore," Teller said. "I think he got that Principal Chief of the Comanches off your own letterhead."

"It is a good thing, this book." Quanah balanced the tome in his hand again. "I will get one of my children to read it to me. I will like hearing of my mother."

Teller glanced toward the pastures that stretched to the west where the Comanche chief's herd of cattle and horses grazed. "Cynthia Ann is why I really came by. I done like I said I would; I wrote those letters. I reckon you know I ain't had much luck. Cynthia Ann died during the War between the States, you know. A lot of records got lost or burned after the carpetbaggers and scalawags come down from the North. I ain't had much in the way of luck findin' her grave. Last letter I got back was from a woman who said she remembered her bein' buried somewheres down around Austin. I'm lookin' into that now."

Quanah glanced at the Texas rancher. Would Teller ever tell

him in his own words what had happened that day so long ago, when his mother had been taken captive by Nermernuh warriors? His hand closed around the book. Perhaps the words on these pages would tell him. "My mother would appreciate what you do for her."

Teller shrugged. "We were friends back when we were knee-high to a grasshopper."

"And I appreciate it, John Teller," Quanah added. "Once, before I reached the age of manhood, I vowed to return her to her family. This is the only way I can keep that promise."

A heavy silence fell over red and white man. Apparently Quanah realized that it was for his mother, not him, the letters were written, Teller reflected. In spite of all the years, the rancher still felt the guilt of the six-year-old boy who had managed to escape his captors without trying to free his playmates.

"I hear you're considering buildin' yourself a house," Teller finally broke the silence.

Quanah's head turned to the Texan. "Not a small house like those other chiefs live in, but a big house like on the ranches in Texas. I have bought some lumber, but do not have money for carpenters and more wood. I have asked the Secretary of the Interior for help, like what was given to the other chiefs."

"Reckon you've got a few cattlemen friends who will help out when they learn you got need." Teller made a mental note to speak with his fellow ranchers about the matter. Quanah Parker was too strong a proponent of range leasing to lose because of a few boards and nails. The time to renegotiate a new six-year lease would soon be at hand. "Also heard Charlie Goodnight mention something about you gettin' yourself appointed as a judge."

A smile slid across Quanah's lips. "Tomorrow we finally have a court of red men to judge the crimes of red men. This is something I have sought for many years. It is a long-needed thing."

Teller tilted his head back toward the west. "Well, your judgeship, I suspect I'd better get back and check on my boys. We brought two hundred head across the Red to fatten 'em up for about a month before drivin' down to Fort Worth."

"Tell Jeff Teller I asked about him." Quanah watched the rancher step into the saddle.

"I'll do that." Teller reined a bay to the west and clucked the animal into an easy gallop.

Quanah's gaze followed the young woman who walked from the room. His eyes then turned to the left and a window that revealed the growing shadows of the approaching evening outside. He glanced at Lone Wolf and Tehuacana Jim, judges who sat on each side of his chair. "It has been a long day. There are no more who need us to listen to them. We will come back in a week."

His fellow judges pushed back their chairs, stood, and followed their last complainant of the day from the Fort Sill briefing room that had served as a courtroom for the afternoon. Quanah remained in his chair, surveying the room's interior with a sense of pride.

It had been a good day; better than the original court Agent Hall had begun and allowed to collapse two years ago. E.E. White, the latest in the long progression of Indian agents who came and left the reservation, seemed more interested in the red man handling legal cases that involved only the red man. Although, Quanah admitted, more than a little prodding had been required to get White to convene the court.

To be certain the judges were limited in their judgments. Fines could not exceed one hundred dollars, nor could jail sentences go beyond six months. Limited or not, this represented a new beginning, one Quanah refused to allow to fall by the wayside as had the first Indian court. Experience was a powerful teacher. Because an agent said something would be was not enough to keep it alive. He and the others must maintain a vigil to assure the court continued.

The justice the white man sought from his judges and juries was not what the red man wanted or needed. Whites concerned themselves with punishing those they found to be wrongdoers. The red man considered aiding those who had been harmed to hold more weight than punishing those who inflicted harm.

Today, the first case had involved a Nermernuh brave who had shot and wounded a Mexican who lived on the reservation. The brave was given ten days in jail and fined thirty dollars to cover all the Mexican's medical expenses. When released from jail, the brave would work in place of the man he had injured until the Mexican was fully recovered—this sentence atop the work the brave did to care for his own family.

In another case, the three judges had ruled in favor of a cast-off wife. They awarded her ownership of four horses that had been foaled during her marriage by a mare she had owned before that marriage. Since the woman's former husband had sold the horses in question, the judges required that he pay her the price received for the animals. In this way, the woman would be able to care for herself and her two children until she found another husband.

A good day, Quanah mentally repeated while he went over the five cases the court had disposed of during its first day. The People would benefit from a court presided over by red men.

He, too, would be rewarded, Quanah admitted. As presiding judge he received thirty dollars a month, and the two other judges were paid twenty-five. All three received extra rations while serving.

When what the government provided was added to the thirty-five received from the ranchers, Quanah mentally tallied, his monthly income was quite handsome, even by white standards. And there was his share of the grass money he received each year from the lease.

Walking the white man's road was not all profit, he realized when he finally stood and stretched. He was still a leader of the Nermernuh. As such, it was his duty to care for those less fortunate than himself. The tipis that surrounded his own swelled to as many as twenty-five during the winter months. None who came to him were denied food for their pots nor aid that would help them stand tall on their own.

Although the white men spoke of their Jesus and loving their brothers, they did not care for other whites as he did for his people. He had seen too many of the old and young die on the plains from empty bellies to allow that to happen when he had the wealth to prevent it.

"Quanah?" Agent White waited for him outside.

"My friend White," Quanah greeted the man. "I was thinking of the words of Jesus I have heard the missionaries speak. I think Jesus must have been Nermernuh. He believed in loving and sharing as we do among the People. This Jesus was a good man."

White stared at him as though the man did not comprehend what he had heard. "It's not religion I need to talk with you about. I received a letter from Commissioner Morgan today. I think you should come to my office so I can read it to you."

Dread pushed away the sense of accomplishment that had

filled Quanah's chest but a heartbeat ago. Once while Hall was agent, he had requested funds to help build a house; Morgan had denied the five hundred dollars. Quanah had then written to Secretary of the Interior Teller, who had returned the matter to Morgan's hands. Morgan again refused to provide any funds as long as Quanah continued the practice of polygamy.

White motioned the chief to a chair while he leaned against a desk on one side of his office and lifted a sheet of paper. "The letter's not long, but it's direct. Morgan writes, 'As it is against the policy of this office to encourage or in any way countenance polygamy, no assistance will be granted Parker in the erection of his house, unless he will agree, in writing, to make a choice among his wives and live with the one chosen and to fully provide for his other wives without living with them.' "

The Indian agent dropped the letter back to the desk. "I warned you this would happen again. When you first came to the reservation, it was easy to overlook the fact you had more than one wife. But this isn't then. All that you've done to help the Indians on this reservation has caught the public's eye. Wherever you travel, there are newspaper stories written about you, whether it be to Dallas or Fort Worth or Washington. Do you understand what I am saying?"

"Other chiefs with more than one wife were given money to build homes like white men. I am no different." Quanah kept his anger under a tight rein. He had heard all this before.

"You are different, Quanah. That's what I'm trying to explain to you. People throughout this country read about Quanah Parker and how he has accepted civilization and leads his people toward a progressive future. Yet, at the same time, they read that he has five wives and almost twenty children." White shook his head. "This is a nation of Christian men and women. It outrages them to read that their government is supporting a Comanche chief who lives like a heathen. It embarrasses those in the government who are trying to help you. Two wives would be enough to do this, but you have five wives!"

Quanah held his tongue. Six wives now lived with him. There was no need to further upset the Indian agent. "The Nermernuh have throughout all of time chose the wives they wanted. To me and my people, it is not for other men to say how many wives a man chooses. It is a matter between that man and the women he loves. If I can care for my wives and children, why should this bother others?"

White released his breath in a frustrated gust. "Because Christians believe in one man and one wife."

"Those you call Mormons are Christians, yet they live with more than one wife." Quanah would not be put aside.

"Mormons have their own problems and have nothing to do with you and your family situation," White answered. "You have to chose one wife and live with her alone."

"Do Christians want to take a man's children away from him?" Quanah stared at the Indian agent. "For me to send away my wives would also mean sending away my children. Would the white man's Jesus want this?"

"Jesus?" White's eyes went round with disbelief. "What do you know of Jesus? In spite of all that his been done to stop it, you and your followers are still eating narcotics and calling that religion."

"I have been to the white man's church and heard the talk of Jesus," Quanah defended himself. "For the red man there must be more. Peyote provides that. The white man goes into his church house and talks about Jesus. With peyote, the Indian goes into his tipi and talks *to* Jesus."

If White heard him, he ignored the chief. "I'm not blind. Every general store bordering the reservation is stocked with cactus buttons. I know white men aren't buying them."

Quanah fell silent. White men did not seek visions to guide them; the red men did. He had trained both Nermernuh and Kiowa throughout the reservation to lead the peyote ceremony. No man who called upon father peyote gathered others to him to rise against the whites, as did those who followed the way of the Sun Dance. Father peyote opened the heart and mind to the gentleness of the world and pointed the way to live in harmony.

"This cactus is no better than guzzling cheap whiskey until a man loses his mind," White continued. "In truth it is worse. It's a narcotic. It addicts a man until he can not live without it."

Quanah remained quiet. Like all the agents who had spoken against peyote, White was ignorant. A man could not live without food and water. The sacred cactus buttons were only a path to the other world of spirits. Whiskey robbed a man of his mind; peyote stretched the mind until it encompassed things that could never be seen with the eyes.

"What do you have to say?" White demanded.

"I have said it all before," Quanah replied simply.

The agent shook his head. "I have been authorized to declare the stores selling peyote off limits to those on the reservation. And I will do that if something isn't done to stop those using the cactus."

"Are there others we can write, about helping me build a house for my family?" Quanah stood, refusing to discuss father peyote with one who was ignorant of his power.

In 1880, the last of the Comanchero wagons had visited the reservation. When the New Mexicans no longer brought peyote, Quanah had found white traders who would. The storekeepers soon discovered that dealing in the cactus buttons was profitable. Should Agent White cut off that supply, he would find another way to bring father peyote to the reservation.

A second disgusted grunt escaped White's lips. "For some reason, I feel you understand everything I've said, but just don't care. Either you can't see, or refuse to see, that the world is changing. You have to change with it, if you intend to survive, Quanah."

"I am trying to change, but the government will not help me build a house," Quanah persisted.

White gave in with a helpless shrug. "I'll see if there is anything else I can do. But I doubt any decent man will listen to an Indian who has five wives."

Quanah turned and walked from the office. It was time to return to his lodge and the six wives who waited there for him.

CHAPTER
TWENTY-EIGHT

The buggy rolled out of Harrold, Texas, along a dusty road that was little more than two ruts cut into the prairie by the occasional passage of ranch and farm wagons. Except for the creak of harness leather or the moan of the rig's springs, no sound punctuated the soft whisper of the wind as it swept across the plains.

John Teller cast a sideways glance at the Comanche chief who rode beside him. Quanah Parker sat with his back rigidly straight and stared directly ahead. The rancher attempted to read the Comanche's face, but could not. Quanah's features held no hint of expression. The Indian might as well have been asleep with his eyes open.

The same was true of the small woman who sat to Quanah's right. If asked to describe the woman's face, Teller would have been unable to do so. When the Texan had met the train, the woman had never looked at him, but shyly kept her eyes downcast. Her name was To-pay, and that meant Something Fell. The rancher knew that; he had read it in the Fort Worth newspapers he picked up at the post office during his weekly visit to town.

Among the most recent batch of newspapers also had been

a letter bearing a New Mexico postmark. The letter inside had been simple—a request for Teller to meet the train in Harrold today and drive Quanah and his new wife back to Fort Sill.

If the lease on the reservation pastures had not been so important, Teller told himself, he would have ignored the letter and let Quanah walk all the way home. In two years, the lease would be reviewed for a third six-year period. Land was not as easy to come by as it had been nineteen years ago when Teller bought his first section. Now, with five sections carrying his brand, he had learned what Texas ranchers had known since cattle had been introduced to the state by the Spaniards. Grass was limited. Once-lush prairies soon became overgrazed. It was a matter of basic economics—either a man cut back on his herd and lost money or he found more land.

With luck the lease would be granted again, securing the reservation pastures right up to the new century. After that? Teller could not hazard a guess. There was growing support in Congress for the President to break up the reservation into private ranches and farms. Quanah and the other chiefs had managed to block such action, but the day was coming when all the Indians' protest would be for naught. Teller saw that clearly, and it was coming quicker than he wanted to consider. The Sooners were starting to complain that the Indians had far too much land that they did not use. When they got loud enough, politicians would listen. And when it came to people who could squall and bawl, Sooners were unmatched on God's green earth.

"How is your family, John Teller?"

Quanah's unexpected question gave the rancher a start. Other than thanking Teller for meeting them at Harrold, the Comanche had not uttered a word.

"Tess is doin' fine, as are the boys and little Carol Ann," the Texan answered.

"Jeff Teller must be grown to a man by now," Quanah said, although his eyes remained forward and did not shift to the Texan.

"He intends to go off to college in Austin come September." Teller gave his head a shake. "Ain't certain how a lot of book learnin' will help him run a ranch, but it's what his momma and he want, so that's the way it will be, I—"

Teller caught himself. His head jerked to the right, and he stared at the Comanche chief. "Hell, I don't know why we're talking about my family. It's your 'much married condition' that's the problem here." Teller used the phrase the newspapers repeatedly employed to describe Quanah's overabundance of wives. "Seven wives! You know you've really gone and stuck your hand down a snake hole this time."

"Six wives," Quanah corrected without a trace of emotion. "Weckeah is no longer a wife. She left my lodge. She said, 'too many wives,' and she left. Still six wives—that is all."

"Six wives!" Teller shook his head in disbelief. "Most men have got their hands full with just one!"

"Maybe that is why white men take only one wife," Quanah suggested.

The rancher ignored the comment. "Then you had to jump up and run off the reservation. Every newspaper in Texas and the Territory carried the story. Half of 'em had you gathering braves for a Comanche uprising, and the other half had you runnin' clear down to Mexico to escape the United States."

"It was best to leave. I feared Eck-cap-ta intended to hurt To-pay. If he had whipped her or cut off her ears or nose, I would have had to whip him," Quanah explained. "I have promised to fight no more. It was better that we left."

Teller realized that slicing off the tip of the nose or the ears was the method by which the Comanche marked wives who were caught in an infidelity. "I thought To-pay was only promised to this brave Eck-cap-ta. I didn't know they were married."

"He had promised two horses, a carriage, and fifty dollars to her father for her hand." Quanah smiled his young wife. "When To-pay told Eck-cap-ta she wanted me and not him, I paid Eck-cap-ta what he had promised for her. This was not enough for him. He threatened to whip To-pay, or worse. So we left the reservation and rode the train to New Mexico. We visited the people of my first wife To-ha-yea, who was not a wife."

Teller could guess why the chief had chosen New Mexico as his destination. The most recent string of Indian agents had all but dried up the flow of peyote into the reservation. Since most of the cactus buttons had come from New Mexico, the rancher suspected Quanah had killed two birds with one stone. He carried To-pay out of harm's way to let his rival cool down a mite while he opened up a new supply and trade route for the peyote he needed for his religious ceremonies.

Nor would the Texan put it past Quanah to have used To-pay as a cover for the real motive for the New Mexico trip. With reservation officials hot under the collar about the chief's new wife and his unauthorized disappearance, drug-laden peyote would be the farthest thing from their minds.

"I wired Lieutenant Nichols when I got your letter," Teller told the Comanche. "I suspect he'll be waiting at Sill's gates, but I doubt he'll have a brass band playin' to welcome you when we ride up."

Quanah did not answer, but lapsed back into his earlier silence. Teller shrugged as he turned his attention to the road, leaving his passengers alone with their thoughts.

Acting Indian Agent Lieutenant Maury Nichols of the 7th United States Infantry strode back and forth across the width of his office while he unleashed the tirade that had apparently been growing within him since Quanah had disappeared two weeks ago.

"If it was my decision, I would lock you in the stockade until you got some sense back into that thick skull of yours." Nichols paused his pacing long enough to stop and glare at the chief. "What you did was wrong, and you damned well know it. Commissioner Browning knows it's wrong, too, but it appears he's afraid to lock you up. He thinks that most of the Indians on the reservation would come running to the fort and tear down the stockade with their bare hands to get you out."

Quanah kept his eyes locked to the man, but said nothing. He had learned long ago that an ill-chosen word at times like these only increased a white man's anger.

"Since Commissioner Browning's the one making the decision in this matter, this is what he's come up with." Nichols snatched a yellow telegram from his desk. The lieutenant read aloud, "In light of prior warnings Quanah Parker has received over an extended period of time about his continued practice of polygamy, and his blatant disregard of these warnings shown by his taking of yet another wife, I hereby order him to give up this most recent wife or suffer removal from the Court of Indian Offenses, of which he has been a member for close to a decade. The choice is his."

Nichols, telegram still in hand, pivoted to face the Comanche chief. "That's the final word. I've sent To-pay back to her father's lodge. You can walk out that door and go after her and lose your place on the court, or you can sign an agreement I've drawn up and remain a judge. Like Browning said, it's up to you."

Quanah blinked. He had expected a reprimand and perhaps some type of punishment such as a cut in rations for a week or two. But this struck straight to the heart. The Court of Indian Offenses was something he had fought for and had kept alive for years.

An icy band surrounded Quanah's chest and contracted. Nichols had no respect for the court. Six months ago he had increased the number of judges who heard cases from three to six. He appointed three "blanket Indians" whom he controlled to these new seats. Should Quanah give up his position as presiding judge, his seat would be open for Nichols to fill with another of his handpicked "good Injuns." It would be only a matter of time before the court collapsed and white men once again sat in judgment over red men.

An image of To-pay superimposed itself over the thoughts that crammed into his skull. Not since the day he had first seen To-ha-yea with the Comancheros had desire for a woman fired his blood more than for To-pay. When she was with him, the years piled upon his back melted away, and he felt like a young brave again, free of all the entanglements that life upon the reservation cast around him like a spider's web.

Quanah drew a slow steadying breath. To-pay or the Court of Indian Offenses—he was given no other choice. Quanah Parker the man and Quanah Parker the chief of his people had never seemed so separate and divided within him.

"How does your agreement read?" Quanah asked the acting Indian agent.

Nichols produced a single sheet of paper and began to read, "This is to certify that I, Quanah Parker, principal chief of the Comanches . . ."

Man or chief? Could they be separate? Quanah had never viewed his life as such.

". . . give my word to the acting Indian Agent Lieutenant . . ."

Man or chief? How could the white men not see that both were one and the same?

". . . that I give up and relinquish all claims to To-pay as my wife and . . ."

Man or chief?

". . . will immediately on my return home . . ."

Man or chief?

". . . give her back to her people."

Man or chief?

"There it is," Nichols concluded. "What will it be? The choice is up to you."

Man or chief? Quanah could not escape the parting of his life Nichols forced upon him. *Man or chief?* He had led his band here, had promised through words and actions to lead them on the white man's road. To abandon them was not within him, he realized as anguish clawed within his heart. He was no mere brave; he was the son of Peta Nocona—principal chief of the Comanches.

Quanah answered Nichols simply, "I will make my mark."

"You all right?" John Teller asked when he drew the buggy up on the road that ran between the dozen tipis that stood beneath the oaks and the Star House.

Quanah glanced at the rancher while he climbed to the ground. "I do not bleed."

Teller was not certain what that meant. "I've got a long ride back. I'd best be on my way, unless I can do something else for you?"

"You have done much." Quanah gestured to the two-story house. "You are welcomed to spend the night in my home."

"I need to be back at the ranch by the morning." Teller shook his head. "Got two new bulls comin' in—rich-blooded Durhams. Got to make certain I'm gettin' what I paid for."

Quanah tilted his head in acceptance. "I thank you for what you have done for me, John Teller."

The rancher nodded, waved off the thank-you, clucked to the bay in harness, and reined the buggy in a wide circle before heading back toward Fort Sill.

Quanah watched the man disappear in the darkness of the early night. After all these years, he still felt no friendship within the Texan's heart for him or the People. Yet, there was a bond between them that could not be denied. Quanah held no words to describe that bond, but he trusted Teller more than most white men and many red men who loudly proclaimed to support him.

The rancher lost in the night, Quanah's attention turned to

the massive ten-room wooden structure he had named the Star House. Lights burned yellow from many of the windows, although no one ran out to greet him. Nor did those in the tipis to his left welcome his return.

It was not surprising. He was certain many had heard the buggy's approach. The People no longer traveled the nights, leaving that for whites. Few cared to interfere with white men who passed their way in the darkness.

Quanah slipped a hand into the pocket of the black coat he wore. His fingers brushed over four peyote buttons nestled there—a promise of the continued supply the Mescaleros would provide for him and the others who followed father peyote.

Quanah turned his back on the Star House. He walked past the dozen tipis of those whose need had brought them to live with him. Tonight the council of men would not bring the answers he needed. He pulled one of the cactus buttons from the pocket and bit into it while he hastened toward a tipi secluded in a clearing among the oaks.

CHAPTER
TWENTY-NINE

Colonel Mackenzie stared up at Quanah and the eight braves he had sent after four Kiowas who had stolen the soldiers' ponies and fled the reservation. "The ranchers have accused you of stealing horses when you crossed their range yesterday."

Quanah looked at the riders mounted to his left and right. "Look at our ponies, Mackenzie. For days we have ridden them long and hard. They can barely walk beneath our weight."

He watched the colonel study each of the animals.

"Would we have stolen such poor horses?" Quanah asked.

Quanah shook his head to clear the memories from his skull and open his mind to the peyote that coursed through him as he sat naked on a sage cushion beside a smoking fire of cedar branches.

The Dawes Act.

Again and again, his thoughts threaded back to 1887, when Congress had passed the General Allotment Act. In spite of his opposition and the protests of all the chiefs on the reservations, the whites had granted the President the right of severalty—the ability to divide the reservations into farms and ranches of one hundred and sixty acres for each brave, with smaller acreage for other members of his family. The remaining acres of reservations would be purchased by the government and opened to settlers.

The old curses deluged Quanah's mind. Even the whites who usually stood beside the red man had voiced approval of the Dawes Act. Their belief was that private ownership of land would hasten Indian acceptance of the "civilized world."

"But the President did not use the Dawes Act." Quanah spoke aloud in the hope it would free his thoughts from the web of the past and bring forth the future.

It did not.

Although there were whites who demanded the reservations be opened, five years passed before David Jerome and the other two men of his commission came to the reservations to negotiate the Dawes Act with the various nations. Jerome came to the Comanches and Kiowas in 1890, and gathered the chiefs and the braves together to hear his words.

We heard and understood him, but he did not understand what we said, Quanah remembered. Nor would Jerome give the price the government would pay for each acre of "excess land" it would purchase from the red man.

Quanah had pressed for that price time and again, and was told it would be "around a dollar an acre." He had asked, too, why the red man was being denied the three hundred and twenty acres granted each brave by the Medicine Lodge Treaty of 1867. Jerome had no answer for that either.

"Inevitable." The word sprang from Quanah's lips. He had learned its meaning from the white man. How aptly it described the white man's voracious hunger for lands he did not possess, his insatiable need to devour all that belonged to the red man.

The Jerome Commission and what it sought to take from the tribes the white man had confined to the reservations was inevitable. Quanah, as did other chiefs, signed the agreement Jerome presented after several meetings. Inevitable as the outcome would be, Quanah hoped to buy time and find the means to delay the inevitable for as long as possible.

For that signature, White Eagle and his supporters shouted that the whites had bought him just as the ranchers bought him with the money they paid him monthly. Quanah had received nothing from Jerome, although he later learned the white men had made special concessions to other chiefs for the marks they placed on the agreement.

Inevitable, he told himself. Had he not signed, half the reservation would have taken his refusal as a sign of open rebellion and risen against the whites, so heated were the tempers at that time.

Nor had the Ghost Dance lessened the explosive nature of the reservation that year. It was then the Arapaho Sitting Bull had told his people he had seen the red messiah Wovoka with his own eyes—a messiah who would lead the Indian nations to freedom from the white man's yoke. Sitting Bull preached the Ghost Dance, with its specially prepared shirts, as the road to Wovoka.

Arapaho though he was, there were those among the Kiowa and the Kiowa-Apaches who listened and believed. A follower of father peyote, Quanah disavowed the Ghost Dance. Again the chiefs who opposed him cried out that he was a traitor to the red man, that his white blood ruled his head and heart.

Quanah's head moved sadly from side to side. Worse were the whites who accused him of following the Ghost Dance during a visit to Fort Worth. The words he had spoken then now spilled from his lips: "Having just got fixed to live comfortably, I would be an idiot to incite my people to do something that would make beggars and vagabonds of them. We have been accused of most everything except being fools, and people who know the Comanches have never credited them with that."

The Jerome Agreement.

Jerome wiggled back into his mind. For two years the President had not employed the inevitable. Quanah and others wrote or visited Washington trying to delay its implementation. For two years they had accomplished that.

"Inevitable," Quanah said the word aloud again as he felt the peyote slowly slipping from his mind.

No visions of the road that lay ahead of him had come, only memories of the past.

His mind reached back twenty years to a vision he had once sought, only to find Cona Cawb-vey waiting to show him that within the past lay the future. Was that what his memories did this night?

Quanah's head lifted and he looked toward the breeze-stirred canvas flap to the tipi. Outside he saw the soft light of dawn. *Did the future lie mired in the past?*

After twenty years of dealing with the white man, he still felt uncertain and inadequate. What the red men were told one year changed the next. Elected leaders came and went, and with them the promises and words changed. None would be bound by what others had done or promised before them. How could a man find the solid footing of rock when governed by sand?

"*Inevitable,*" the word came from his lips again as he tried to sort through the memories the peyote had awakened.

As hungry as the white man was for Indian land, he wanted to swallow all that was the red man in his belly. It was not enough that the People abandoned their tipis for houses, but they must cast aside all that made them Nermernuh. Like the white man, they could take no more than one wife. Nor were they to wear their hair long, but allow barbers to shear them like sheep. To walk with father peyote, too, was wrong; only the Christian church with its dead god Jesus was proper for worship.

And the white man's schools, Quanah thought. Even he had been forced to send his sons and daughters away from their family to the Carlisle School in faraway Pennsylvania. That eleven of the first sixty students sent to this school died did not matter to the white man. The red man *must* learn to be white.

"Inevitable," Quanah said, as he began to see the direction his vision pointed.

Quanah had led his people to the reservation and promised to show their feet the white man's road. What he did not see then was that the white man's road was a constantly changing path. Even the whites did not know which way it ran, or what twists and turns lay ahead. How could men who had ridden freely across the prairies be expected to follow such a route in a mere twenty years?

No Nermernuh embraced the white man's road more than he. The chief dwelled in a fine house equal to those claimed by Texas ranchers. His herd of more than four hundred cows grazed on forty-four thousand acres beside one hundred and sixty-five ponies. White hands, whom he hired, cultivated crops on one hundred and thirty-five acres. And he raised hogs, although he had never developed a taste for their meat. All this he did because this was the white way.

Like the white men, he leased acres to sharecroppers and ran white men's cattle along with his own for the money they paid.

And in the white way, he accumulated wealth. No chief or brave on the reservation had prospered as had he.

This was not enough. No matter how much he accepted the whites' customs, the white man wanted more. They cared not how deep they wounded him to get what they wanted. He had told John Teller that he did not bleed, but taking To-pay from him had torn into his heart as nothing the whites had ever done before.

Nor did the whites stand with him against those who opposed every word he spoke or step he took. White Eagle and his supporters remained as strong as ever. No matter which direction he turned, they were there, screaming that he betrayed his people for the white man's wealth.

"Would they have given up one they loved to serve their people?" To-pay's image filled his head, and tears welled from his eyes to trickle down his cheeks. "Would they have forsaken a wife to provide for the ones they lead?"

How could times be so bountiful and still be so dark? How could a man know such wealth and feel as though his feet precariously balanced on the edge of a yawning precipice?

The answers eluded him no matter how deep he probed within his head. A yearning for the time his greatest worry was whether he returned to his lodge with fresh meat for Weckeah's stew pot filled his breast. How free of the convoluted machinations of the whites those distant days seemed. The white man was easier to comprehend when he was an enemy rather than a friend.

Quanah leaned to his left and dipped a hand into a bucket of water he had brought with him into the tipi. After two handfuls to quench his thirst, he bathed his face in the coolness of the water. The rippled reflection that stared up from the bucket was a man he did not know. The man was old, the creases of nearly fifty years etched around his eyes and across his forehead. Peta Nocona had not seen the passing of so many years when he entered the Valley of Ten Thousand-fold Longer and Wider.

Would his father recognize his own oldest son when they once again hunted together? Few braves lived so many *taum* when the bands wandered the plains. Those who did were revered for the experience of their years and the wisdom they had garnered from life. They did not have to endure constant accusations from the likes of White Eagle.

"Inevitable," Quanah repeated aloud once again.

White Eagle and those who hovered under his wings were as inevitable as the Jerome Agreement. Perhaps that was what the vision revealed to him. He was to prepare himself and his people for the inevitable, when the white man's road would abruptly shift beneath their feet and send them hurling off into a new direction.

Slipping his legs into black wool pants, he gathered the white man's coat and shirt from the floor of the tipi. Later, when he had returned to the comfort of well-worn buckskins, he would again ponder what he had seen throughout the night and plan ways to postpone the inevitable. For now, he must tell his family that he had come back to the reservation. Not only did his eyes hunger to see his wives and children, but his stomach growled as loudly as a bear to remind him that he had not eaten in more than a day.

He stepped from the tipi and nearly stumbled. To-pay stood waiting with a basket in her hands.

"Quanah Parker asks his wives to become peyote woman for the men who enter the peyote lodge, does he not?" To-pay lifted the basket. "And does not peyote woman bring the braves who have seen through the eyes of father peyote food and drink?"

"I thought you were in your father's lodge." Quanah was not certain the vision belonged to him or was merely a lingering trick of the peyote. "I signed an agreement with Agent Nichols that I would not claim you as a wife."

"I know. Word spread quickly of what Nichols forced you to do." To-pay placed the basket beside her feet in the grass. "When my father heard, he said that I could come to you if that was my wish. Nichols's agreement does not stop me from claiming you as my husband."

As much as Quanah wanted her and all she offered to him, he could not accept. "When Nichols finds out that you are in the Star House, he will—"

She stepped to him and placed a finger against his lips. "My tipi is among the others. I will not live in your house—at least, not for now. When Nichols has forgotten me, or he leaves like all the other agents, then I will live in your house. Until then, you can visit me when you wish to be with me."

Quanah's arms opened and enfolded the young woman. Her own arms circled his waist. Man and woman, husband and wife, they held tightly to each other in the light of a new day.

CHAPTER
THIRTY

Quanah's gaze lovingly moved over the faces of his children, savoring the familiarity of their features and smiles while they seated themselves at the restaurant table. Even the black uniforms they were forced to wear at the Carlisle School, or the short cut of their hair, did not disguise their Nermernuh features.

"Are you on your way to Washington, Father?" Wanada, the oldest of his daughters enrolled in the Pennsylvania school, asked.

"I have visited Washington and return home," Quanah answered.

"Did you discuss the Jerome Agreement?" Harold asked. "They taught us about it here. Our teachers say it is a good thing."

"Your teachers are white and not red." A gentle smile touched the Comanche father's lips. "What is good for the whites is often not good for the People."

Quanah considered his most recent visit to the nation's capitol. If fortune rode with him, he had delayed the inevitable once again. Although the whites still held the Jerome Agreement like a raised stick, they remained hesitant to strike with it. One day in the near future that stick would fall and the red man would feel the full force of the blow.

"Your brother Herman Lehman visited our family before I traveled to Washington." Quanah accepted menus a waiter brought and passed them to his children. The fifth menu he placed on the table, unable to read its words. "Although his blood parents are Mexican, he still feels that he is one of the People. He asked me to say that he often thinks of his brothers and sisters and wishes to join them one day."

"I remember his last visit," Esther said while she studied the menu. "It was before you built Star House."

"Was he impressed with our home?" Laura questioned.

"He was." Quanah nodded. "He said his adopted family was richer than his blood one."

"Maybe that's why he wants to come back to us." Wanada winked at her father, then read him the fare the restaurant offered.

Quanah selected steak and potatoes, which Wanada ordered when the waiter returned.

"Are we really rich, Father?" This from Laura.

"Richer than many, poorer than some," Quanah replied.

"Father"—Harold's eyes turned to Quanah—"we heard our teachers talking about trouble back at the reservation. They mentioned your name. I heard them say that your enemies were trying to ruin you. Is that true?"

Quanah pursed his lips while he gathered his thoughts and shaped them into words. Although White Eagle and the others had always stood against him, he had never thought of them as enemies, but as opponents. In truth, he realized, there were those who followed White Eagle who would delight in seeing him transformed into a pauper.

"The other students whisper that you have stolen money from reservation funds." Esther's dark eyes peered at her father over the top of her menu.

Quanah ignored the arrow that drove to his heart. His children should not see the pain that such words brought him; pain that was tripled because the words came from those closest to him. "There are men whose hearts are green because I have prospered. Their accusations are not new."

When he saw that all four of the children hung on all he said, he added, "The only money I have ever taken came from white men. I did this because I worked for them in ways that made profit for both the white and red man. I have never taken money from the red man. I have always given to those in need; that is the Nermernuh way. It is the old way, and I have tried to walk the white man's road, but to provide for those with less is an old practice I can not forsake. When a chief helps others, he gains support from those he helps. His opponents call this buying supporters. If a chief let those in need starve, he would be called cruel and without a heart or soul. His opponents will find fault in whatever direction he steps."

As the waiter brought their meals, Harold questioned, "Is it true your enemies want to remove you from the Court of Indian Offenses? My teachers have said this."

"They try," Quanah answered without hesitation. "They have tried before and failed."

That seemed to satisfy his daughters and sons, who began their meal and discussed their classes. Quanah, however, could not shake the unrest their questions had awakened in him. Although he had managed to sidestep every attempt to divide his family since Agent Haworth had suggested he consider taking only one wife those long years ago, he had never felt such pressure as there was on him now.

Since Agent Nichols had attempted to separate him from Topay four years ago that pressure to conform to the white man's way had grown steadily. This year, Commissioner of Indian Affairs William A. Jones had ordered the present agent, Captain Frank Baldwin, to remove Quanah from the court, along with the Kiowa judge Apiatan, for their refusal to enforce a ban on polygamy among the bands on the reservation.

Baldwin, whose respect Quanah had won, repeatedly aided the chief by nominating replacements for Quanah and Apiatan whose histories were less than spotless. Time and again Commissioner Jones rejected the nominees and ordered Baldwin to select others. In the meantime, Quanah and Apiatan retained their seats on the court.

Of all the Indian agents who had come and gone during his twenty-three years of reservation life, Quanah had never known one to fight for him as Baldwin did. Nor was it just for an aging chief he battled. Baldwin had uncovered more than one "squaw man" who leased Indian lands for a few hundred dollars, then subleased the same lands for thousands to white men. Baldwin, too, looked the other way when white inspectors and missionaries complained of the continuing use of peyote among the People, usually pointing a finger directly at Quanah for keeping this practice alive.

Yet, in spite of Baldwin's maneuverings, Quanah had never felt his seat on the court to be so shaky as it was now. Baldwin was, after all, merely an Indian agent; there was only so much he could do and comply with orders from his superiors.

Commissioners change as quickly as Indian agents, Quanah thought, while his gaze returned to his children. *I must quietly ride through this storm. I will still be on the reservation when Commissioner Jones is gone.*

"Father"—Laura looked up from a plate half filled with vegetables, none of which were familiar to Quanah—"will you talk to the students at Carlisle as you did when you visited us last time?"

"Not this time. There is much waiting for me to do at home," Quanah answered. "But if I did, I would tell them what I always tell you—go to school and get an education, and walk the white man's road."

"What of Nermernuh ways?" Harold pressed. "Are we to forget that we are of the People?"

"Never forget that. Hold it close to your hearts," Quanah replied. "But do not let it rule you. The old ways will not provide for our people in this world. They must learn the white ways to survive. Only fools, who would doom themselves and their families to be no more than beggars, cling to dreams of a time when the buffalo thundered across the prairies. The buffalo are gone and will never return. That is the truth of it."

Quanah silently prayed to Father Sun and Mother Moon that his children heard and understood what he said. Unless they did, the People now called Comanches would vanish from the face of the earth, without even a lingering memory of the great warriors who once were called lords of the plains.

Quanah sat quietly while Speaks Softly drove the two-horse team northward toward the reservation. The chief listened quietly while his aging friend recounted all that had occurred during his absence.

"The whites press in around us wanting our land." Speaks Softly brushed aside a stray strand of silvered hair the wind blew into his face. "The newspapers in Oklahoma named you an 'old chief who is stuck in the past.' They say you stand in the way of progress. Even newspapers as far away as Kansas City demand you help open our lands to white settlers."

Quanah smiled. "I am *old*, my friend. Did either of us ever expect to see the coming and going of so many *taum*?"

Speaks softly grunted. "Speak only for yourself. I am not old. Ask my wives if you think differently. My heart and mind are still those of a young brave ready to ride long and far with the rising of the full-faced moon."

As are mine, Quanah reflected. Yet, he could not deny the nagging aches that filled his joints each morning when he rose from his bed. The aches had not been there when he first came to the reservation.

"Even the store owners, who have lived on the red man's money for all these years, cry out that you are like a log in their paths," Speaks Softly went on with his report. "They say that the reservation blocks the construction of a road that would connect them with the white men to the west."

Since the passage of the Jerome Agreement, the whites' demands for Indian land increased daily. Their reasons for wanting the land were as varied as the colors that streaked the stones of a stream. At the heart of the whites' words always lay the same thing—money. The white men saw Indian land as a means for putting more money in their pockets.

When Quanah originally agreed with the whites' wants, he had been called progressive and civilized. Although his views on the management of Indian lands had not changed in the years since the leasing had begun, he now was viewed like a wheel of a wagon that was axle deep in mud. Settlers, merchants, newspapers, and even the Rock Island Railroad all cried out for the reservations to be dissolved and the land opened for whites.

Quanah's mind returned to his trip to Washington. Since 1892, he had made eight such journeys, each meant to delay the final adoption of the Jerome Agreement. Like those that had gone before, this one had been paid for by the Texas ranchers, the only white men who benefited from the reservations remaining untouched.

The politics the white man taught his red wards were as twisted and changing as the white man's road. White Eagle and Lone Wolf and their followers once again stood with Quanah in opposition to the Jerome Agreement. It was the "squaw men" and younger braves among the bands who rose to support the division of the reservations. To them, the land they would receive offered an opportunity for quick money. Land could be sold to whites clamoring for it in the blink of an eye.

When the land was gone? What would they have left? Nothing! This is what they could not see, what Quanah tried to show them. Land was the whites' measure of a man's worth. Without land the red man would be nothing.

"There is another matter." Speaks Softly's voice dropped to a barely perceptible whisper. "Commissioner Jones is at the agency headquarters."

Quanah's head snapped around. "Jones? Commissioner of Indian Affairs?"

Speaks Softly's head bobbed up and down. "Agent Baldwin said if you came to Fort Sill, he would ride with you to Anadarko. Commissioner Jones wants to palaver with you."

A floe of ice as cold as the bitterest winter coursed through Quanah's veins to form a squeezing fist around his heart.

"Weckeah, Cho-ny, Ma-cheet-to-wooky, To-nar-cy, To-pay, A-er-wuth-takum, and Co-by," Jones read from a piece of paper in his hand. "And Pop-e-ah-waddy. Eight women! All of them your wives. Eight wives, Parker! This is outrageous! In spite of all the orders to abandon the practice of polygamy, you continue to flagrantly ignore them and flaunt your wives in the face of authority. Eight wives! The mere thought of this harem shocks the senses of Christian men and women!"

"I have five wives," Quanah countered. "Weckeah, A-er-wuth-takum, and Co-by are no longer wives."

Jones tossed the paper aside and glared at the chief. "Five wives, four, three, or even two—it doesn't matter. The Indians of this reservation were ordered to abandon their polygamist ways. More than one wife is too many for you or any other man here. Do you hear what I am saying?"

"I hear." Quanah gave his head a tilt. "But I do not understand. It has been the way of my people for all of time to take more than one wife. All that is required is that man be able to feed, shelter, and clothe his wives and children. I have provided more than these necessities for my family. Why is that not enough for you?"

"Because it isn't the Christian way, the way we white men live." Jones made no attempt to contain his frustration. "You loudly say that you follow the white man's road, yet you stubbornly cling to the practice of polygamy. I think you understand everything very clearly and are simply throwing your 'much married condition' in our faces."

"Among my people, a man or woman does not have to stay with one he or she does not love. If either is unhappy, they move on to one they can be happy with," Quanah explained. "I love my wives and they love me. Were it not so, they would leave. Except for To-nar-cy, all my wives have borne me sons and daughters. Twenty-four in all have been born—nineteen still live. Most attend the white man's schools.

"If you and the other white men say I must have only one wife, then so be it. But I can not choose which of my wives will stay and which of the others I must drive from my house. You choose which of my wives will be my one wife."

Jones's mouth opened, but only a strangled sputter escaped his lips as his eyes narrowed and glared at the Comanche chief.

Ten minutes later Quanah walked away from the meeting. Jones, as he had feared, had stripped him of his seat on the Court of Indian Offenses. But five wives still dwelled within Star House.

CHAPTER THIRTY-ONE

"Are you certain?" Speaks Softly eyed his old friend. "They say deer have been sighted in the mountains. We can track and hunt them with our bows as we once did. It will be good to do so."

Quanah shook his head. "It would be good to hunt deer again in the Wichita Mountains, as I once did with my father Peta Nocona. And fresh venison would taste rich on my tongue. But not today. Today I will sit here on my porch and rest."

Speaks Softly sucked at his teeth in disgust. "Sit and rest! You sound like an old man."

"I am old, and am due the respect of an elder." Quanah laughed. "Besides, hunting parties are for young braves, not silver-hairs like you."

Waving off the comment with a flick of his wrist, Speaks Softly climbed onto the back of a bay, after one false start that carried him only halfway to the saddle. "Stay in your rocking chair, if that is what you want. Me, I will hunt deer. And when I return, I will build a campfire in front of your door. When you come out to sample the sizzling venison backstrap

I roast, I will tell you to go away, that you are too old and have no teeth to chew real meat."

Again Quanah laughed while his friend rode toward the mountains to relive younger days on the deer trails there. If Speaks Softly had visited him on the morrow, perhaps he would have taken up bow and quiver and joined his friend in the dreams of old men. Today, he was tired. His mind and body needed time to regroup and find strength. The year that had passed since Commissioner Jones had removed him from the Court of Indian Offenses bent his shoulders with the weight of ten years.

Every minor squabble and major fight that had ever flared on the reservation seemed to have found new fuel to feed its fires in the past twelve months. While he and others fought to hold back ratification of the Jerome Agreement, Captain Baldwin was replaced with a new agent, who was in turn replaced by James Randlett.

Amid all that turmoil of change, Commissioner Jones assigned a special agent to the reservation to oversee the leasing negotiations. In spite of being political allies in their opposition to the Jerome Agreement, White Eagle and Lone Wolf and their followers once more attacked Quanah, branding him a white man who used Indians to line his own pockets with riches.

Unlike those who had come before, this special agent sided with White Eagle. Special Agent Pray sliced the land Quanah controlled in half, and then reduced the Comanches' rent-free pastures from twenty-three thousand acres to five thousand, to force Quanah to accept a lease weighted heavily in the white man's favor.

Quanah eventually did sign the lease—after two months and days upon days of negotiating on his own with the help of the newest Indian agent, Randlett. Although the final agreement cut heavily into the land Quanah once controlled, he had bartered with that land to increase the acreage from five thousand to ten thousand each Comanche might use rent free. Pray found himself cut off at the knees.

And Quanah found himself once again facing Commissioner Jones to answer the old charges, that he had stolen Indian money. Quanah openly admitted to taking money from ranchers, because he worked for them, not because they bribed him. Never, he emphasized, had he ever taken a single penny from red men that was rightfully theirs. The claims that Quanah was a bought Indian fell aside when his opponents could produce no evidence to support their accusations.

Pray's parting shot before leaving the reservation was a commission from the Indian Office that named White Eagle "a principal chief." For Quanah, who had claimed to be the principal chief of the Comanches, this commission gave his longtime adversary an equal footing the former shaman had never enjoyed.

Randlett was quick to understand the undercurrents White Eagle's commission created—currents that could swirl into a maelstrom that would rip the reservation apart. He also recognized that Quanah was a stronger ally.

Quanah let his eyes rove over the farmland that stretched to the pastures he rented from the reservation. Although the ten-cent-an-acre price he now paid, thanks to the new lease agreement, substantially cut his acreage, the battle that had raged for a year had brought him more than land and wealth.

He slipped a letter from inside his buckskin shirt and opened it. Although he could not read the words written there, he did recognize the signature of Commissioner Jones. Jones had written the letter at Randlett's request to end the constant bickering that threatened the reservation.

Even though the written word remained alien to him, Quanah had memorized the letter's first sentence:

"This is to certify that Quanah Parker is recognized as the chief of the Comanches."

For the first time in the history of the Nermernuh, a single man led the People. Not even Peta Nocona and all the great warriors who had gone before him could make that claim. Quanah smiled as he rocked in his chair and enjoyed this day of long-needed rest that had finally come for the chief of the Comanches.

A drizzle fell from the sky, rain that touched the skin with a coldness kissed with winter rather than the heat of an August day. Quanah silently thanked whatever spirit had convinced the clouds to blanket the sun and shed their tears on the earth. Within the clouds' tears, he hid his own as they ran down his cheeks.

He had come here today not as the newly certified chief of the Comanches, nor as the leader of the People. He had come to this grave as a friend. And as a friend, he stayed after the family and other mourners had driven away in their buggies to escape the summer shower.

Alone beside the fresh mound of turned earth, he stripped away the woolen suit he had worn during the funeral ceremony. Naked except for breechclout and moccasins, he slipped the hunting knife hung about his waist from its sheath. Twice he raked the razor-honed edge across his chest to open thin lines of crimson that welled heavy drops which rolled down his body.

Quanah lowered himself cross-legged to the wet ground and began to chant a song of mourning. His sing-song words praised the strength and courage of a young brave who feared no enemy. His choruses told of a man who loved and cared for his family. He then chanted of a friend who was always at his side and loyal as any he had known. Finally the song became a prayer to all those who awaited in the Valley of Ten Thousand-fold Longer and Wider to gather themselves together and welcome another brave in their midst.

When the song ended, Quanah remained on the ground staring at the grave. "Old fool, how could you go and get yourself thrown from your pony? Did your promised taunts of roasting venison mean so much that you had to ride out and break your neck?"

Quanah's body shuddered as tears rolled anew from his reddened eyes while he gathered his clothes from the ground and stood. "You will be missed sorely, Speaks Softly. Know that this is true. You will be sorely missed by Quanah Parker."

Glancing one last time at the grave of his friend, the chief of all the Comanches began the long walk back to his home.

CHAPTER
THIRTY-TWO

John Teller winced as he shifted his weight on the driver's seat of the buckboard, and cursed beneath his breath. Gradually he managed to straighten his right leg and relieve the damnable throbbing in his knee. In spite of the doctor's reassurances the injury would heal "as good as new," the knee had nagged him like an aching tooth for the five years since he had banged it up when thrown from the back of a frisky three-year-old gelding.

He muttered another curse while he surveyed the prairie from atop a gently rolling rise. The knee was why he was sitting in the driver's box, rather than helping his two youngest sons and ten ranch hands below gather five hundred head of cattle. Even on the best of days, he could sit a saddle no more than an hour before the knee's pain grew too intense to bear.

The fact that the knee had served his body well for sixty-six years never entered his mind as he berated the physician who had treated him as a quack and charlatan. It was not right that he sat up here while his sons did all the work below. He had not been raised that way; a man was supposed to carry his own weight.

Not that I'm needed, Teller thought with more than a bit of pride. Phil and Tom had proved themselves to be more than capable of handling the situation. That the two young cowboys were his sons only caused his chest to expand to the point where his shirt threatened to pop its buttons.

The rancher's thoughts drifted south to Austin where his oldest son Jeff continued his studies. Teller sucked at his teeth and cocked his head to one side. He was not certain exactly how he felt about the course in life Jeff had chosen for himself. The Texan's vision of the future placed Jeff beside his brothers, running the ranch, when the good Lord finally called their father. Jeff, however, had ideas of his own.

Teller smiled. *Inherited that mind of his own from me. Reckon I can't complain.*

The rancher cast a half glance at the yearling hitched behind the wagon. His oldest might have himself buried hip deep in books, but his feet were firmly planted on solid soil. The boy had a good eye for horseflesh.

Teller's attention returned to the Oklahoma prairie, gradually surveying the full sweep on the grasslands around him. His eyes stopped when they came to a pair of scrubby red cedars a quarter of a mile from where he sat. Although time had required the rancher to employ the pair of spectacles he carried in his shirt pocket whenever he was required to read the printed word, there was nothing wrong with his eyes when it came to distances. He did not recognize the bay horse tied to one of the evergreens, but there was no mistaking the six-foot Indian dressed in buckskins who stood watching the roundup.

Save me a long ride later. Teller lifted the reins and clucked to the pair of horses in harness. When the animals brought the buckboard to an easy roll, the rancher edged their heads toward the unexpected visitor.

"John Teller," Quanah Parker's familiar voice called when the buckboard rolled within earshot. "I was afraid I would not find you."

Teller halted the wagon beside the Comanche chief. "You came lookin' for me?"

Quanah motioned to the cattle being herded below. "I heard you had come to take your cows home."

Teller nodded. "What with the Dawes Act passed and the reports I've heard about rustlers, I thought it best to pull out of Oklahoma before it got any worse."

"I'd pull out too, but there is no other place for me and my people."

The rancher caught a note of sadness underlining Quanah's voice. It surprised him. The chief rarely displayed emotion, whether it be in his expression or in his tone.

"It's as bad as they say, then?"

"Worse." Quanah's dark eyes turned toward the Texan. "When Congress ratified the Jerome Agreement, we were told it would be a year and one month before the whites would move onto what was once our land."

Teller listened while the Comanche explained that with Congressional passage of the agreement, Sooners immediately swarmed over the reservation in an attempt to lay claim to parcels of land.

"The soldiers drive them away, but they come right back, or they take Indian cattle and horses when they leave," Quanah continued. "I tell my people to pick the best land, but that does not stop the white men."

Those would-be settlers who tried to jump the gun on the opening of Indian land were exactly why Teller had driven across the Red River. He wanted his cattle south on his own range before the Sooners got the idea Texas beef would be just as easy to steal as were Indian steers.

"And the white men bring whiskey with them." Quanah's gray-streaked braids tossed from side to side when he shook his head. "Whiskey runs like a river. White men give braves whiskey, and the braves sign papers that say they have sold their lands."

Teller did not know how to answer. Once the Comanches raided white lands. Now the roles had somehow reversed themselves. The trouble with the Sooner raiders was that they weren't satisfied with simply making off with a few head of horses or cattle; they wanted to rob a man of his home as well.

The rancher glanced back at his sons and cowhands who worked his herd. He recalled the critics in the East who had decried the leasing of reservation pasturelands. They had accused cattlemen of robbing the red man of what was his. At least ranchers had paid for the use of the grasslands; they had not stolen the land out from under the Comanches like the government had.

"I read where Congress added some four hundred thousand

acres to the Jerome Agreement." Teller looked back at the chief. "Will that be up for lease?"

Quanah shrugged. "The Big Pasture is for all Indian stock. It will go to our children. That is what Congress says—today."

Teller pursed his lips and nodded, realizing Quanah understood that politicians' promises were not worth the paper they were written on. "I'd like to know about it, if the land does come up for lease."

"One hundred and sixty acres is not enough." Quanah's gaze scanned the prairie. "A man can not raise cows on one hundred and sixty acres."

Teller knew that well enough. The majority of Congressmen came from the rain-rich lands east of the Mississippi River. A farmer with a hundred acres there could feed half the nation with his crops if he had a good year. The plains were not farm lands, but grasslands. In dry years it took as many as twenty-two acres to feed a single steer. One hundred and sixty aces did not give a man a shot at raising a herd.

"You might consider buyin' a parcel or five of land for yourself," the rancher suggested. "Once the government opens the reservation, the price will go up like a skyrocket on the Fourth of July."

"No money," Quanah answered with another shake of his head.

"What?" Teller's head cocked toward the chief and his eyes narrowed. "Surely you got something socked away?"

"Debts," Quanah replied. "Still owe for the Star House. Money the ranchers paid, I used for my people or for leasing land."

By all accounts Teller had heard, Quanah was a rich man. Then again, his banker told him that he was a rich man, too. If one looked only at the tally sheets and ledgers, it could fool a man. He did not know one independent rancher he could call rich. The men who ran the big cattle companies might be, but not a man who worked his own spread.

After considering the Comanche's words for a few moments, Teller offered, "Look, if the times get bad for you and your family, I can always use hands who can handle a horse and a calf. You might send some of your sons down my way."

"Thank you, John Teller." A sad expression crossed Quanah's

face. "But I send my sons and daughters to the white man's school. They will not be land-poor Indians like their father. They will understand the white man's world."

"Oh!" Teller sat upright in the buckboard. "I'm gettin' forgetful in my old age. You mentionin' sons and daughters reminded me. I got a present for you. Jeff bought himself a mare down in Austin and bred her to that stud you gave him years ago. He said I was to give you the first colt she threw. Haven't been up this ways in a while, so I was a little late gettin' him to you."

Teller motioned to the rear of the buckboard and the yearling tied there. "Ever see a horse spotted like that?"

Quanah grinned as he walked to the colt. The animal lifted a bald face and stared at the chief, snorted once, then let a leathery hand stroke his head.

"White face, black neck and shoulders, but a spotted rump." Quanah eyed the colt carefully. "He is truly of unusual markings."

"Jeff said he's called an Appaloosa. His kind was originally bred by a tribe of Indians up Montana ways, I think. I would have cut him, if he had been mine, but I remembered Comanches prefer stallions."

"He is a fine horse. Will his children carry such markings?"

"Some do and some don't, the way I understand it," Teller replied. "Anyway, Jeff said you were supposed to get him. Said it was payment for the gray you gave him the first time you two met."

"Tell Jeff Teller his gift makes a old man's heart sing." Quanah untied the colt and led the yearling to the cedars where he lashed the lead to a limb near his mount. "Does Jeff Teller still go to school?"

"Yep. Decided he wants to be a lawyer. Damned if I know why." Teller gave his head a befuddled shake. "Reckon if he learns his trade well enough, he can keep his old man out of trouble."

"Lawyer?" Quanah turned back to the rancher. "Too bad he is not a lawyer now. I would hire him to help see my people got a fair shake from the government."

Fair shake—the words, the thought, seemed out of place coming from a Comanche's mouth. The decades parted, and Teller once more stood beside the bodies of his young wife and their son. Had they been given a fair shake?

The rancher caught himself. That the world had changed since those days when he and his father had farmed near San Antonio, did not erase the pain or the memories. So why did something twist inside him when he heard the chief recount the problems faced by the Comanches?

Suddenly aware that Quanah stared at him, Teller looked up. A smile touched the corners of the chief's mouth. "What are you grinnin' at, old man?"

"Another old man—an old enemy who remembers as I remember," Quanah answered. "It is why we have often talked these long years, John Teller. Your footsteps have shaped my world, as mine have shaped yours. Now the footsteps of others threaten to erase our footsteps from the sand. This sits heavy in both our hearts."

Teller's eyes narrowed. He had no idea what the old chief meant. He turned his head and looked back to the herd. His sons drove the cattle southward. "Looks like they're leavin' without me."

He lifted the reins and raised them to give the team of two a healthy pop on their rumps. Abruptly he stopped and glanced at Quanah again. "Hell, I am getting old. Jeff gave me something else to pass along to you."

Teller shoved a hand in the back pocket of his breeches to pull out a folded slip of paper, which he handed to the Comanche. "That's Jeff's address. He said you were to write him. He thinks that he might know where Cynthia Ann is buried."

Quanah's eyes widened. "He has found my mother's grave?"

"He's not sure," Teller said. "But I reckon he'll be more help to you down in Austin than I can be up here. Write him like he asked."

"I will do that, John Teller." Quanah carefully placed the folded paper in a leather pouch hung from his waist. "My mother and I thank you."

"Thank Jeff, when and if he does something." Teller lifted the reins again and snapped them atop the horses' rumps. "Remember what I said about your sons comin' down to my ranch."

With a wave, Teller moved the buckboard toward the herd that moved south toward the Red River. Although he did not look back, he felt Quanah's eyes on the back of his neck for the

next five miles. He did not like the sensation. It reminded him
of the days he had ridden into Comanche territory to face an
enemy that would have happily hung his scalp from a lodge pole.
Worse, it reminded him that today that same enemy was being
robbed of its lodge poles.

CHAPTER
THIRTY-THREE

The Winchester's report came like a crack, shattering the morning's stillness. A coyote running through the high grass of the Big Pasture gave a sharp yip-whine when a slug of lead slammed into its body. The impact stole the animal's balance, toppling it to its side. The coyote struggled to get its feet beneath its body. It lifted halfway from the ground before collapsing back to the earth—dead.

"A fine shot, Mr. President—a damned fine shot." Charles Goodnight grinned at Theodore Roosevelt.

The recently inaugurated twenty-sixth President of the United States gave his head a disgusted twist to one side and adjusted his spectacles with forefinger and thumb. "A good enough shot, Mr. Goodnight, in that it got the job done; the coyote is dead. But it was far from fine. The kill was not instantaneous. A good hunter should always have respect and reverence for the game he stalks. His shot should be quick and clean, so that the animal does not suffer. I was off my mark slightly, and the coyote suffered. Not long, I'll grant you, but it still suffered."

The Texas rancher shook his head. "I think you're being a

mite too hard on yourself, Teddy. I still say you made a fine shot."

Roosevelt arched both eyebrows and glanced. "Ask Chief Parker. He'll tell you that I was off of my mark."

Quanah's gaze shifted from the body of the dead coyote to the President and rancher who stared at him. "The President is right. Among the Comanches, the coyote is considered to be one of the wisest of animals. If he must be killed, he should killed quick and clean."

President Roosevelt looked back at Goodnight and gave his head a single sharp tilt that signaled the final judgment had been rendered on the subject. When he looked back at the Comanche chief, he asked, "Is that why you have shot only jackrabbits this morning, Chief Parker? Because of the Comanches' respect for the coyote and its wisdom?"

"I can eat rabbits," Quanah answered simply. "Coyote does not taste so good."

Roosevelt's face split in a wide grin. "Now that is a straight-forward practical answer. All men should be so forthright, especially a few businessmen I know, as well as a herd of Democrats. This country would be far better off for it."

A lone trooper astride a sorrel with a star in the middle of its forehead galloped across the prairie and drew his mount up near the President. After a snapped salute, the soldier in his starched khaki uniform announced, "Mr. President, breakfast is ready back at camp. Hot coffee, fried eggs, and wheatcakes, as you ordered, sir."

"And ham?" Roosevelt questioned.

"And ham, sir," the soldier corrected.

The President glanced at the fifteen men who accompanied him. "Gentlemen, the cool Oklahoma air has created a ravenous hunger within me this morning. I suggest we all mount and retire to the camp. After that, we can continue our quest of ridding these plains of pesky varmints."

With the others, Quanah mounted and rode after the newest President of the United States. The chief admitted to himself that he liked this man. He spoke with a clear voice, and his laughter came from deep in the belly. Of all the Presidents, only Roosevelt had visited the reservation. Nor did he visit merely to give speeches; like the People, Theodore Roosevelt was a hunter. And Roosevelt was a warrior, a man who had proven himself in the war against the Spanish. These were good things; things that Quanah understood.

Nor was Roosevelt like President McKinley, whom Quanah had met in Washington shortly after the ratification of the Jerome Agreement. When Quanah had begun to speak of the red man's need for more acreage, McKinley's underlings had quickly hastened the Chief of the Comanches and the other chiefs with him from the President's office.

Quanah had first met Roosevelt two months earlier when he, Geronimo, Hollow Horn Bear, American Horse, and Little Plume had walked in a great parade in Washington the day Roosevelt took office. Then he had merely shaken the President's hand. This morning, before the sun rose, when the rest of camp still slept, he and the President had shared coffee by a campfire and talked.

Quanah had told Roosevelt of all the hardships that had plagued his people in the five years since the Jerome Agreement had become law. The President had listened to all the chief had described, from the smallpox epidemic of 1901 to the white bootleggers who grew wealthy off the red man's thirst for whiskey.

When Quanah outlined the troubles with the Big Pasture, the additional four hundred and eighty thousand acres of grasslands the Jerome Agreement had granted the red man, the President already seemed to know of the ranchers' squabbles as they vied for leasing rights. He had also been aware of small towns that had grown up around the reservation since 1900, and the demands of the whites to open the Big Pasture for settlement.

"I will use my influence to see that any future land leases will have provisions for employment of the red man by those leasing the land," Roosevelt had said. "I know unemployment is high among the Indians. This should provide some relief, though not solve the problem. But it will be a beginning."

And Roosevelt had promised that any actions he took as President would be fair to all men, white and red.

Quanah found a trust in this President's words. He sensed a sympathy for the red man and sincerity in Roosevelt's feelings. Perhaps this white man would finally brush away the obstacles to the white man's road over which the People had stumbled for thirty years. The time for such a man among the whites was long overdue.

A smile moved across Quanah's lips when the President's mounted entourage reached the camp of white tents. John Teller stood beside a buggy with a steaming tin cup of coffee in his hand. Instead of reining to the soldiers who waited to care for the mounts, Quanah directed his horse toward the rancher.

"John Teller, long years have passed since we last talked." The deep creases of age that lined the Texan's face surprised the chief.

"Not much reason to come up this way." Teller stepped forward and shook Quanah's hand when he dismounted. "I wasn't lucky enough to get a piece of the lease lands. But when Charlie invited me to the hunt, I thought I'd drive up and meet Teddy Roosevelt. Never met a President before, you know."

Quanah noticed a cane leaning against the buggy; he pointed to it. "A stick to walk with?"

Teller shrugged. "My bum knee—on cold mornings it acts up a mite."

Quanah understood stiffness in the joints. He faced the same each morning. He had even visited a white doctor for relief. The physician had pronounced that he suffered from rheumatism and there was nothing he could do to cure the ailment. Although the doctor did say the affliction was still a long way from Quanah's heart.

"Well, Mr. President, how do you like the Indian guide we arranged for you?" a voice from beside the campfire carried to Quanah's ears.

"Chief Parker is a fine old chief," Quanah heard Roosevelt answer. Then he turned his attention back to the aging rancher.

"Jeff Teller has written me. He found my mother's grave," Quanah said.

"That's what he told me." Teller nodded.

"I have written to the Texas governor asking him to help me move my mother here."

"Jeff said it would probably take some time to get all the paperwork cleaned up," Teller commented. "But he said that he thought that eventually you'd get everything worked out."

"Jeff Teller has been good to me. He has worked without asking me to pay. This is welcome since money had been hard to come by."

Teller looked at the chief. "You mean you haven't invested some forty thousand dollars in the Quanah Line, like I read in the newspapers?"

"Railroad pay me a little to talk up their business, that is all." Quanah shook his head. "Their money helps pay my bills. Besides, their railroad is small—only twelve miles to help carry gypsum from the mines in Texas. Too little to ever make Quanah Parker a rich man."

Teller smiled. "Don't reckon either one of us will ever get rich in this world. Paying the bills is the best a man can do, it seems."

Sometimes more than a man can do, Quanah reflected. The wealth that had once been his quickly disappeared after the Jerome Agreement's ratification. Although his family lived in the warmth of the Star House and there was food on the table, there were always bills to be paid, some for which there never seemed to be money.

"John!" Goodnight called to his fellow rancher. "Come over here. There's someone I think you should meet."

Teller looked at the Comanche chief. "We'll talk more later. Right now there's a President just waitin' to shake my hand."

Quanah watched as the rancher lifted the cane and walked to the campfire with a heavy limp. In one way white men and red men were the same—time took its toll on all.

"This is the form you have to use for your expenses." Indian Agent Randlett placed a piece of paper on the desk in front of Quanah. "Let me help fill this out this time, then you can use it as an example for the others you will file in the future."

Quanah watched while Randlett's pen filled in the date and then the year, 1908. The agent asked for the cost of each item the chief had incurred during his trip to Anadarko.

"Twenty-eight cents for the electric cars and one dollar and forty-four cents for the railroad ticket." Quanah began to recount the small sums spent to travel to the reservation's headquarters to sign lease papers. "I spent fifty cents for two meals and twenty-five cents for a hotel room."

"All for a grand total of two dollars and ninety-seven cents," Randlett said while he added each item to the form. "Now you sign your name right here."

Quanah did, writing his name rather than making the mark he once had used. "Now you pay the money owed me?"

"I'm afraid not. You work for the United States government now, and the government takes its own time to reimburse its employees. You file this form now, and in two or three months, the government will send you a check for what is owed you," Randlett explained.

Quanah nodded heavily. He offered no complaint. After all, it had been Randlett who had arranged for Quanah's employment as a farmer in the West Cache farmer's district. The chief had never planted a row of seeds in his life, nor did he now. But the government paid him twenty dollars a month for the advice and aid he provided to the agent. Randlett had even arranged for a telephone to be installed in the Star House so that he could talk with Quanah without requiring the chief to make frequent trips to Anadarko.

On more than one occasion Quanah had thought that Randlett was the only white man in all of the world who cared about the red man. Even President Roosevelt had turned his back on the Indians. Although he had provided for more money per acre than originally offered for the Big Pasture's four hundred and eighty thousand acres, he still had taken the land from the reservation two years ago. The prime land that had been promised to yet unborn Comanches was given to whites who had illegally settled the Big Pasture.

Randlett, however, again and again displayed his concern for the chief of the Comanches and his family. The agent had gotten Quanah's daughter Wanada a job at the Fort Sill school for a yearly salary that equalled the one Quanah now drew from the government. And the agent also had arranged for a five-room house to be built for three of Quanah's other children. When Quanah's son Harold had died of tuberculosis, Randlett had succeeded in securing Harold's land in Quanah's name.

Quanah's memories slipped back to the day he had reluctantly sold that land for three thousand dollars. His intent had been to use the money to clear away his debts for once and for all. Instead the government took the money, deeming the sum to be too large to be trusted in the hands of a red man, and doled small amounts after months of formal requests. Quanah's bills with storekeepers remained and continued to grow.

"Here, take these with you." Randlett handed the Comanche chief a small stack of expense forms when Quanah rose. "You can fill them out at home and send them in, rather than waiting until you come to Anadarko."

"That is good." Quanah nodded and turned to leave the agent's office.

"And, Quanah," Randlett added, "if you need anything else, just call me on the telephone."

Again, Quanah nodded and walked outside. *Need*—in spite of all his help, he wondered if Randlett truly understood the red man's need—if any white man could? Throughout the years, he had tried to explain. His words, whether spoken to the endless line of Indian agents who came to the reservation or to the leaders in Washington, always fell on deaf ears.

Quanah reached the train station and climbed aboard the first car. He found a seat beside a window and gazed outside when the train jerked to a sudden start. The homes and buildings of Anadarko rapidly slipped by to be replaced by the white man's ranches and farms. No matter in which direction he looked or how far his eyes sought, he saw the whites' houses and barns.

Closing his eyes, Quanah leaned his head back and allowed the gentle rocking of the train to lull him toward sleep. While he napped, he would let the train carry him across the prairies where he had once led raiding parties toward the farmers' lands in Texas and Mexico.

CHAPTER THIRTY-FOUR

"Follow after the white way, get an education, know well work, and make a living for yourselves and your families." Quanah stood beside the grave and spoke to those gathered at the Mennonite mission at Post Oak. "Learn the white God, then all will be ready for death like my mother, and all will lie together."

Quanah fell silent. The funeral ceremony ended. He watched while family and friends filed by the grave wherein his mother now rested. After more than half a lifetime, he had fulfilled a promise and returned Cynthia Ann Parker to her family. It was a good end to a decade this sunny December day.

Now and then friends took his hand and shook it while they leaned forward to softly utter their well-wishing in his ear. He smiled and nodded, paying half attention to their words. His focus was on the children who placed flowers on his mother's grave. Where they had found blossoms at this time of year he did not know. Their fragrance filled his nostrils. His mother would have liked them, of that he was certain. Hadn't she named her first born Quanah—Sweet Aroma—after the prairie flowers of spring?

Children—there were children. His chest expanded. After all the People had met at the white man's hands, there were children. The Nermernuh survived; they had not been wiped from the face of the earth. His mother would approve of that, too, as would his father and his uncle Cona Cawb-vey. As long as there were children, there was hope.

"Mr. Parker."

Quanah's head snapped up. While his mind gathered wool, the line of well-wishers had passed and moved to the buggies hitched beside the mission to make their separate ways home. He did not know the young white man who stood before him in a three-piece black suit and starched white shirt with black tie. Yet, there was something familiar about the man's blue-gray eyes. He could not place a finger on the familiarity, though.

"Mr. Parker, I just wanted to say that I'm sorry I missed you when you were in Austin. A business matter in Corpus Christi called me away," the young man said. "I also want to extend my father's apologies for not being here today. I'm afraid he's home in bed recovering from a long bout of influenza."

Influenza? Quanah had received a telegram from John Teller that said the rancher would not attend Cynthia Ann's burial because he had been confined to his bed with influenza. Quanah's eyes narrowed when he leaned forward to closely study the young man's face. He smiled. He recognized the familiarity now.

"Jeff Teller? Is that you, Jeff Teller?"

"Yes, sir, it is." The young man grinned when the chief grasped his shoulders and squeezed. "I guess I should have introduced myself before I went on telling you about my father."

"You have grown into a fine-looking man, Jeff Teller." Quanah stepped back to eye the younger Teller from head to toe. "It has been a long time since I gave a small boy his first pony."

"That it has, sir. Fact is, I just gave my fiancée one of his daughters. The prettiest dapple gray filly you've ever seen. Mary, my fiancée, was just about as tickled to get that filly as I was to get that colt you gave me way back then," Jeff answered.

"Your father should be proud to have raised such a fine man." Quanah gave the young man another thorough inspection.

"I suppose he is, although he really hasn't taken a shine to me becoming a lawyer yet—but he's slowly getting used to it."

"A lawyer—someday you will go to Washington and become

a famous man. Maybe become President," Quanah said. "Maybe you help my people then, the way you helped me find my mother."

"I'm afraid President is a long way from an attorney trying to get himself established with a decent practice." Jeff shook his head.

Quanah gestured the young man's hesitancy away. "No, you will be like your father, Jeff Teller. You will make a name for yourself."

Jeff chuckled. "It's you who have made a name for yourself. I saw you back at the state fair in Dallas two years ago. I tried to introduce myself then, after your talk, but by the time I got through the crowd, you were gone."

"Too bad, we could have eaten dinner together and talked of ponies."

"I also saw that picture show, *The Train Robbery*, you were in," Jeff continued.

Quanah chuckled. "White men tried to make Quanah Parker an actor. I was no good."

"My husband." Quanah's wife To-nar-cy approached from behind and touched the chief's arm before the young Teller could comment. "We must be going. The others will be gathering at our home."

Quanah looked at his wife and smiled, then turned back to Jeff Teller. "Many family members and friends are coming to the Star House to celebrate my mother's return. Will you come with us? Without your help, she would still be lost to us."

Jeff Teller grinned widely. His expression immediately transformed into a frown. "I would enjoy that, Mr. Parker. I truly would. But I have a train I must catch in two hours. If I miss it, there is no way I can get back to Austin in time for a court case I have Wednesday. I hope you understand."

Quanah nodded. "We all have work that must be done. Tell your father I am glad his health returns to him. Our footsteps still fall in each other's worlds."

Jeff Teller frowned again, but said, "I will tell him that. I'll tell him exactly what you said."

"That is good. Now I must go and join my family, Jeff Teller." Quanah shook the young man's hand once more before turning with To-nar-cy to the buggy that waited for him.

In the driver's seat was Herman Lehman. Although the young man still used the name his blood parents had given him, this year he had requested to be officially adopted by the People. Quanah had seen to it that his adopted son's request was granted.

It has been a good year. My mother and a son have come home.

"Quanah, come to my side."

Quanah's eyes blinked open when the medicine man thrust the sharpened eagle bone into his throat.

"Give him water now." The healer's voice filled the chief's ears, but behind it was another voice.

"Quanah, come to my side."

Cona Cawb-vey! It was his uncle who called to him!

Quanah's eyes fluttered closed as water trickled into his throat. How cool it felt.

"I don't know what else can be done." Quanah recognized the voice of the white doctor who had treated him in the Cache railway station. "The heart stimulant I gave him doesn't seem to be helping."

"Quanah, come to my side."

Quanah tried to answer, but his lips and tongue were swollen. He turned his head to one side and then the other. Cona Cawb-vey was nowhere to be found. All he saw were the faces of his wives and children gathered around the bed on which he lay.

He closed his eyes. Did the peyote linger in his mind? In search of a cure for the weakness that now caused his body to shake uncontrollably, he had traveled north to a Cheyenne shaman who claimed to hold a peyote cure for the ailment. Was it another peyote vision that gave life to his uncle's voice?

"You are my son. You are blood of my blood."

Father? Was it Peta Nocona that spoke to him? *Father?*

No answer came. Certainly it was peyote lingering in his mind that brought the voices. He should have been wiser than to trust a Cheyenne's medicine. Once before he had done so, and it had led to the disaster at Adobe Walls.

"Can't you stop him from shaking?" Fear tightened To-nar-cy's voice. "What is wrong with him?"

"It is his rheumatism," the physician answered. "It's reached his heart. There's nothing I can do. He either ..."

Quanah closed his ears to the white doctor's words. Too much remained unfinished. He could not surrender to the weakness of his body. He was Quanah Parker, Chief of the Comanches; the People needed him to lead them as he had throughout his life.

"Quanah, come to my side."

Uncle, it is not time. He refused to answer Cona Cawb-vey's call.

"You are blood of my blood."

Nor did he acknowledge his father. They did not understand the world that threatened to devour the Nermernuh, a world that would swallow them and erase all trace of the People from the face of the earth. The Kwerhar-rehnuh still required a warrior chief, one armed with words and the white man's law, to guide their footsteps.

"Remember the flowers, my son. Remember the sweet aroma."

Mother?

"Remember the flowers."

Flowers? Of what use are flowers when facing the white man?

Quanah's eyes fluttered open. He searched the faces hovering over him for his mother. She was nowhere to be found. *Mother?*

"Remember the flowers, my son."

The coy scent of blossoms mingled in the air. How could this be? The bitter cold of February reigned outside the warmth of Star House. Where did blossoms grow in the middle of winter? Flowers now would be as unusual as those the children had placed on his mother's grave last December.

"Remember the flowers."

The flowers—a gentle calm suffused Quanah's trembling body with a soothing liquid warmth. He saw the direction his mother's words led. He saw the children who had brought the flowers and carefully placed them on the grave. *The children.* He recalled his own thoughts. The children—they were the future of the People. He had given the Nermernuh that—the opportunity to bring new generations into a new world.

"He dies!" To-nar-cy's voice grew even tighter. "I can feel it!"

Quanah's lips parted. He wanted to tell To-nar-cy, to tell all his family, it was all right. There were children, and where there were children, there was hope. A sudden cough frightened the words from the tip of his tongue. He drew a gasping breath in an attempt to find the voice squeezed in his swollen throat.

"Quanah, come to me."

Yes, Uncle. Quanah closed his eyes and accepted. *It is time that I joined you.*

CHAPTER
THIRTY-FIVE

"Look! Billy, an airplane!"

His grandson's abrupt exclamation awoke John Teller from a drowsy half-sleep. Blinking his eyes to clear the sleep cotton, he sought the droning of an engine that rose above the rumble of the automobile's motor. He tilted his head outside the open passenger window and found the bi-winged mechanized bird of wood and red-painted fabric as it gracefully did a slow turn in the air, then swooped downward toward an open pasture.

A red-winged hawk screeched and launched itself from atop a telephone pole as the man-made invader of the air leveled out three feet above the ground. Teller could see two people, faces hidden behind glass goggles, seated in the tandem cockpits of the aircraft while it gradually drifted to the earth and rolled to a bumpy stop.

"What'd'ya think it is? A Spad, or maybe a Newport?" The excitement in seven-year-old Billy's voice echoed the enthusiasm contained in his brother's shouted airplane alert.

"No," Glenn answered with the wisdom of the two additional years he had on his younger brother. "It's a two-seater. I think it's a new plane we haven't seen before."

"You boys keep it down and stop acting like a bunch of wild Indians! You two have seen airplanes before." Jeff's eyes left the road long enough to cast a reprimanding scowl at his sons in the automobile's rear seat. "Your grandfather was napping until you woke him."

"Sorry, Grandpa." Billy leaned forward and touched Teller's shoulder.

Before the retired rancher could lift his own hand to give his grandson a reassuring pat, Billy bounced back in the seat and pressed close to Glenn in an attempt to get a better view of the airplane. Teller smiled, trying to remember the days when his own body brimmed with such energy.

"Pa, are you okay?" Jeff gave his father a sideways glance.

"Fine," Teller answered. "Just a little groggy. Sorry I drifted off. I forgot how long it took to get to Fort Sill."

Jeff grinned. "We're making a lot better time today than when you first took me with you to the reservation. Almost doubled my speed on that stretch of paved road back yonder."

"Daddy!" Glenn shouted from the backseat. "Look, they're giving rides in the airplane. There's a sign by the gate."

Teller glanced toward the barbed-wire-enclosed pasture. A yellow-painted sign with red letters proclaimed that for a mere five dollars anyone could "EXPERIENCE THE THRILLS AND EXCITEMENT OF FLYING!"

"Daddy, you said you'd let Billy and me take a ride one day," Glenn continued.

Jeff shook his head. "This isn't the day. You're here to keep your grandfather company, remember?"

"But Daddy, you said."

"Young man, I said that this isn't the day," Jeff repeated with finality.

Although his oldest grandson offered no further protest, Teller heard a disgruntled snort come from the backseat. For a moment the image of Teller's father stepped into his thoughts, and the broad belt he had worn that would have quickly punished the smallest display of disrespect. *That was a long time ago—a hell of a long time ago.*

"Things don't look changed much since I was up here for Cynthia Ann Parker's funeral," Jeff said while he scanned the countryside. "A few more houses, I guess, but pretty much the same."

Teller turned back to the window to hide his expression. His oldest son did not like him "telling yarns about the old days." Jeff's world was all modern, with gleaming steel and machines that growled their power. This was the world his sons would inherit, he had told his father on more than one occasion. Glenn and William needed to prepare themselves for that world; their grandfather's reminiscences of Indian battles would not do that.

Maybe Jeff did not remember the first time he had driven him to Fort Sill, but Teller did. Even then, when the Comanches were settled into reservation life, this land had been wide open. The countryside that raced by outside was sliced into barbed-wire-enclosed patches. Whitewashed houses and red barns were scattered across the plains in all directions. More years than he wanted to count had passed since the Texan had hunted coyotes with Teddy Roosevelt in the Big Pasture, but he had not grown senile in that time. Nor had he lost his eyesight. There were changes—changes everywhere.

The automobile slowed, and Jeff shifted into a lower gear.

"There's a sign ahead." Teller's oldest son tilted his head toward the road. "Looks like they're expecting a crowd to go and put signs out."

Jeff turned left down a narrow dirt road, to follow the white sign with its arrow and single word—"Dedication."

"There *is* a crowd!" Jeff tilted his head again. "Must be a hundred cars parked up there."

And at least a hundred buggies, Teller thought as he took in the scene a quarter of a mile up the road. "It's the old Mennonite mission. Didn't realize they were puttin' up the monument there."

"It's where he's buried, alongside his mother and sister," Jeff answered. "That's usually where they put monuments."

Teller's mind drifted back to a small newspaper article he had read in 1915. The few short paragraphs recounted the desecration of Quanah Parker's grave. Apparently grave robbers took a diamond brooch Quanah had been buried in. The article had placed a value of four hundred and fifty dollars on the piece of jewelry. Teller had been certain at the time that the thieves had been white. No red man would ever disturb the final sleep of one of their own.

"Looks like the ceremony has started," Jeff said while he slowed and pulled toward the parked automobiles. "If you don't mind, I'm going to stop back here. We'll be able to get out easier. Pa, sorry we didn't make it in time. There were a lot of bumps in the road."

Teller waved away his son's apology. "I didn't come here to listen to a lot of words by some politician who doesn't know a Comanche from a cigar store Indian. I just wanted to see what kind of stone they put up."

While the Texan opened the automobile's door and stepped outside to lean heavily on his cane, Jeff looked back at his sons. "I want you two to mind your p's and q's. We're here to pay our respects to one of your grandfather's old friends. You two act like gentlemen, understand?"

"We understand," Glenn answered.

"Good." Jeff opened their door and let the two boys slide out. "Now go stand with your grandfather and give him a hand, if he needs one."

Old friends? Teller pursed his lips. Quanah Parker had never been a friend. Old scars ran too deep for that. There was respect, the retired rancher admitted that. He was certain Quanah had returned that respect for an "old enemy who remembers as I remember." It *was* memories that brought him here today. When a man had lived as long as he, the future had given up all its promises.

"Grandpa, are you ready?" Billy asked when he and Glenn took their places at his arms.

"Reckon we ought to wait a bit." Teller looked at his oldest son. "Seems they're breakin' up. Let's let the crowd thin a mite."

Jeff nodded, his expression saying he understood that his father was "too old" to be jostled by crowds.

Teller ignored him. If he wanted to get through the small mob of people who surrounded the marble monument, he damned well could. After all, he held a cane and was still capable of giving it a good swing if the situation warranted.

"Grandpa, Daddy said the man buried here was an Indian chief. Is that true?" Billy looked up at his grandfather, head twisted slightly off to one side like a young pup giving the world an inquisitive gander.

"The first and only chief of the Comanches," Teller confirmed.

"How'd you meet him?" This from Glenn.

"I was the man who brought him in to the reservation." Teller caught Jeff's disapproving frown out of the corner of an eye. He remembered a similar expression on Tess's face when he first had tried to tell Jeff about the day Cynthia Ann and he were taken captive by the Comanches. "It's a long story, boys. Maybe if there's time, I'll tell it to you on the way back home."

The frown disappeared from Jeff's face, and Teller's answer seemed to satisfy his grandsons. And for the moment, it satisfied Teller himself.

However, during the drive home, whether Jeff approved or not, he intended to recount everything he knew about the Comanches to Glenn and Billy. He had never told Phil all those stories, and now it was too late. The war to end all wars had left Phil buried in a grave somewhere in France. He would not make the same mistake with his grandsons.

Your footsteps have shaped my world, as mine have shaped yours. Teller had often thought about what Quanah had meant by those words. He understood now. He also understood the rest of what the chief had tried to tell him—*footsteps of others threaten to erase our footsteps from the sand. This sits heavy in both our hearts.*

Fences barricaded the open range, automobiles eradicated trails opened by wagons drawn by oxen, weeds overgrew the forgotten graves of those who first came to this land—all footsteps of others that erased the traces of those who had come before them.

"Pa, folks are starting to leave." Jeff's voice drew Teller back to the present.

Engines coughed alive and sputtered as drivers pulled their automobiles away. Here and there, above the rumble of motors, came the crack of a whip or a sharp whistle to awaken horses harnessed to buggies. Teller looked back at the monument; the crowd had thinned enough that he could reach it without having to employ his cane.

"Ain't no need for y'all to come with me," Teller said to his son. "You can wait here if you want. I don't reckon this will mean much to the boys."

"If you want to be alone, it's ..."

Teller closed his ears to Jeff's words as he limped through the men and women who made their way to the waiting vehicles. *Quite a footstep,* he thought while he studied the marble monument he approached. Standing a full ten feet tall and at least a yard wide, the three-piece structure was designed to endure the passing of decades of footsteps before it was erased. He suspected the massive monument would have met with the old chief's approval.

"If you ask me, this is a total waste of the taxpayers' money. Why spend funds to erect a monument to a man who exploited his own people to make himself rich? The money could be used for social programs to help the Indians."

Teller's head turned to two young men who whispered loudly beside the monument. Both appeared to be in their early twenties, with that college-cut appearance about them.

"You're full of it, Cal," the second answered with a determined shake of his head. "He was a great man. The Comanches would have been walked all over if he hadn't made a stand and fought for them. He's a perfect example of the noble savage!"

Again Teller closed his ears. He had heard all the arguments about Quanah many times before. To those who opposed him, he was a greedy devil who lined his pockets with money that should have rightfully gone to his people, a half-breed who sold himself to white ranchers. For those who supported Quanah, he was a strong leader who tried to make a place for the Comanches in a bewildering world.

Reaching out with his right hand, the Texan let his fingertips trace over the words chiseled into the marble monument:

RESTING HERE UNTIL DAY BREAKS
AND SHADOWS FALL AND DARKNESS
DISAPPEARS IS
QUANAH PARKER
LAST CHIEF OF THE COMANCHES
BORN—1852
DIED FEB. 23, 1911

Quite a footstep, Teller thought again. *You'll be remembered a damned sight longer than most men—white or red.*

"Noble savage? The Indians were no more than Stone Age people who ran head-on into technology. In case you've forgotten, that's why we're here. The government is paying us to drag these people into the modern world."

The continuing argument drew Teller's attention back to the two young men. *Social workers,* he realized from the last statement.

"The Indians were closer to nature than we are. They were in harmony with the world they lived in."

"Baloney! Mystical rhetoric! Just because a man defecates on the ground doesn't make him in harmony with nature. Besides, what has that to do with Quanah Parker or the way he exploited his people? He was rich when he died. They say he was buried wearing a diamond brooch!"

"And what about his long fight to keep Indian lands for the red man," the second young man countered. "The government would have stripped the red man of every acre it had given him if it weren't for chiefs like Quanah Parker."

The man thrust a finger to the monument. The gesture caused both to look up and discover Teller staring at them. Instead of a blush of embarrassment at the attention their argument drew, one of the men asked, "Were you a friend of his?"

Teller glanced at the monument and stepped away. "I don't reckon I'd call him a friend, but I knew him just about as long as any white man, I guess."

"What do you think?" the man pressed. "Was he a great leader, or did he exploit his people?"

"He was a man," Teller answered after a moment's reflection. "He was just a man. That's all, just a man."

The drone of an engine drew Teller's gaze to the sky. The bi-winged airplane sailed through a clear Oklahoma sky again, carrying passengers for five dollars a ride.

Leaving the two men staring after him, Teller started back to where Jeff and the boys waited. He managed to slip a battered billfold from the back pocket of his suit pants by the time he reached them. Twenty dollars—two fives and a ten—nestled inside.

"I've seen what I came to see," he announced. "I reckon it's about time we went and saw about getting these boys a ride on an airplane."

He was immediately rewarded with a chorus of joyous shouts from his grandsons, plus a series of grateful hugs.

He also drew a reprimanding glare from Jeff. "Pa, I don't think—"

"Ain't nobody askin' you to think, just drive us down the road to where that airplane is givin' rides," Teller cut him off. "If you won't, me and the boys have got legs to get us there. The more I think of it, I just might take myself a ride in that airplane."

"Pa, you aren't serious. You're almost nin—"

"I know damned well how old I am. Which is why I might as well take a look at this earth from the sky today. Might not be here tomorrow." He winked at his son while he pulled the twenty dollars from the wallet and flashed them at Jeff. "And if you're a good boy, Jeff, I just might pay for you to take a ride."

Jeff stared at his father with mouth agape. Then with a shake of his head, he laughed. "You're one stubborn old cuss, did you know that?"

"Yep. I was born with a stubborn streak a mile wide."

"Come on, boys." Jeff opened a back door and waved his sons into the backseat. "Your grandfather wants to take us for an airplane ride, so I guess we're going to see what it's like to fly."

Teller smiled as he watched his son and grandsons. Men left all sorts of footsteps to mark their passage through this world, and they did not have to be chiseled in marble. He would leave a few of his own, and right now those footsteps wanted to ride in an airplane.

ABOUT THE AUTHOR

GEO. W. PROCTOR, a prolific Western writer and lifelong Texas resident, has also written science fiction. His previous Western novels include *Enemies, Walks Without a Soul, Comes the Hunter,* and *Before Honor,* which was a Spur Award finalist in 1993. Mr. Proctor and his wife currently reside in Arlington, Texas.